ROSE

AND THE VENGEANCE OF

CANNONFLASH JONES

BY
J. R. KNOLL

Email: Vultross@aol.com

ARTWORK BY
JEFF FAIRBOURN

faile35.deviantart.com

ISBN: 1452813086
ISBN-13: 9781452813080

For my First Mate,
My True Love,
My Rose O' scarlett,
Jami Lynn Knoll

The little pirate woman who sailed into my life and stole my heart with a single smile, made calm the turbulent sea I was lost in, filled my sails with a true wind and took my side as we sailed into an uncertain future to forge a new life.

Together we are invincible, our two hearts, both once broken, are strong as one.

To my dearest Love,
Yours always,
Cannonflash

Chapter 1

WANTED WOMAN

Festive as always, the tavern on the outskirts of town was a smoky, noisy place, but those at the round, wooden card table in the center of the room barely noticed. This was a sturdy place but of poor construction. Many of the wooden planks that made up the floor were twisted and bowed up and creaked when they were stepped on. The bar was old and made largely from the wood of wrecked ships, and the three people working behind it were kept busy by the patrons who haunted the place frequently. Almost all were mariners, men and a few women whose blood was the sea itself, and among them were many pirates.

In the sixteen hundreds, the law on this scattering of islands in the Caribbean was supposed to be the governments who had established themselves there. The largest presence on Jamaica was the British and the fort on Port Royal was an ominous symbol of their supremacy there. It was, however, something of an inconvenience for those who operated outside of British law. During this time, with European countries fighting amongst themselves, the colonies in the Caribbean found themselves on their own for the most part and local governors were frequently at odds with each other and almost always at odds with the

 1

numerous privateers and pirates who haunted this part of the world.

Among these would be a woman who, on this day, escaped her troubles with a mug of rum and a game of cards. Dark green eyes were framed by very long, very thick lashes and were fixed on the thin built man who sat across from her. He was not attractive, nor did he pretend to be. His long hair was very thin as was the mangy, un-kept beard he wore. This was a man who spent long periods of time at sea and clearly spent little of his time sober.

Her interest in him was far from a romantic one. He had much of her money on the table before him, and a taunting look in his bloodshot eyes.

She pursed her full lips a little and her eyes narrowed just slightly. This was a woman who could easily catch the eye of any man who saw her. Long brown hair was restrained in a single pony tail, but for what was feathered and dangling from her temples and forehead. Her face was one that was not heavily painted with make-up, nor did it need to be. A very lovely woman, she was not a thin woman, rather thick bodied but thick in all the places with curves that would would turn any man's head, and her bleached white shirt was open halfway down her chest, perhaps to relieve some of the Caribbean heat, or perhaps to distract the other card players at the table, and she had ample breasts to do just that. The cuffed sleeves concealed more than her arms and she would have to demonstrate a pirate's slight of hand to make her move. The man across from her was watching her like a hawk, as was everyone else at the table. The ace up that right cuff might just get some of her gold back, unless she was caught. Again.

The man strummed his cards across his fingers, not quite smiling.

She reached to her mug of rum and gently picked it up, her eyes shifting to it as she raised it to her lips. A couple of swallows later she gingerly set it back in its place. Her eyes shifted to her ever shrinking stacks of coins, then to the enticing pile of coins in the center of the table. Only two hands were still in play, and hers had to win. Looking back to her cards, she reached up with that right hand and scratched under her ear, then slowly slid her knuckles down her neck and over one breast and back to the table. That's all anyone saw.

Setting her elbows on the table, she grasped her cards with both hands and examined them closely, then turned malicious eyes on the man across from her. Now, she had *three* aces in her hand to work with. That right hand slowly reached to her stack of coins and she picked one up, tossing it carelessly to the pile in the middle as she snarled, "Call."

He smiled slightly and slowly laid a straight flush down to the table.

She closed her eyes and slapped her cards down, trying to ignore him as he laughed and drug the pile of coins toward him. That's how her luck had been for months.

A young man who had entered unnoticed made his way to her through the crowd of people who milled about in the tavern. Facial hair was not yet his and his hair was neat and orderly as always. The hat he wore was a three pointed mariner's hat. His white shirt was dirty as was the brown vest he wore. His brown trousers were dirty as well and a sizeable hole was worn in one knee. His boots seemed too big and awkward for him as he walked.

Reaching her, he gently placed a hand on her shoulder and reported, "Captain, they've raised the new mast and the crew's working on getting the rigging in place. We should be good to go by this evening."

Without looking at him, she nodded and replied, "Okay. Get everyone ready to shove off by dark."

"Aye, Captain," he responded as he spun around to leave.

Reality was coming back to her even as she watched new cards slide her way. One by one she picked them up, not liking what she saw and sneering a little as the last one made it to her.

A thin man with graying hair and a white beard strode up behind her with a mug of something in one hand. His other hand was at his belt, his thumb hooked there near the cutlass he always wore. The gray shirt he wore was well kept and the black vest he wore over it looked new. His trousers looked like they had been recently pressed and he was well groomed, almost like a dignitary of some kind. He watched her for a moment as she tossed yet another coin toward the middle of the table. Not waiting for her to receive another card, he cleared his throat to draw her attention, which he got without even a look.

"Give me a moment, Bugs," she murmured.

He took a gulp from his mug and watched that moment as she lost yet another hand.

"At your convenience," he said to her as she dropped her head into her hands.

Heaving a sigh, she gathered up what money she had left and shoved it into a pouch on her belt, then stood and reached for her own mug, offering, "Thanks for the game, mates."

"Thanks for the money, Lass." one of them countered.

She responded with a smile and a sneer and turned to follow the gray headed fellow to another table near the back, and everyone at the table she just left watched her, keeping their eyes on the red, form fitting tights that covered her legs and hips and left little to the imagination. As they sat down, she rubbed her eyes with one hand and pleaded, "Just give me good news."

"Okay," he complied, "they haven't caught you yet."

She stared off into nothing and nodded.

"You're pushing your luck, Rose," he informed. "The Governor's got an even bigger price on your head now, so big that I don't know who you can even trust anymore."

She turned her eyes down and nodded again.

"How's your ship?" he asked before taking a drink from his mug.

Her lips tightened and she replied, "She got pretty banged up. I barely got her to port in one piece, and without my main mast." Looking to him, she offered, "I guess I should be thanking you for what you did out there."

He smiled slightly. "I just distracted them. And there's no British frigate made that can outrun the *Silver Falcon*. Besides, it's nothing you haven't done for me a hundred times."

With a smile and a nod, she said, "Well, maybe I'll live to do it a hundred more. I guess that price they have on me is not yet high enough for you to turn me in."

"Nor will it be," he informed straightly. Taking another drink, he shook his head and advised, "You need to get yourself away from Port Royal, missy. You've been damn lucky they haven't noticed that wreck you brought in. I'm surprised they haven't a detachment of guards come after you."

"Just as soon as the *Dragon* is sea worthy," she assured. "I'm just going to lay low until then." She shook her head. "I had to call in my last favor from the shipyard just to get her in."

"I noticed her flying British colors," Bugs observed. "Nice touch."

"Just one of many captured flags," she said straightly. "I'm going to try and get out this evening whether the repairs are done or not. I think we can limp to Tortuga with what we've got in a couple of days."

He nodded. "Right through all the sentry ships that are waiting for you. Why don't you let me get you out of here tonight?"

Shaking her head, she took a gulp from her mug and insisted, "I won't leave my ship and crew behind."

"The gallows won't care about your loyalty, Rose."

"I know," she said softly, looking into her mug. "We lost some good mates on that last outing, didn't we?"

Bugs nodded again and confirmed, "Aye, we did." He raised his mug to her and added, "But we've still got each other, Lass."

She smiled and bumped his mug with hers and they both drank.

"I sure don't know what I'm supposed to do now," she informed, staring back into her mug. "Seems like every navy in the world is gunning for the *Scarlet Dragon* and her captain."

"I know the feeling," Bugs agreed. "Rose O'scarlett is almost as infamous as Blackbeard, Sparrow and that lot. Best be keeping your head down, Lass."

"Aye," she said, nodding slowly.

"You could leave the sea," he suggested. "Not too late for you to start a new life."

"Could you?" she countered.

"I'm too old and set in me ways, Rose. Take what's left of your youth and settle down somewhere."

"I have to see this through," she insisted. "I have more than just myself to think about."

"Aye," he said with much sarcasm in his voice. "I'm sure the gallows will love to know that."

She rolled her eyes. "Aye, you said that last time, too." She huffed another sigh and insisted, "I'll be all right once I'm at Tortuga. I can regroup there."

"If you get there," he added.

An unnatural hush fell over the tavern as the door slammed. The creaking of the floor and clop of heavy boots drew everyone's attention to the door, and many quickly looked away and ducked down, trying hard not to be noticed.

The man who entered was of enormous stature with thick arms and a bulky chest and back. Black hair reached nearly to his shoulders and his black goatee added menace to his already imposing features, which were primitive with an exaggerated brow and very heavy jaw. Faded black trousers looked like they had been recently dried of sea water and big boots found the floor with purpose. He wore no shirt over his titanic frame, only a black jerkin that showed off the muscular bulk of his chest and arms. Cruel green eyes scanned the tavern as he strode in and found the bar. This was a man who knew he was feared and made no secret that those who did had good reason to.

And many of the patrons, about half the people in the tavern, quietly slipped out the door. Those who remained were no longer so festive and many of them hunched down and murmured amongst themselves as they tried not to be noticed.

One of the men behind the bar was quick to grab a pitcher and reach to one of the barrels of ale, turning the valve as quickly as he got the pitcher under it. As the big man arrived, the barkeep turned with the nearly full pitcher and set it down in front of him.

Grabbing it by the handle, the huge man in black turned toward the room and leaned back against the bar, propping his elbow on it as he raised the pitcher to his mouth and took a few gulps from it.

Rose had her eyes locked on the big man and was unaware that her lips hung open at the sight of him. She raised her chin toward him and asked, "Who is that?"

"No one you want to associate with," Bugs warned. "Keep your distance from that bloke and stay out of his way. I've never heard of him granting quarter to any under his guns."

"Really," she drawled in a challenging tone.

"Miss O'scarlett, if you only take one piece of advice your entire life then take this one and keep your distance from that pirate."

6

"Pirate, is he?" she asked absently. "He looks like a rough one. Think he's for hire?"

"Everyone's for hire, Rose, except Captain Jones over there. You really don't want to throw your lot in with him."

"You haven't told me why I shouldn't," she pointed out, still staring at the big man. "He might just be the one to get a girl out of some copious hot water."

"Or turn you over to the Reds for a handsome profit," Bugs countered.

"Do you know him?" she asked.

"Only by reputation," was his answer.

Another of Rose's crew slipped in, creeping along the far wall as if to keep as much distance between himself and the big man at the bar as he could. His bald head shined a little in the light of the oil lamps and he wore no shirt over his impressive build. His eyes never left the big man as he took a chair across the table from Rose and reported, "They'll have the ship seaworthy by tonight, Captain, but she's in a hard way. Lots of British soldiers snooping about, too."

She absently nodded.

Bugs cleared his throat.

The crewman bade, "Captain? Ye hear me?"

"Yes!" she barked, suddenly irritated. "The snoopers are too brittle, I heard!"

He exchanged looks with Bugs.

Rose noticed him staring with wide eyes at the big man and she asked, "What do you know about that big bloke over there?"

"Nothin' I like, Captain. I heard tell he once took on a garrison of British 'cause one of 'em looked at him wrong and killed half of 'em bare handed. I also heard tell he sank four frigates in one day and nary took a cannon hit to his ship. Bit a shark and killed it once, I hear. Never offered quarter to those under his cannons and takes not a prisoner, I hear. Killed a man not long ago in a tavern in Tortuga who he thought was cheating him at cards, broke the poor soul's neck with his bare hands. Comes from the deepest part of Hell, me think. Davy Jones himself avoids him."

"And his name?" she prodded.

"All the men I know just call him Sir."

Rolling her eyes again, she looked to Bugs and asked, "Does he have a first name?"

He answered straightly, "Only name I've heard for him is Cannonflash Jones. He captains the most feared ship on the seven seas, a giant two hulled monster called the *Black Dragon*."

"I like the name," she drawled.

"Don't get you any ideas, Rose," Bugs warned.

She looked down at her mug, then gulped down the last of what she had and stood, informing, "I'm empty. Be right back." Ignoring the groans of her friend and crew member, she strode with a sultry walk to the bar and stopped a few paces down from the big man, leaning onto the bar as she slid her mug to the barkeep across from her. The commotion in the tavern went unnoticed as her thoughts were consumed with the big man beside her. She pretended to ignore him, but this was difficult as she wanted to see him close up.

A young woman who was rather thin and half a head shorter than Rose approached from the other side of the bar and took her mug. Long straight black hair was kept perfectly brushed and combed and was restrained behind her with a red ribbon. She wore a forest green dress that had a very low and lacy neckline and short sleeves. Very pretty in the face, her big brown eyes were locked wide on the huge pirate who stood beside Rose. She absently took the empty mug and pulled it toward her, then finally looked to Rose and asked, "More rum?"

"Aye," Rose replied, "that would be wonderful, Maria. Thank you."

The barmaid took a black bottle from beneath the bar and filled Rose's mug, turning her eyes back to Jones as she did. Looking back to Rose with an arched brow, she shook her head in slight motions.

Rose smiled back and nodded.

"You're just as impressive from behind," someone behind her complimented, his accent unmistakably British and his speech very direct and proper.

Maria backed away, her eyes darting about behind Rose, who casually raised her brow and looked over her shoulder.

Fanned out behind her were four navy guards in bright red uniforms. They were heavily armed and three had their hands on their weapons. The fourth had his arms folded.

"Did you think you would go unnoticed here in Port Royal for long?" the officer asked, smiling as he raised his chin slightly.

Rose shrugged. "Well, I was hoping." Her right hand moved down toward her cutlass.

Metal rang as the three soldiers drew their weapons.

Now she was feeling cornered, and near panic. Ever so slowly, she turned and leaned her elbows on the bar, raising a leg to prop her boot against it and allowing her scarlet tights to show off her shape. "Well I'm glad to see the law around here is on its toes. God only knows what could happen to a girl in these parts."

The officer raised his brow. "Do you mean like a trial and hanging?"

"Not what I had in mind," she countered. "Um, would you gents mind if I were to finish the drink I just ordered?"

"I'm afraid I would," he replied.

She looked back and took the mug anyway, her eyes on it as she said, "Oh, come now. Can't a girl have one last drink before the gallows?" She raised the mug to her lips, then swept it to make the rum splash into the faces of three of them.

Taken off guard, the fourth took a step back as the other three reached for their burning eyes, and before he could get himself set with his weapon she kicked him hard in the chest and knocked him into the table behind him.

Swiftly, she grabbed the officer's arm and spun herself around, flinging him into the soldier who was trying to quickly right himself.

Four more soldiers burst into the tavern.

Her brow arched and she sighed, "Oh, great," then she pushed one rum-blinded man into the other and grabbed a chair, hurling it at the four men who had just stormed in.

Bugs and her crewman were already in action and jumped the officer and one of the soldiers as they tried to get her from behind.

The other patrons simply stayed out of the fray.

Rose pushed a table over and rolled it toward the four charging newcomers, then she darted around them and reached for a mug on another table. Someone grabbed that arm, and before she could react, someone grabbed the other. Her arms were twisted behind her by two men and she was turned to see the officer striding toward her, still rubbing his eyes. As he neared, she noticed Bugs and her crewman being held at sword point by three of the British, and Bugs' hand was on his cutlass, ready to draw it. As their eyes met, Rose subtly shook her head, hoping to call him off before he ended up arrested as well.

Shaking his head, the officer stopped a pace away and folded his arms. "I didn't expect you to come quietly, Miss O'scarlett, nor did the chap who turned you in. I think it's time for you to just stop this nonsense and come along now."

She drew deep air, trying to catch her breath, then she nodded. "You're right. No more nonsense." She kicked him hard in the gut, pushing off of him and sending herself and her two captors stumbling backward. They ran into something, and ale splashed all over them.

The officer's eyes grew wide.

Rose wrenched one arm free and half turned to take on the other soldier, then she froze as she looked up into the face of the big man at the bar.

His pitcher was still in his hand and the ale that had once been in it covered him. He was staring down at her, and he did not look happy.

She smiled sweetly and offered, "Sorry."

He brushed some of the ale off of him and slammed the pitcher down, his gaze shifting to the soldiers who held her.

The officer took a few steps back, pointing a shaking finger at the big man as he shouted, "This doesn't involve you, Jones!"

Not known for a forgiving nature, Cannonflash took the shirt of one of the soldiers with one hand and hurled him over the bar, slamming him into the mugs and glasses on the other side. As he fell to the floor and was covered with bar wares, the second soldier drew his sword and tried to thrust, but his arm was caught and the big man's arm torpedoed fist-first into his face, knocking him out cold. He was thrown into the officer as another soldier charged.

The three holding Bugs and Rose's crewman at sword point abandoned them and charged the big man, who responded by throwing a heavy table at them.

This time patrons fled the bar.

Rose slowly backed away, watching this bear of a man take on five of England's finest, and as he mercilessly beat them down,

Bugs and the crewman grabbed her arms and pulled her toward the door.

"Time to go," Bugs insisted as they negotiated around overturned furniture.

She did not resist, but she did protest, "We should help him."

Bugs laughed and shook his head. "You just keep thinkin' that, Lass, and while you're at it let's give him some distance."

Out of the tavern, they slowed their pace to stroll unnoticed through town and toward the water.

"Well they know you're here," Bugs observed. "They'll no doubt be looking into finding your ship. We need to be shoving off now!"

She raised her brow and looked to him. "*We*, Mister Nailhall?"

"Yes, we. Your rigging isn't set and your *Dragon'll* not take the wind well without her main sails." He looked over his shoulder, squinting against the sun that plunged toward the horizon. "Should be dark in a couple of hours. I'll tow ye out to sea and keep the lines on until your sails are set." When he heard an angry sigh from her, he added, "Put your pride away, Lass. You'd do the same for me if I liked it or not."

"Aye," she conceded softly, her gaze on the path before her. Looking up, she saw a tailor shop and said, "Got to make a stop first. Mister Larson, get to the ship and get 'er ready to get under way."

"Aye, Captain," the crewman replied, hurrying on his way.

"Another shopping spree?" Bugs asked grimly.

"They know what I look like by now. Gotta make sure they don't recognize me."

"Be quick, then," he sighed.

This took nearly an hour and she emerged from the tailor's shop looking like a different woman. Her hair was up and worn under a large brimmed black hat that had a long white feather stabbed into one side. Her white shirt was traded for a red one with a black vest, and dark pink trousers conformed to her shape as well as her old ones had. Black boots went nearly to her knees.

Seeing Bugs, she ran her fingers along the brim of her new hat and asked, "What do you think, Captain Nailhall?"

He nodded and dryly said, "Beautiful. We need to go."

She rolled her eyes and took his side.

"Two navy soldiers were lookin' for you a while ago," he reported. "The place is crawling."

"They aren't looking for the big fellow?" she asked.

He huffed a laugh. "Look what happened the last time they found him. Today they're interested in a troublesome woman named Rose O'scarlett."

"Never heard of her," Rose joked.

As they reached the dock, they stopped suddenly as they saw a sea of red uniforms swarming about.

Rose's eyes darted around and she murmured, "Not good."

"Aye," Bugs replied.

"Now is when that big berserker from the tavern would come in handy," she observed.

Pursing his lips, he nodded. "Aye, but right now we'll have to rely on our wits."

Her eyes scanned the many soldiers scattered about the beach, dock and shipyard. "Think they'll notice if we just stroll right up the dock to your ship?"

"I can't see you drawing any attention in that outfit," he replied.

Rose recognized the sarcasm in his voice and shook her head slightly. "This isn't an outfit they'll be looking for."

"No, they're looking for the woman in it."

Rose smiled slightly and wrapped her arms around one of his. "Well, perhaps they're not looking for a lady who you are bringing aboard to show a good time."

His eyes slid to her. "Why Miss. You must think me a hussy."

She laughed loudly and drew in close to him. The British soldiers were taking notice, but in a fleeting way and her face did not hold their attention long enough to be recognized by anyone. Fortunately, her body was a good distraction here. It was a long, tense walk to the dock where Captain Nailhall's ship waited.

Moored across from a small Navy warship, Bug's ship was not a huge one by any means. Small and fast, and heavily armed, it could sail shallow waters that the larger British patrol craft could not. His crew worked at a moderate pace to ready the ship to return to the sea and a few of them carried supplies across the planks that accessed it from the pier.

Almost there, more eyes found them and both began to feel more and more unnerved.

Thirty yards away they passed a stack of crates that had been inspected by the Navy soldiers and Rose saw that one was still open and the packing was straw. A number of clear, corked bottle tops protruded from the straw within the open crate and her hand swept in with a fluid motion and removed one. She clamped down on the cork with her teeth and pulled it free, spitting it the other direction, then she raised the bottle to her lips and took several long gulps.

Bugs glanced down at her. "How is it?"

Rose grimaced a little and replied, "A little dry for my taste, but not a bad wine for a white." She looked up at him and offered him the bottle. "Try some?"

"Later," he mumbled, his eyes locked on a Navy officer who was watching them approach.

This was a tall man with a sword on his left side, pistol on his right, decorations on his chest and a ruthless look in his eyes. He was clean shaven and perfectly groomed, wearing his hat perfectly. Behind him were two red clad soldiers with muskets in their hands, and they looked like they were ready and anxious for action.

Glancing around, Bugs saw far too many British soldiers on the pier to risk a confrontation, and there were even more on that patrol ship. A breath growled out of him as the officer and two armed soldiers with him approached, and he warned, "Be on your good behavior, Lass."

She took another drink from the wine bottle and assured, "You'll have no worries from me, Captain Nailhall." As the soldiers approached and stopped to block their path, Rose laughed and leaned heavily on Bugs' arm, slurring her words a little as she said with loud words in a thick British accent, "Why Captain! I think surely you should have more, I do!" As all three soldiers looked right at her, she pulled the brim of her hat down with the hand she held the bottle with, spilling some of the wine as she looked to them with a flirty smile. "Well 'ello, gentlemen."

The officer cleared his throat and looked back to Bugs. "Captain Nailhall, I presume."

Bugs nodded and confirmed, "Aye."

Raising his chin, the officer went on, "Seems to be some problems with your manifest. You mind telling me of your cargo?"

Bugs shrugged. "Not much to tell of. Farming supplies for Tortuga and such."

"And one pretty lady," Rose added in that thick accent. She leaned toward the officer and loudly whispered, "He's the captain of his own ship. Got me a man with a heavy purse, I do."

"And your manifest?" the officer pressed. "It appears to be missing."

"Not missing," Bugs corrected. "Many pirates about these days, especially working the docks. Many more working behind desks. That manifest stays locked up until I see the cargo meself. Wouldn't want any numbers changed on it, now would we?"

Nodding slightly, the officer agreed, "I suppose that's a wise precaution."

With a slightly wobbling head, Rose looked to Bugs and complained in that high voice, "You told me you'd show me your ship! I'm here to have me a good time, I am!"

Bugs glanced at her, then looked to the officer and raised his brow.

Folding his hands behind him, the officer leaned in close to Bugs, whispering in his ear, "I would just keep that one drunk, and when you leave Tortuga, make sure she stays there." Stepping back again, he raised his chin and announced, "You appear to be in order, Captain Nailhall. Carry on."

"Thank ye, sir," Bugs replied, leading the woman at his side past the navy men as they stepped aside.

Walking across the plank to get aboard was no special ordeal really, but Rose acted as if it was, barking a scream halfway across as she acted like she was about to fall off.

Once aboard, Bugs approached one of his crew and asked in a low voice, "Any Reds aboard?"

The man shook his head and looked around. "Came aboard a while back and sniffed about. Checked out our holds. Looked hard and asked lots of questions."

"They take anything?"

"Wanted the cannons. I told'em we've hired on to privateer for his Majesty's fleet against those pirates what keep raiding the merchants."

Bugs smiled and nodded. "Earned ye some extra gold, mate. Take your station."

"Aye, Captain." The old sailor looked Rose up and down and raised his eyebrows, nodding as he observed, "You'll be bringin' a man's heart to the deck, Captain O'scarlett."

She smiled back and curtsied to him. "I thank thee, kind sir."

He offered her a smile back and went about his tasks.

"We'll get you out to the *Dragon*," Bugs informed, "and we'll attach the tow lines and get you under way."

"You don't have to do this, Bugs," she informed solemnly.

He nodded.

Chapter 2

TWO DRAGONS

Getting Rose back aboard the *Scarlet Dragon* was easy enough and once there they attached the towing lines to her bow and they were off in short order.

Hours after dark, Rose stood behind the wheel of her ship, not really concentrating on keeping her course true as her mind was occupied with the problems at hand. The British had a growing presence on Tortuga and many of the mariners there, many of them pirates themselves, would not hesitate to turn her in for that reward. She had changed her clothes—again—and was wearing her scarlet tights again and a white shirt that had baggy sleeves, open down her chest and tied off high on her belly. A bandana was around her head and the wind in her hair was one of the few things she had left to look forward to.

With the ship largely blacked out with only a few lights burning, her men could do nothing aboard but sleep, and she had sent most of them to do just that. The next day would be a trying one. Short on money, she wondered how she would finish repairs to her ship and pay for some of the supplies she had coming in. Her crew had not been paid for almost a month and she knew they were growing restless and she also knew she would have to get her ship back in order and back to plundering, and do it quickly.

One of her crew climbed to the top of the wheelhouse and was slow to stride to her. A man in his fifties, he was not well groomed; his graying black hair was as unkempt as his scraggly beard as he strode to her with long steps and a slight limp. Wearing a faded blue shirt and black trousers with a brown three point hat on his head that was worn by many mariners, his eyes showed strain and concern as they found her.

She did not even glance at him as she turned the wheel to make a slight adjustment to keep the ship's direction.

Turning to face forward, he folded his arms and stared ahead at the heavy sloop that pulled them steadily toward Tortuga. Finally he nodded and said, "That Captain Nailhall is a good bloke."

Rose nodded.

"Might be the last of your favors with him," he added.

"Aye," she agreed. "He's a good man, Mister Smith. I'd do the same for him in an instant."

With a slight nod, Smith observed, "Aye, but not so profitable." He finally turned his eyes to her. "We need to start bringing in some money, Captain O'scarlett. The crew'll not keep so long with no pay in their pockets and it's been more than a month."

Tight lipped, Rose nodded yet again and informed, "I've another shipment waiting in eastern Cuba and a couple of buyers. Once we resupply at the port in Tortuga then we can—"

"That kind of trade ain't what I mean," he snapped. "You know what I mean, Rose. The Merchant ships south of here are full of gold and the like coming and going and we've not gone after one."

"They're also escorted and heavily armed these days," she countered. "Until this ship is back in form we'll not sail into another pitched battle only to limp away empty handed. Not again."

He huffed a laugh. "So now we're a merchant vessel."

"We'll do what we must," she insisted. "With more heavy cannon we'll be able to take anything out there."

Smith loosed another hard breath, then looked to the East, to the pre-dawn glow. "Mornin's coming. Think we'll miss the patrols out here?"

"I'm hoping so," she admitted. "We aren't exactly in condition to fight at the moment."

He looked around, then behind, and he raised his chin. "Captain, we've got a problem."

She finally looked his way, then over her shoulder, her eyes widening.

Following them were four ships, their white sails just barely visible in the dim light of pre-dawn and filled with the wind.

"British?" Smith asked.

"I can't see merchants sailing in formation like that," she answered. "Rouse the crew and do it quietly. Let's see about getting what sails we can up and get our guns ready for them."

"You mean to turn and fight?"

Rose loosed a hard breath and replied, "We won't outrun them and we'll need to be ready when they overtake us."

Shaking his head, Smith turned to carry out his orders.

As the glow in the eastern sky grew a little brighter the crew of the *Scarlet Dragon* was frantically at task to get up what little canvas the rigging was in place for. Slowly, as the lower of her sails filled with the wind, the ship lurched forward just a little faster, and with Bugs' ship pulling her she made much better speed, but the ships pursuing her continued to close on her. It would take more than an hour to raise more canvas, and that was an hour they did not have.

The chase did indeed drag on and the British closed to within a half mile before that first hour. The sun was not yet up but was making its presence known all around and its light was an unwelcome addition to what had been a blind race. Bugs' ship could easily outrun the four frigates behind them. The *Scarlet Dragon* could easily outrun them, with all her sails up.

With better light her crew was up in the rigging and working frantically to get it set. The next step was to lighten the ship, but without her full sails the *Scarlet Dragon* would still not be able to outrun the ships behind her. As a sail was rigged it was opened and filled with the wind, and ever so slowly the ship began to gain speed.

Rose looked behind often and could only watch helplessly as the British ships drew closer. If she was caught, her next stop would be a short trial, then the gallows, and probably her entire crew would accompany her. Looking forward again, she looked to Bugs' ship that desperately pulled her toward safety. Few pirates were so unified and her loyalty to Captain Nailhall was absolute. She would not risk him being captured as well.

The crack of a cannon sounded behind and she wheeled around as a ball slammed into the water right behind her ship. As the fountain of water settled back into the sea, she stared with wide eyes and open lips at the ships that pursued and steadily gained on her. They were only firing warnings. Just two or three more and she would face all their guns, and she knew her ship was not in any condition for such a fight.

Smith ran up the ladder and took her shoulder, pointing off the port side as he announced, "Fog bank!"

She looked, and almost smiled. "You figure we can make it?"

"At the rate they're gaining, probably not, but it's better than no chance at all."

Rose looked to Bugs' ship yet again. There was finally a chance to escape, slim as that was, but she would have to afford her friend the same chance. "Take the wheel," she ordered, and when Smith grasped the wheel she darted around it and down the ladder to the first deck. Running past her working crew and dodging around everything littering the deck.

As she reached the bow she turned her eyes to the two thick ropes that tethered her ship to Captain Nailhall's. Her eyes darted about and finally she saw what she was looking for, hanging on the front wall of the superstructure for the second bow deck. She took the axe in her hands and turned to the ropes, swinging hard over her head and cutting the first of them halfway through. Two more chops and it snapped and sprang toward the towing ship. Turning to the other, she did not even hesitate with the axe, chopping through it with only two swings. She felt the *Scarlet Dragon* slow down and watched as Captain Nailhall's ship began to quickly open the distance.

"Godspeed," she whispered to her old friend.

Her crew watched her in disbelieving silence as she hurried toward the wheelhouse, and she ignored their stares. Taking the wheel from her first mate, she ordered, "Get down there and get this ship ready to fight. If we don't make it to the fog then this could get messy."

He glared back at her and pointed out, "We might have made it still under tow."

"Just get the wind in our sails," she snapped, "and get ready to turn hard!"

Responding only with a sneer, he headed to the lower deck.

Another shot sounded and struck just off of their starboard side, very close. The marksmanship of the British sailors was legendary and she knew they could hit her at any time. Looking over her shoulder again she saw them a quarter of a mile or less away from her. With a sharp tack they could bring the fury of all their broadsides to bear on her. She figured she had one more warning shot before they did just that.

Ahead and to her left was that fog bank. It appeared to be almost two miles away and very dense and when she turned toward it her ship would slow considerably, and the British would be upon her in moments. She would have to time this perfectly, and she knew that her chances were slim even if she did.

The final warning shot fired, this time from another of the navy ships and this time hitting close to her port side. They had issued their final warning.

"Mister Smith!" she called. "Angle those port guns as far back as you can and be prepared to fire as soon as they're in your sights!"

"Aye," he called back.

She knew that a barrage of eighteen pounders would do little against the ships behind her, but it would send a message. If they meant to take her down, she would go down fighting.

Looking back yet again, she saw them less than three hundred yards behind her, and they appeared to be making ready to attack her.

"Hold on!" she shouted. With all her strength she wrenched the wheel over and began to spin it as hard as she could and her ship responded with an eager lurch to port and the starboard side listed toward the water.

With surprising speed the *Scarlet Dragon* turned hard toward the fog, but the British seemed to expect this. One turned to pursue, two stayed on course after the *Silver Falcon* and were ready to fire as they passed the *Scarlet Dragon*, and the forth turned to the right, bringing its guns to bear on her from directly astern where the ship was most vulnerable.

This had been a fatal miscalculation! Experience was not conspiring against Rose this day, but her enemies had learned well from previous encounters with her and this time were ready.

She saw the maneuver and turned the wheel hard the other way, shouting down to the deck, "Get those starboard guns directed to the stern and fire as you get'em into your sights!"

The British were denied a direct shot at the *Scarlet Dragon's* stern and when their guns fired many of their cannonballs hit her side at too sharp an angle to damage her and glanced off, but many others connected and ripped into her side. By the time she was in a position to return fire only eight of her guns were able to reply and only five of them connected. Smoke poured from the *Scarlet Dragon's* starboard side and the men on the gun deck worked feverishly to control a couple of small fires, right two cannons and move the dead and injured away from the area they needed to work in.

Though it would slow her further, Rose turned the wheel back to the left, redirecting the ship hard back toward the fog which was now only five hundred yards away. Once inside she could hopefully get out of the sights of the British guns and limp to safety. As she neared the fog, the wind began to die down and her ship slowed. Turning desperate eyes up to her sails, she watched as a couple of them began to go limp.

"Captain!" one of her crewmen shouted up to her. When she looked down at him he was leaning over the rail of the ship and pointing ahead and a little to starboard.

"Sweet mother of God!" another shouted.

She looked that way.

A truly horrible apparition exploded out of the fog with frightening speed. It was huge and black. Two hulls were joined as one and they were propelled by black sails that were rigged in a total of six masts, three on each hull. The hull itself looked to be more than twenty feet taller than the *Scarlet Dragon's* and it was easily more than eighty feet longer, twice her overall size! From both of the highest masts it flew the colors of a pirate, but not a flag like she had seen before: A cannon and cutlass were crossed beneath a skull that appeared to be frozen in a horrible battle cry.

It was only a hundred yards away and coming right at her, yet Rose found she could not react. Her eyes were locked wide on the leviathan before her ship, one that was less than a hundred yards away and closing on her with frightening speed.

A few seconds of clarity was all she needed and it struck her like lightning. With strength and speed she did not know she possessed, she began to wrench the wheel over to the left and her ship responded smartly.

Then the cavernous maws of eight huge cannons caught her eyes. They were facing forward, four on each hull of the massive warship. She had never seen guns so big, not even mounted on any of the British or Spanish forts she had visited!

Thunder and fire exploded from the bow of the huge black ship as the eight giant cannons fired almost simultaneously, enveloping the front of the massive ship in thick smoke.

Rose felt the concussion all the way to her bones and she was sure her ears would explode. She dared a look behind her, her mouth falling open as she saw the entire bow of the ship that was pursuing her blow apart in fire and smoldering wood. Bodies, cannons and smoke-trailing timbers were hurled into the air and the navy ship disappeared in a plume of black smoke.

The *Scarlet Dragon* veered from the path of the monster that was bearing down on her and still the hulls of the two ships scraped for about ten feet as they passed, and the *Scarlet Dragon* shuddered.

Keeping the wheel hauled over, Rose looked to her left to watch what was happening. Nothing remained of the ship that had been chasing her but the cabin at her stern and some floating debris. With one salvo the front of the ship had been completely destroyed and she was quickly going down by the bow. Rose expected the other navy ships to move in and attack, but instead they turned to run.

Cannon fire erupted from the black leviathan again, this time from its left flank and another of the British ships was pounded by cannonballs, half of which exploded when they hit. The main mast of the stricken ship fell and drug down much of the rigging with it. The black ship turned hard and much faster than one would think possible and brought its starboard broadsides to bear on another of the British ships. There were two decks of twelve guns, twenty-four in all, and they fired a murderous barrage into the unfortunate navy ship. This one managed to return fire and Rose raised her chin as she watched the cannonballs that hit the black ship simply bounce off. One of these glancing shots slammed into her own ship, penetrating the forward deck.

It was time to go.

Turning the wheel the other way, she directed her ship into the fog where it disappeared.

Even as she fled toward safety, Rose could still hear the thunderous sounds of battle growing more distant and she knew that it would follow her for some time even after she could no longer hear them.

Chapter 3

OSCARLETT IN NEED

The *Scarlet Dragon* anchored in a secluded cove on the other side of Tortuga to escape notice both from patrolling British ships and those who would turn her in for the bounty on her captain. Repairs could continue, her injured and dead could be attended to, and hopefully she could formulate a plan to get her back on the path she needed to be on.

Walking up the beach in snug fitting gray tights and a white button up shirt which was tied at her belly and left open otherwise for some relief against the tropical heat, she had her favorite cutlass on her black belt, her pistol, dagger, and a few pouches full of money and other items. The red bandana around her head would hopefully keep the sweat from her eyes as well as keeping her hair under control.

Smith strode at her side, and he was shaking his head.

"I know you don't like it," she snapped, "but if we're to get to safe waters then this is how it is going to have to be."

"I understand, Rose, but this place was crawling when we left and they'll be looking for you now. They find this ship and it's over before it begins."

"Then make sure they don't find her." She clenched her teeth. "Listen carefully. If I'm not back before dark then make sure the rigging is finished and get my ship to Santiago."

"Without her Captain?" Smith grumbled.

"The crew will follow you as they do me, Mister Smith and we both know they will. Just know that I'll never abandon you or the crew. We'll see this through, I promise."

"Aye, Captain." He growled a sigh and looked away. "Just be sure that you return before dark, savvy? The crew's grown restless and there's been talk. You'd best be showin' them something soon, and something profitable."

With a nod, she conceded, "I know, Mister Smith. With any luck I'll be back with good news by dark."

"About a galleon full of gold, I hope," he grumbled.

She stopped and he stopped beside her. She was staring down that trail that led into a thick jungle, and her eyes were focused and strained. Drawing a deep breath, she finally said, "Just remember my words, Mister Smith, and if I don't get back before dark then get my ship to Santiago." She looked to him and finished, "You have the *Scarlet Dragon* until I return."

Tight lipped, he nodded to her, then turned and strode back toward the ship.

Rose would not watch after him, but she turned one more look to the *Scarlet Dragon* before starting the long trek into town.

* * *

Tortuga's only civilized village was not what the rest of the world would call civilized. Though the British were trying to expand their presence and even the Company had established itself, most of what could be found here were farmers, fisherman, and mariners, and most of the mariners who haunted the taverns and other businesses near the docks were considered unsavory types at best. This was a stronghold for pirates and the British had all but accepted this.

Stone and timber made up most of the buildings that lined the few streets. Some parts of town more inland had been fortified with stone walls to repel native aggressors or invaders from unfriendly countries who would wish to colonize the island.

The walls were very old, but still in good form, whitewashed in the heart of the village where businesses thrived, but more run down toward the beach where the seedier lot spent most of their time.

And near the water is where Rose was heading. Sure there was an appealing aspect to the more civilized part of town, but she needed to be where the ruffians could be found, and she needed to call in some favors.

The tavern that overlooked the main pier was as it had always been, rowdy. The furnishings were all old and appeared to be second hand, and most of them had been repaired more than a few times. The inside of the tavern was as dingy and weathered as the outside and made of gray planks and timbers. It was not a place where one would see people of high society, rather its opposite. Lit by old, rusty lamps on the walls and tables, it was a shadowy place where a lady would not go willingly unless she had business within, and many of the women within had just that, making an easy living off of drunken mariners. She strode in to catcalls and long, hungry stares, but knew to ignore them all. There was business to conduct here, assuming she could find the people she needed to conduct it with.

Only a few steps in from the door, she stopped and set her hands on her hips, scanning the tavern slowly. She did not immediately see who she was looking for and pursed her lips. Looking to the bar, she decided it was time for a drink.

Wading between tables, passed out men on the floor, overturned chairs and the like, her eyes still darted about in a search for some people she knew, people who often haunted this tavern.

Leaning an elbow on the bar, she half turned and looked out into the crowd.

"Captain O'scarlett," a gruff, gravely voice greeted from the bar.

She turned her head and offered him a little smile.

This was a rough looking man, one who had belonged to the sea for most of his life. Gray hair was thin and white eyebrows were long and bushy. He had a ragged beard and no mustache and regarded her with strained eyes. His was the long sleeved white shirt of an old mariner, though the shirt was dingy and had not been properly washed for some time, as the smell from him would attest.

Resting an elbow on the bar, he leaned in close to her, his pale blue eyes piercing into hers as he grumbled, "Got ye quite the reputation, haven't ye, Lass?"

With a little nod and a raise of her eyebrows, she confirmed, "More than I'd like, Mister Greun. Can you offer a girl a drink?"

"No taste for me ale still?" he asked, and when she shook her head he smiled and turned to the back where the waiting mugs and liquor were neatly stacked on the shelves above the rough cabinets behind the bar. "Woman of the sea and your only interest is me expensive rum."

"Women like expensive things," she reminded.

"Easy to see that in ye, Lass." He turned back with a waxed wooden mug full of rum and water and handed it to her, then leaned his elbow on the bar again and leaned toward her. "Come for that favor I owe ye?"

She shrugged and took a drink. "Honestly, I could use a hundred of them. The reds are coming down on me like spring rain, me ship's shot up and I could really get her into a shipyard if I can."

Greun shook his head. "No shipyard here, Lass. Reds are watchin'em like a dog watches a lame cat. Taken many a ship, they have. Keep yer distance and get yer pretty little self out of here when ye can."

Rose huffed a sigh and took another gulp of rum. "I simply can't believe my foul fortune lately. Can't believe it."

"Fortune is as ye make it, Lass."

"Speaking of which," she started before taking another gulp of rum, "I need money. Any word on a buyer for my last shipment?"

"Had a buyer, straight up," Greun informed, then he shook his head. "That was one of the ships that was seized by the reds. Had good money and they took him to the gallows and that governor at Port Royal got his gold."

"As usual," she grumbled.

"Aye, the place is crawling, Lass. You don't need to be here."

She glanced around the bar. "Well, as soon as my rigging is ready to go then I'll be off to Cuba. I can get my wits back about me there."

"And no worries about the reds," Greun added. "Just don't get yeself in bad with the Spanish over there and you'll have no worries, aye?"

"Aye," she confirmed. "I've been good about leaving their ships alone. Let's just hope they don't hear about the bounty that Governor Berkley has on me." She looked to him again and asked, "Any sign of Captain Nailhall of late?"

Shaking his head, Greun confirmed, "Not hide nor hair, Missy. If he's coming this way then I'm usually one of the first to see him. At least he likes me fine ale."

They both enjoyed a little laugh, then Rose saw him look toward the door and something unnerved him. Knowing not to turn herself for a look, she asked in a low voice, "Reds?"

"Aye," he replied. "Get that drink and find ye a table to the rear, and slip out when ye have the chance."

Rose did just that, and with very good timing. Daring a glance back, she saw a young officer and four heavily armed soldiers in the red coats of the British Royal Navy approach Greun, and he looked nervous. Finding a table in a relatively dark place, she took her seat and subtly blew out the lamp in the middle of it, and she turned her head slightly to hear what was said.

The young officer raised his chin and asked, "Have you been here all day?"

"Since morning," was Greun's curt answer.

"We're conducting a door to door search for a particular pirate," the officer informed. His speech was very clear, very deliberate, but his voice betrayed youth that he could not conceal. "Big chap wanted by the crown. Perhaps you've seen him?"

Greun shook his head. "Lot's of blokes come in here, some big, some not so big."

"You'd know him on sight," the officer insisted. "He's best known around these parts as Cannonflash Jones. Quite the notorious sort. Shot up a squadron of His Majesty's finest ships early this morning and I mean to bring him in for trial and hanging."

Laughing a hearty laugh, Greun shook his head and barked, "*You* mean to take Cannonflash? Boy, you'd best head back to your mama and send these men where they'll be safe."

Setting his jaw, the young officer grasped the hilt of his saber with his left hand and said loudly, "Now see here, old fellow. I mean to take him in for trial and hanging and if I find out you are harboring him then you'll join him on the gallows. In the meantime—"

"You got a whole garrison waiting outside?" Greun interrupted. "If you mean to have a go at Cannonflash with just you and four men then you'd better have your affairs in order." He raised a finger and added, "I tell you what, mate. How about a drink on the house for the five of you condemned men, aye? One last drink before he sends you all to your maker."

Everyone within earshot laughed with hearty laughs and the young officer's eyes narrowed as he glanced about.

When the laughter died down, he looked back to the barkeep and warned, "You'd best be telling me if you see him come in here, old boy, otherwise things will not be so easy for you in the future! Do we understand each other?"

"Oh, we understand," Greun chuckled. "I like ye, boy, so if Cannonflash comes in here I'll not send you his way, aye? Let ye grow up to manhood that way!"

Once again the bar erupted in laughter, but this time the officer turned on his heel and stiffly led his men back out.

Rose returned to the bar and rested her elbows on it in front of her, offering the old barkeep a little smile and a shake of her head. "Mister Greun, you are a man who takes a lot of chances."

"No more than that little boy!" Greun shouted back at her, and this time Rose joined the patrons in a good laugh.

The door slammed and quick boots striking the floor approached from directly behind her and Rose stiffened with wide eyes as the young officer leaned onto the bar right beside her.

"One last thing," the young man said loudly. "I'll not be spoken down to by the likes of you. You'd best consider how you would speak to His Majesty's officers or you could likely find yourself in a rather foul place! We wouldn't want this establishment shut down and confiscated by the crown, now would we?" When Greun shook his head, he finished with, "I thought not. Now be a good chap and just police those words a little better from now on." He turned his head and looked right at Rose.

Nervously, she looked back at him and offered a little smile.

He tipped his hat to her and offered, "Miss," then he turned and strode back out with those quick, clopping steps again.

And Rose finally allowed herself to breathe out, and her head sank all the way to the bar to lie on her crossed arms.

"Heh," Greun laughed. "Guess I'll be pourin' ye another drink, aye?"

Without lifting her head, she nodded.

Rose and Greun would talk for over an hour of things that were not even related to her current situation. From this old barkeep she had collected much wisdom over the years, much useful information, and she found her association with him to be a close one, more so than most others she knew. During that time many people came and went and from time to time the kindly barkeep would excuse himself to go and attend to one.

Still, her problems would not allow her to rest, even for a moment, though she did her best to relax as best she could, just to feel less of a burden if even for that fleeting moment.

Someone sat down beside her and she recognized Bugs' voice as he ordered, "Stoutest ale you've got, Mister Greun."

"Aye, Captain Nailhall," the barkeep said as he went to task.

When Rose looked to her old friend, she found his eyes already on her and some strange mix of fear and concern was there.

He raised his chin and said straightly, "Didn't expect to see you here, Captain O'scarlett."

She flashed him a friendly smile and picked up her mug, countering, "A girl sometimes needs to have her thirst quenched, Captain Nailhall. Why would that surprise you?"

As she drank, he replied, "Because your ship sailed more than an hour ago."

Rose coughed and slammed her mug down on the counter. Getting her breath back, she turned bewildered eyes to Bugs and barked, "What?"

"I thought you were on board," he reported. "Didn't know what to think when I came in and saw you here."

She turned her eyes ahead again, wide eyes that struggled for answers. "They must have been seen by the Reds. Passing patrol got a glimpse of them or something."

"You'd better hope that's all it was," Bugs warned as he raised his mug to his mouth.

Rose vented a sigh and raised a hand to massage her eyes. "I need to find a way to Santiago."

"Your ship's heading that way?"

"Aye, I've ordered Mister Smith to get her to the cove over there, but I told him not to leave unless I didn't make it back before dark. Don't know what he's doing out there in broad daylight with so many navy patrols around."

"Couldn't tell ye, Lass. If ye can wait a few days I can take you there meself. Got the ship laid up at the shipyard at current."

Her eyes shifted to him and widened. "Reds caught up to you after all, didn't they?"

"No run in with the British," he confessed. "Had a run in with a sizeable log that nobody on watch saw. Put a hole in me side."

"Ouch," she said sympathetically. Gulping down the last of her rum, she patted his shoulder and offered, "You be well, my friend, and keep your head down. The Reds are everywhere today."

"You do the same, Miss O'scarlett."

Rose made it to the docks with no problem. The British had thinned out and were otherwise engaged in conversations with each other or with many of the women who haunted the area in search of a mariner with a lonely ache and loose pockets.

Out in the open, she set her hands on her hips and scanned the area, looking for a ship captain who might need to make some quick money, and she had just enough gold on her to entice some ship captain to divert there. Not only her ship awaited her, but other issues involving shipments of material to her secret cache on the big island.

She strode down to the pier to look for ships that might be docked there. Across the bay was a ship that was very familiar to her, and captained by her friend Bugs Nailhall. Sure enough, the *Silver Falcon* was moored at another pier and was being unloaded, and timbers and tools were being taken out to her. With tight lips, she looked about again, finally seeing someone step off one of the small sloops that was moored halfway down the pier. As she approached, she hesitated. He was a dirty looking fellow with scraggly clothes, long unkept hair and wearing no shoes or boots. He also had a bottle in his hand. If he was the captain then she knew she would not be able to trust him. The search would have to continue.

About a hundred yards away she would find the shipwright. She knew him well and they had traded favors many times. Ever the pleasant fellow, she had always felt that she could trust him no matter the circumstances. She also felt that he would pay a heavy price to see her without her clothing, but he was ever the gentleman and never spoke openly of such things.

Nearing the open doors and the counter that kept him separated from his patrons, she could see the many wares he sold behind him, including coils of rope, block and tackle sets and parts, signal flags and many other items that were displayed on the walls behind him. He also sold cannons and shot for them, but they were not displayed for the authorities to see.

Almost there, she stopped as a huge, ominous form entered her field of vision and her eyes widened slightly as she watched the huge man in the faded black trousers and black jerkin stride right up to the shipwright. Looking to her old friend, who was a small fellow anyway, she saw the horror in his eyes as Captain Jones approached him, and he backed away as the huge pirate captain slammed his thick arms onto the counter.

Rose half turned her head and slowly approached, listening to what was said.

"What are you tellin' me?" Jones demanded in a deep, gruff voice. "I said ten kegs and you said you'd fill me order before today. Where is me powder?"

Swallowing hard, the shipwright tried to explain, "They seized the ship that was carrying it here and the shipment is being held! I—I—I've sent the seven I had to be taken aboard your ship and they should—"

Jones slammed his fist onto the counter and roared, "I said ten, ye mangy housecat!"

Raising his hands before him, the shipwright assured, "I'll make it worth your while, Captain Jones! By the time you're ready to sail to Cuba—"

"I'm leaving for Santiago in two hours," the big pirate yelled.

Rose raised her brow and pursed her lips.

"I'll have your powder when you return, Captain," the slight man assured, "me word on that! I'll even throw in an extra for your trouble!"

Raising his head, Jones growled, "Make sure that you do. When I come back I'll have me powder or I'll have your guts for fish bait, savvy?"

"Aye, Captain Jones. Not to worry! I'll have what you need, me word!"

Jones grunted and turned to walk away, leaving the shipwright shaken and breathing a sigh of relief that he would live a few more days.

Rose watched the big man stride toward town and, without thinking, she set about pursuing him. With his long strides he was not easy to run down, so she called after him, "Captain Jones." He did not even hesitate so she repeated, "Captain Jones! I would have a word with you."

He glanced back at her and scowled, growling back, "Be quick about it, wench," but he never really broke stride.

With some effort, she caught up and looked up at him as she offered, "I want to thank you properly for what you did out there."

"And what was that?" he grumbled.

"Mine was the ship that you saved from the Reds this morning. Had us a close scrape and I have you to thank for—"

"You got in me way," he snarled. "Do it again and I'll send you to the bottom like I did them."

"You saved my hide out there," she pointed out, "and I've a debt to you."

"Forget it," he growled.

"Well perhaps I would ask a favor from my savior."

"Favors aren't given lightly, Lass."

"All I would ask is passage to Santiago."

He scowled again. "I don't run a passenger ferry."

"You're going there, anyway," she reminded.

"Aye, and it looks like you'll be staying here."

She felt herself becoming frustrated but refused to succumb to it so quickly. Clearly, this man was not going to be easy to get through to, so a different tactic was called for.

She grabbed his big arm and stopped, tugging back to spin him around, and stumbled a few steps to keep her footing as he was not so easy to stop.

He finally stopped, looking down at her hand on his arm with eyes that threatened death.

Wisely, she removed her hand and folded her arms, raising her chin as she introduced, "I am Captain Rose O'scarlett. Perhaps you've heard of me."

Looking over his shoulder at her, he regarded her coldly and shook his head.

"I'm the most wanted woman in the Caribbean, considered famous in some parts." She raised her brow. "You mean you've never heard of Rose O'scarlett?"

"I have matters to attend," he informed rudely as he turned to continue on his way.

She set her jaw and pursued him again. "I'm only asking for passage to where you're already going. I can pay you if you like."

"Keep your shillings," he suggested. "If you're that hard up to go to Cuba then it's only a few days by dinghy."

Rose stopped and pursed her lips, then finally, loudly informed, "I have powder."

This time he also stopped.

"I stockpile it in a little cove near Santiago. It's kept all warm and dry."

Without turning around, he asked, "How much?"

"Eight, ten kegs at least," was her answer, "and I've another shipment due in the next couple of days."

He half turned his head.

"Got to keep my ship and my mates supplied," she went on, "for a price, of course." With a loud sigh, she looked away and wistfully said, "I'd hoped you could be one of my mates, but I suppose not."

"Powder and what else?" he asked sharply.

Smiling just a little, she turned her eyes back to him and replied, "Perhaps a few crates of navy muskets, perhaps some navy swords and pistols, perhaps all sorts of cannon shot. You said you need powder, though. So are you me mate or not?"

He just stared into the distance.

"You said you need three more kegs," she recalled. "I think I can spare three."

"Four," he corrected.

"I said I can spare three," she reminded.

"Cuba's a long swim, Lass, and I'll be wantin' pistols and shot for 'em."

She loosed a deep breath and looked down at her fingernails, considering his offer.

He turned and folded his huge arms. After a moment he prodded, "Well?"

One more quick check of her fingernails and she reluctantly nodded, then approached him with a sultry walk. "You drive a hard bargain, Captain Jones." She gasped as his big hand seized her shirt and she was pulled brutally toward him with strength she had not even imagined.

He snarled, warning, "You'd better be tellin' me the truth about this powder, Lass, or there will be some lucky shark or gator with you in his belly."

Wide eyed, she swallowed hard and nodded, assuring, "You'll see, Captain. I've no intention to cross you. I'd like you to stay on my side, if you please."

"See that you don't cross me," he advised, pulling her closer and her shirt up dangerously high on her chest. "I get me powder or your ship and your mates will get in me sights, savvy?"

She raised her chin. "Well, then. Sounds like we have an accord." When he released her she straightened out her shirt then raised her hand to shake his, and was a little relieved when he did. "Four kegs and a crate of pistols and shot." She raised her chin slightly. "So why not gold?"

He turned and continued on. "I get what I need with me cannons."

Rose followed with a slight smile. "Aye, so I've heard. So where are we going?"

Jones stopped and set his hands on his hips, looking up toward the sky as he vented an impatient breath.

Wisely stopping behind him, she just raised her brow, expecting an answer.

"I've things to attend, wench," he growled. "Go to the dock and wait for me there."

"Perhaps I want to make sure you don't sail without me," she lied, her eyes glancing over his big, muscular back. "Besides, if you want your powder and pistols you'd better make sure nothing happens to me. Many pirates about who would love to make off with a lovely lady like meself."

He growled, then shook his head and continued on his way.

"You never answered me," she informed.

"I don't like a lot of talk," he snapped. "I've no use for it."

"You're the Captain," she agreed.

"And best you remember that," he growled.

He had many errands that day and terrorized many people in the process. Though she had not heard of him until a day ago, he seemed to be well known to this place that she often visited.

Back at the docks, he entered a stone and timber structure near the main office for the shipyard, one that was well maintained and one of the few that actually had painted wood. The heavy, ornately carved wooden door had a polished brass handle which he pulled the door open by. Inside, it was a little smoky, and though it was well decorated with fine furnishings, paintings and statuary, the feel of the place was an ominous one. Many well dressed people were already there and all eyes found them as they entered. Once again conversation and activity stopped at first sight of the big pirate. Across the room was a long counter with a desk on one end. Bins full of parchments could be seen behind it and many pigeon holes were also behind the counter, most of those containing rolled papers, perhaps maps.

The man behind the counter was well dressed in a white shirt and a blue vest, both of which had been recently pressed. His dark hair was perfectly groomed and his eyebrows were very thick. A thin fellow, he did not look like he could hold his own in a fight and his eyes widened a little as the big pirate strode right up to him.

Jones rested his arms on the counter and glared down at the thin fellow, who swallowed hard under the attention of this huge man.

Without a word, the thin man turned to one of the pigeon holes and withdrew a rolled parchment, setting it down on the counter before the big pirate. It was bound with twine, which he removed by pulling one end of the knot.

Unrolling the parchment, Jones' eyes narrowed as he studied the words and drawings.

Drawing a breath, the thin man finally said, "I've had them delivered directly to your ship, Captain Jones. They're all in good order and still crated when they were delivered. Figured it best to keep them from unwanted eyes."

With a grunt, the big pirate nodded, his eyes still on the parchment.

Raising his eyebrows slightly, the thin man observed, "Never heard of guns that big on a ship before."

"Nor will you again," Jones growled.

Rose noticed a heavy set fellow in a black mariner's uniform watching them, and in an instant she recognized him. Her eyes widening, she turned away, back toward the counter. Anyone could see how tense she suddenly was and she hoped the man did not recognize her.

"Is it to your liking?" the thin man asked.

Jones nodded, ever so slightly. "Think they'll work. And me other items?"

Taking a half step back from the counter, the thin man nervously replied, "Um... Uh, the ship that carried them was seized."

The big pirate's eyes snapped to the thin man, and he did not look happy. "Seized by who?"

"Navy, I think, but most likely English Trading Authority." The thin man forced a smile, his eyes glancing toward the black clad man who was now standing behind Rose with his arms folded. "Suspected them of piracy. I expect the ship to be released in the next couple of days. Can't blame the Company for looking out for their interests."

"The Company?" Jones growled.

"English Trading," the thin man replied. "Well established in these parts. Good for business, they are."

"I know who they are," Jones snarled.

Rose felt something pressed against her back, something that felt much like the muzzle of a pistol. She half turned her head, her eyes cutting back that way as someone took a firm grip on her shoulder.

"Now then," the hefty fellow in the black uniform started in a low voice. "I think it's time you and I stepped outside for a little chat."

"I don't think that would be wise," Rose informed straightly.

"I don't care what you think, Miss O'scarlett," the man countered. "You are coming outside with me. You can walk or I can drag your limp and bleeding body out of here."

"You would shoot a lady?" she asked a little louder, hopefully loud enough for the pirate at her side to hear.

Jones slowly turned his head to look over his shoulder.

"You're a pirate," the English Trading officer sneered, "and your capture has been a long time coming."

Slowly, she looked up at Jones, raised her brow and shrugged. "Well, Captain Jones, it looks like you don't get your pay after all."

The officer's eyes widened and he looked up at the big pirate, declaring, "Jones!"

The big pirate's eyes narrowed and he turned toward the English Trading officer, ever so slowly.

Swallowing hard, the officer backed away, lowering his pistol as he said in a shaky voice, "I… I didn't… I thought you were still out at sea."

Jones took a few steps toward the retreating officer, locking the man's gaze in his own.

"This… This woman is wanted by the crown," the officer stammered. "My orders are to bring her in."

Rose took the big pirate's side and folded her arms. "So, you would mean to bring a girl in and collect that bounty yourself, would you? Perhaps Captain Jones is interested in the bounty on me. Think you'll be depriving him of that?"

His eyes narrowing, Jones took a step closer and bent toward the smaller man, a scowl on his face as he growled, "You mean to get in me way again? I have an accord with those over you, and if I have so much as a spit of trouble from any of you then your ships will find themselves under me guns again. You want to be the cause of that?"

Shaking his head, the officer assured, "No, Captain Jones! Um, I'll see to it that you aren't troubled again."

Jones turned back around, grumbling, "See to it, and see to it me cargo is released today."

When the officer looked to Rose, she raised her brow and asked, "Isn't there something you're supposed to see to?"

He nodded and fled from the place.

When she turned back to Jones, taking his side again, she smiled and observed, "That went well, I think."

He did not look at her, instead keeping his eyes on the parchment as he asked, "You know those four kegs of powder you owe me?"

She nodded. "It's five now, isn't it?"

"Aye," he confirmed.

They left the shop and she found herself keeping up with his long strides with some difficulty. A dinghy awaited them, and four of his crewmen were already there. They were a rough looking lot and all of them eyed her with mistrust. They were big men, all well armed with cutlass and pistol and dagger, and Rose found herself questioning the wisdom of this decision. She knew she could quite likely find herself chained in the hold of Jones' ship with he and his crew doing anything they wanted to her, and she knew that only the promise of those kegs of powder kept her from being turned in for that bounty or a fate worse than the gallows.

They boarded the small boat and the four men went to task getting it under way. Dark was a few hours away and they appeared to want to be away from the port as quickly as they could. Jones himself stood by the mast, holding onto it as the boat rocked and pitched. For protection more than anything, Rose stayed as close to him as she could. Horrible images of what could happen to a woman aboard a pirate ship flashed through her mind, but she did her best to dismiss them. She was a pirate herself, after all.

Many ships were at anchor beyond the bay, mostly those that did not want to be noticed. She knew this part of Tortuga was not well accommodating to larger ships, and what she had seen of this *Black Dragon* gave her the impression that it would be the largest out there.

And she would not be disappointed.

They passed fairly close to the ships that were at anchor at the mouth of the bay and she recognized a few of them.

And as they rounded one of them, a weathered and battle weary frigate that had once belonged to the French Navy, her eyes were filled with the ominous black form that was a quarter mile out, and her eyes widened as she saw it for only the second time.

Bugs' description had been right on the mark and memories of seeing it explode from the fog that morning charged fresh into her mind. The ship was black and made of the hulls of two heavy frigates. Each of these hulls was twice as large as her ship, and the *Scarlet Dragon* was a rather large ship in her own right. It was facing out to sea and they were approaching from astern. Her sails were furled and the deck was a beehive of activity. Many men were aboard, some up in the twin rigging of this behemoth as they worked with the black fabric of the sails. Drawing closer, she saw cannon barrels facing backward, which was unheard of. Four were on one hull, four on the other, and two more on the heavily built center spar that held the two hulls together and about twenty feet apart with the ship's rail continued across as if it had always been one vessel. The rigging appeared to be tethered together to work as one unit and the masts were shorter than they seemed they should be. Despite its bulk and massive displacement, it rode high in the water and seemed to have a very shallow draft for a ship so enormous.

Rose had seen firsthand what this monster could do to other ships and she felt a little unnerved about actually going aboard her, yet there was an anticipation here as well. This was the most feared ship at sea and she was almost giddy at the prospect of actually stepping onto her deck.

The dinghy sailed between the hulls and the men aboard, including Captain Jones, grabbed onto ropes that were lowered from both sides. Rose watched in amazement as the ropes were quickly tied off to four corners of the dinghy and two of the men broke off of this task to take down the sail.

One of them, a big, bald fellow who wore no shirt or shoes and looked as if he was forged from the sea itself looked to her and barked, "Don't just stand there gawking, Lass. Give us a hand with this canvas."

Knowing what to do, she helped them lower and secure the sail.

Looking up, Captain Jones shouted to someone overhead, "Bring us up true."

Some kind of mechanical working could be heard, much like an anchor hoist, and the dinghy was lifted from the water and toward a hole in the deck above.

Rose looked up to where they were going, swallowing hard as she saw many more men looking down at them, and an uncomfortable number of them had their eyes on her.

Finally reaching the top, the men jumped from the dinghy which fit nicely and very snugly into the opening. Wooden pegs were hammered into place to keep it there, fitting securely through holes in the deck trim and through the dinghy's hull. The big bald pirate turned back as he jumped from the dinghy, which sat a little lower than the deck, and offered her his hand. When she took it he pulled her almost brutally from the boat and onto the ship.

Jones had his arms folded as he looked around at the activity aboard his ship and he turned slightly and shouted, "Secure that gun or you'll be going overboard after it!"

"Aye, Captain Cannonflash!" a skinny man with no shirt shouted back.

Rose took his side, marveling at the spacious deck and massive firepower she saw. Each rail was armed with a dozen swivel guns to compliment the ten heavy cannons on each side to augment the two dozen from the decks below, and her eyes widened as she saw the ten massive hundred pounders that were facing forward. Four were on one hull, four on the other, and two more securely on the center structure. The rail that should have been up front was not there, but the deck was raised in front of them with what appeared to be iron plate. This ship was huge, solid, and judging from all of the black canvas that the men in the rigging were dropping it was very fast.

The activity aboard looked like total chaos, and yet there was an order to it. Jones was not barking out orders for everything that needed to happen, his crew just knew as if they had done this hundreds of times.

Another big mariner, nearly the height of Captain Jones and nearly his size and build, strode right up to Jones and raised his chin, combing his long brown hair back with one hand as he reported, "Ship's in good order, Captain. We're ready to sail on your word."

Not looking at him and instead watching what happened around him, Jones asked, "The crew eat tonight?"

"Aye, Captain. Next watch is awaiting you in the galley."

Sweeping his eyes across the deck once more, Jones finally nodded and said, "The word is given, Mister Cannonburg. Take your station."

Cannonburg shouted back, "Aye, Captain!" Striding around his Captain, the big pirate barked out, "Drop the canvas and fill 'er with the wind. Hoist the colors and let's get this fine ship under way. Helm, give us a heading to Santiago."

Looking to the two huge, new cannons facing forward before him, Jones watched as his ship turned and lurched forward, into the sea beyond, and he finally said, "Welcome aboard the *Black Dragon*, Captain O'scarlett."

Continuing to look around her with wide eyes, she nodded and complimented, "This is the biggest ship I've ever seen."

"Or will ever see," he added. As he turned and strode toward the rear of the ship and to a waiting door, his guest was quick to spin around and catch up to him.

He took her below, to the second deck and the room that was near the inside of the hull they were in. Looking around her at the lamp lit interior, Rose could see why this ship was so formidable, and so feared. The cannon hatches were closed and a dozen cannons, twenty-four pounders from the looks of them, stood ready with shot and powder bags between them. The bulkhead had extra bracing that held iron plate in place that was riveted onto the planks of the outer hull. Each plate appeared to be an inch thick and no gun at sea could put a round through it. There was all kinds of reinforcement here and from the looks of it this ship would shrug off even being rammed by a heavy frigate! It also looked heavy. To the inside was a solid looking wall with small ports in it every so often and a couple of doors. Less than a quarter the width of the hull, this chamber was no doubt here for battle and battle only. It was narrower than the gun deck on the *Scarlet Dragon* but was clearly more solid.

Rose did not realize that she was just standing there, staring down the gun deck until she heard Captain Jones clear his throat. Looking that way, she saw him standing at an open doorway, looking back at her with impatient eyes. She casually strode to him, still glancing about as she observed, "Your ship is the most solid I've ever seen."

"Or will ever," he replied. "If you mean to eat at me table, quit making me wait for you."

She entered ahead of him, looking up at him over her shoulder with a flirty smile as she said, "Why thank you, kind sir."

"Just get in there," he grumbled.

Looking ahead of her, she saw a long table that was flanked by timber benches, but had one high backed and plush looking chair on one end. All kinds of food was laid out, bottles of wine and rum and ale, fruits and two well roasted pigs among other things. Many of his crew awaited him, almost thirty of them, and when they saw their captain they raised mugs and cups and erupted in cheers, and all of them stood.

Jones took his place at the head of the table, looking down to a tall tin mug that awaited him. A young man, perhaps sixteen or seventeen and wearing the cleanest white shirt on the ship with black trousers and no shoes, was quick to pour something from a silver pitcher into the mug that looked and smelled like stout ale.

Rose stood beside him, glancing about nervously. The crew was acting like a fanatical mob in the presence of their captain.

Jones held his mug up and his crew followed suit, and when the Captain drank, the crew drank, and Rose quickly found a mug and drank with them. The ale was a little bitter and she squinted against it, but it was flavorful nonetheless.

They all slammed their mugs and cups down and the crew waited in silence to be addressed.

Looking them all over slowly, Jones nodded and started speaking, but softly. "You'd be rich men serving aboard my ship. The sea will give you gold or take your lives. It will give you vengeance or strike you down with it. But tomorrow," he suddenly shouted, "it will give us its bounty!"

Once again the crew cheered him.

Jones held his hands up to silence them. "Me men, we have those dogs from the Company running from us and the Brits avoiding us. Eat now. Collect your strength. Tomorrow, we take the sea and spread the fear of the *Black Dragon!*"

Once again the room exploded into cheers and everyone finally sat down, and the feasting began.

None of this is what Rose expected. Jones had said very little all day, and when he did speak it was some kind of threat to someone. She expected his crew to live in fear of him as well but these men admired him and the respect she could see from each of them as they looked his way was not respect born of intimidation.

Almost reluctantly, she reached for the bounty of Captain Jones' table and joined their feast. The food that was prepared was excellent, something else she did not expect to find aboard this ship. This meal was a banquet, a party, and it seemed to be almost routine to the men, as if they ate this well all the time. Thoughts that she was aboard the most feared pirate vessel in the world began to fade and she actually began to feel a little less out of place.

An older fellow with stringy white hair and a raggedy white beard took a few gulps from his mug, then slammed it down and reached for the pitcher. As he poured another mug of ale, he asked, "What brings a pretty lass like yourself onto a ship of ruffians like us?"

Rose nervously looked to Jones and as he looked back at her she did not see anything in his eyes that told her to keep her intentions a secret, and yet there was that familiar warning in the pit of her stomach that told her to respond with caution. Maintaining her bearing as she always did, she looked to the turkey leg she picked at and replied, "Captain Jones needs some supplies that I have, so we worked out some barter."

His eyes still on her, Jones took a long drink from one of the pitchers, then picked up a blackened piece of meat and bit into it like some ravenous shark.

Chewing on something himself, the old sailor asked, "Be ye stayin' aboard the *Dragon* for a spell?"

She finally turned her eyes to him. "Believing the old tale that a woman on board is bad luck?"

"Heh!" the old mariner barked. "This ship makes her own luck." He motioned toward Jones with his head. "Cannonflash there would spit in the eye of Davy Jones himself if he saw fit, and Davy would do not but ask for more!"

"Finest and most feared skipper on the seven seas, Cannonflash is!" another of the crew nearby shouted. "The sea gods themselves look to him for good fortune!"

This raised a cheer and Rose slowly turned her attention to the big captain at her side. He was not really responding to the accolades and continued to eat his meal.

"You haven't heard tell much of Captain Cannonflash, have ye, Lass?"

She shook her head and took a drink of ale. "No, not much."

The older fellow elbowed her and nodded when her eyes found his. "Three years ago I found meself in a bit of a scrape with some of those reds. Outnumbered, I was, four to one with me mates, ship afire and nowhere to go but the gallows. Looked pretty grim that night, it did, but we heard cannon fire and a ball hit right in the middle of the British regiment. Blew 'em apart, it did, and when we looked we saw Cannonflash standin' there with a deck gun in his arms, smokin' from the muzzle. He threw it down and picked up another and let'er rip right into their ranks again, then he threw it down and drew his pistols. He jumped right into the middle of 'em and sent 'em packin. A few held their ground and one of 'em shot him right in the chest. Shrugged it off, he did, and killed the red that shot 'im with 'is bare hands. Rescued me and seven of me mates that night and we'll not forget." He looked to Jones and held up his mug as he shouted, "Aye, Cannonflash?"

Jones looked to him and picked his mug up, reaching across Rose to slam it into the crewman's, then the crew erupted into cheers again and everyone drank.

Rose had never seen men act this way, even those who were partying in the taverns. Looking to the older fellow, she asked, "So... Do you feast like this every night?"

He answered, "Night, morning... Whenever we eat. And we eat well and often, right mates?"

Another roar of agreement sounded.

Turning her eyes to Cannonflash, Rose smiled slightly and observed, "Well. There would seem to be much more to Captain Jones than one would first think."

The older fellow nudged her again and said for all to hear, "Every soul aboard this ship would kill or die for Captain Cannonflash. He's pulled us all out from the pit at one time or another and he'll do it again if he needs. I tell you, Lass, if you mean to come aboard as his mate, you've chosen the right ship."

 46

She shook her head slightly and asked, "You aren't afraid that the British or the Company will attack you in force some day?"

A quiet washed through the room and men looked to each other, then they all looked to Jones, and all at once they exploded into a roaring laughter, men beating on the table and throwing spent turkey and chicken bones across the table at one another.

Rose's eyes shifted around, her brow arched high over them. Finally her gaze locked on Captain Jones.

He just smiled and shook his head and went about his meal.

A red haired fellow, middle aged perhaps, who was sitting across the table and halfway down it shouted to Rose, "You've never heard of this ship? Ye been kept in a crate ye whole life?"

They roared in laughter again.

She smiled back and replied, "Well, I once heard tell that this ship sank four frigates one day."

The room grew quiet again and all eyes turned to Jones.

The older fellow raised his chin and asked, "I hadn't heard about four, Captain."

Raising his brow, Cannonflash looked back to him and asked, "Don't remember that night?"

"Aye, I do, Captain, but as I recall we took down a whole fleet, not just the four frigates."

The red haired fellow laughed. "Maybe the frigates is all anyone remembers, mate!"

Laughing, the older fellow looked to Rose and informed, "It wasn't just the frigates, Lass. Jones took this ship head on into an entire fleet of thirty ships. Our cannon barrels were glowing red by the time it was over. We fired broadsides from both port and starboard, fired our forward guns, fired muskets into 'em, took down corvettes and galleons and frigates and everything they had."

"Truthfully," a black haired fellow a third of the way down the table on the other side, one who wore a recently cleaned red shirt, interjected, "three of them got away, and I think it was only twenty-four ships in that fleet."

Wide eyed, Rose looked to Jones and barked, "You sank twenty-one ships in one day?"

He shrugged and did not look back at her as he replied, "I didn't count 'em. Those that came around to fight I obliged.

When the smoke cleared it was hard to tell how many we'd sent to the bottom."

"You're the 'Black Issue' the British were plotting against last year," she breathed.

He shrugged again and tore a piece from his turkey leg.

"Black Issue?" the old fellow asked.

Turning to him, she answered, "I raided a ship last year that was bound for Port Royal from England. No gold on board, no treasure or taxes or anything. There was only a chest with letters within and a sealed envelope to the Admiralty."

"And you took their letters," Jones laughed.

Looking back to him, she confirmed, "I read them that night, especially those with the King's seal. They were cryptic, but the message said that the fleet that was meant to deal with the pirate problem here in the Caribbean fell victim to the Black Issue that they'd had problems with before."

The crew fell silent again and their eyes fell on her.

"What more did they say?" the black haired fellow demanded.

Rose shrugged and looked to her plate. "Many references to this Black Issue, a few about Navy Ships being destroyed while merchant ships did not fall victim to it." Her eyes slid to Jones. "Only a very bold man would attack the Navy so."

The older fellow shouted, "And you're looking at the boldest there is!"

Once more the room erupted.

When Jones looked to her again, she found herself feeling an admiration for him that was shared by his crew, and she smiled ever so slightly. "I think that fleet never arriving is what kept many of us alive this last year." She looked to the crew and raised her chin. "I also think I might have one more crate of new Navy pistols that is not spoken for as of yet."

The red haired fellow across the table stood and glared at her, demanding, "What be your name, Lass?"

She regarded him with steely eyes as she replied, "I am Rose O'scarlett, captain of the *Scarlet Dragon*."

His eyes narrowed, then he picked his mug up and looked around, yelling, "To Captain Rose O'scarlett!"

Cheers and shouts erupted again, and this time for her.

Rose knew she was blushing and looked to Jones with a little smile.

Stone faced as he almost always was, he just raised an eyebrow and attended his plate of food.

* * *

Evening found Rose at the bow of the ship as it sliced through the water like the unstoppable beast it was. She was leaning against one of the huge hundred pounder cannons on the left hull. A nearly full moon bathed the sea in its soft light and sparkled off of the wave tops in the night. The wind blew her long brown hair freely behind her and over one shoulder. She often enjoyed little pleasures like this on her own ship, a vessel she missed. Running a ship was hard enough work, especially running it on the wrong side of the law. It seemed that she was always looking over her shoulder and wary of any sails she saw on the horizon, and wary of any treachery among her own crew. This imposing juggernaut she was on seemed to have no worries. There was no fear aboard this ship, only a light hearted and almost festive feeling. Most of the crew was not even drunk! The captain did not live in fear of his men nor did they live in fear of him. Maintaining order and some degree of discipline had proven to be a monumental undertaking for her, but here it seemed to happen on its own.

Her thoughts danced about freely for the first time in years. The price on her head, pirates and Navy alike gunning for her, not knowing who she could trust or if the next port would fire on her... They all seemed distant. Foremost in these thoughts was the big captain of this ship, this Cannonflash. He was an imposing sight, a frightening man with a short fuse and a temper like the cannons he wielded, a beast of the sea with no soft side that could be seen, no soft underbelly, but he would not leave her thoughts. Something told her that there was more to him than she could see, more than anyone could see. She had left him to attend to matters below decks, a place she did not seem welcome, so up in the wind was the place to be.

With her arms folded against the passing air, she watched the sea for an unknown time, her mind and heart finally feeling some peace. Looking over her shoulder, she turned at the waist to see behind her. Many men were still on the deck and she had the attention of a number of them, but they would not approach her, probably for fear of their captain's wrath. Lights burned from the masts, the wheelhouses and many other points. Aboard a pirate ship this was unheard of. Such a ship had to be invisible in the night lest it be set upon by the Navy patrols. This ship had no fears and went about its way without a care.

Seeing her looking their way, the crewmen went about their tasks.

From the rear of the ship, where the ladders were that went to the lower decks, a huge form wearing a black vest emerged. The rear of the ship was not that well lit, but she knew who she saw.

Jones scanned the deck, then he strode to the center, between the hulls, and inspected something there. When another crewman approached him, he turned toward him and folded those huge, thick arms. They were too far away for Rose to be able to hear what was said and she really did not care. Her gaze was consumed with the huge pirate captain. She did not know how long she stared at him but her eyes remained fixed on him as he went about inspecting more of his ship. As he bounded up the ladder to the wheelhouse she marveled over how easily he moved his bulk around.

Ever so slowly, she turned and leaned her hip against the cannon, tightening the fold of her arms as she watched him talk to the man at the helm. They spoke almost casually, not captain to crewman, but more as two men just conversing. The foul tempered berserker she had come to know was not to be found aboard his ship and she watched him with growing interest.

When he left the wheelhouse and strode toward the other hull, she turned her attention to the sea once again, and the uncertain future that awaited her. Her thoughts returned to her own ship, her crew, and the friendships she had forged with others. Bugs Nailhall had rushed to her aid on many occasions and she to his. The Code of the Pirates took loyalty only so far, but this code was forgotten between them. He had never interested her romantically and she was sure she did not interest him. Sure, they found one another appealing, but that three year friendship would not allow it.

And romantic stirrings pushed her thoughts back to Cannonflash, and as much as she tried to rid her mind of him, she could not. She had been with many men over the years, some out of necessity and some out of womanly need. Always selective, she had been with many who appealed to her, but only for the moment.

Womanly need was speaking loud and clear this night. It had been a while and she wanted someone. Aboard a shipload of ruthless pirates, taking care of that need would prove to be no problem, but there was only one she was really interested in on this ship.

Rocking her head back, she closed her eyes and shook out her long hair, just for the feeling of doing so, then she vented a deep breath and gazed out into the sparkling nothingness of the sea. Many matters awaited her, and getting her ship back in fighting form was only the first of them.

Finally, her thoughts were pried away from the pirate captain, but were now consumed with things she would rather not think about, but knew she had to.

"Lookin' for sails out there?" Cannonflash asked from behind her.

She shrieked and spun around, a hand over her heaving chest as she turned wide eyes up to his. Calming her nerves a bit, she finally managed a smile and admitted, "I didn't hear you come up on me."

He was staring out into the dark sea and nodded slightly. "Absence of your senses can get you killed in this business."

She combed her hair back behind one ear with her fingers. "For some reason I feel safe aboard your ship, safer than I've felt for many years."

Still he did not look at her and just nodded again.

Silence gripped them that next moment.

"Have you thought about where I am to sleep tonight?" Rose asked, leaning her head subtly.

Jones slowly shook his head.

She raised her brow and said almost meekly, "I don't think I would be safe down there with your crew. There is no telling what could happen to me among all of those girl hungry men."

He finally lowered his eyes to hers.

51

"We wouldn't want me to get violated or worse now, would we, Captain Jones. If I'm too rattled I may just forget about where me powder's hidden."

With the slight lifting of an eyebrow, Jones told her without words of his annoyance over what she had said. He finally told her, "Perhaps you should have thought of that before coming aboard."

She smiled just a little. "How badly do you want that powder and pistols? Badly enough to share the Captain's cabin?"

He growled a sigh and looked back out to the sea.

Half turning, she sat back against the enormous cannon and looked across the ship, and she arched backward to be sure he got a good look at her generous curves. "I need to turn in soon, Captain. Got to keep rested and keep my wits about me."

Silence found them again.

Jones finally turned and conceded, "Go on, then. Get rested. Me cabin's at the back of the port side."

As she turned and watched him walk away, she called after him, "Aren't you coming?"

"In me own time," he replied.

* * *

Rose entered slowly and cautiously, finding a single light burning on the wooden table in the middle of the Captain's cabin. This was the most spacious room on the ship it seemed, easily fifteen feet deep and twenty feet wide. A single bed was against the wall to the right, right under the partitioned window. A sofa and chair were on the other side. At the very back of the room was a work table of some kind with many rolled parchments scattered about it. About nine feet wide and almost four deep, it had a chair pushed into place and drawers on both sides. Shelves were at the back almost six feet high and were laden with many things from parchments to cannon balls. An old pistol lay in the center of it. An assortment of swords and cutlasses hung on the walls. To her right, on the same wall as the bed was a huge wooden wardrobe that was closed and secured with a lock. It looked a little out of place on this ship. A big sea chest was at the foot of the bed.

Then her eyes found the painting above the bed and she slowly approached. It was fine work, a beautiful blond haired woman in a white gown sitting by a window with the sea behind her. Only the hint of a smile was on her lips and something almost seductive in her eyes. Drawing closer, Rose saw words painted on the bottom. Taking the oil lamp from the table in the center of the room, she held it to the painting to see the words, her lips slowly parting as she read aloud in a whisper, "To my dearest love. Yours always. Emily." She looked over her shoulder to the door as if to see the big pirate through the wall. With one more look at the painting, she tried to dismiss it as something he had taken in his piracy and finally turned to walk away from it.

Setting the lamp back on the table, she strode to the couch and sat down. With a little strain and effort, she pulled her boots off and laid them down on the floor beside her. Rubbing her eyes, she finally felt the fatigue of the day taking its toll on her. She was tempted to undress and slide into his bed, but was afraid at the same time. Her flirting was met with a cold response and she did not want to be on this huge man's bad side, especially this far out at sea.

Looking about, she did not find many comforts, and apparently blankets and such were either locked in that wardrobe or in the trunk at the foot of his bed. Slowly, she unlaced her shirt and undressed down to her undergarments. She allowed herself to succumb to her weariness and curled up on one end of the couch and pulled her shirt over her. With her head resting on her arm, she closed her eyes and loosed a long breath. The Caribbean night was growing chilly and she curled up a little tighter beneath her shirt

At some point, rocked slowly by the sea, she drifted off to sleep.

Many hours later she awoke, but barely enough to be coherent. The evening had grown a little colder and her hand groped over her shoulder, finally finding the edge of the blanket and she pulling it up to her neck. Snuggling into her pillow, she drew a breath and curled up to drift back to sleep.

Then her eyes flashed open. She groped for the blanket again. And it was soft and wool, and very warm. The pillow was also very soft and felt like one that was stuffed with goose down.

The lamp in the middle of the room was burning low and she sat up and looked first to the blanket, then the pillow, then to the bed across the cabin.

Cannonflash was fast asleep, lying on his back with his face directed toward the wall. He was not wearing that vest she always saw him in and was covered halfway up his chest by his blanket. Even in this dim light she found herself captivated by him, and a deeper curiosity about him stirred. No, he was not attractive in the face, but with that body he did not have to be.

Slowly, she swung her feet to the deck and stood, wrapping herself in the blanket against the chilly air. Padding lightly, she crept toward the sleeping pirate, cringing every time the wooden floor beneath her creaked. Only a few feet away she stopped and just stared at him for a moment, watching his huge chest rise and fall as he slept. Part of her wanted to slip beneath that blanket with him, to feel the warmth of him against her, but most of her still feared him and what he could do to her if she awakened him, or surprised him. Taking a step back to return to the couch, she kept her eyes on him, and the floor beneath her heel creaked loudly.

In an instant he swung his arm over and Rose shrieked as she found herself staring down the cannon-like maw of his pistol— and the hammer was pulled back! Her chest heaved as she struggled for breath and finally she met his eyes, knowing hers were wide with fear. When his eyes narrowed, she cleared her throat and managed, "I see you are a light sleeper."

His lip curled up slightly and he just glared at her.

"I was cold," she informed softly.

"That's why you have a blanket," he growled back.

She nodded. "I… I also wanted to thank you, for the blanket and pillow."

He just stared back at her, his steady hand keeping the muzzle of his weapon trained on her.

Rose swallowed hard and after long seconds admitted, "I'm rather frightened to move. What would you have me do?" She secretly hoped that he would demand that she join him in his bed.

His thumb moved to the hammer of his pistol and very slowly, very deliberately, he lowered it over the cap. Finally, he ordered, "Get back to your bed and go to sleep."

She nodded and slowly backed away, keeping her gaze locked on his. "Good night, Captain. Sorry to have disturbed you." Daring to turn fully, she strode back to the couch and pulled the blanket from herself. Just to give him a good view of her, she bent over and fluffed her pillow, then she threw the blanket over the couch and took her time as she bent over and straightened it, running her hand over it to work out the wrinkles. Half pivoting, she raised her arms over her head and stretched, arching her back and she rolled her head back and drew in a deep breath. Even wearing her undergarments he should have been able to get a good look at her shape. Twisting one way, then the other, she finally looked toward his bed.

He was already facing the other way, and starting to snore.

Rose angrily folded her arms and turned fully to him, and she was really tempted to find something to throw at him. Better judgment prevailed, however, and she slipped beneath her blanket and laid her head to the pillow, curling up on her side and facing the back of the couch. Trying to clear Cannonflash from her thoughts was simply not to be, and he was still there as she drifted back off to sleep.

Chapter 4

THE JAWS OF THE BLACK DRAGON

Rose did not notice as the blanket was slowly, gently pulled from her in the early morning sunlight. She lay curled up on her side, one leg drawn to her and she was hugging her pillow with both arms and soundly in a deep sleep. She did not feel the eyes on her, the warm Caribbean breeze working its way through the cabin, or the sounds of the crew hard at work on the deck right outside the door.

A hard, open handed slap to her behind sounded almost like a gunshot and she screamed "Ow!" as she rolled over and sat up, reaching for her stinging backside as her wide, barely alert eyes locked on the big pirate captain who stood a couple of feet away.

Cannonflash looked back at her with steely eyes and finally ordered, "Get yourself up and get dressed. We've sails ahead and we're at battle stations."

Still just barely awake, Rose reached for her trousers and asked in an excited tone, "What kind?"

Jones turned from her and walked to the wardrobe, pulling a key from his vest pocket as he replied, "Schooner from the look,

 57

fast and the size of a galleon. Riding low in the water and painted in white and red. Too pretty for a warship."

As she stood to buckle her belt, Rose looked to him and suggested, "Perhaps a passenger ship, taking people back to England."

"Coming from England," he corrected as he rummaged through the locker. He removed a thick belt which he wound around his waist and she could see at least four holsters for pistols and keepers that would hold his cutlass and dagger.

Quickly pulling her shirt on, she asked, "Is she armed?"

Cannonflash began removing pistols from his wardrobe and slipping them into the holsters, and he shook his head. "Hasn't fired if she is. Won't matter anyway."

Rose retrieved her own weapons from the table and put them in place as she followed the big pirate out.

On the deck, she found it to be a hornet's nest of activity. Deck guns were being loaded, and swivel guns, but not the big hundred pounders at the bow. Following Jones to the center of the ship, she asked, "You aren't going to use the big ones?"

"No need," he growled back. "Save them for warships. We'll not fire on that ship unless we have to."

She stood beside him and set her hands on her hips, watching the activity aboard as she observed, "Not what I expected of you, Captain Jones."

"And what did you expect?"

"I've heard that you grant no quarter to those under your guns."

He huffed a rare laugh. "Bet you also heard I'm ten feet tall and swallow sharks whole. You can see I'm not ten feet and I've never swallowed a whole shark. Take me word for that."

"I will," she assured, "but I can see where people would think you're ten feet."

Their eyes met, then they looked back to the activity on the ship.

Raising his chin, Jones called, "Mister Cannonburg!"

The big fellow she had seen the night before stopped mid stride and turned, then hurried over to his captain.

Cannonflash looked to the fleeing ship, now less than a quarter of a mile away. It was a two mast ship with sleek lines, bright white paint and every stitch of canvas in the wind. Amazingly, the huge *Black Dragon* was gaining on it. His eyes narrowing, Jones ordered, "Send two twenty-four pounders their way, one across the bow and one on their flank. Let's see if they'll stand to."

"Aye, Captain," Cannonburg replied as he turned. Darting to the deck guns on the starboard side, where their intended victim was, he barked his captain's orders to two of the gun crews.

Jones folded his thick arms, his eyes locked on the fleeing schooner.

Nodding, Rose observed, "Definitely a passenger ship. Think there's anything of value aboard?"

"We'll see in short order," he answered dryly.

Two cannon shots rang out and geysers of water burst from the sea in front of the fleeing ship and to its side.

The chase lasted another few minutes and Jones just watched as his ship drew closer, and his eyes narrowed. Raising his chin again, he shouted, "Mister Cannonburg. Put a round into her stern and see if *that* will convince them to lower their sails."

Another cannon fired and this time an iron ball slammed into the back of the ship near the deck. Chunks and shards of wood exploded from the stricken vessel.

A few minutes more passed and as they drew closer they could see activity aboard the schooner and in the rigging. Almost reluctantly, the schooner's sails were furled and she began to slow, and the *Black Dragon* closed rapidly and turned to come along side.

Rose followed Jones across to the other ship. Despite all of the weapons he carried, he did not draw any of them and just strode onto the forward deck as his crew assembled the people on board in a straight line. These were ordinary looking folks, those who might be seen in an English village or wandering about the markets at Port Royal. Many of them were dressed very nicely, and all bore looks of horror as the pirates raided their ship and held them at gun and cutlass point. About fifty in number, they were lined up along the rail on the ship's starboard side. The ship's crew, all dressed in white uniforms trimmed in blue, were assembled on the opposite side.

Cannonflash addressed the thirty crewmembers first, his eyes scrutinizing them as he slowly walked before them. The officers were at the far end of the line, and this is where the big pirate paused.

An older fellow with white hair and a white beard stepped forward to confront the big pirate, and he wisely kept his hands at his sides. Jones was a head height taller and turned fully to face the older man.

Raising his chin, Cannonflash asked, "You're the captain of this vessel?"

The man nodded and confirmed in a proper English accent, "I am. I would ask fair treatment for my men and passengers."

With a slight nod, Jones growled back, "We'll see." Looking over his shoulder, he barked, "Weapons?"

Cannonburg strode to him. "Not much. No ship's armament, just a few muskets and pistols and a saber or two."

Jones nodded and looked down to the saber that was still at the captain's side. Reaching to it, he seized the hilt in his big hand and pulled it from the scabbard, looking it over with interest.

The schooner's captain nervously watched him.

"Fine blade," Cannonflash observed. Taking it by the blade, he offered it hilt first to the captain, who hesitantly took it.

Rose found herself growing anxious as she followed him to the passengers.

The first one he reached was a middle aged woman who had a young son who looked like he was eight or nine years old, and her breath caught as the boy, dressed as a sailor, produced a wooden cutlass and held it in a challenging posture toward the big pirate captain. The woman seized her son's shoulders from behind and pulled him to her, her wide eyes locked on the big pirate in a horrified, pleading stare.

Jones stopped and looked down at the boy, and he set his jaw. "Ye hold that blade well. Protecting your mother, are ye?" When the boy nodded, he nodded back and turned to pace on his way, ordering, "Carry on, boy."

None of the other passengers really interested him as he walked down their line as an officer would during an inspection. He wore no expression for the most part as he slowly strode toward the other end of the line with many of his crew and Rose following.

Several of the *Black Dragon*'s crew emerged from the cabin at the center of the deck and four of them carried two wood and brass chests, each of which was four feet long, perhaps two high and three wide. From the strain on the men's faces, the chests were heavy with something. One of the men with them shouted, "Captain! We've a find!"

Jones turned and strode to them as they set the chests down on the deck. Some of the schooner's crew and officers became uneasy and exchanged nervous glances.

"Open them," Cannonflash ordered.

"Stop!" one of the officer's shouted as he stormed toward them. This was a younger man with blond hair and a thin build.

Jones' men just watched him and did not try to intervene, and many of them wore humorous smiles as they anticipated the inevitable. The big pirate ignored the young man as he watched one of his men fumble with a lock that sealed the first chest.

"I said stop!" the young man shouted again as he reached the pirate captain.

Rose turned toward him and backed away a step.

Jones finally looked over his shoulder at this impudent man who dared to address him.

"That is the property of the crown," the young man insisted, "and the likes of you shall—"

Cannonflash's hand slammed palm-first into the young man's throat and gripped like a hawk. As the young man struggled to get air past the big pirate's fingers and fought to pry the hand from his throat, Jones drove him backward a few steps and growled, "These chests are mine now, savvy?"

While Rose felt for the foolish young man, she could not help but also feel a certain arousal at watching this big pirate manhandle him. Wisely, she said nothing as Jones pushed the young man backward toward the rail and the schooner's crew got out of the way. The rail itself was only about waist high and stopped the young man's retreat, but Jones pushed him back anyway, arching his back over the side.

Holding his victim precariously over the rail, Jones yelled to him, "Anything else to say before I feed you to the sharks?"

"Wait!" Rose heard herself shout.

Silence gripped the deck of the schooner and all eyes focused on her.

Jones slowly looked over his shoulder, his brow low over his eyes as he glared at her.

She nervously glanced around, then strode toward Cannonflash, her eyes on the young man in a narrow leer as she asked, "How does he know about the chests?"

Raising his chin slightly, Jones eyed her for a moment, then he pulled the young man back from the rail and released his throat, taking his shirt at the shoulder instead as he directed him toward Rose.

Cannonburg strode up behind Rose and folded his arms. "Perhaps he's Navy, or an agent for the Company."

Her eyes narrowing, Rose grabbed the sailor's collar and yanked him toward her, demanding though bared teeth, "What is in the chests?"

"Why don't you check for yourself," he hissed back.

She pushed him back, just glaring at him for a moment, then she wheeled around and drew her pistol as she strode to the first chest. With a quick, careful aim, she shot the lock from the first crate, then tossed her pistol from her and reached for the lid. Something quaked in the pit of her stomach and she hesitated. Looking over her shoulder, she turned fully and set her hands on her hips, her eyes on the young sailor as she ordered, "Come over and open it."

His eyes widened.

"Now!" she demanded.

Cannonburg took his arm and hurled him across the deck and he stumbled and landed at Rose's feet. Ever so slowly, he turned his eyes up to her, eyes that betrayed fear.

"I said open it," she snarled.

His wide eyes shifted to the chest.

"You're baiting us, aren't you?" she snarled. Looking to Cannonflash, she informed loud enough for all to hear, "Captain Jones, this whole thing is a trap."

His gaze locked on her, he half turned his head and asked, "How figure you?"

"He won't open the chest," she explained. "It's packed with explosives. They sent this ship this way knowing that pirates would intercept it, and as we all know, when treasures are captured it is most often the captain who opens it first. I suppose when you didn't he had to interest you in doing so."

Jones' lip curled up and his narrow eyes slid to the man on the deck. With three long strides the big pirate was upon the young man and he hoisted him from the deck by the shirt, holding him at eye level with his feet dangling from the deck as he growled, "That true, boy?"

"I have nothing to say to you," the young man hissed.

Cannonflash turned and carried the young sailor to the rail again, lifting him higher as he shouted, "Perhaps you've something to say to the sharks!"

The *Black Dragon*'s men shouted in approval and the terrified young sailor clutched at Jones' arms as he struggled not to be thrown over the rail.

Rose rushed to them and grasped Jones' shoulder as she cried, "Captain, wait. He may still be useful to us."

Glaring into the sailor's face, Cannonflash snarled, "More useful to the sharks, I think."

Looking to the young sailor, Rose folded her arms and raised her brow. "Well, I'd say you have one last chance to stay dry today. So, are you going to answer a few questions or shall Captain Jones drop you overboard and that chest with you?"

Raising his chin, the young sailor glared back at Jones and sneered, "God save the King."

"Before you throw him over," Rose suggested, "why don't we let him watch one of these English citizens open that chest."

Jones slowly looked over his shoulder at her.

Her eyes slid to him and she raised her brow.

Looking back to the sailor, Cannonflash narrowed his eyes, then he turned and hurled the man toward the chest and watched him slam onto the deck and roll to a stop. Glancing around, he finally found a suitable victim, pointing to a young woman as he ordered, "You! Step forward!"

Wearing a long, spring dress of a light yellow material, the young woman who could have been no older than twenty shrieked and grasped her chest, and she backed away a step.

Rose strode toward her, taking her arm as she ordered, "You heard Captain Jones." Pulling her brutally from the line, she led her to the chest and ordered, "Open it. Let this gallant young English soldier watch you get yourself blown to pieces."

"Stop!" the young sailor shouted.

Rose stopped beside him with the young woman still in her grip, and she looked down to him. "You had your chance, boy. Now she takes your turn."

"What kind of people are you?" he yelled.

Smiling, Rose leaned her head and sweetly replied, "We're pirates, the same heartless cutthroats that you meant to kill with whatever's in there. Now live with this on your conscience." She shoved the young woman toward the chest and barked, "Open it!"

The young sailor scrambled to it and slammed his hands down on the lid, tightly closing his eyes as he insisted, "You can't! Don't do this!"

"Then open it yourself!" Rose shouted.

He stared back at her with wide eyes for long seconds, then his attention turned slowly to the chest and his lips tightened.

Jones ordered, "Mister Cannonburg."

Cannonburg nodded and looked around him. Seeing some thin rope hanging from the rigging, he pulled some down and cut it with his dagger, then he approached the chest and tied it off to the hasp on the lid. As he backed away, he advised, "Stand back, mates," and when everyone backed away, he carefully pulled the lid open from a safe distance.

With the lid not even a quarter of the way up the top of the chest exploded straight up with the sound of a cannon and many of the people aboard dropped to the deck, including Rose. Cannonflash and most of his crew merely flinched back. A bright, smoking projectile of some kind was fired straight up, and as Jones watched it ascend, his eyes narrowed. Seconds later, hundreds of lead balls began to rain down on the ship and the surrounding ocean. When the last of them fell, all eyes turned to the young man who still crouched on the deck.

Motioning with her head to the other chest, Rose demanded, "That one too?"

He nodded.

Jones looked to a couple of his men and ordered, "Throw it over the side." As the chest was carried away, he strode up to the young sailor and folded his arms, looming over him as he demanded, "Who's the signal for?"

The young sailor was hesitant to answer, but finally replied, "There is a squadron of ships following. They'll be along in short order so you'd best be on your way and you'd best hope you can outrun them."

Jones huffed a laugh.

Rose turned her eyes up to Jones and informed, "This *was* a trap, a very well thought out trap. Kill the captain and a-few others and then the rest of the ship should be easy to capture."

Someone still aboard the *Black Dragon* shouted to them, "Sails!"

Everyone turned and looked, then someone pointed to the rear of the ship and shouted, "There!"

Jones and Rose and many others went to the rail and looked behind the schooner and the *Black Dragon*, and the pirate captain's eyes narrowed again. Looking to his ship, he shouted, "Get to your battle stations and load those hundred pounders! Get the ship ready to get under way!" Wheeling back around, he ordered, "Get yourselves back to the ship!"

As the *Black Dragon*'s crew scrambled to return to their ship, Rose grasped Jones by the arm and cried, "You mean to attack them?"

His eyes slid to her and he snarled, "If you mean to question me then you'll be left here."

She backed away a step and watched him follow his crew back to his ship. Glancing at the passengers and crew of the schooner, she called after him, "What about them?"

Jones looked over his shoulder and shouted back, "They'll have a story to tell when they reach port. You coming with us or staying with them?"

Rose looked to the young sailor as he stood, raised her brow and shrugged when he met her eyes, then she hurried after Jones and his men.

Back aboard the *Black Dragon*, sails were unfurled and the massive ship lurched forward. With Jones in the center of the ship calling orders, a man at the helm turned the wheel and the *Dragon* began to turn hard, and much faster than Rose thought it could. With six masts of sails full with the wind, the ship lurched over slightly as she wheeled around to face the eight ships that bore down on her from a couple of miles away.

The scrambling about the ship was not as it had been before. Men waited at their posts, cannons were loaded and ready and others stood by the rails with muskets.

Rose took the Captain's side again and folded her arms, staring ahead at the ships that sped toward them. A moment later she cleared her throat and finally said, "So the stories about you are true."

He looked down at her, meeting her eyes.

Raising her brow, she observed, "Looks like I get to see the great Cannonflash Jones at his best and doing what he does."

Jones looked forward again and growled back, "There's only eight of 'em. Should be a short fight."

Also looking forward, Rose informed, "Most pirates have the good sense to run when the Navy comes after them in force like this."

"I'll not run from the likes of them," he snarled. "They want a fight with the *Black Dragon* then I'll unleash all their worst nightmares." Raising his chin, he called, "Mister Cannonburg!"

Cannonburg strode to him and answered with a smart, "Aye, Captain."

"Reposition the heavy fronts," Jones ordered. "Four to the port on that first frigate port, four starboard on the next to the right, and keep the center two on that corvette ahead. Let's put the fear of God in them with our first salvo."

Nodding, Cannonburg complied, "Aye," and he turned to hurry off.

"Johnny," Jones called after him.

Cannonburg stopped and half turned.

"Put the first ten of our broadsides forward on them low and fire into their gun decks, and have the swivel guns have at them on the deck."

With a little smile, Cannonburg wheeled around and continued on his task.

"Should we find cover?" Rose asked grimly.

Jones shook his head. "If they get a shot off at us then they deserve a chance at me. I aim to be seen on the deck through this fight."

"Well, Captain Jones, I've seen what this ship and her crew can do to three other ships, but this is eight on one." She turned nervous eyes up to his, and he reassured her with a single look.

"If you're that nervous," he offered, "then wait in me cabin until it's over."

"Not a chance!" she barked back, folding her arms. "I've not run from a sea battle for many days."

He huffed a laugh and looked to the closing British ships. "Not since the last fight you were in."

"I was at a disadvantage," she pointed out. "But you seem to have all of the advantages here, except you're outnumbered and outgunned."

"Outnumbered, Lass, not outgunned." He suddenly shouted, "Put your sights on those first three and fire at two hundred yards, then stand by the twenty-four pounders!"

A tense moment followed as the *Black Dragon* closed on the fleet that meant to sink her. Two hundred yards away Rose could see the deck guns and the swivel guns of the British ships swinging forward to deliver a first strike, but when she glanced up at the big pirate captain beside her, she did not see concern, only a level of focus she had never seen before.

Cannonburg, standing at the bow of the ship, looked back at Jones, and when Jones nodded, he turned forward again and shouted, "Hundred pounders, open fire!"

Horrific thunder and fire belched from the front of the *Black Dragon* and deadly projectiles struck three Navy ships true, and when the huge cannonballs slammed home they exploded with devastating force. The entire bow of the first frigate exploded. The second frigate was hit at the bow and amidships and the timber hull was opened in a cascade of fire and fleeing wood and metal, and cannons and men were blown overboard. Only two of the hundred pound balls struck the corvette and they penetrated the deck halfway between her bow and mainmast, and when they exploded, they took her powder kegs below deck with them and the ship blew apart in a hellish explosion that sent the main mast a hundred feet into the air and ripped the ship in half.

The hundred pounders were withdrawn to be reloaded and the twenty-four pounders were turned sharp forward on the deck, and those holding the firing lines looked back at Cannonburg.

Johnny slowly raised his hand, and seconds later thrust it down as he shouted, "Fire!"

Twenty-four of the Dragon's main guns fired almost as one and cannonballs ripped into the two damaged frigates, and the mainmast of the ship on the left slowly rocked forward and fell, dragging down the sails with it.

The remains of the corvette sank, the stricken frigate to the right veered off, the frigate to the left was crippled and floundered on the sea and as the *Black Dragon* charged between them, her crew raked their decks with rail cannons and muskets. With the battle only a minute old, one Navy ship was sunk, two were crippled, and the other five, one frigate and four corvettes, turned their flanks to bring their guns to bear on the deadly pirate marauder.

Jones shouted, "Reload those forward batteries with high explosive and stand by the aft broadsides. I want that frigate down first! Helm, turn us into 'er!"

As the corvettes moved to flank the *Black Dragon*, she turned with purpose toward the last heavy frigate, which was only three hundred yards away, and the ten hundred pounders forward were moved back into position.

Cannonburg barked to the men on the hundred pounders, "Put your sights on 'er forward and let'er have it at a hundred yards!"

The men on the heavy cannons worked with precision and speed that Rose had never even seen aboard the Navy ships she had observed. One man knelt down behind the cannon and looked along the top of the barrel, directing the other two who moved the huge cannon to aim it.

The twenty-four pounders on the deck were moved back into position and aimed the same way, though elevated slightly higher.

Cannonburg looked to one side, then the other and barked, "Broadsides, fire at will!"

Cannons from both sides of the ship fired almost sporadically and in a hail of cannonballs, half of which exploded as they struck the smaller ships while the other half tore through the decks and sails and splintered masts.

Still, not a single shot had managed to land on the *Black Dragon* herself. Men at the rail cannons and manning the rail with muskets fired almost continually. Younger crew members knelt behind them, reloading muskets and handing them off to the men who fired them.

In a moment the frigate had closed to a hundred yards and began to turn and bring her broadsides to bear on the pirate, but not quite halfway turned, the big hundred pounders fired again, and this time all ten slammed into the side of the one ship and blew her flank apart and the ship nearly in half. Even before the debris began to settle the powder kegs exploded almost all at once and the ship disappeared in fleeing chunks of wood, burning shards of timber, cannons, crates and the bodies of British seamen.

As the huge ball of fire began to burn out and yield to black smoke, Jones turned his eyes up, then he shoved Rose aside as he almost ran through her.

She turned and stumbled backward, clutching for his big arm, then she saw the smoking cannon barrel slam onto the deck right in front of where they had been standing and spin to a stop after rolling about twenty feet.

They both stared at it as it lay smoking on the deck right behind where they had been standing.

She looked up at Jones.

He looked back at her and half smiled. "Hell of a way to get a cannon, but I'll take it!"

Her brow arched.

The *Black Dragon* wheeled around to port as the big guns were reloaded and her broadsides and swivel guns continued to pound back at the attacking corvettes.

Jones looked over his shoulder and shouted, "Get those aft guns turned and ready to finish those bastards as they come into your sights!"

Rose glanced about, then she noticed one of the corvettes on the left was finally in position and only about seventy yards, and despite the damage it had already taken, its ten port broadsides flashed to life, and ten cannonballs slammed into the *Black Dragon*'s flank. One penetrated and Rose could hear it creating havoc below decks through the open hatches. Immediately the guns of the *Black Dragon* retaliated and ripped at the deck and flanks of the passing ship.

A thunderous boom sounded from the other side and she wheeled around, watching a rolling cloud of fire and smoke rising from the wreck of one of the British ships. Jones' men knew right where to hit their enemy and their aim was deadly accurate.

As the British ships maneuvered desperately to get into position to fire, the *Black Dragon* fired almost continually from her broadsides and deck guns, and as a Navy ship passed too close she was raked with rail cannons and muskets.

The *Black Dragon* took two more broadsides, but neither seemed to cause damage as the solid steel balls simply bounced off her flanks. The hundred pounders at the bow fired again as a corvette crossed the Dragon's path a hundred yards away, and the British ship was blown to pieces and in a moment nothing remained of it but floating, smoking debris.

In ten minutes it was over and one last corvette was turning to flee with a ship eight times its size turning to pursue.

"That was amazing," Rose observed almost dreamily. "I've never seen so much damage done to the Navy so quickly."

Jones just nodded, his eyes on the fleeing corvette.

She glanced up at him. "Shouldn't you just let it go? You've won the day already."

"I've won the day when that ship has been sent to Davy Jones' locker," the big pirate captain snarled.

Rose drew a breath, hesitant to speak again, but finally managed, "It may be more valuable to you if it escapes."

He set his jaw, his eyes locked on the fleeing ship, and after a long silence he snapped, "You keep saying those words, O'scarlett, and I keep not seeing."

She drew and released another deep breath. "Well, Captain Jones, it's very simple. If you leave no survivors then who will tell of the horrors of meeting the *Black Dragon* in battle?" When she looked up at him she first noticed that his gaze was still locked on the fleeing Navy ship, but he did appear to be considering her words. "Of course," she added, "they should limp into port with a few holes shot in them and maybe a mast or two shot off, just so that all will know they were released simply because you wished to let them go."

His eyes slid to her.

With a little shrug, Rose folded her arms and said, "That's what I would do, let all of them know about the dangers of facing a ship like this. Stories told by survivors of such encounters tend to become stories of legend."

"I don't need stories feeding my ego," he snarled.

"Of course you don't, Captain," she agreed, "but such stories can keep the fear that precedes you everywhere solid and fresh in the hearts of your enemies." Looking up to him, she offered him a little smile and cocked an eyebrow up.

His eyes narrowed.

She smiled just a little more. "You're a man who puts fear into the hearts of other men, and envy in the hearts of all who encounter you."

"So I'm to show mercy to that ship?" he grumbled.

Rose shrugged and turned her eyes forward, folding her hands behind her as she replied, "Depends on what you mean by mercy, Captain. Spare their lives, or some of them, and condemn them to a lifetime of fear and nightmares. I can't say which is the worse fate, but I do know their stories would spread that fear." She glanced up at him. "I'm just thinking out loud, Captain Jones. Pay me no mind."

He eyed her with suspicion for a moment, then demanded, "Why would you be concerned with stories of me ship and me?"

She looked back to him and her eyes glanced over him up and down. Looking forward again, she shrugged yet again and replied, "I've no answer for you, Captain Jones."

Cannonflash set his jaw as he leered at her, then he looked forward and shouted, "Mister Cannonburg! Put a hundred pounder into her aft and blow her stern off."

Responding quickly to the order, Johnny directed a single, forward facing cannon to take aim at the fleeing ship, and it belched fire and thunder with horrific purpose.

As all aboard the *Black Dragon* watched, the cannonball drove home and exploded with horrific purpose causing much of the rear of the ship where the captain's cabin was to blow apart. When the debris fell and the smoke began to clear, a huge part of the corvette's stern was gone. Smoke still poured from the gaping hole and more parts of the ship and pieces of furnishings and other objects fell from the ship as it continued to run.

One of the men at the cannon that had fired turned and shouted, "That ought to make'em a bit lighter, aye?"

Most of the men on the deck roared with laughter and Cannonflash himself smiled just a little.

Turning, Jones shouted back to the wheelhouse, "Helm! Give me a heading to Cuba and take a true course."

"Aye, Captain," the response came.

As the ship turned, Rose looked up to the big pirate captain and observed, "You are just ruthless, Captain Jones."

"Best you remember that," he snarled back.

She turned fully to him and raised her brow. "Will you buy a girl breakfast?"

He looked down at her and just growled.

* * *

The rest of the day was uneventful and bordered on boring. The *Black Dragon* cut through the water with ease and the spirits of the crew were still high after the battle. The one cannonball that did any damage had entered through an open cannon port but was stopped by the heavy timber and iron plate behind the cannons and did no damage to the ship overall. None of the crew was even injured despite being so outnumbered. Rose marveled at how brutal and short the battle was and how the big ship and its crew emerged virtually unscathed. Seven British ships had been destroyed, one had been damaged and allowed to flee to safety, and the dreaded *Black Dragon* had casually gone about its way. Captain Jones had an appointment with some of Rose's supplies and he seemed eager to collect. Rose herself was quickly getting used to life aboard his ship. During the course of the long day she did what she could to help, but the crew knew their routine and did their jobs without complaint or direction. Jones himself stayed on the deck most of the day, but also patrolled the ship and even took the helm for a while. He seemed to enjoy his time at the wheel and the look in his eyes was different when he was there. He seemed more at peace and almost lost in distant thoughts.

As the sun approached the Western horizon, a grand feast was served in the galley, and this time Jones and Rose joined another shift of his crew, and the mood was just as festive.

Evening came quickly as the sun plunged beyond the horizon and Rose found herself standing at the bow of the ship again and staring at the approaching water and the horizon beyond. Santiago, Cuba was less than a day away and she did not look forward to departing the *Black Dragon* for good, even as her own ship, the *Scarlet Dragon* called to her.

With a wistful sigh, she turned from the bow and strode with slow steps toward the Captain's cabin. She did not know why but she was tired. Her mind raced about concerning what would happen when morning came. Cuba would be on the horizon when the sun came up and her stay aboard the *Black Dragon* would end. Thoughts of departing the big ship were laced with reluctance. Her own ship awaited her, but so did the price on her head, the hunt for that ship, and more importantly the whole reason she went to sea to begin with.

Entering the cabin, she knew Jones would not be there but glanced around for him anyway. A shallow sigh escaped her as she walked to the couch she slept on and sat down. Absently pulling her boots off, she stared straight ahead at nothing with blank eyes. If other obligations were not calling to her, she would have given the big pirate captain everything in her stores and joined him aboard this magnificent, menacing ship. Setting her boots down on the floor beside the couch, she rubbed her aching feet for a moment, still staring absently ahead of her. Just as absently, she reached to the laces on her shirt and loosened them with one hand. As she pulled the shirt over her head, her hair snagged on something and such a simple thing, done hundreds of times, suddenly became an ordeal. It took a moment, but she freed the stubborn lock of hair and pulled the shirt off, throwing it hard to the floor and she glared at it for long seconds after. Leaning her head back, she shook her hair out and combed her fingers through it a few times. After, she stood and unfastened her belt and trousers and pulled them from her hips before sitting back down and pulling them the rest of the way off. There was not much to her undergarments, only a lacy half top and tight fitting white silk over her hips and upper legs.

Sitting there with barely anything covering her, she remained lost in thought, and really did not care if the big pirate found her like that. Secretly, she hoped he would.

The painting over Jones' bed caught her attention again and she found herself approaching it before she realized. Standing only a few feet away, she gazed back into the eyes of the lovely woman portrayed and studied her with her full attention. Leaning her head slightly, she began to wonder. This had to be more than a prize taken from another ship. Judging from its placement, right where the big pirate slept, this meant something to him. And the words on it, *To my dearest love. Yours always. Emily.* This painting was made for someone, someone very special to the woman.

"Who is she?" Rose asked aloud. The big pirate captain's silken approach had not gone unnoticed this time, even as she was lost in thought. When she looked over her shoulder, Jones' eyes were on the painting, but snapped to her and narrowed.

"She is no concern of yours," Cannonflash snarled.

Looking back to the painting, Rose leaned her head and observed, "She's beautiful."

"Aye," Jones agreed softly.

Rose cut her eyes aside as if to see him, but she did not look back. The pirate captain's simple, subtle answer was laced with loss and she could hear sorrow behind his voice. She turned her gaze back to the painting and gently asked, "What happened to her?"

Jones did not answer.

Finally turning to him, she looked up to his eyes, seeing his locked on the painting. "I see she is still very dear to you."

With a low growl, Cannonflash turned and strode with heavy steps to his wardrobe. "There are matters you should not pry into, O'scarlett. That is one."

She nodded and turned her eyes down. "I understand, Captain. I didn't really think you were steel all the way through, anyway."

His activities suddenly stopped and he just stared inside the wardrobe.

Rose would not look at him and instead half turned and sat on his bed. Staring across the room to the couch she would sleep on again as she said with tight lips, "One doesn't need but to guess that she—"

"Enough!" he roared, spinning to face her.

She flinched and her wide eyes found him, and she cringed as he stormed to her.

Grabbing her arms, he easily jerked her from the bed and held her firmly before him, glaring down at her as he shouted, "Don't speak of it further, woman, or you'll go over the side, powder or no powder, savvy?"

Rose dumbly stared up at him. His grip on her hurt, but she did not care. Tears filled her eyes, and in an explosive moment she shouted back, "Do you think you're the only one? Did you stop to think that others have lost their dearest love too?"

He snarled in response, "Do you think I care what you've lost?"

She twisted and forced her arms from his grip and when she tried to back away she fell back and found herself sitting on the bed again. Her angry gaze locked with his, she spat, "Go ahead, Captain Jones. Keep it penned up. Make certain that nobody in the world knows you are able to love someone. Maybe that's what will keep up this mystique about you while you rot from the inside!"

"I've heard enough!" he warned.

"Oh, I'm certain you have," she countered. "You lost someone and now it's just too painful to even think of openly, so you'll come in here and brood over her painting every night."

"You've no idea what you're speaking of, woman, and it's not something for you to be concerned over."

"Maybe not, Jones. Maybe I should just let you appear strong for everyone and I'll wander about knowing how weak you really are on the inside. I lost my husband years ago to the British, but you won't see me disgracing his memory by mourning my life away like you are!"

Enraged, his lips rolled away from his teeth and raised a hand to strike her.

Rose sprang up and pushed him back a step with both hands, glaring back up at him as she shouted, "Go ahead, big man! Hit me as hard as you can! Knock me out cold and throw me over the side to drown. You know you want to!"

He hesitated. His eyes were still locked on her and wild with rage, and yet they widened when she had said that. Slowly, he lowered his hand.

She pushed him again and yelled, "Go on!" Tears began to roll from her eyes and her voice began to break. "Come on, Jones. Hit me! You wouldn't be the first!" She quickly wiped the tears from her cheeks and looked away. As she clenched her hands into tight fists, she snarled, "Go on, then. Just hit me and have done with it. That's what big men like you do, isn't it? Put me in my place and get it over with."

"Why would you want that?" he asked with a hint of concern in his voice.

Long seconds passed, and she finally breathed, "I don't." Where the sudden surge of anger had come from she did not know nor did she care at the moment. An old wound now felt fresh, reopened by a man who she had extended a kind hand to, and this was a bitterness that she could not easily dismiss. Not looking back at him, she walked around him, her arms crossed over her as if for protection as she strode toward the couch across the cabin. She felt his eyes on her but would not look his way. Removing the blanket, she laid down to her side, facing away from the pirate captain. Covering herself to her shoulders, she curled up as tightly as she could and tears poured from her eyes as she tightly closed them.

There would be no comfort for either of them this night. As Rose curled herself up tighter to protect herself from an old pain, the light from the lamp dimmed and she heard the floor creak as Jones strode slowly to his bed.

It seemed like hours later when Rose had cried all she could, and at some point she drifted off to sleep.

Chapter 5

TREACHERY

Her eyes opened slowly and she realized that the light in the cabin was the sun and it was morning. She still felt wounded from the night before and had no wish to face the big pirate again, but she heard him across the room rummaging about in his wardrobe, and she still felt a little anger. Not one to back down easily, she slowly sat up and pulled the blanket from her, staring down at the floor for some time to allow herself to awaken fully. Her clothes were still on the floor where she had dropped them, right beside her boots.

She finally turned her eyes to Cannonflash, who was standing at his wardrobe, inspecting a pistol. Drawing a breath, she still felt an allure for him, for some reason now more than ever. She reached for her trousers and slowly pulled them on, one leg at a time, then stood to pull them up over her hips. Her attention was fully on what she was doing, but her mind was on Jones.

"Killed by the British, was he?" Cannonflash asked unexpectedly.

She hesitated, then pulled her belt tight and buckled it. "Aye, that's what I said last night."

"Hmm," he growled. "Ye picked an odd way of revenge."

 77

"What do you mean?" Rose snapped as she reached for her shirt.

"Get you a ship," he replied, "and go after them at sea."

She had slipped one arm into her shirt and stopped what she was doing, her eyes still on it as she corrected, "That isn't why I do this."

"You're too well spoken to have been raised by the sea," he observed, slipping his pistol into one of the holsters on his belt. "Been educated, I think."

Rose pulled her shirt down and snarled, "What of it?"

Finally turning to face her, the big pirate folded his arms and gave her that same stone-like look he always did. "Why are you out here, O'scarlett?"

She only glanced at him.

"Revenge isn't a game for the meek," he pressed, "nor is piracy against the Reds. You have a ship that can barely hold its own against a schooner and you say of yourself that you're famous, as everyone should know you by name and reputation."

Rose finally looked to him with an enraged glare. "I owe you five kegs of powder and a crate of pistols, Captain Jones, and that is all I owe you!" With that she turned and stormed to the door, slamming it on her way out.

Storming to the bow, she locked her gaze on the landmass before her. With less than five miles of water between her and Santiago, it was just about time to pay her debt and leave the *Black Dragon* forever. The massive ship was at full sail and slicing through the sea at her best speed and it seemed as if the ship itself wanted rid of her. No matter. She wanted away from Jones and his ship even as they both sent her heart into constant turmoil.

As Cuba drew larger and larger, closer and closer, heavy boots also drew closer from behind and as they stopped right beside her, she would not look that way.

Jones folded his arms as he also stared at the shoreline beyond with blank eyes, and finally he informed, "I'll need a heading to get ye close to me powder."

"Just drop me at the main port," she said with sharp words. "I'll go from there and have it back at the dock before nightfall."

He vented a hard breath and corrected, "You'll be going with Mister Cannonburg to get me powder."

"I don't need a keeper," she snarled.

"He's going with ye," the Captain growled.

"So you can find my secret cache? I don't think so, Jones."

"And I don't think you'll just be dropped to disappear into that Cuban jungle.

She huffed a sigh, her lips tightening. "I saved your life on that schooner, possibly some of your crew. Don't you think you owe me some kind of consideration for that?"

"Trust is a dangerous game in this business, Lass, and business is what this is. You and Cannonburg go for the powder or I turn you in for that bounty instead."

Her eyes cut to him.

He looked down at her.

Her chest heaved as she forced another hard breath from her, then she turned her eyes ahead again and snarled, "Fine."

"I've no interest in where you stash your pathetic little stores," he growled. "Once I have me powder and pistols then you'll be rid of me for good."

Rose turned her eyes down, her mouth tightening to a thin slit. She nodded and agreed, "Aye, and you'll be rid of me."

Jones turned and shouted, "Mister Cannonburg! That boat ready to put to water?"

"Aye, Captain," came the answer from across the ship.

As the big pirate captain turned and stormed away, Rose took one more good look at the magnificent black ship before she departed it.

* * *

It was still early, not many ships were about and the small port of Santiago was not so busy. Just as well. The few people about took little notice of Rose and Cannonburg as they made their way to a jungle trail that would ultimately take them to the camouflaged cave where she kept her stores. It took hours to get there and she hoped that the twists and turns were doing their job of confusing the big pirate with her.

Once at the hillside, she took him around a grove of trees in front of the cave so that they would approach it from a different direction, walking another path that circled back for almost half an hour before they finally arrived. Rose had planted a few thorny trees that people would avoid at the entrance and left just enough room to walk comfortably between the thorns and the rock face of the cliff to get to the cave opening. Snug under an outcropping and wrapped in oiled burlap were a couple of old oil lamps that would provide light. Once they were lit, she handed one to Cannonburg and led the way into the old cave.

Inside, it had clearly been mined for something in years past and some of the old equipment was left behind. The room they entered was about thirty feet deep and awkwardly oval, fifteen feet at the widest point. A pile of stones and rubbish was ahead that went all the way to the ceiling and an old wooden wheelbarrow lay on its side at the far base of it.

"Okay," she announced in a low voice. "Here we are." She stopped and looked back at him, directing her lantern around to illuminate him as she continued, "Remember, only five kegs and one crate of pistols and shot."

He nodded and growled back, "I heard the Captain."

She led the way around the pile of stones and rubbish and entered another room, one that had old timbers holding up the entrance. This room was almost square, twenty feet in any direction and had a lattice of wooden timbers that seemingly held the walls together and kept the room intact. It was unusually dry within for being underground and Rose stopped dead in her tracks as she entered, her eyes widening as she found the room empty! Shining the light around, she gasped as she found every corner devoid of the stores she had stockpiled there. The powder, the ammunition, the food, the captured treasures... All of it was gone!

Cannonburg looked around and asked, "So where to from here?"

"I don't understand," she breathed, her mouth agape as her wide eyes swept the room once more in disbelief.

He looked down at her and asked, "Where is the powder."

Rose shook her head and shouted, "It's gone! Everything's gone!" She wheeled around and stormed out of the room, out of the cave and outside where she stopped by the outcropping and set her lamp down. Shaking her head again, she looked aside and said as if to herself, "This just can't be. Nobody knew about this place…" Her eyes widened and she raised her head, breathing, "Oh, no." She blew her lamp out and shoved it back into the outcropping, then turned and slapped Cannonburg in the chest with the back of her hand as she ordered, "Come on. Let's go."

He followed suit with his lamp and pursued her, demanding, "Go where? Where is the Captain's powder?"

"It's been taken," she replied, hurrying along a path that took them away from the cave and downhill.

This was not the direction they had come from and Cannonburg was growing uneasy. Still, he followed but pressed, "Where are we going, O'scarlett?"

"There's a cove not far from here," she informed. "It's where I hide the *Scarlet Dragon*. It's deep enough for a large shallow draft vessel to go almost up to the shoreline. They can't have sailed already."

"You saying your crew cleaned out the cave?"

"Aye, that's what I'm saying. Dammit, why did I put my trust in him?"

They emerged some time later on a white sand beach and Rose turned to the East and walked at a brisk pace along the water. Cannonburg did not speak further as he walked at her side. She was angry and distraught and he seemed to be able to tell that something had gone wrong. Foremost in his mind was the powder and pistols his captain wanted, and to this end he remained wary.

The beach turned inland and Rose raced up the sand toward the jungle again. Finding an obscure path, she rushed past trees and vines and emerged onto white sand again. They had found the cove that was surrounded by tall trees and grasses. The cove was ringed by white sand and was a quarter mile wide and about that deep and was mostly concealed by the peninsula of plant covered sand and stone that wound around it from the far side. The water was a dark blue, deep from the look of it and kept calm by the natural surf breaker.

And anchored in the middle was Rose's ship, the *Scarlet Dragon*.

Rose stopped as she saw it, and her eyes darted about to the activity on the beach, the boat that returned to the beach from the ship, and the stacks of crates and other items that were near the water's edge. Her lips slid away from her teeth as she stormed down toward the beach, toward the flurry of the activity near her supplies. There was a hundred yards of sand to cross, but for some reason nobody took notice of her as she drew closer.

Her eyes fixed on one man who stood by and barked orders at the others, directing a few to the waiting stack of crates. He was far better dressed than she had last seen him and as she got closer she noticed him in new boots and he wore a big hat with a long feather in it.

As he pointed to the boat, which had just landed, she grabbed his arm and swung him around, shouting, "What do you think you're doing, Smith?"

He turned fully and smiled as he folded his arms, greeting, "Well, if it isn't Rose O'scarlett. Heard you'd been taken off by savages on Tortuga."

"You knew where I was and where I'd been, Smith. Why was the mine cleared out?"

"Business, Miss O'scarlett."

Her eyes narrowed. "I didn't order any of that to be taken aboard."

"I did," he announced. "I'm afraid we've had a change of command, Miss O'scarlett."

Rose's brow lifted, her lips parting slowly as she shook her head and breathed, "What are you saying?"

"Call it mutiny, if you will," Smith replied, "but the crew and I lost confidence in you. Lost a lot of good mates out there during that last fiasco you put us all through."

Taking a step back, she shook her head again and said just above a whimper, "You can't mean that. We built this crew together! We—We've taken—"

"And," he interrupted, "your so called leadership has almost been the death of us all. You must understand, Rose, that this is business, that's all. It isn't personal." He raised his brow. "It could be, but it isn't."

The shock began to wear off and she clenched her teeth as she found her anger. "Mister Smith, you'd be wise to stand down and do it right now!"

"Or what?" he spat back.

She went for her pistol, then froze as half a dozen of her men drew theirs and trained them on her.

"It's over," Smith informed coldly.

Her eyes darted from one man to the next, and slowly her hand moved away from her pistol. He had not noticed that Cannonburg was about ten feet behind her and watching. Tight lipped, she asked in a soft voice, "Can I at least have my personal affects?"

Smith eyed her for long seconds, then he looked over his shoulder and barked, "Take that next load to the ship and bring back Miss O'scarlett's chest." Looking back at her, he smiled and shook his head. "You had to know it would come to this sooner or later, Rose. But, I'm sure you'll find opportunity elsewhere." He glanced at Cannonburg and ordered, "Now if you want what's yours then you'll walk back up to the edge of the jungle and sit there where I can watch you until we depart."

She closed the distance between them with two steps and stopped less than a foot away from him, glaring up into his eyes as she hissed, "I will remember this, Mister Smith."

"I'm sure you will, Miss O'scarlett," he countered.

Rose stared up at him for a long second, then turned to storm away, but he grabbed her arm and brutally turned her back to him.

With a wicked smile, he offered, "Maybe you'll give me what you should have a long time ago, and maybe I'll let you sail with me as me first mate. What say you, Miss O'scarlett?" He raised his chin slightly as the tip of her dagger pushed against his throat.

With bared teeth she snarled, "Perhaps your little worm can end up on a hook to catch a little fish. What say you to that, Mister Smith?"

He loudly cleared his throat and three of the men who were working with the cargo turned to them and drew their pistols, training them on Rose.

Smith smiled at her and informed, "They'll pump you full of lead balls before you can bleed me, puppet."

Cannonburg reached over Rose's shoulder and pressed the muzzle of his own pistol against Smith's cheek as he growled, "Even if they fire you'll be just as dead. Now release Captain

O'scarlett and back yourself away." He pulled the hammer back and added, "Now!"

Wisely, Smith released Rose's arm and raised his hands before him as he slowly backed away. He was still smiling even as he turned his eyes to the big man behind her, the big man who still held the pistol on him with a steady hand.

Raising another pistol to train on the man to the left, Cannonburg' eyes narrowed as they shifted from one man to the other.

Rose stared back at Smith for a moment, then she turned and strode away, ordering, "Come on, Mister Cannonburg."

Warily, Cannonburg backed away, and as the other men lowered their weapons, he did the same, slipping them back into their holsters as he turned to follow Rose.

Nearly to the tree line, Rose turned and sat down on the sand, watching with blank eyes as her former crew and former first mate loaded the last of her supplies aboard her ship. Good to his word, Smith directed a sea chest to be dropped on the beach near the water, then he looked up the hill and waved before getting onto the boat to return to the *Scarlet Dragon*.

As she watched her ship sail away, Rose drew her legs to her and rested her chin on her knees. Finally, the *Scarlet Dragon* was out of sight and she closed her eyes.

Cannonburg had been sitting beside her unnoticed for most of the time they had watched Smith stealing her ship, her crew, and her supplies. He had not spoken, as if he sensed that she did not want conversation, but with the *Scarlet Dragon* gone, he finally drew a deep, loud breath, one that growled out of him.

She slowly turned her head to look up at him.

His eyes narrowed and he scowled as he said, "I can't abide mutineers. Traitors should be shot and given to the deep, says me."

Rose nodded and could say nothing.

He finally looked to her, his eyes stern as he informed, "I have me orders, Captain O'scarlett. Got to bring the Captain's powder or you back to the ship in irons."

She nodded again and offered, "I understand." She smiled, just a little. "You didn't have to do that down there."

"Aye," he agreed, "but as I told you, I can't abide mutineers. Far as I can see, that's still your ship out there."

Her lips tightened and she softly offered, "Thank you, Johnny."

He smiled back at her and nodded. Looking back to the beach, he stood and offered her his hand. "Okay, Captain O'scarlett. Let's get that sea chest and be on our way."

As they approached the old chest, which was about two feet wide, two high and a foot and a half deep and was rather old and gray and showing its years, Rose clenched her teeth as she saw the lock had been cut off and the chest opened. Kneeling down in front of it, she opened the lid and began to remove a few belongings, mostly clothing that had been rummaged through and shoved back in haphazardly.

Johnny folded his arms and asked, "Did they leave any of your valuables?"

Still removing clothing and placing it into the open lid, she replied, "They didn't know about the valuables in here." She took out the last of the clothing, a half empty perfume bottle, a large handbag and a small wooden chest that was painted white and pink which she put down with care beside her.

His brow lowering, Cannonburg leaned closer as she reached into the empty chest again.

Wedging her fingernails into the wood at the bottom near the back, she strained against the wood and tried to pry it up.

"What are you doing?" Johnny asked.

"False bottom," she replied. When something tapped her on the shoulder, she looked and saw the hilt of his dagger, and she offered him a little smile as she took it. The dagger made prying the bottom up easy and she removed the wood and tossed it aside. Looking over her shoulder again, she raised her brow and ordered, "Give me those pistols of yours."

"What?" he questioned.

She removed two heavy caliber pistols from the bottom, new looking pistols with heavy barrels and large wooden grips. They were adorned with polished brass and were expertly made, very fine looking weapons that she offered to him handles first with the words, "Trade?"

His eyes narrowed and he removed one of his pistols. It was old, well used and not as high a caliber, nor was it as attractive a weapon. They had been stolen from the navy after a fierce battle and were nothing one would want to trade for, though they were reliable and fired true. With suspicion in his eyes, he demanded, "Why?"

"Won these in a card game," she explained, then she raised her brow and went on, "They kick like mules and hurt my wrists like hell to fire. I figure someone as big as you would prefer more hitting power and not be bothered by the kick."

"Function over form?" he asked.

With a little smile, she nodded and confirmed, "Aye. I must say, though, it was the most profitable pair of Jacks I'd ever held."

He chuckled and pulled his other pistol, agreeing, "Deal."

It only took her a moment to stuff a couple of dresses, some undergarments and many other items into the handbag. Reaching in, she also removed two suede sacks full of coins and stuffed them in as well. The last thing she removed was a thick sealed envelope of brown paper which she slipped in with much more care.

The envelope is what caught Johnny's attention and his eyes narrowed again as he as asked, "What would that be?"

Her movements hesitated, but she slowly closed the handbag and replied, "It is absolution."

"Not sure what you mean," he admitted.

Rose drew a breath and nodded, then she finally stood and slipped the strap over her shoulder. "I won't burden you with it, Mister Cannonburg. You've been too good to me."

He nodded. "Aye, and now I have to take you back to the *Black Dragon* to face Captain Cannonflash's ire. Wish I didn't have to."

A smile touched her lips and she nodded back to him. "You are a rare gem in this world, Johnny. I think someday you'll make a wonderful captain, yourself." Looking across the cove, she sighed and said with regretful words, "Well, we should be on our way."

As she walked at a moderate pace down the beach, he followed, but protested, "Where are we going? The port's the other way."

"Aye," she admitted, "but my sloop's this way."

"Your sloop?"

Giving him a sidelong glance, she informed, "Smith did not have my absolute trust, Mister Cannonburg, nor should he have. I have many resources he did not know of. Do you think you could find your way back here?" When he nodded, she went on, "Can you find your way back to the cave from here?"

"Aye," he replied. "Why?"

She shrugged. "Because you do have my trust." With her brow high over her eyes, she looked up at him and offered a little smile.

"Don't know why I would," he grumbled.

Rose laughed and bumped him with her shoulder. "I just follow me heart, Mister Cannonburg."

In short order they were across the cove and Rose turned toward the jungle. Still in the dark as to where she was going, he did not speak up this time, though he clearly remained wary of her.

The jungle path she led him through was narrow and treacherous and as tall as he was the going was difficult, and he kept up with her with some difficulty. Finally, he lost sight of her and found himself almost desperate to catch sight of her again. He stopped to get his bearings, looking around him through the thick growth of the jungle, and finally he stormed forward again, scowling as he rampaged through the dense trail.

He emerged in a clearing near what appeared to be a river and stopped again, scanning the area for any sign of her. To his right was what appeared to be an ancient stone structure, an ideal place to hide. It was covered with vines and was not easy to make out, so he followed the wall and wheeled around it as he found the edge, coming face to face with a human skull! With a loud gasp he backed away and drew his pistol, stumbling a few steps, then he yelled and wheeled around as someone grasped his shoulder.

Rose looked irritated and hissed, "Would you stop messing about and come on!" She looked behind him to the alter of gray stone and raised her brow. "Aye, it frightened half the life from me when I first saw it, too. Just about wet meself."

As he slid his pistol back into its holster, he wiped the sweat from his brow with the back of his hand and followed her again.

Across the clearing and down a slope they went and then back into the jungle for another hike down an obscure trail. This time, when the trail opened up again they could hear water lapping on the rocks ahead and they stepped out onto the bank of a river.

Rose set her hands on her hips and looked ahead of her to the sloop which was tied off to a couple of trees. It was a run-down ship, not more than eighty feet, though it looked far too big to be where it was, as the river itself was only about a hundred feet across. It had only one mast and the sail was furled and covered and bound tightly against the storms that would rip at the place. Three bronze deck guns faced them and three more opposite. There was a swivel gun mounted on the bow and ports for three more cannons were closed and sealed. The hatch that opened to the lower deck was sealed with a bolt and old padlock. From the way it sat in the water, it appeared to be beached and rocked slowly back and forth with the wind and the movement on the water.

It was a short jump across to the old vessel and Rose got a running start of a few steps and cleared the four foot span to the edge of the ship easily, as if she had done so many times. Cannonburg, with his long stride, merely stepped across and was aboard right behind her.

Going right to task, Rose began to untie the bindings that held the sail in place, shooting him a glance as he just watched her. A little smile touched her lips as she announced, "Welcome aboard the *Scarlet Enchantress*. She was my first ship. I guess I held onto her all these years for sentimental reasons."

Nodding, Johnny took her side and helped her with the sail. "I can see why, Captain. She seems a stout ship." Glancing around, he asked, "How do you propose we get her off the bottom?"

She glanced back at him. "We'll go below and remove the ballast. I have copper tanks down there that I fill with water to half sink her when she's not sailing. Weighs her down enough to put her bottom against the sand and hold her in place."

He nodded again.

The sail down the river was a short one and in short order they were out to sea. The *Scarlet Enchantress* was a smooth ship and took the wind eagerly. She turned hard and Cannonburg found himself holding onto the mast as Rose turned the ship hard toward the port a few miles away. This was also a fast ship and they were turning toward the pier before he realized.

Like the expert mariners they were they put the little ship to the side of the pier and had her secured bow and stern in no time. Santiago was well known for harboring unsavory types, just the kind of place that pirates would blend into. A few British wandered about with their sabers on their belts and muskets on their backs, but they did not seem interested in enforcing any laws. This was still Spanish held territory and the small claim the British had here was not one that was especially secure.

A pub was in the center of the little community and here is where Rose led Cannonburg. They found a table and took their seats and were quickly served mugs of local made ale that was very stout. It was a noisy, smoky place but even the activity about could not distract a woman who did not realize she was lost in thought. Johnny barely noticed as his eyes darted about in a search for something or someone unspoken.

Perhaps a half hour passed when Cannonburg finally noticed Rose had not taken a drink and just stared at her mug as she absently turned it a little at a time. "Captain?" he finally summoned.

Her eyes snapped to him, then back to her mug and she offered, "Sorry. Just thinking."

"Aye," he said with a nod. "You'll be owing Captain Jones those five kegs or you'll be seeing him rather cross."

She nodded and added, "And pistols." Venting a sigh, she shook her head and mumbled, "Why does everything go wrong all at once like this?"

He picked his mug up and replied before taking a drink, "Just the way of things, Captain."

A smile touched her lips and she looked fully to him. "I can see why Cannonflash likes you. Your kind of loyalty is a rare thing."

"Some loyalty is earned, Miss," he explained.

Looking back to her mug, Rose grumbled, "Aye, I should have earned a little more from that mutinous crew of mine."

"Or been more selective about them," he suggested.

"Sometimes you take what you can get, Mister Cannonburg."

 89

"And we saw the result of that today. Now you've no ship, no crew and no payment for Cannonflash."

She raised her brow. "I just need to think of something, that's all. Perhaps I have favors to call in." She turned a stern look on him and insisted, "I will find a way to pay him what I owe."

"By tonight?" Cannonburg asked.

Rose lowered her eyes, then shrugged, softly replying, "I don't know. Thank you, Johnny."

"For the drinks? You bought them as I remember."

She smiled and looked to him. "No, for the time. You could already have taken me back to the ship in irons as your captain ordered."

He raised his brow and looked back to his mug. "We've time for all that later. Better I return with Captain Jones' powder than you in irons, I think."

"You're a good man, Mister Cannonburg."

Johnny smiled and winked at her. "Good man and a pirate. There's a mix for ya."

The door slammed and drew their attention, and Rose lifted her brow high over her eyes as she saw the tall, well made young woman enter.

With her dark blond hair restrained behind her in a long pony tail, the green eyed young woman was surely an alluring sight to the men about the tavern, but she had a menace about her, and a hard look in her eyes that would serve warning to any who would approach her. As tall as most men Rose knew, she was broad shouldered for a woman with big, muscular arms and thick legs. She did not have a tiny waist but was generously put together in both hips and bust. Hoop earrings dangled from her ears. She wore a dark pink bustier that showed off much of her chest and left her arms and broad shoulders free and unencumbered. Tight fitting red trousers conformed to her like a second skin and looked like they needed a good washing. On her broad, black belt hung two pistols and a dagger on her right, and a huge cutlass on her left. Her black boots were knee high with tall heels that added to her already statuesque form.

She set her hands on her hips and quickly scanned the tavern. This was a very pretty girl and she had the eye of every man there, though none seemed to be able to muster the courage to approach her. Striding to the bar with long, heavy steps, she slammed her palm down on it and said with a loud, young voice, "You there! I've gold to spend and a parch to quench!"

Johnny raised his chin and shouted to her, "They don't serve ruffians the likes of you in here, Missy."

Rose's eyes widened as the big woman's attention snapped to him and she held her breath as Cannonburg and this woman stared each other down.

As he stood, the woman turned fully and strode toward him, a glare in her eyes as she snarled, "And what mangy dog would speak to me?"

His eyes narrowed and he spat back, "A mangy dog that'll send you out the door or bed you, wench."

"Oh boy," Rose mumbled, her eyes shifting from one to the other. "What are you doing?"

The tall woman strode right up to Johnny, her brow low over her eyes as she stopped only a foot away from him. He was noticeably taller than she was, much heavier built and clearly fearless of her, and she seemed just as fearless of him. After a short pause she sneered, "You'd best watch who you talk of bedding, dog."

He smirked. "Afraid you'll want more?"

She set her hands on her hips and raised her chin. A smile forced its way to her mouth and she reached to him, pulling him forcibly to her for a kiss. Johnny wrapped his arms around her like a hungry bear and crushed her to him.

Watching them kiss each other, Rose rested her elbow on the table and her chin in her palm, her brow arching slightly.

The big woman pulled away from Cannonburg slightly and turned her attention to Rose, snarling, "Who is that tramp you're sitting with?"

Her eyes narrowing, Rose slowly moved her other hand to her cutlass.

Johnny turned slightly to her and warned, "Careful, Angie. This is Captain O'scarlett. She's worked out some trade with Cannonflash and I'm along to see to it everything goes smoothly.

The big woman nodded slightly, snarling, "Just so long as she knows what to keep her grimy little hands off of." Looking back up to Cannonburg, her demeanor changed again and she offered him a broad smile. "Saw the *Dragon* at anchor and knew you'd be here. Maybe you'll be showing a girl about, aye?"

"Maybe so," he replied, "but got business to attend first."

Turning her narrow eyes back on Rose, the big woman made no secret of her disapproval.

Rose easily dismissed the hateful look and turned her attention back to Cannonburg, offering, "You kids just run along and have your fun, Mister Cannonburg. I've a few errands before we return to the ship."

He raised his chin slightly and his eyes narrowed as he did.

"I'll meet you back here in a couple of hours," she assured. "We don't want Captain Jones irritated about problems with his shipment."

Nodding slowly, Johnny hesitantly said, "A couple of hours."

"And don't be late," she warned. "I've much to attend to tonight.

He nodded again and assured, "I'll be back then." Turning with the big woman at his side, he strode with her toward the door, looking back at Rose once more before he left.

This would be an ideal time to escape the fate she had coming, but as she had voiced before, she did not want Jones and his crew hunting for her as well. She gulped down contents of her mug and left the tavern herself. There was indeed much to do, and a debt to be paid.

On the other side of the small village was a solid looking warehouse, one that was some distance from the beach. Big double doors were the only way in or out and a well worn path led right to them. Many barrels were lined up on one side of the door and stacks of crates, some of them four high, were everywhere. Rose knew that this big structure was not just here to store things. She walked inside and past the few men who worked there. As she strode toward the back, a place she had visited many times before, she did so anticipating an end to the crisis at hand. However, a new hiding place would have to be found for her stores and this was on her mind as well.

A long counter spanned much of the warehouse which was packed with many more crates, barrels and other items including cannons, rolls of rope, tools, huge mounds of rolled canvas and countless other items. The big fellow who stood behind the counter was who she sought. He had a full beard but no mustache and he was balding. His hair and beard were light brown and streaked with gray. He wore spectacles before his eyes and a dirty white shirt and brown leather apron over it.

With his eyes and attention on the manifest on the counter before him, he did not seem to notice her approach, but as she was close enough to gently set her hands on the counter he greeted, "Be right with you, Rose."

She nodded and waited for a long moment as he scribbled something into the book he studied. When he finally closed it, she offered him a smile and said, "Good to see you again, Patrick."

He nodded, but did not smile back. His eyes were strained as he looked back at her, and slowly he removed his spectacles.

"That shipment I've coming tomorrow," she started.

He put his spectacles back on and reopened the book. "There's no shipment."

A chill shot through her and she raised her brow, asking as calmly as possible, "What?"

"It's business," he replied. "Our dealings have to end. There's a price on your head and too many gunning for ye, and I can't afford to be known to associate with ye."

Slowly shaking her head, she desperately informed, "Patrick, I need that powder!"

"They've been here six times this week!" he barked, finally looking back to her. "They've rummaged through everything, took me books and made it clear that my neck will stretch too if they find I've had dealings with you! I have a family, Rose! I have to think of the wife and wee ones."

She looked away, clenching her teeth as her mind scrambled. Looking back to him, she suggested, "Look, Patrick, perhaps you can just give me five kegs."

"I can't, Rose," he insisted.

"I've already paid you for twelve, Patrick! And I've paid you for much more than that! You owe me!"

He slammed his fist onto the counter and shouted back, "Then you be paid in full! I didn't turn you over to the Reds and I'll not today, but I make no promises about tomorrow!"

She took a step back, slowly shaking her head. "We've been doing business for three years, Patrick. Three years. I've called you my friend all that time."

Looking back to his book, he nodded and softly admitted, "I know. It just has to end."

Desperation was in her voice as she cried, "I need that powder!"

He loosed a hard breath and said, "I can't risk it."

Setting her hands on her hips, she shouted, "But it's bought and paid for!"

His eyes snapped to her and he countered, "Ye got papers?"

She raised her chin, then clenched her teeth and hissed, "You know we've never worked that way!"

"You need to go, Miss, and don't come back here."

Tight lipped, she stepped back toward the counter, grasping the corner with both hands as she pled, "Patrick, please! Don't do this to me!"

"Good day!" he shouted, looking back to his ledger.

Her jaw shook as she glared at him, then she wheeled around and stormed toward the door, only to stop halfway there and wheel around. "This isn't over, Patrick! Believe me this isn't over!"

Right outside the door, she strode out with steps as long as she could make them, then she paused near some double stacked crates. They had the seal of one of the local distilleries on them and her eyes narrowed as she saw these seals. Drawing her dagger, she wedged the blade under the lid and pried it up with loud creaks from the protesting nails, then she grasped it with her free hand and wrenched it off. Inside, packed in straw, were several bottles of the local made rum. She slid her dagger back into its sheath and reached in to remove one.

A big man in black trousers and a dirty blue shirt with no sleeves burst from the warehouse brandishing a cutlass and shouted, "You'll be putting that back, wench!"

In one quick, fluid motion, Rose spun toward him, leveling her pistol on him with a steady hand and her thumb pulling back the hammer with two loud clicks. With a low brow, she shouted, "You got something else to say to me?"

Wide eyed, the big man backed away as he lowered the cutlass.

With narrow eyes, she snarled, "I'm still owed for what I paid and you'd be a fool to believe I won't collect!" She raised the bottle to her mouth and pulled the cork out with her teeth, spitting it toward him before she took a few gulps of the rum within. Locking a glare back on the big man, she slowly lowered the hammer of her pistol and with slow movements she slid it back into its holster, and before turning to leave she took one more bottle from the crate.

* * *

Cannonburg returned to the tavern without the woman he had left with. Setting his hands on his hips, he scanned the smoky room and finally locked his gaze on a table in the back corner, and his brow arched as he saw who he was looking for.

Still grasping the second bottle of rum by its neck, Rose was laid over the table with her chin resting in front of her and her half open eyes staring straight ahead. The first bottle she had taken lay on its side in the middle of the table and that is where she seemed to be looking, though she was really looking at nothing specific. Her hair was pulled over one shoulder and much of it lay on the table beside her head. Her other arm was stretched out across the table. When heavy footsteps approached and a shadow fell over her, she rolled her head over and planted her cheek on the table, turning her unsteady eyes up to Johnny as she tried to bring him into focus. Drawing a deep breath, she asked with slurred words, "You ever have a really difficult day, Misser Camelbumps?" Closing her eyes, she giggled. "Camelbumps!" she squealed. "That is so funny! I said Camelbumps!"

Johnny folded his arms and informed, "It's time to get ye back to the ship, Captain O'scarlett."

"Okay," she sighed, pushing herself up with great difficulty. When she went to stand, she stumbled over the chair she had been seated in and the big pirate caught her before she could fall all the way. As he held her up, her head wobbled to and fro, back and forth, and finally she looked up at him and suggested, "You should take the helm, Misser Candlebarn."

Nodding, he agreed, "Aye, Captain. I'll do just that."

95

Getting her to the dock to board the dinghy was an ordeal in itself as she could barely walk. Still, she had a firm grip on that bottle of rum and would not let it go. As he helped her into the boat, she took yet another swallow, then looked up at him and observed, "You a really good looking boy, Jimmy. Really good looking boy."

He propped her up against the mast and replied, "Thank ye, Captain."

She nodded a wobbly nod and asked, "Which way to the side?" Looking around, she let go of the mast and, still clutching the bottle in her hand, stumbled over to the side of the dinghy and fell to her knees. With her hand firmly grasping the edge of the boat, she leaned over and vomited over the side.

Cannonburg groaned and rubbed his eyes.

Once aboard the *Black Dragon* it only got worse. He had to hold her up as he escorted her to the captain's cabin and she gratefully had one arm around his back as she staggered along with him under the watchful and curious eyes of everyone aboard.

"I love this ship!" she declared loudly. "Bess ship in the world, it is! Think I'll stay here." Looking up at Cannonburg, she smiled and assured, "You'd make a swell cabin boy, Jimmy!" Taking another swallow from the bottle, which had only a quarter of its full contents left, she reached down and grabbed his buttocks, and when he shot her an irritated look she assured, "I'll fight off that big pirate woman wrench, I will. You juss show me where she is and I'll give 'er me big boot and kick 'er over the side! You mine now, boy!"

"Uh, huh," he grumbled as he opened the door and escorted her into the cabin. Once inside, he gave up trying to walk her and just picked her up, carrying her to Cannonflash's bed.

"Why Misser Cabin… something," she slurred. "I'll not be taken so easy, you ruffian!" She laughed again and corrected, "Oh sure I will. Take me all ye want, handsome!"

He dropped her onto the bed and she exploded into hysterical giggles.

"That was fun," she squealed.

"Wait here for the Captain," he growled as he turned to leave.

"Not leavin' me alone, are ya?" she shouted. "Bring me more rum, cabin boy!" Rose watched after the door for some time after it closed, then she yelled, "Where's me rum?" Raising her other hand, which still clutched the bottle, she smiled and declared, "Oh, there it is!"

The bottle did not quite make it to her mouth before her head rolled back and she passed out, and slowly she slid off of the bed head first.

* * *

A whole bucket of cold saltwater hit her square in the face and she awoke with a gasp, sucking much of it down her throat. Coughing ensued and she sat up and clamped a hand over her mouth as she hacked up some of the sea water she had inhaled. Once that subsided she raised a hand to her throbbing head and finally opened her eyes, groaning as some large black boots came into focus.

Finally, slowly, she turned her eyes up and squinted to see Johnny Cannonburg standing over her with a wooden bucket in his hand and his brow held low over his eyes.

"Get yourself down to the galley," he ordered. "Captain Cannonflash'll be having words with you after."

Rose watched him turn and stride from the captain's cabin, and as he closed the door she had an ominous feeling in the pit of her stomach, something that overshadowed even the terrible hangover she had. Looking around, she realized she was sitting on the floor, and had slept there.

Still holding her head, she wandered into the galley and stopped at the table. The crew had already eaten and everything was in order here. She pulled out the chair near the captain's chair that she had sat in since coming aboard and gingerly sat down. Resting her elbows on the table, she slowly lowered her forehead to her palms and closed her eyes.

A man entered carrying a pot that had a ladle hanging out of it and alerted her to his presence as he slammed it down onto the table hard near her.

Her head popped up, then she groaned and closed her eyes again, rubbing her forehead as she snapped, "Shh!"

The man laughed a deep, hearty laugh and patted her shoulder. "Got what ya need right here, Lass." As she leaned back, he set a wooden bowl down in front of her and a spoon beside the bowl. Lifting the lid to the pot, he carefully removed the ladle and dumped some of the steaming concoction from the pot into the bowl. Two more times he did this before putting the lid in place.

Rose finally looked up at him.

He was a tall man with nearly black skin, very plump lips and a bald head. He was nearly as large as Cannonflash and had a massive uncovered chest and thick arms hanging from very broad shoulders. He wore blue trousers and a cook's apron that was clearly not washed often. Clean shaven, he had a very pleasant look about him and offered her a big smile as he ordered, "Well, dig in, Lass. Worked hard all mornin' on that."

She looked down to the bowl and did not recognize what was in it. It had a unusual smell, but not an unpleasant smell. Drawing her head back, she looked up at him again and raised her brow.

He pulled out the captain's chair and sat down, resting his arms on the table as he stared back at her, and after long seconds he urged, "Go on, Missy. Eat it or it'll eat you."

Rose turned her attention back to the bowl and finally asked, "Um, what is it?"

"Menudo," he replied. "Best remedy for a night of too much rum."

She gingerly picked the spoon up and dipped a little out, hesitantly slipping it between her lips. It tasted unusual, but it was good and she raised her brow and nodded to him.

"My own recipe," he informed proudly. "I make the best menudo in the Caribbean."

She took another bite and finally asked, "So what's in it?"

Shaking his head, he smiled again and assured, "Believe me, you don't want to know."

Rose suddenly stopped chewing. When the black man laughed, she forced herself to swallow and looked back to the bowl.

He produced a spoon from his apron and removed the lid to the pot, dipping some out and eating it himself.

They sat there in silence for a few moments and enjoyed the food he had prepared. She quickly found that she was enjoying this new and exotic food and also found her stomach settling and her head beginning to feel better.

"I've seen you around the ship, I think," she said to him.

He nodded and took another bite from the pot. "Aye, I man a deck gun and will board from time to time when the captain needs another hand, but I stay in the galley for the most part." He looked to her and boasted, "I'm considered the best cook at sea so Cannonflash makes sure I'm taken care of."

She smiled and took another bite. "You are definitely the best cook I've run into for many years. How did you end up aboard the *Black Dragon?*"

He looked back to the pot and took his time spooning more out, and also took his time to answer. "I was just a boy when I was brought to this part of the world. Got sold to a plantation as a worker. Not a good life, so I left one night."

"I can imagine that the plantation owner was not very happy about that," she guessed.

He smiled and shook his head. "No, he was not. Called together a hunting party and came after me. Chased me for many days. I ended up in a village near the sea and was not well received. You see, it is illegal for us negroes to learn to read and write."

"I'd heard that somewhere. I assume you learned?"

"Aye, that I did. Looked for work and finally they caught up to me." He loosed a deep breath, staring into the pot before him. "I didn't want to go back, and I didn't want to be killed that day. They were going to do one or the other so I ran again with five men chasing me. Ran to the docks, and down the pier and saw this huge, beautiful ship anchored beyond. She was taking on supplies, so I thought they could use one more hand and tried to blend in and help them load the dinghy, but I was seen." He turned his eyes to her, looking more serious than she had seen him since he had walked in. "I didn't want to go back and I fought and hit one across the jaw. That's a death sentence for us black folk." His eyes drifted away. "They had me and knew it, but I had a friend I knew nothing about." He looked back to her with a little smile. "They were beating me down, and then Cannonflash appeared from that dinghy and took them all on. Three of them went over the side of the pier and the other two ran away when he was through with them. Took me aboard, he did, and put me to task. I told him I could cook for him such meals to make him smile and he put me in the galley to prove it." He took another bite and finished, "Been here ever since."

Rose smiled.

"Owe me life to Cannonflash," he added, "and I'll not forget. He's hungry, he'll get me best meal. He needs another sword or gun at his side, old Harold will be there."

"Got a price on your head, then," she observed, "just like me."

"Just like everyone on this ship," he added. Raising his brow, he asked, "Runnin' from the law, are ye?"

With a little nod, she looked to her empty bowl and softly confirmed, "Aye."

The older fellow who had been so talkative her first night at this table staggered in and took the chair across from Rose. He groaned and raked his fingers through his thinning white hair, then looked to her bowl and asked, "Through with that, Missy?" When she nodded he took the bowl and spoon and dished out some of the menudo, then began to shovel it into his mouth.

"Go easy," Harold warned. "I don't want to see that again after you've swallowed it."

The old mariner grunted back.

"Had you another rough night with the bottle, did ye?" Harold asked.

"Aye," the old man confirmed. His eyes snapped to Rose and he recalled, "Ah, I'm to tell ye to get to the captain's cabin and wait for him. Time for your reckoning, I think, Missy."

She looked away and loosed a hard breath, then nodded and asked, "Think he'll shoot me before he throws me to the deep?"

"He might," Harold replied, "and he might not. If he's in a good mood—"

"Okay!" she barked. Standing, she reluctantly turned to the door to the galley and mumbled, "Wish me luck."

It was a beautiful, clear day outside, the *Black Dragon* was sailing fast with the wind and there was no land in sight. She took a moment to enjoy it and allow the wind to blow through her hair. Her shirt was still damp with sea water and she wished she could change. No matter.

 100

When she entered Jones' cabin she close the door gently behind her and leaned back against it. Her eyes wandered about, finally fixing on that painting. Then her eyes caught her handbag which was lying on the table near the lamp, and she smiled as she remembered the garments within.

Living on the run most of the time, Rose learned to change quickly and was soon in a low cut white blouse with frills about the cuffs of the half sleeves and the neckline. A short skirt that was scarlet red and ideal for walking on the beach complimented the scarlet button-up vest she wore over her shirt that accentuated her bust line. Finding a hairbrush in the make-up box, she brushed her long brown hair and restrained the sides behind her head with a bright pink barrette. Her boots did not well suit this outfit and the slippers she had last worn with it were still on her ship, so she wore no shoes at all. Changed and feeling more a woman than a pirate now, she opened the box again and looked at her reflection in the small mirror that was mounted on the inside of the lid. Now she took her time. When Jones entered the room, she was certain he would kill her, and she at least wanted to die feeling pretty. Still, she had one last card to play, although she was confident that it would make no difference at all, but a slim chance was better than none at all.

She brushed pink powder on her cheeks, darker pink powder over her eyes and rubbed on hot pink lip gloss from a small jar with one finger. Working her lips together to distribute it evenly, she managed a little smile and blew her reflection a kiss. The last time she had made herself up like this had been for her husband many years ago. Perhaps she would meet him in Heaven or at least catch a glimpse of him on her way to Hell. Her love for him had never diminished, but she had somehow moved on.

The door to the cabin closed hard and she flinched at the sudden bang. Slowly, and with both hands, she closed the make-up box and just stared down at it with tight lips as she braced herself for the inevitability of her death.

Heavy boot steps approached.

She tensed, and swallowed hard.

Jones' heavy boot kicked one of the chairs half way around.

Rose looked to the chair, then slowly turned to the big pirate, raising her eyes to his with her brow arched and held high.

She swallowed hard again and sat gingerly in the chair, awaiting the worst. She folded her hands in her lap, pressing her legs together out of pure fear, almost as if she wanted to ball herself up so tiny he could not see her.

His eyes were as stones. With his massive arms folded and his brow tense and low over his eyes, he was death personified and as frightening a sight as she had ever seen. When he finally spoke, his voice tore through the room like his cannons through enemy ships. "Had me a talk with Mister Cannonburg. Had me a long talk with 'im."

Her eyes still locked on his, she nodded ever so subtly.

Jones was looming over her and raised his chin just slightly. "Me powder?"

Rose felt a grip around her throat and a crushing weight on her chest. She could barely breathe. But this was more than fear of the big pirate. She had always paid her debts. Always. There had always been a way. Today, she owed a debt she could not pay, and felt she ashamed. Lowering her eyes, she softly admitted, "He took it. He took everything, my supplies, my ship, most of my... He took it all."

"This Smith bloke?" Jones demanded.

She nodded. "It was just business, he said, and after those last few outings I can't say I blame him and the crew. I've not made many profitable decisions the last few months." She heard him take a step back and raised her eyes to him again. "I've more supplies on Grenada, but he knows about them as well." She shrugged a little. "The local garrison commander there might also have it in for me."

Jones' eyes narrowed.

A little snarl took her lip and she turned her eyes away from him. "His name is Colonel Thomas Digby and... Well, he had me cornered. He, um... He wanted to work out a deal to keep me from the gallows. He wanted to bed me and after... I might have robbed him and had the crew make off with most of the fort's supplies."

Jones raised an eyebrow. "What kinds of supplies?"

Rose shrugged. "Well, anything that he did not have watched. Apparently he was bold enough in his reputation to think that nobody would go into the actual fort on a raid. Didn't want to upset his reputation so we went in and did it real quiet like. Of course word might—"

He barked louder, "What kinds of supplies?"

She cringed and replied as she glanced about, "Just what an army garrison would have mostly: Stores of food, ammunition, rifles, powder, some of their clothing—"

"Where?" he demanded.

Slowly, Rose turned her eyes up to his again. A new opportunity had just presented itself, one given over to her by Jones himself. "Now it seems my life is reduced to a few words, Captain Jones." Her lips tightened slightly and she went on, "What would be worth sparing my life today?"

"Me powder," he snarled back.

Drawing a deep breath, Rose stood and held her arms tensely and carefully at her sides. "Captain Jones, I've nothing left, no ship, no crew and by now Smith is on his way to Grenada to rob the last of my holdings there. I pay my debts and I pay timely. Get me to my stores on Grenada before Smith can wipe them out and all that's there is yours."

He raised his chin. "Everything?"

She nodded. "Everything you'll have. It's in a cave there about a mile from the fort."

"And you don't think anyone's found it there?"

A little smile touched her lips. "It's well camouflaged and in a place nobody goes."

"How much powder?" he asked.

Rose shrugged and leaned her head slightly. "I don't recall, really, eight, perhaps ten kegs."

"And rifles?" he pressed.

"Captain Jones, try to imagine everything a British garrison might need to sustain it, little things like swords and food and clothing and shot..." She raised her brow.

Jones pursed his lips. "So, I'm to sail all the way to Grenada now and assume that you've got more stores there that you mean to trade for your life. That what I'm hearing, Missy?"

"It is more than enough to pay my debt to you," she insisted. "Of course, there is the issue of that squadron of ships that guards it. Not sure how we would slip by them in a ship this big." She cringed as he closed the space between them with a single step and shrieked a gasp as his hand clamped around her hair and forced her head back. With her eyes locked wide on his she trembled and her lips parted in both fear and wanting.

Jones' eyes narrowed again. "And you tell me that this Smith fellow may have it cleaned out before we can get to it. What am I really to find there, O'scarlett?"

When he jerked her head back further she grasped at his arm and realized that breaths entered her reluctantly, and this was not purely out of fear. "Please listen to me," she begged with desperate words. "Right now it is there and the *Scarlet Dragon* has a half day ahead of us. Get me there quickly and we can stop him before he takes everything."

Looking away, Jones released her and backed away a step, then turned his eyes back to her and growled, "Your word you've got stores there."

Rose crooked her jaw and confessed, "To be honest, Captain Jones, I have stores almost everywhere. The one in Santiago is actually the smallest of the lot."

He raised his brow.

"I'm a pirate," she explained, "but I don't rely on ships and cannons to take what I need. I have people who work for me at every dock and supply depot in the Caribbean. That's where most of my money comes from, not the sea."

He half turned his head and demanded, "How am I to believe this?"

Rose shrugged. "Believe what you will." Looking to his belt, she reached to him and pulled a pistol from its holster, then she offered it to him. "Or kill me and throw me overboard and never collect what I owe you, and all of this would have been for naught."

He slowly took the pistol from her.

She folded her arms, raising her chin to look up at him. "You a gambling man, Captain Jones?"

"No," he replied straightly.

Rose smiled. "I'll bet you are."

He turned away and strode over to his wardrobe.

"What do you use all of that powder for?" she asked.

"You saw that yesterday for yourself," he grumbled back.

"Explosive cannonballs," she answered herself. "Ten kegs would load lots of shot for your cannons, I think."

He returned to her with a rolled up map and brushed her belongings off of the table with his arm.

She was quick to spin around and catch her make-up box on its way to the floor.

Jones unrolled the large parchment, the map of Grenada, and he demanded, "Show me where."

Rose set her box down in one of the chairs and folded her arms again. "Or you'll kill me?"

"Or I'll make you wish I had," he growled.

"I want something first," she insisted.

His eyes were devoid of patience as he turned them on her like weapons.

She did not waver or flinch and raised her chin almost in a challenging fashion.

"You are in a position to demand nothing, wench," he growled.

"Then I would ask, Captain Jones, purely out of womanly curiosity, of course." She half turned and looked to the painting.

"The cave!" he demanded.

Turning her eyes back to him, she asked in a casual voice, "Who is she?"

He growled a sigh. "You're testing me patience, woman!"

"Then I'll answer your question of last night, Captain Jones. Yes, my husband was killed by the English Navy. He also served in the English Navy."

Jones drew his head back.

Pain was evident on Rose's face as she turned to the handbag that had been brushed onto the floor and picked it up. Setting it onto the table, she reached inside and down to the bottom, finally producing the brown envelope. She stared at it for a moment, memories and tragedy wrenching at her from within. "This is why they killed him. The documents within would bring down the governor of Port Royal and dozens with him, but getting it to the Admiralty in London is impossible now."

"What is it?" Jones asked in a low voice.

Rose drew a breath and a tear rolled from her eye. "It is evidence of extortion and murder and theft and piracy by the Navy itself on his order. The then Admiral Berkley sought fortune and profit from his new assignment. My husband knew what he was doing and was careful to document what he had observed, careful to obtain manifests and orders from the Admiral. There are many things within here that would see him hanged, many things I'm sure I don't even realize. I've never even opened it. I safeguard it still on the chance that I can finally carry out what he meant to do."

"You had a ship," Jones pointed out. "Why not just take it to England yourself?"

"Because I also had a price on my head and Berkley's tentacles reach so far I don't know who can be trusted, here or in England. The man Jeffery thought he could trust..." She spun around and cried, "I'll show you my every store on every map and give you absolutely everything I have left if you would only get this to London. On your word, Captain Jones!"

He hesitantly took the bound parchment from her, his eyes on hers, and finally he asked, "How much are we speaking of?"

"You would likely never need powder again," she admitted softly. "Do as you will with me, Captain Jones, just please get that to London and..."

"How did you get it?" he asked suspiciously.

"Jeffery entrusted it to me," was her answer. "I've kept it hidden from Governor Berkley for more than four years. That is truly why there is such a price on my head. The infamous Captain O'scarlett was of his own invention. My ship and crew..." She loosed a hard breath and turned her eyes down. "I suppose I tried to live up to the stories at some point. I've kept hope that I would someday make it to London with those documents, but that hope fades year after year."

"You'd have made it by now," he growled. Turning, he slammed the documents onto the table and strode back to the wardrobe. "You're not so helpless, O'scarlett, and we both know it."

As he pulled rolled maps from the top of the wardrobe, one by one, she simply watched, knowing that she was about to be made to show him the locations of the last of her stores. When he returned and laid the charts down, she heard herself breathe, "He has my son."

Jones froze and just stared down at the table for a moment. His eyes slid to her, but his expression did not change.

"He's had little Jeffy for more than three years," she continued in a meek voice. "I haven't seen him in that time and I pray he still remembers me. Jones, if I go to London and if..." She raised a hand to her mouth and turned away from him. "I need the Admiralty to have those documents and take Berkley to the gallows as they should, but I don't know what he would do to my son. If I know they are coming to get the governor then I can get my son out of there, but... But that means I would have to act as the British come to take him, while he is distracted."

"Why don't you just go and get the boy?"

She shook her head. "I can't. He's on the other side of Jamaica and in a state home there where they keep the children of mariners and those lost. Berkley has guards and spies everywhere and the last time I tried..." She sucked a hard breath through her mouth and covered her eyes. "They said they would kill him if they saw me there again. I don't dare return to that side of the island."

With slow steps, Jones approached her, looming over her again as he folded his arms and demanded, "He has a price on your head, he has your boy, and he's had opportunities to get you to the gallows, and yet here you are."

Rose nodded and confirmed, "Yes, here I am. Got the biggest price on my head of any woman in the Caribbean and I'm running for my life every day." She finally turned and looked up at him. "It's all his price to keep my son alive. I have to be all the pirate menace he's made me out to be and more. I have to be such a notorious threat that the Admiralty will continue to give him whatever he wants to combat me. Don't you understand? He's been using me for three years! I didn't capture the *Scarlet Enchantress* he gave her to me!" Her mouth shaking, she slowly shook her head as tears rolled from her eyes. "I'm no pirate, Jones. I'm a woman with simply everything to lose and no way to win. If he captures me then he gets to be a hero, I go to the gallows, but my son gets to grow to manhood. If he doesn't capture me then he gets to continue this sick game of his. He'll get what he wants no matter what."

"Berkley, ye said?" Cannonflash asked, half turning his head.

Rose nodded. "My husband was once very loyal to him, and then he found out what a monster the man really is."

"This Berkley wouldn't have commanded a ship once, would he?"

Rose glanced away, then nodded again. "Yes he did, many years ago before he was promoted. Fighting pirates here in the Caribbean, I think. That's what got him to Admiral so quickly."

"How so?" Jones growled.

"He was a ruthless pirate hunter," she explained. "Jeffery once told me that he sank or captured fifteen vessels in less than four months. He later learned that some of the ships that Berkley sank were not pirates at all, just merchant ships. That's part of what is documented there."

"Bound for England," Cannonflash growled, "or returning." He spun away, back to the table and leaned over the map of Grenada, his big palms planted on the edge of it. "Show me these stores of yours."

She padded lightly over to the table, sensing a new resolve within the big pirate. Dragging her finger along a path marked there, she finally tapped one point behind the mountain and dangerously close to the British fort. "It's in a cave right here. A big boulder and lots of rubbish blocks the entrance from view and I've strewn rocks and bushes along the path to obscure it from unwanted eyes." She glanced at him. "Maybe a booby trap or two about as well."

His eyes shifted to her. "Not a pirate, eh?"

Rose smiled and shrugged slightly. "Well, perhaps just a wee bit." With a lifting of her brow, she asked, "So something tells me that the great Cannonflash Jones is already formulating some plan to get his powder, perhaps a little of his secretive vengeance against the Reds."

He nodded in subtle motions.

Her eyes remained fixed on his as she said, "I would be part of that plan, Captain Jones, if you'll have me."

"So what's in that cave is mine?" he asked.

She raised her chin slightly and assured, "It is, Captain Jones, that and much more, everything I have."

Jones pushed off of the table and turned fully on her, looming over her anew as he announced, "Then we have a new accord, we do." He jabbed a finger into her chest and reminded, "Just make sure you don't cross me, Captain O'scarlett."

With strain in her eyes, Rose corrected, "It's *Miss* O'scarlett, Sir."

He half smiled, an ominous smile. "Miss O'scarlett until ye have your ship under ye again. So, we have an accord or no?"

Another smile took her mouth and she took his hand. "We do, Captain Jones."

* * *

The galley was as loud and festive as always, and then Rose walked in ahead of Cannonflash. On sight of her the table was quiet and the eyes of all the men present were fixed on her.

She glanced about nervously, and finally realized that this was the first time Jones' crew had ever seen her dressed up so. As she walked to the table one of the crew sprang up and pulled her chair out for her and she offered him a shy smile as she sat down.

Jones took his chair and looked to his empty mug, then to the pitcher that was just out of reach. When nobody reacted and just stared at the woman next to him he slammed his fist down on the table so hard that the bang was felt and heard through most of the ship!

Rose flinched, her eyes snapping to him.

The older fellow sitting to Jones' right was quick to grab the pitcher and hand it to his Captain, but his eyes did not stray long from the lovely woman who sat at the table with them.

Cannonflash stood and raised his mug. "Mates, we've a new accord this day and we've some supplies to collect from Grenada. Might be a British warship or two along the way so let's stay sharp and keep our cannons at the ready."

One of the crew looked to him and announced, "A new accord, Captain? Sounds like an occasion to break out some of the Captain's rum, aye?"

All eyes found Cannonflash, some nervously.

Jones looked to Rose, and she merely raised her brow at him. With a rare smile and a nod, he lifted his head and loudly agreed, "Aye! Is time for rum!"

The galley exploded into cheers.

Turning toward the kitchen, the older fellow shouted, "Harold! The Captain would have that rum brought out, if you please!"

A moment later the big black fellow in the apron strode out among the cheers of the crew, and he was carrying a crate with British shipping marks on it. The top was off and as he set it down he smiled broadly and produced the first bottle. Pulling the cork with his teeth, he spat it toward the middle of the table and offered the bottle to Jones, who took a few gulps and handed it back to him. Taking a few gulps himself, Harold handed the bottle on and pulled out the next, this time offering it politely to Rose.

She smiled and took the bottle, drinking from it with the same enthusiasm the crew did.

Hours later, after walking about the deck of the *Black Dragon*, Rose stood on the bow, leaning against one of the huge hundred pounder cannons again as she enjoyed the wind in her hair. The sun was on the starboard side and almost down and casting its orange light across the sparkling sea as if to say its goodnights, and she took in every glimmer of it. In the galley she had done what she had for years and kept pace with the drinking of the men as if she was one of them. Tonight, feeling well beyond tipsy, she still held a mostly empty rum bottle as she stared ahead of the great ship, her eyes dancing on the water as she enjoyed the passing air. She really did not notice how it blew under her skirt, lifting it high above her knees to display the shape of her legs, and this had the attention of many men aboard, especially one big fellow.

Half turning her head, she smiled as she saw Jones out of the corner of her eye. He was watching her, and she was enjoying his gaze upon her. Finally she greeted, "Would the Captain care to join a young lady to watch the sunset?"

He strode slowly to her, taking her side as he stared ahead of the ship with his big arms folded.

They watched the horizon for a moment, and as the last of the sun finally plunged into the ocean, he announced, "I'll be turnin' in early. Busy day tomorrow and I'll be needin' me rest."

Rose nodded and said, "I should, too. The cave's quite a hike from the water. I wonder if my clothes are dry?"

He shrugged.

With a glance at him, she turned toward the cabin and started that way, then stumbled and fell to the deck.

As she pushed herself back up, Jones grabbed her arm and took the bottle from her as he pulled her to her feet. "You'll be needin' no more of that, Lass."

"One more drink?" she asked sweetly in the voice of a little girl.

"Don't think so," he growled. Looking to one of the men near the rail, he called, "Mister Haley!" then he threw the bottle to the crewman and escorted the intoxicated woman to his cabin.

As the cabin door closed behind them, Rose turned and slipped her hands around his neck, pulling herself close to him as she smiled and asked, "Jones, do you find me pretty?"

He grasped her waist and pushed her away as he replied, "I find you drunk."

"And I find you sexy," she drawled.

Jones did not seem at all comfortable with her clinging to him so, but she really did not care at the moment. She had been too afraid for the most part to put her arms around him so, even though she had really wanted to, but in that drunken moment where good judgment and moral fortitude were not to be found, fear of him was absent and she did what her inhibitions would not allow her to do otherwise.

"Okay," he finally growled, "off to your bed."

"No!" she barked. "Off to yours."

He forced a sigh from him and took her arms, pulling them from his neck as he ordered, "To your own bed, wench. We've a long day tomorrow and I'll need ye rested and with your wits about ye."

She clung to him anyway and insisted, "I have all the wits I need, Mister."

"Go!" he ordered, still pushing her off of him.

"You're going to hurt me feelings!" she squeaked. When he reached down and picked her up behind the knees, cradling her in his big arms, she thought *Finally!* But, disappointment was only a few steps away and he flung her the last four feet onto the couch where she almost bounced off onto the floor. Lying there with shock and disappointment in her eyes, she could only stare back at him and feel rejected and hurt.

"Now go to sleep," he growled.

Rose watched as he walked to the table, turned down the lamp and finally removed his jerkin as he sat on the edge of his bed. Pulling his boots off one by one, he dropped them angrily to the floor before rolling to his back and laying his arm across his eyes. She drew a breath and pulled the pillow under her head as she laid down fully, her eyes still on the big pirate captain. She was tired and sore, and now a little heartbroken. She had never been rejected by anyone before. Ever! And this only made her want him more.

More from drunken misdirection than conscious thought, she sat up and reached over her head, grasping the back of her shirt and slowly pulling it off. Standing, she unlaced the skirt, then slid her thumbs between the skirt and undergarment and her skin at the hips, slowly sliding them off of her. She reached up once more, working with the barrette and finally got it unfastened, then dropped it, unaware that it was still clinging to the back of her hair.

She stood there naked for long seconds to collect her nerve, then slowly she crept forward, her eyes on the big pirate who surely had drifted off to sleep by now. The ship rolled gently and she was used to this, but with so much rum in her walking on solid ground would be a challenge and she found herself unable to walk the straight line between the couch and the bed, though she was barely aware of this. Way off course, she ran into one of the chairs at the table and it made a horrible scrape on the wooden deck. She grabbed the chair to quiet it, then pushed off and walked wide around it. The barrette fell from her hair and hit the floor with a loud crack and she spun around and raised a finger to her lips, loudly ordering, "Shh!" Turning toward the bed again, she glanced about to get her bearings, the ship pitched and she stumbled into the chair once again, this time falling over it and rolling to the deck.

Cannonflash did not move during all of this.

Her hands grasped the edge of the table and she pulled herself up to peer over the table at him. The dim light from the oil lamp was just enough to blind her a little and she could not see him, so she stood and looked about, finally turning to continue to the bed. Once there she reached down to nudge him, summoning in a whisper, "Hey," and found him not there, then she realized she was standing on her blouse and backed up a step. She had returned to the couch. Looking over her shoulder, she saw Jones across the room with his arm still over his eyes.

"Son of a bitch," she snarled as she turned to start the journey over again.

Finally there, she stopped and stared at him from about four feet away. She was unable to stand steadily, but did not seem to be aware. Remembering the first time she had approached in the night and awakened him, and the gaping maw of the heavy caliber pistol she did not want to see trained on her again, she reasoned out that a different strategy was called for, so as gently as her drunken state would allow, she summoned, "Psst!"

He did not stir.

Rose repeated, "Psst!" When he still did not move she said just over a whisper, "Jones! It's Rose. You awake?"

Slowly, his hand on the other side of him rose up, clutching his pistol and directing it toward the ceiling, and just as slowly his thumb pulled back the hammer.

Her eyes narrowed and she set her hands on her hips as she stepped toward him, informing with slurred words, "You don't scare—" She did not see his boots there and collapsed to the deck again.

Heaving a heavy breath, Jones lifted his arm from his eyes and turned his head to see her hand grasp the blanket he lay on.

Rose pulled herself up onto her knees and looked him right in the eyes. With a big smile she waved with her other hand and announced, "Ahoy, Captain Jones."

Cannonflash raised a brow and ordered, "Back to bed with ye, wench."

"I'm not a wrench, dammit!" she insisted. "You know, it's supposed to be hot here but the nights can get very chilly at night." She pushed herself up and stood before him, folding her hands behind her and swinging her shoulders slowly back and forth. "You never answered me. Am I pretty?"

He stared up at her face, not allowing himself to look to her body at all, and he raised his brow. "If I say you are pretty, will you go to bed?"

She offered an unsteady salute and assured, "Yes sir!"

"You're pretty, O'scarlett. Now get to bed."

"You're the captain," she agreed, then she just stood there.

"Go on," he prodded. "Back over there and get to sleep."

"I'm sleeping with you tonight," she insisted with slurred words.

"I sleep alone," he snarled back.

Rose clenched her teeth and looked away from him, folding her arms as her jaw began to quiver. Finally, she asked, "Why? Am I not appealing? Am I so ugly?"

He laid his arm over his eyes again and growled, "I'll not have you drunk."

She stood there long seconds more, then laid down beside him anyway, curling up as close to him as she could and laying a leg over his.

Jones lifted his arm again, staring at the ceiling as he grumbled, "What are you doing?"

"I... I won't be dunk... drunk by morning," she informed, "and I'll be right over here when you wake up." Snuggling in closer to him, she closed her eyes and slid her hand across his broad chest.

He growled, making no secret of his irritation but she ignored him and allowed the rum and the slow rocking of the ship to lull her quickly off to sleep.

An unknown time later she awoke with a start as she slammed onto the floor with a thump. Looking around her in the darkness, she rolled over and sat up, trying to get her bearings and figure out where she was. Looking to her left, she met Jones' eyes and her lips parted slowly, nervously. Long seconds passed and she raised her brow and offered, "Sorry. Guess I fell out."

"Guess ye did," he confirmed.

Rose drew her legs to her and wrapped her arms around them, loosing a deep breath as she grumbled, "I hate waking in the night like this." Grasping the edge of the bed, she stood and turned back toward the couch, offering, "Sorry to wake you, Captain."

He seized her wrist and spun her halfway around, then jerked her back toward him.

She stumbled sideways and was sitting on the edge of his bed before she realized. Turning at the waist, she looked down at him with wide eyes, fearing what he could do to her, and wanting him to do it all. She shrieked a breath in as his arm wrapped around her waist and pulled her with brutal force over the top of him, slamming her onto the bed on his other side. As she lay on her back trying once again to regain her bearings, he was upon her.

Jones grabbed her wrists, clamping down on them with the grip of a vise and he slammed her arms to the bed beside her head. Wide eyed, she could only stare up at him, at the hungry, powerful look in his eyes. He released her one wrist and his hand found her throat, forcing her chin up and she whimpered at his strength and how helpless it made her feel. Her chest heaved with each heavy breath she forced into her. Even with one hand free, she was too terrified to move, and too exhilarated to beg him not to hurt her.

Ever so slowly, his mouth descended to hers, and once there his lips took hers with a gentleness that surprised her. Everything in her that was woman was suddenly electrified and on fire and her whole body tensed at the taste of his powerful lips and the scrape of his mustache against her soft skin. He pulled back slightly and she finally realized she was not breathing, and forced it once again. Without warning, he took her mouth again, this time like some ravenous animal and with brutal force and she screamed a little behind the savage kiss he forced upon her. His grip on her throat finally loosened but his hand did not leave her. Instead it caressed its way down her body, over her breasts, her belly, gliding with purpose over her hips and to her thigh, which she drew up as if responding to an unspoken command.

He drew back again and she gasped for each breath, this time reaching to him and sliding her hand up his arm and over his huge shoulder. Her hand continued on its way to his neck where it grasped a handful of his thick hair and she pulled him back down to her, and when his mouth took hers as before, she did not surrender. This time she closed her eyes and took his.

His hands explored every part of her body, sometimes gliding over her soft skin and others grasping her like a predator would grasp its prey. His lips found her neck and she almost screamed at this new level of sensation, her whole body moving involuntarily to his touch and what it did to her. Unexpectedly he clamped his teeth into her neck right below her ear and she cried out as pain and ecstasy collided within her. His touch became less and less gentle and she found herself feeling more and more of his strength, and wanted more yet. He finally rose up over her, his arms and legs straddling her body as he was up on all fours right above her. She stared up at him for long seconds, staring into eyes that were commanding, frightening, alluring. She dared to reach to his chest, slowly sliding her hands down his belly and to his trousers where she began to unfasten them. This is what he appeared to want from her. His orders were body language, primitive grunts and how he touched her. He was taking complete control of her, and for the first time in her life she liked it.

He allowed her to pull the trousers from his hips and squirm from under him just enough to work them off of him. Without warning, he turned and grasped her throat again and she shrieked as he threw her forcibly back down to the bed. Planting a knee between her thighs, he grabbed her leg behind the knee and pulled it up toward him, then he descended toward her.

When he entered her it was all of the exhilaration of the last few moments all at once and she threw her head back and cried out as he took her with all of the savagery she had feared and hoped and imagined, and much more! His hand left her throat and clamped over her mouth, forcing her head back into the pillow. Still, she screamed with unholy pleasure as he imposed his will on her in this way, hard and horribly animalistic. She had been with many men, but none had ever come close to what he was doing to her in this moment.

Only moments later she could stand no more and her climax was a torturous one that racked her entire body. It seemed to last forever and drove him to take her even harder. Finally drained of strength, she went limp beneath him and gasped hard for each breath.

He was far from done with her.

Most of the night he used her body like he would one of his possessions and for the most part he was very rough with her, but finally, what seemed like hours later, he finished with her, and she had climaxed twice more during the process. Even as he lay down beside her, she was still out of breath and covered with sweat, both his and hers. As he lay on his back to catch his own breath, she rolled to her side and pressed her body to his and laid her head on his outstretched arm, her fingertips slowly gliding along his chest in large circles. She was exhausted and hoped he was as well.

He finally turned his head to look at her, and did so with eyes that were no longer so hard and cruel.

She stared back at him, her own eyes at peace and vulnerable for the first time in so long.

They just stared at one another for many long moments as her fingers glided along his chest, and the arm she laid on curled over and she felt his fingers slowly combing through her hair.

"You make love like a bear," she told him.

"Been with many bears?" he asked.

With a little smile, she replied, "Only you, Captain Jones." She gazed into those eyes in the dim light a while longer, and she whispered, "I finally feel safe."

A smile touched his mouth and he asked, "Even after all that? Losing me touch, I am."

Rose giggled, then snuggled into him and closed her eyes. As he pulled her closer to him, her whole body relaxed for the first time in many years and she was claimed by a deep sleep she had completely forgotten existed.

Chapter 6

A TWIST IN CIRCUMSTANCE

Morning came with the *Black Dragon* still slicing through the water at amazing speed for a ship so large, her sails full with the wind and her crew going about their duties with some leisure about them. With nothing but open water on all sides, a good wind and no enemies to contend with, this black leviathan seemed at peace and raced along with the speed of a sloop. Dolphins had no fear of this ship and rode the wake at her bow. Seagulls kept up as best they could, waiting for the ship's cook to dump his leavings over the side as he always did.

The hatches for the cannons were closed and the guns of the *Black Dragon* were pulled inside for a good cleaning. Even the big hundred pounders up front were retreated from their positions to have their insides brushed out and their outsides treated with some kind of black oil for protection against the salty air.

At the rear of the ship, inside the captain's cabin, Rose O'scarlett slumbered peacefully for the first time in many years, immersed in a sleep that was free of both troubles and nightmares. A long day awaited her, her many troubles awaited her, but in the moment she was not bothered by any of them. The sun was up and selectively lighting the inside of the cabin and her eyes opened very slowly. Her first realization was that she was not sleeping on that couch on the other side of the room, but she was in the huge bed, snug beneath the blankets and facing the timbers and planks of the cabin wall. Memories of that night charged into her mind and a little smile touched her. For a few moments she was not aware of anything around her and just swam in the pleasure of what had happened. She had wanted to be taken, actually wanted it for days, and when it finally had happened it was far beyond what she had dreamed about.

Knowing that the only thing to make this morning perfect would be the big pirate captain still lying with her, she did not want to move or look to him to find him already gone and to task with something, so she imagined that he was still there with her, if even for a moment.

Drawing a leg up, she shifted ever so slightly and closed her eyes again, allowing her imagination to find Jones still lying with her.

A strong hand gently brushed the blanket from her shoulder and her eyes opened wide. When the hand grasped the blanket and slowly pulled it from her, a little smile touched her lips and she turned her head to see Cannonflash staring back at her.

"Now the morning is perfect," she whispered to him.

He took her arm and pulled her over to her back and she drew her leg up as she allowed his hands to glide over her body again. His touch was gentle and soothing, and perfect. His fingers glided up her belly, between her breasts and to her throat where he gripped her there right under the curves of her jaw and gently forced her head back. His mouth took hers again, almost tenderly at first as the night before, then with more and more of an animalistic hunger. She relished every second of his brutal kiss. Losing her breath again, she gasped to reclaim it, and slid her hand up his arm and to his thick neck, grasping his hair as she had before and forcing him down to her even harder, and he responded with even more brutality.

When she felt his leg drag over hers and settle between her thighs, she suddenly pushed against him, trying to push him away. It took all her strength but she finally managed to separate his mouth from hers and hold him just a little away from her.

Jones seemed a little confused by this and raised his chin slightly, his eyes narrow and locked on her with a predator's stare.

Rose also narrowed her eyes, showing her teeth as she hissed, "I'll not be taken so easily a second time, Captain Jones."

One of his eyebrows cocked up and he growled, "Won't ye, now?"

"Nope," was her challenging reply, followed by a subtle little wink.

As before, he took her wrist in the vise grip of his hand and brutally pinned her arm down beside her head, then the other. With all her strength, she struggled to free herself of him, her whole body squirming beneath him and helpless whimpers escaped her as she fought with everything she had to free herself. His strength was overwhelming and she was simply no match for him.

When he bent to kiss her, she turned her face away and barked, "No! You can't have me again."

His lips found her neck in that certain spot right below her ear and her entire body responded as before, but she fought back still and her whimpers and protests only drove his lust.

"I said no," she whimpered. "You can't have me!"

Jones mouth glided up to her ear and he whispered, "I *do* have you, woman."

She smiled as he kissed that place again and she struggled harder, informing, "I'm not yours yet, Captain." She shrieked as he clamped his jaws down on her behind her ear. It both hurt and excited her and she knew he could bite her much harder! "Let me go!" she whined. "I'll not be taken again!" Her mouth gaped and she sucked a hard breath in as he entered her, and she cried, "Oh, God!" as the sensation lanced through every part of her. Still, she fought him with everything she could.

Once again he made love to her with all of the brutality she had hoped for and more, and yet there was a gentle sensitivity to his touch that invaded from time to time. Her struggles to free herself predictably yielded to her body moving in sync with his. She wanted him to feel the same ecstasy that she did. She wanted to know that she was enough woman to satisfy the animal that dwelled within him. She wanted him satisfied first this time, but he appeared to want to finish her first as before and was working very hard and very thoroughly to that end. Here, too, she resisted him and put off the inevitable as gallantly as she could, but he knew right where to touch her, just how to move, and each time she thought she could stave off the climax of the lust she felt for him, he found a new way to defeat her.

And again he did not finish with her until he was ready to, and it took a while.

Exhausted again, she lay beside him as before, but this time curled up and with her arms drawn to her. Her head lay limply on his thick arm, which was curled around her, his fingers gently caressing her shoulder. She was completely spent and could not even open her eyes. Just getting her breath back had taken time.

Finally, after they had just lain there for some time enjoying the moment, she asked, "Captain?"

"Aye?" he responded.

"Is this just something that comes to you naturally or is it the result of conquering woman after woman at each port?"

He huffed a laugh. "No, just in me blood, I suppose."

Rose managed a little smile and purred, "Oh. Just as I was hoping."

"We'll be at Grenada by morning," he suddenly announced.

Her eyes opened slightly.

"Might have to fight our way through," he went on, "might not. Last time I visited there they gave the *Dragon* a wide berth."

She nodded. "So, it looks like you'll have at least one more night to have at me, aye?" She turned her eyes hopefully up to his.

Jones offered her but a glance and raised his brow. "You offering?"

"Perhaps," she teased, "but I think you'd rather force your way with me. I think you'd like to have me as a pirate would have a woman."

"I think you'd like that more than I would," he countered.

She snuggled against him, getting as close as she could and closed her eyes, a little smile on her mouth as she said, "Maybe."

A knock on the door provoked a growl from the big pirate captain and he barked, "What is it!"

Apparently, the man on the other side knew not to open the door and reported from the other side, "We've sails on our flank and angling into us."

Jones heaved a growling sigh and he ordered, "Get the crew to stations and make us ready. We'll follow explosive shot with solid. Get Mister Cannonburg on that looking glass and find out who they are."

"Aye, Captain," came the response from the other side.

Rose snarled, "If they're British then I want to put the first shot into them!"

Jones patted her shoulder and commended, "That's me girl."

The formerly peaceful deck of the *Black Dragon* was now awash with swarming activity as cannons were made ready, ammunition was taken to them and muskets were loaded. Men were preparing for action and many of them were looking over the starboard rail at the ship that drew closer to them. It was a big ship, a warship, and it was very fast. Even a mile away, one could see that it was closing on them with purpose.

Jones and Rose emerged on the deck fully dressed and armed for action. Rose was back in her red tights and white shirt but wore her red vest over it this time. Her hair flowed freely behind her but the sides were once again restrained with that barrette.

She followed the Captain to the starboard rail, her eyes on the sails that were angled into them and drawing closer.

His eyes narrowing, Cannonflash turned to the wheelhouse and shouted, "Give me a course into them."

As the huge ship turned to intercept the unknown ship, Cannonburg bounded down the ladder and hurried to his captain, a telescope in his hands as he summoned, "Captain!" Reaching them, he raised his chin and reported, "They have their colors up. It's the Commodore."

Jones raised his chin as he stared at his first mate, then he turned his attention to the approaching ship and ordered, "Stand down. Let's prepare to receive them."

* * *

With her sails furled and the anchors of the *Black Dragon* in the water, the other ship slowly came alongside and furled her own black and gray striped canvas. Flying the same flag as the *Dragon*, this other ship was painted an ominous dark gray and would be next to impossible to see when darkness descended. This was a heavy frigate that appeared to be Spanish in design and was bristling with firepower, similar to the *Black Dragon*. A reinforced forward deck bore two of the same hundred pounder cannons that the Dragon was armed with, but it appeared that provisions had been made for two more to be mounted right outside of these.

Rose did not have to look sharp toward the bow of the ominous ship, raising her head slightly as her eye found the ship's name painted there in bold red colors: *Black Revenge.*

A long plank was extended across from the *Black Dragon* and secured to the deck of the other ship and Rose watched as an older man with a white beard and long sideburns walked from one ship to the other as if he was walking on solid land. He wore a black jerkin that was almost identical to the one Jones wore, faded black trousers and buckled black leather boots. A little better groomed, he also shared Jones' green eyes and titanic build, though he was just a little leaner in the arms and chest, and perhaps a couple of inches shorter. A broad cutlass hung on his left side from his thick leather belt along with a pistol and a dagger and another pistol hung from his right.

He strode with purpose onto the deck of the *Black Dragon*, his eyes on Cannonflash as he approached.

Jones raised his chin as the older fellow stopped right in front of him, and he offered his hand, greeting, "Commodore."

The older fellow shook Jones' hand and replied, "Captain." Looking behind Jones, the Commodore nodded and said, "Good to see you again, Mister Cannonburg."

Johnny stepped forward and took his hand, greeting, "Commodore."

After greeting a few other of Jones' crew, the Commodore's eyes fell onto Rose and he hooked his thumbs in his belt as he asked, "And what have we here?"

Jones answered, "This is Captain Rose O'scarlett of the *Scarlet Dragon*. We've worked out some trade and she's en route to Grenada with me."

The Commodore looked her up and down, then took her hand in his far more gently than he had the men present. "My compliments, Captain."

She nodded politely to him and replied, "Thank you, Sir. It is a pleasure to meet you."

Looking back to Jones, the Commodore motioned toward the back of the ship with his head and ordered, "Open a bottle of rum, Captain. You and I need to speak."

"Would you like that cargo transferred to your ship?" Jones asked.

Raising his bushy white eyebrows, the Commodore considered, then he nodded and replied, "May as well, I suppose. Sea is calm today and I don't see a reason to wait."

Jones looked to Cannonburg, who nodded to him and assured, "I'll see to it."

When Rose met Cannonflash's eyes, she felt reluctant to leave him, but retained her composure and would not reach to him like a clingy little girl would—or a woman who had just had her entire world shaken by a night of animalistic passion.

"The galley should be ready for you, Captain O'scarlett," Jones informed in his usual harsh tone.

"Aye, Captain Jones," she accepted with a nod. "Thank you."

She just stood there and watched as the two men walked across the deck, to the rear of the ship and disappeared into the captain's cabin. Looking behind her, she asked, "Mister Cannonburg, what was that about?"

He approached her, his eyes also on the closed door as he replied, "Nothin' to concern you, Captain. Harold has made a fine morning meal and I'd suggest you get there before this crew finishes it off every crumb."

Rose strode into the galley and found it empty again. She took her usual seat and leaned her elbows on the table as she stared ahead at nothing, and she barely noticed Harold stride in with a plate full of food for her.

He set the plate down and sat in the captain's chair, his eyes on her as he asked, "Rough night, Lass?"

Her eyes darted to him and she smiled. "In a manner of speaking, yes."

Harold laughed a hearty laugh and patted her shoulder. "You'd better eat and get your strength back then. Big day coming tomorrow."

She picked up her fork and raised her brow. "Hopefully a big night tonight."

Laughing again, Harold rose from his chair and turned toward the galley door. "I'll fetch ye something to drink, Lass."

By the time Rose emerged from the galley more than an hour later the cargo had been transferred from one ship to the other and the meeting between Cannonflash and the Commodore was over. She emerged onto the deck just in time to see the two men striding from the captain's cabin. Eager to be at Jones' side again, she knew to be patient and not give away any hint that the two had been intimate, lest the risk upsetting Jones' confidence among the crew.

The Commodore's eyes found her first and met her without expression. Walking to Jones' right, he carried some kind of leather satchel casually in his left hand and at his side. Cannonflash himself still seemed to be all business and kept his attention on the older man as he continued to speak.

As she was close enough to hear, she heard the Commodore say to Jones, "You just don't worry over this matter, and remember what I told ye. You know what has to be done, boy."

With a nod, Cannonflash almost reluctantly agreed, "Aye." He finally noticed Rose coming up on them and raised his chin, though his expression remained as stone.

They all stopped and the Commodore raised his chin to her. "Cannonflash here makes tell that you've powder ye trade for."

"Aye, Sir," she confirmed. "I've plenty of stores about with plenty supplies."

"Do ye now? Mind if a gentleman asks how ye come about it?"

She smiled ever so sweetly. "A gentleman may ask, of course, but he must know that some of a lady's secrets must remain with her."

The Commodore half smiled and said, "Aye, perhaps so, Lass. Perhaps so. We should talk business. Might be some profit in there for ye. I've got me three more ships to outfit properly and maybe a lady is what we need to keep supplied."

126

"I would love to talk business with you, Sir. Captain Jones and I have an arrangement worked out already, and perhaps we could talk over a bottle of rum, at your convenience."

He nodded and confirmed, "Aye, and it'll be soon." He looked to Jones and finished with, "See you at Tortuga in three days, then we'll discuss matters further, aye?"

"Aye," Cannonflash agreed.

The two of them escorted the Commodore back to his ship, the plank was withdrawn and the mooring lines were taken loose. The *Black Revenge* took the wind quickly and headed out on her way and the *Black Dragon* resumed her course toward Grenada.

Hours later Rose found Cannonflash standing at the stern of the ship with his hands folded behind him. She was slow to approach him as he looked lost in deep thought. Even after the night they had shared he still was not open, and remained very difficult to read.

The wind blew her hair freely but this time she took little notice. Taking his side just out of arm's reach, she also looked to the sea behind them, but soon her eyes strayed to the big pirate captain and stayed there. He was quiet. He knew she was there, but would not acknowledge her.

Moments passed and she enjoyed the sun on the sea, the wind that blew the ship on its way, and the closeness she felt with this man who she still knew little about.

"Am I disturbing you?" she asked at last.

Stone faced as always, he shook his head.

"I suppose I shouldn't ask about what you and the Commodore spoke of in there," she guessed.

"It wouldn't be wise," he replied.

Nodding, she looked back to the sea, and a moment later she confessed, "I want badly to be held by your big arms again. I know we can't at the moment, I just…" She sighed. "I suppose the crew should not know what happened last night."

"I'm sure they know by now," he informed. "You're not exactly a quiet one."

Rose turned her eyes down and could feel herself blush. "Aye. Sorry about that."

"Don't be," he ordered.

Silence found them again as they stared out at the sea. The wind in the rigging and the occasional creak of the ship's timbers spoke for them.

Her eyes cut to him again and she asked, "Will you be having me again tonight, Captain?"

"I suppose," he sighed.

She smiled slightly and reached up to unconsciously twist her hair. "I may not let you."

His eyes finally slid to her. "Won't you, now?"

"Maybe," she teased. "I might fight you off this time."

Just the hint of a smile touched his lips. "We'll be seeing about that, woman."

"After dinner I'll be retiring early," she informed straightly. "Mister Cannonburg tells me that we should have Grenada in sight by first light and I'll need to be rested."

"Hmm," was his response as he looked to the sea again. "Might be turning in early, meself."

A flirty smile took Rose's mouth and she asked, "Would a lady be out of line to snuggle up to the ship's captain in broad daylight?"

"Yes she would," he answered directly.

She rolled her eyes and grumbled, "Fine."

Chapter 7

PIRATES IMPERILED

Grenada was an imposing place that seemed to mean sure death to anyone foolish enough to set foot on it, but the other side of the island was actually inhabited and had quite a flourishing population. There were farms on the other side and plantations of trees, sugar and spices. One would never guess that from the desolate look of this side, near the fort. Little grew here for some reason, only thorny bushes and scrub brush. Much of this side was simply bare rock and seemed very easy to defend from invaders as it was flat near the water with a wall of cliffs and the mountain that dominated it inland.

The *Black Dragon* had no trouble with the British patrols. In fact, they seemed to steer away from her as she sailed toward the island. These were bigger British ships that were more than able to hold their own against French or Spanish marauders in the area or almost any pirate, but the behemoth that approached was known to have devastating firepower and seemed invulnerable to the weapons wielded against her, so they kept a watchful distance and seemed determined not to fight unless forced to.

Jones only took a trusted few ashore. These included some young men with strong backs, Harold the cook, and the older

 129

fellow who often dined to his right, a fellow who seemed to have a gift for reading maps. With Rose, the landing party numbered nine strong. Taking a path through the simple village that made its living off of those stationed at the fort, they acquired a mule drawn cart to carry the supplies they needed back to the boat, as Rose expected to clean out this cave and leave nothing to her former crew.

The path took them up the side of the mountain and after a couple of hours Rose, who led the way, finally stopped and sat down on a boulder, leaning over to rest her forearms on her thighs. Her head hung low and she seemed uncomfortable, struggling to catch her breath. Back in her trousers and shirt, as her dress would be unwieldy for such a hike, the island heat, sore muscles and aching joints were taking their toll on her this day as seemingly never before.

Cannonflash turned to her and folded his big arms.

She took the water bladder she had hanging by a leather strap over her shoulder and raised it to her mouth, taking a long drink from it, then she shoved the stopper back into place and looked up at the pirate captain, her brow low over her eyes.

"Tuckered out already?" Jones asked.

Her eyes narrowed and she spat, "After what you did to me last night I'm surprised I made it this far!"

The rest of the team's attention was suddenly fixed on her, and the Captain.

Jones smiled. "Didn't think I was that hard on ye. Thought the wailing as pure pleasure."

She rolled her eyes, then took another drink. "I can assure you it was, Captain, but once in a while a lady needs a gentle touch. The way you manhandled me I didn't know if you were going to break me in half or save some of me for later."

Eyes widened and the crew exchanged a variety of looks.

"Saved enough of you, I think," he assured. "Up on your feet, woman. You can rest back at the ship."

She just stared up at him as he offered her his hand, and finally she took it and he pulled her to her feet. As she took his side again to continue up the mountain, she grumbled, "I don't expect you'll be allowing me to rest on the ship, either."

He nudged her with his elbow. "Would ye rather?"

Venting a little sigh, she looked up at him and straightly answered, "No."

The trek continued for about another hour and Rose and Cannonflash spoke little during that time. Mumbles behind them were not meant for their ears, but some reached them anyway and it was clear that new stories about the infamous and dreaded Cannonflash Jones would quickly spread through the Caribbean, much to the joy of the women who awaited him at every port.

A boulder that was the height of a man and twice as wide lay in the trail fifty yards ahead of them. Those who had walked the trail before, including animals, had formed a new trail around it. Scrub brush grew tall on the far side of it and dead branches, brush and pieces of old crates had been piled between it and the side of the mountain.

Her eyes locked on the boulder, Rose stopped suddenly and slammed her arm across Jones' chest. Everyone else stopped behind them.

Cannonflash looked down at her.

"Something's wrong," she said in a low voice.

"What do you see?" he asked, also in a low voice.

"The way the branches are piled in there. It isn't right."

"You think Smith was already here?"

She shook her head. "I don't know, but if he was I don't see him going to the trouble of putting the branches back in."

Jones raised his chin, his eyes on the branches piled between the boulder and mountain. "What doesn't look right about them?"

"I always stack them in there vertically so that it looks like the plants just died there. Those were laid in place, and I don't remember putting broken crates in with them." She looked up at him. "We're being watched, Captain Jones. Someone's laid a trap for us."

"For you," he corrected. "I'm guessin' me powder's not in there."

She shrugged.

"Harold," Jones summoned.

The big black fellow took his side and answered, "Aye, Captain?"

Staring at the boulder before him, Jones informed, "We've an ambush ahead, mate."

Harold raised his chin, his eyes also locked on the boulder. "How many, you think?"

"No way to tell," was Jones' reply.

"We need to go," Rose urged through clenched teeth.

Cannonflash shook his head and corrected, "We'll go nowhere. Reds are probably all over." He drew his pistol and grabbed her by the hair, directing the muzzle to the side of her head as he shouted, "I'll not tell you again, wench!"

A gasp shrieked into her as he jerked her head back.

Jones looked over his shoulder and ordered in a loud voice, "Spread out and find that mine. It's covered out here somewhere. Just remember the red on the map."

His men went to task, half of them slowly grasping their pistols.

"What are you doing?" she whimpered.

"Quiet!" he ordered, yanking on her hair again. "Mister Mueller, see that what she said is true and not just so much fire and smoke."

A thin man with no shirt and a brown jerkin strode by, toward the boulder as he shouted back, "Aye, Captain."

"That treasure's close," another of the men said loudly. "Two of you give me a hand with this wagon."

Rose heard three of Jones' men jump into the back of the wagon and she heard the hammer pull back on at least one musket. She also heard a few pebbles and some sand slide down the side of the mountain only ten or so feet above them. Now what the Captain was doing was clear and her eyes shifted to him, and she bared her teeth, shouting, "I'll tell you no more, pirate!"

Jones yelled back, "I said quiet, wench!" He threw her to the ground and drew his other pistol. "We're already on top of it and ye know we are!"

She rose up on her knees and turned at the waist to glare at him, her hands reaching subtly to her belt. "You'll never find it. I'll die before I give up me mates!"

He aimed his pistol at her and growled, "Then you'll have your secret safe with you in Hell just as soon as I..." He looked to Mueller and shouted, "Fire!"

Unnoticed to all eyes was the thin mariner working with his flints, igniting a small fire in some brush and grass at the base of the boulder, and as he heard the disguised order from his captain, he lit the fuse on a hand-held bomb and tossed it over the stacked brush, then he wheeled around the other side of the boulder.

Jones dropped to one knee and turned his attention and his guns down the mountain, into the thick brush there.

The bomb detonated, blowing the brush away from the entrance in a thunderous explosion.

Rose fell to her back, drawing her pistols as she did and directing them to a ledge ten feet above them, and when she had the two British soldiers in her sights she fired both guns at once, hitting one of them.

The other ducked down and backed away.

Mueller lit another bomb and threw it up to the ledge, and seconds later the explosion threw off the body of the second British soldier.

Cannonflash directed his fire down the hill and into the thick brush growing there and two more fell.

As the British forces finally charged, Jones' men in the wagon and those who had dispersed blunted their assault with a volley from pistols and muskets, and those who did not fall took cover behind whatever they could. Another bomb hissed as it flew down the hill, exploding over the heads of a group of them that had closed to only twenty feet or so.

Mueller called to Jones, "Two left!"

As the British began to fire back, Jones finished reloading his second pistol, then he nodded to Mueller and pointed to a clump of brush down the hill.

The next bomb landed right in the middle of it and exploded and three soldiers rolled limply down the hill.

Rose had reloaded and gotten to her knees, scanning the area all around for a target, then she ducked slightly as a bullet hit nearby. She quickly realized they were surrounded and looked to Jones with desperate eyes as she cried, "We need to get everyone into the mine!"

"We'll be cornered!" he growled back. Taking quick aim, he fired and downed another.

"Trust me," she insisted. Without waiting, she stood and fired her pistols one after the other as she hurried to the now exposed entrance.

Jones followed.

One by one the crewmen made it into the cave, finding it emptied of supplies with only a few empty crates and packing straw remaining. It was only about ten feet wide, thirty feet deep and was pitch dark inside. Mueller entered with an improvised torch, one that would not last long.

Holstering her pistols, Rose groped to a flat stone leaning against the wall near the entrance and strained to pull it down. Behind it were three oil lamps and she wasted no time getting the first one to Mueller. As he lit the first, she handed him the next, then the last.

"Now what?" Jones growled.

Holding the last lamp, she looked up at him and motioned toward the back, then she looked to Mueller and ordered, "Give me that last grenade." When he did, she led the way to the back of the cave.

The very rear of the cave, leaning against the back wall were many rotted out timbers that looked to have once been used in a mine somewhere. They were big and appeared heavy, but Rose took the first and pulled hard against it, toppling it over.

"Come on!" she barked.

Men scrambled forward and toppled the other dozen, revealing a passage that led deeper into the mountain.

Looking to Jones again, she half smiled and informed, "The Reds don't know about this part. Okay, everyone. Go on and go quickly!"

Jones stayed near the entrance, pistols in hand, and hustled his men to safety, then he looked to Rose and motioned her through.

"Go," she insisted. "I'll be right behind you. And get everyone as deep in there as you can!"

As she put the fuse of the bomb to the lamp, Jones raised his chin, then ducked down through the tunnel opening and hurried along.

With the fuse lit, Rose tossed it toward the entrance, then turned and fled.

The British outside were sure they had the pirates cornered and a couple of them fired awkwardly into the cave, then one threw a grenade in, one that landed a few feet from Rose's.

They seemed to explode together and smoke erupted from both sides of the boulder outside followed by plumes of dust that were forced out as the entrance to the cave collapsed. The hillside above the entrance and boulder also collapsed and a landslide ensued, one that the British desperately retreated from.

Deep in the mountain, Rose stopped in a larger room and spun around as the rumble of the collapsing tunnel behind them shook the very ground they stood on. Raising her chin, she half smiled again before looking up at Cannonflash.

He raised a brow and commended, "Ye planned this out rather well, O'scarlett. Do ye have shovels to dig out or do we dig with our hands?"

"We don't dig out," she corrected, striding past him. "We walk."

They followed her into another tunnel, one that was shored up with heavy timbers. The going was slow and single file for the most part as this tunnel, clearly dug out my men, was only about six feet wide and about that tall. Cannonflash and Harold were hunched over, avoiding the ceiling and the beams that were only high enough to allow a normal sized man to pass walking upright. Nobody but Rose knew how long they would be in the cramped, humid tunnel and the men started to become uneasy in the heavy, close air.

At long last it opened into a huge, natural cavern, one that seemed to go on forever. Years, perhaps decades ago miners had flattened out the floor and shored up weak sections with timbers. Tunnels had been bored deep into the walls over many years. What they had been searching for had been forgotten long ago and the mine itself had been abandoned and forgotten. It was perhaps the Spanish explorers looking for gold, nobody was sure, but a few pirates were thankful for their labors.

When Cannonflash caught up to Rose and took her side, she was staring at the floor before her and unconsciously shaking her head.

"You're puzzling over something," he observed.

"How did they know we would be there?" she asked absently. "Smith obviously got there first."

Harold speculated, "He turned us in, he did."

"Aye," Cannonflash agreed. "They just didn't expect more than Captain O'scarlett."

Rose grumbled, "Mutinous bastard. Next time I see him I'm gutting him like a fish!"

Another of Jones' men said from behind, "You'd better get to him first, then."

She sighed and shook her head again. "He must have come straight here. He knew I'd come after this store next. Somehow he knew."

"Probably after that bounty on ye," Jones guessed.

Harold stopped. "Does he know about these tunnels and these caves?"

Everyone else stopped as well.

Rose stared ahead of her into the darkness with wide eyes and she breathed, "Oh, no."

"They were ready for us to do this," Cannonflash growled. "Probably got a whole garrison waiting to meet us when we leave here."

Her eyes darting about, Rose's mind scrambled, and finally she looked to her right and took off that way, bidding, "Come on!"

They followed, though reluctantly.

"Where to now?" Jones grumbled.

"Remember when I said he didn't have my absolute trust?" was her reply. As he caught up to her, she turned her eyes up to his and continued, "I didn't tell him everything and he never took the time to explore these caverns."

Harold took her other side and prodded, "Go on."

"I found a map of this place a couple of years ago when we raided the fort. It was left behind by the Spanish, I think. The fort the Reds currently occupy was built by the Spanish. They abandoned it when they didn't find any gold and the fort remained intact and abandoned for years until the Brits found it. They added on and fortified it and they've been there ever since."

"All very interesting," Jones snarled. "How does that serve us now?"

She smiled at him and replied, "Because I know right where we're going."

"And that would be?" he asked.

"The Fort," was her quick answer.

Jones stopped, and so did all of his men.

Rose turned toward them and set her free hand on her hip. "How do you think I really got all of that stuff back there? I sent Smith and most of the crew out the front gate in the middle of the night, told them about the cave and told them to get back to the ship and wait for me. The other end opens into a basement that is right under the commander's office. There are wooden shelves built in front of the entrance to this tunnel, I guess to conceal it."

Raising his brow, Harold said, "And this basement room is..."

Rose smiled. "Where they store their munitions."

The men all glanced at each other.

"How well guarded?" Jones questioned.

She shrugged. "Depends on how many they have out here chasing us."

Cannonflash and Harold exchanged looks, and Harold grinned.

* * *

The wooden bookshelf pushed with unusual ease, and just enough to allow Harold to peer into the storage room. Slowly, he extended his arm into the room, gripping one of the lamps. Scanning the room, he saw no one there and beckoned those behind him to proceed out of the tunnel.

One by one they emerged into the large storage room which appeared to have been cut out of the very rock that the fort sat on. Heavy timbers held up the floor above which was a good four feet over even Cannonflash's head. All around were shelves, stacks of crates, more shelves, some of which were laden with jars of preserved food. There were barrels of fresh water and, as promised, crates of muskets, bayonets, pistols and shot. There were also many kegs of powder along one wall and a stack of cannon barrels.

Rose found a few more lamps near the entrance and lit them all, handing some off to some of the men and then distributing the rest around the basement, hanging many on hooks that waited on the pillars. Other lamps were already in place and she lit these as well. Something caught her eye and she strode over to a wooden crate that was left open. Looking inside, she removed a white shirt and held it against her chest. On a shelf to the left were more of them, all neatly folded, along with red trousers. To the left of this were many red coats, all neatly hung by a rod between that shelf and another.

Hearing the floor creak, everyone turned their eyes up. The footfalls and creaking sounded like two sets of boots walking from one end to the other, toward the stairs that would lead them down to the basement.

Rose crept over to Cannonflash and whispered, "Take some of the men back into the tunnel."

"We all should go," he whispered back.

"No time," she argued. "Besides, they'll know we were here."

A few moments later the door at the top of the wooden stairs opened and light swept in. Two men entered, one after another, and they were engaged in a casual conversation about unimportant personal issues. Dressed in the uniforms of the British army, less their coats, their white shirts had the sleeves rolled up. They wore no hats and their hair was well groomed. Neither had a beard or mustache.

"I don't know," the older of the two complained. "Some women just won't listen to reason."

"You're in the army for a reason, mate," the other responded. "She married a soldier and knew she married…"

Halfway down they stopped as they saw the activity in the storage basement.

"Hello?" the older of them greeted nervously.

Dressed in one of the British uniforms, less the coat, Mueller turned toward him, gripping a fist full of papers in one hand and a feather pen in the other. His hair was slicked back and he had an old pair of spectacles over his eyes. Glancing from one to the other, he calmly asked, "Can I help you gentlemen?" His British accent was flawless.

Two other of Jones' men also turned from what they were doing, one stacking a crate on top of another and the other appeared to be counting the uniforms on the shelves. Rose kept her back to them. She was the only one wearing the red coat of the British uniform and this thankfully concealed her long hair. Her hands glanced along the coats as if she was counting them.

The older soldier's eyes narrowed and he asked, "What would you men be doing down here?"

Mueller sneered and replied, "Got on someone's bad side, I suppose. Got to have an inventory by the end of the day, that and we have to pull for a ship that's coming in to be resupplied."

"Which ship," the other soldier asked suspiciously.

Looking down at the papers, Mueller replied, "The Prince Edward, looks like."

"Really," the first solder drawled. "I thought the Prince Edward was still in England."

Mueller shrugged and turned back to the crate of pistols. "Not for me to say. They tell me to resupply a ship, I don't ask why, I just get their goods. So what is it you gentlemen need?"

They glanced at each other, and the older one finally replied, "Came for some blankets. Got us some men coming to the rotation sometime today."

Nodding, Mueller absently said, "Probably on the Prince Edward. You don't happen to have a requisition, do you?"

"Um," the older soldier stammered, "I don't."

"Of course not," Mueller grumbled. "Come on and take what ye need and give me a count."

They descended the rest of the way in and strode to the shelves right beside Rose, and she tensed up as they neared, turning away slightly as she ran her finger along the labels on the small crates at the bottom.

Each soldier took five and as they turned the younger of them looked to Rose and asked, "Haven't I seen you before?"

She shook her head and continued on with what she wanted him to think she was doing.

"I'm sure I have," he insisted with narrow eyes.

Mueller looked to him and barked, "Quit your gabbing or you'll be messing up the counts! I'm behind schedule as it is!" He lifted the top sheet and asked, "Ten?"

"Aye," the older soldier confirmed.

"Very good," Mueller said with a nod. "Oh, and perhaps you can do me a favor."

The older soldier raised his chin, eying the so-called clerk with suspicion.

Mueller handed him the top manifest. "Can you have a detail take these to the pier? My men and I are overtaxed and we'll never get out of the Colonel's sights if this isn't done by tonight."

"Hmm..." the soldier growled.

Mueller sighed and looked across the room. "Perhaps you'd find a bottle of brandy down here tonight if it all gets done.

The soldier raised his chin, smiling ever so slightly as he took the manifest and confirmed, "I think the Prince Edward will find her supplies in good order."

"You have my thanks," Mueller grumbled, looking to the papers again.

The two men headed back up stairs, the older adding, "And a bottle of your brandy. Cheerio!"

As the door closed, Mueller looked up that way and smiled, saying, "Aye, you just keep thinking that, limey."

Rose finally turned around, looking up at the door first, then she nodded to Mueller, complimenting, "You are amazing."

He raised his brow and informed, "I once served in His Majesty's navy. I might know me way around their ways still."

"How did you come up with a manifest of supplies for a navy ship?" she asked.

Mueller shrugged and admitted, "Found it over there."

Rose shook her head and offered him a big smile, then she turned to the book case as one of the men pulled it from the tunnel opening.

Cannonflash emerged and glanced around, then nodded to Mueller, who nodded back to him. His eyes finding Rose again, he informed, "We're not in the clear yet, O'scarlett."

Her brow arched and she confirmed, "Aye, Captain." Glancing about, her mind scrambled anew as she pondered a way to get them all out unnoticed.

"Well," one of the crewmen said grimly, "looks like we're cornered."

"We need a diversion," another advised.

Harold pointed out, "They have many men out there chasing us, so perhaps that's diversion enough."

"And," Cannonflash added, "the Dragon's at anchor within sight of the fort."

Rose slowly raised her head and looked to the big pirate captain. "And they haven't attacked."

Mueller shook his head. "They know not to fire on that ship."

"Unless they have her captain," she countered. Looking to Cannonflash with wide eyes, she assured, "There's no way they could have known we were coming here, and if they did there is no way they could have gotten word to the fort in time."

"Coincidence," Jones grumbled. "They smell opportunity."

"So do I," Harold informed with a smile. When he had their attention, he glanced at each of them and continued, "Slave trade comes right through here."

Jones considered, then nodded. "Aye, it does." He looked to Mueller and ordered, "Find what insignia you can down here, high ranking as possible, and everyone get a uniform." He looked to Rose again and added, "Except you. Get out of that one and into as little as your modesty will allow."

She raised her brow.

* * *

Not where she expected to be.

Rose found herself stripped to her trousers and undershirt, no boots and her hands shackled behind her. Walking right behind her, Harold only wore his trousers and his hands were also shackled behind him. Flanking them were six British soldiers, all armed with muskets and sabers and four of them recently shaven. One officer was among them, an average fellow with slicked back, thinning hair. He bore the insignia of an army captain and led the way, his hand on his newly acquired saber as he strode confidently out of the main fort complex and into the open grounds that were contained by a high stone wall.

They all glanced about. As hoped, the British soldiers here did not number strongly and most of them appeared to be in the field searching for the invading pirates. Still, the cannons on top of the wall were manned and no doubt loaded and ready. A few men paced on top of the wall, but inside of it there was little activity.

The main structure they marched out of was built of stone and was clearly constructed by the Spanish. Arched doorways and windows of the two level structure were of fine stonework, something the British presence in the area never thought necessary. Balconies were closed with ornate railings about waist high. Gun positions and a couple of cannons were on the roof and a few guards milled about the second level balcony with their muskets over their shoulders. Well groomed grass grew in most of the open area between the main building and the wall surrounding it. The fort backed up into the mountain and a few smaller structures were built into the side of it. On one end of the fort was the original mission, a church that was also constructed of local stone but was more crudely made and clearly much older.

The main gate was flanked by two towers that were built into the twenty foot high wall itself and stood ten feet high over it. Here is where the gates were hinged, and for some reason they stood wide open. Through them one could see the road that led directly to the pier a quarter mile away, and the mass of soldiers and sailors on the pier would provide yet another obstacle once they were clear of the fort.

Rose fidgeted as her undershirt began to drift off her shoulder as she walked. Cannonflash walked at her side in a British uniform that fit him very tightly in the chest, back and shoulders, and she glanced at him often.

In a low voice she grumbled, "I can't say I'm comfortable with this, Jones."

"You aren't supposed to be," he murmured back. Giving her a hard look, he ordered, "Just look as a prisoner like you should and we'll get to the ship without problems."

The heavy iron shackles that were clamped around her wrists were becoming painful to wear and she complained, "Couldn't you have used rope or something? These hurt."

"Had to look like the real thing," he informed. "Now stop your gabbing."

She glared up at him and hissed, "Don't get any ideas about doing this to me tonight."

He smiled slightly and countered, "Too late."

"Stop the detail," a man with a thick English accent ordered from behind and to the right.

Rose knew that voice and her breath froze within her, her eyes locking wide ahead of her.

Mueller looked over his shoulder and shouted, "Detail, halt!" When the procession stopped he turned fully and approached the heavy set man in the well decorated red uniform.

Black hair beneath the officer's hat was unattended and he had a face that was not easy to look at long. His uniform was in good order but was faded and past its prime and fit him a little too tight. Dark eyes glanced about from the approaching Mueller to the prisoners and back and were laced with suspicion.

Stopping a few feet away, Mueller was respectfully at attention as he asked, "What may we do for you, Sir."

The officer met him with a hard look up and down, then looked to the prisoners again and demanded, "Were are we going with these two?"

Mueller glanced over his shoulder and replied, "Escaped slave and one that was aiding him. Bound for Port Royal for trial, I think, and then probably back to Havana for him."

"I see," the officer said softly. "I trust you have papers on them?"

"I was not issued papers, Sir. I was informed that everything was in order and to escort them to Port Royal." His eyes narrowed slightly. "I was also informed that there would be no problems."

"We've a ship out there," the officer informed straightly, "one captained by a well known pirate."

Mueller half turned his head, then looked back and countered, "I don't hear any gunfire. Either the battle's over or you've not ordered the patrols to engage her."

Slowly, the officer shook his head and countered, "We don't engage that ship with what we have here, and I'll not provoke a fight against her." He raised his chin slightly. "Two boats were seen coming ashore a few hours ago, presumably from the pirate's vessel, and my men pounced on a group of them as they tried to recover some stolen property."

Nodding, Mueller assumed, "You got them, then?"

The officer looked to Rose and replied, "Not yet, but very soon." He strode around Mueller and approached her.

She heard him coming and faced away from him as best she could, angling her face downward to allow her unrestrained hair to conceal it as much as possible. When he took her arm and brutally turned her toward him she kept her head down, but knew the game was already up. He grabbed her hair and jerked her head back, and her eyes met his fearfully.

Slowly, a smile overtook the officer's mouth. "Well now. Look at who has returned to the scene of her crime. It's good to see you again, Miss O'scarlett."

Rose forced a smile back and raised her hand from behind her to waggle her fingers at him in greeting.

Folding his hands behind him, the officer raised his chin as he stared down at her with a foreboding look. "I've so looked forward at our reunion, my dear."

"I'll bet you have," Rose mumbled as she looked away.

He raised a hand to shoulder height and gestured to the guards behind him, then he informed, "I'll be taking this woman into custody myself."

As the two guards walked around the officer and took Rose's arms, Mueller followed them and barked, "I have my orders!"

"Now you have new orders," the officer countered.

Mueller set his jaw and sternly informed, "My orders come from Governor Berkley himself, so you'd better be taking it up with him."

The officer turned to face Mueller and advised, "You'd best find your place or you can share a cell with her. If Governor Berkley asks about her then you tell him that I have taken her into custody, and if he would like for her to be released to the Port Royal authority then he will come here personally to see to it. Now take your other prisoner and remove yourself from this outpost."

Rose looked nervously at Mueller, who glared back at the officer. When he turned his eyes to her she subtly nodded.

His eyes narrowing, Mueller looked back to the officer and raised his chin, saying straightly, "Aye, Sir. But be sure that *my* head will not be the one to roll when I return without her." He spun around and snapped his fingers and the men with him followed.

The officer watched them approach the pier, and watched longer as they began to board one of the boats there. Finally looking back to Rose, he cupped her jaw in his hand and informed, "We have some catching up to do, my dear." As he turned back toward the main building, he ordered, "Bring her to my office."

* * *

The office itself was as Rose remembered it from almost a year ago. The simple wooden desk was an older one that was left by the Spanish when they had abandoned the island. Many of the furnishings were. Two book cases flanked the largest window behind the desk and a modest table with a lamp, stack of clean paper and inkwell were beneath the smaller one to the left. Books and papers burdened the old shelves and the desk as well as rolled maps. On the other side was a small table with crystal flasks and carafes, the more ornate with crystal stoppers and the rest with wood or cork sealing them. Crystal glasses were lined up neatly in front of them. This was the only part of the office that seemed to be in order. Two chairs sat ready in front of the desk, older chairs that were of simple wood construction.

Behind Rose were two armed guards in the red coats of the British Army. She could feel their eyes on her but would not return their stares. They had her standing in front of the desk, just behind the chairs, and they stood there in silence for a while. Her undershirt had migrated fully off of her shoulder and made her feel even more vulnerable than she felt half unclothed.

Venting a deep sigh, she looked around her yet again, then shifted her arms, grasping her wrist to massage the worsening soreness from it.

Finally turning toward one of the guards, she asked in as sweet a voice as she could manage, "Could one of you chaps be good enough to remove these?" Her eyes darted from one to the next as they stared back at her in an awkward silence with blank eyes. She turned back around and mumbled, "I suppose not."

After another long wait, the hefty officer finally strode into the office with a handful of parchments. "Sorry about the delay," he apologized.

"Oh, no worries," Rose assured. "Just been enjoying the conversation of your charming men."

Stopping behind his desk, he smiled and nodded to her, then extended his hand to one of the chairs and offered, "Please, have a seat."

The guards did not wait for her to respond as they took her arms and brutally forced her to one of the chairs, yanking her back into it.

She looked up at one and barked, "Easy! I'm a woman, you ruffian!"

The officer also took his seat and said, "Sometimes, one wonders. How have you been, Rose?"

Turning her attention to him, she shrugged and replied, "Oh, about the same, Thomas. Pillaging, plundering, drinking... You know."

"Some things never change," he sighed, looking down at the parchments. "Except now you've entered into the illegal slave trade."

Raising her chin, her eyes narrowed as she demanded, "Since when is the slave trade illegal?"

"Since you are dealing in escaped and stolen slaves," he replied, still studying the paper.

Rose looked away and mumbled, "Oh. I suppose there's that."

He folded his hands on the desk before him and looked to her with his brow held high. "So I suppose now is when we begin the business of bartering for your life. Do you remember the last time? I certainly do."

She would not meet his eyes as her lips tightened, and with a nod she softly confirmed, "I remember."

"And to think," he went on, "I thought you actually wanted to live. You have more to repay me for than the theft of the fort's property, Rose, much more."

Through clenched teeth she reminded, "I did what you wanted me to that night. I did everything you wanted me to."

With a slight nod, he confirmed, "Yes, you did, didn't you? But then I can hire a woman of loose scruples to do that, can't I?" He leaned back in his cushioned chair, which creaked as he shifted in it. "Now, Miss O'scarlett, perhaps you will tell me what you will offer for your life this time. What have you left? Obviously not your dignity."

She clenched her teeth and turned her face away from him.

He stared at her in silence for a long moment, then, "Governor Berkley will no doubt be sending a ship to retrieve you in the next few days, then you'll be off to a well deserved trial and hanging. I wonder if I should take the time to attend. I would be delighted to see you get your treacherous little neck stretched." He looked down to his hands. "Then again, that seems like such a waste. Of course, I have no illusions about you keeping your word should we come to an agreement."

"I kept my word last time," she snarled.

"And then you and your men robbed this outpost of everything you could take," he reminded.

Rose finally, slowly turned her eyes to him. "I never said I wouldn't, nor did you make that an arrangement of our bargain, so I kept my word to you."

He raised his brow and nodded, conceding in a low voice, "I see." He drew a long breath and released it through his nose, his eyes fixed on her as asked, "So, any word from your son?"

Again she looked away from him, clenching her teeth anew.

"A shame you will never see him again," he sighed. "More so that he will grow up knowing that the mother who abandoned him was a criminal and was hanged. Once word of this gets out... Well, children can be so cruel to other children when armed with such knowledge."

Her brow low over her eyes, she looked back at him with a deadly glare.

He casually looked down at his fingernails. "Haven't paid the bond for his release, I take it. Now you have quite a price on your head. Such a price could very well make one a rich man, wouldn't you say?"

"What is it you want?" she hissed.

With a subtle shrug, he folded his hands again and looked back to her. "Back to business? Very well, Rose. Perhaps we should discuss your future, or what there is of it." His eyes shifted to the door as someone entered.

Another soldier, a young man with short blond hair and a uniform in perfect order entered and snapped to attention. "Reporting as ordered, Colonel. The pirate's ship has departed."

"As I thought they would," the Colonel drawled, turning his eyes back to Rose. "The code of the pirates, yes?"

Rose turned her eyes down, now feeling completely abandoned, and alone.

"You seem to need time to think, Miss O'scarlett," the Colonel observed. "Guards, take her to the stockade outside and keep her under heavy guard. Make certain she is not disturbed. She has some reflecting to do."

They took her arms and were not gentle as they hoisted her from the chair and turned her toward the door.

"Oh, and Rose," he called after her pleasantly.

She stopped and half turned, her eyes glossy with tears as she turned a venomous glare on him.

"Consider wisely the next few hours," he warned. "I've enough just here to convict and hang you, or you could just disappear into that mine beneath the fort where you can live out your days as a plaything for the men and I. Decide how you want your end, Rose, quick with the stretch of your neck or long and drawn over many years. Or, perhaps, you'll consider our original arrangement. Either way I win, and you belong to me." He motioned with his head and the guards yanked on her arms and removed her quite brutally from the office.

Chapter 8

DESPERATE ACTS

The day crept by and the small cell she was in grew darker and darker. This stockade backed up to the sheer stone cliff of the mountain the fort was built into and was in fact built right into it. Open space was on both sides between the perimeter wall and the stockade, and the stockade and the thick stone wall of the main building. A second level balcony overlooked it from the main building and guard posts on the wall side. Even if one escaped from the stockade itself it was fifty yards to the nearest cover, and after reaching that the guards still had clear shots from many positions. The only hope would be to reach the main gate, avoid the muskets of the guards there, avoid the cannons on the wall and get down to the pier where...

It was pointless to think about.

The place stank as no wind could get in or out. She was in the first of four cells that were constructed of heavy stone block. The floor was solid volcanic rock. Heavy iron bars were across the ceiling and the one door which was made of thick timbers that were bound together by thick iron strapping had the only window to the outside, and it was a small one. The cell was about six by eight feet and would accommodate up to four men.

Wooden racks were the only beds and were hinged to the stone wall on the left and rear of the cell and held in place by thick hemp rope. It was not comfortable, but at least it was not the floor.

Rose had been here before and preferred the lower rack at the rear of the cell. Laying on her side with her arm curled under her head, she stared blankly at the one window of the cell, watching the light outside slowly dim into night time. At some point she expected the Colonel to send for her. His bed would be more comfortable than this rack, but that meant spending another night with him, and the thought disgusted her. However, that was not where her mind was. Once again her thoughts were consumed with the big pirate. Sharing his bed in two nights of animalistic lust was something she would remember for the rest of her life, short as that seemed now. With that mingled the realization that he had abandoned her, and that stung. She had convinced herself that they had made some kind of bond, that some piece of his heart was hers now, but it clearly was not so. She had unintentionally given him hers, and his betrayal had crushed it.

Still, this had been business. She had promised him gunpowder and other things and had not delivered. She would not blame him for leaving her there. At least he had not killed her outright, and at least she had those two nights with him.

Rose drew a deep breath and closed her eyes, releasing it gently as she tried to relish the little glimpses of the softer side of this monstrous pirate captain. She finally resigned herself to her loneliness, to her destined fate at the gallows, and to never seeing her son again.

She had almost drifted off to sleep when the lock outside was turned with a few loud clicks and her eyes flashed open. Raising her head as the door was opened, she watched two guards enter, then she clenched her teeth as a third man entered, an unpleasant looking fellow who had not shaven for days, wore a faded uniform and had hair that was unkempt beneath his hat. As he smiled at her, he revealed rotten teeth that were brown and blackened in places. He fortunately only entered the cell half way.

The disapproval of him was evident in Rose's eyes as she watched him leer at her like some hungry animal.

He ran his gaze along her body from one end to the other and back again, and finally wiped his mouth with the back of his hand. When he finally spoke, he had the voice and accent of someone who was not exactly of status, had never been, nor would ever be. "Got somethin' for ye, puppet." He held the wrapped package before him and informed, "Colonel Digby wants to see you in this when we take you to him, and you've got a half hour to get ready." He tossed the package to her and it landed on the rack beside her.

Rose looked down at it, then back to the unkempt man and straightly said, "Tell Colonel Digby that I respectfully wish for him to go straight to Hell."

Smiling broader, the man nodded and replied, "Aye, he thought you'd say that, so he said you'll be wearin' that when we take ye, or ye can be brought to 'im naked." He folded his arms and leaned his head. "Still want me to tell 'im to go to 'ell?"

Turning her eyes away, she slowly took the package in her hand and answered, "No, I'll just tell him myself." She swung her legs to the floor and stood, pulling the string to open the brown paper package, then she hesitated and looked to the man who still leered at her, raising her brow. "Do you mind?"

"Not at all," he drawled.

"Step outside," she ordered.

He shook his head. "Don't think so. Keeping me eyes on ye so ye don't escape."

Rose glared at him as she pursed her lips, and finally vented her irritation in a deep breath and tossed the package on the rack before she began to undress under the watchful eyes of the three men.

The dress that Colonel Digby had sent for her was a pretty one, bright yellow with a very low neckline and a lightly made skirt that only covered her just below her knees. It fit her very tightly around the waist and her chest bulged out of it, just as he no doubt planned. He had not sent shoes so the walk from the stockade to the main complex was not a comfortable one.

Once inside, she expected to be taken right to his bed chamber, but instead she was taken to the officer's dining hall on the second level, a well decorated room with four arched doorways and lavish furnishings. It was a big room, clearly meant to entertain many people. The wooden table in the center was covered by a long white cloth and was at least fifteen feet long. This evening it only had two chairs pushed up to it: One at the far end and one to the right of it. The place settings were in position. Four silver candelabras, each with five candles burning, were evenly distributed along the table. There was wine, a silver pitcher of water, a bowl of fruit... This man went all out to impress her, and she raised her brow as she took it all in.

She was escorted to the far end of the table and made to stop there. Glancing about, she saw a guard posted at each entrance, and each guard had a musket on his shoulder, a pistol in its holster and a sword hanging on his belt. Digby wanted to impress her, but he clearly also wanted her to know that she was going nowhere that he did not want her to.

When they were halfway down the table, one of the guards strode ahead of her and pulled her chair out, his eyes on her in a hungry stare.

At this point it would just be easier to comply, so she strode toward the chair with a sultry walk, grabbing an apple out of one of the fruit bowls as she passed it. She sat daintily in the chair as she reached it and was helped to pull it up to the table. The three guards who had escorted her in departed the way they had come, but kept their eyes on her as long as they could.

He meant to make her wait, so she leaned forward and propped her elbows on the table, glancing about as she absently took a bite out of the apple with a horribly loud crunch. It was very sweet and, despite how hungry she was, she chewed slowly as she scanned the room, and in the back of her mind she continued to calculate her chances of making a successful escape.

A long moment crept by and she took another big bite of the apple as loudly as she could. A few more moments ticked slowly by and her eyes fixed on a wine bottle in the middle of the table in front of her, one that had the cork only halfway into it so that it could be easily opened. In short order she finished the apple and tossed the core over her shoulder, then she half stood and reached for the wine bottle, settling back into her chair as she looked into the clear bottle full of red wine. Raising her brow, she glanced at one of the guards, then took the cork in her teeth and pulled it from the bottle, spitting it across the table where it bounced twice and disappeared over the other side. She raised the mouth of the bottle to her lips and took several big gulps, then she looked down to the bottle and raised her brow again. Looking to one of the guards, she commented, "This is really good wine!"

The guard only glanced at her and nodded.

He looked vaguely familiar but she dismissed that thought with another drink from the bottle.

"Wouldn't you rather have that in a glass?" Digby asked as he entered from the same door she had.

Rose looked that way, seeing him in a new and perfectly pressed dress uniform, all his medals in their places and the buttons and buckles shined to perfection. His hat was in his hand and his hair was, for once, perfectly groomed. He had even shaved!

She took another drink, then shook her head and answered, "No, this is fine." His prim and proper little dinner party would not go as smoothly as he'd hoped, and she would see to that. After taking another couple of loud gulps, she belched loudly and daintily blotted the tip of her napkin on her lips as she set the wine bottle down on the plate in front of her and leaned back in her chair. "So, I assume you got me all dressed up to come here for a good dinner? Or is this a prelude to something else?"

He sat down and also leaned back in his chair, his eyes on hers as he replied, "Perhaps both, my dear. Perhaps this would be a good time to renegotiate our arrangement of a year ago."

Rose looked back to the wine bottle and nodded. With the whole day to consider this little scenario she had managed to conclude nothing. Her ship was gone, she had no crew, the friends she had made around the Caribbean were slowly turning away out of fear of knowing her, and the big pirate captain she had wanted since the first time she had seen him had abandoned her. She knew what Digby wanted and now she had to decide if it was better than the gallows.

The Colonel cleared his throat, but could not seem to summon her attention.

Two black women entered, both rather young and dressed in white servant's attire, and both held their eyes low and their heads down. They were both rather well made, both with pretty faces, and both carried dishes covered with silver domes.

One approached Rose and reached for the wine bottle, snapping her hand back as Rose slapped it and grabbed the bottle. She shot a look to the Colonel, then hesitantly set the dish down on the plate in the bottle's place and backed away. The other served Digby, slowly backing away with the first.

The Colonel casually took his napkin and laid it in his lap, and as he removed the silver dome he said, "I hope you like pheasant. I had them brought here to hunt a few years ago and they've done rather well."

Rose picked the small bird on her plate up with her hands and savagely took a bite out of the breast, chewing for a moment before she shrugged and informed with a full mouth, "I've had better." Something in the kitchen beyond the door behind Digby crashed and she flinched and looked that way.

Ignoring the disturbance, the Colonel picked up his fork and knife and attended his own meal. "I've had quite a banquet prepared so I'm sure you'll find something to your liking."

"Maybe so," she countered with a nearly full mouth. Taking another swig of wine, she belched before biting into the pheasant again.

Their meal continued without further conversation. Rose had not eaten since that morning and was famished, and made no secret of it. She ate like a savage with primitive upbringing and in short order had finished the bottle of wine, upending it to let the last drops drain into her mouth before slamming it onto the table. Daintily wiping her mouth, she looked to Digby and asked, "Don't have any good rum around here, do you?"

His eyes locked on her for a few awkward seconds, and finally he answered, "I'll see about finding you some." He set his fork down and wiped his mouth, then he pushed his half empty plate back and folded his hands on the table before him, his gaze locked on her as he suggested, "I think it is time to discuss your future, Rose."

Feeling a bit tipsy from the entire bottle of wine, she set her elbow on the table and rested her cheek in her palm, offering him a flirty smile as she agreed, "I think you are right, Thomas.

Maybe you'll tell me what you have in mind. And if you say gallows even once then our whole evening is over, savvy?"

He smiled and nodded. "That doesn't have to be discussed at all. In fact, I'd rather avoid it myself."

"So much for wanting to see my pretty little neck get stretched," she said with slightly slurred words.

He drew a breath, then informed, "Perhaps it is time for Rose O'scarlett to disappear. You could leave the sea and stay here with me."

"As your consort," she added.

"Call it what you like," he sighed, "but I'm certain you would prefer that life over the noose that awaits you. Bear in mind that I could attain considerable wealth just by turning you in to be hung. I would be a hero in these parts by simply sending a message to Port Royal."

"Aren't they already coming for me?" she asked.

Digby shrugged. "Most likely. Coming for you is one thing. Finding you is an entirely different matter." He reached for another bottle of wine and pulled the cork from it. Carefully, he poured his glass full and continued, "There are hundreds of places on this island to hide you and tales of your attempted escape and subsequent demise trying would surely carry over to every island in the Caribbean, and eventually on to England." He reached to her place and took her glass, slowly pouring it full as well. "No more worries, Rose, no more price on your head. No more running."

She watched him slide her glass toward her, her eyes blank as she considered.

A squeaky wheel coming from the kitchen distracted her, but barely. She glanced that way, absently seeing a tall, thickly made black skinned man pushing a metal cart to the table. He was dressed in white servant's attire that seemed too small for him. The only thing that seemed to fit him was the kitchen hat he wore, and his attention was on the cart he pushed.

Rose looked back to her wine, her cheek still resting heavily in her hand. Slowly, her other hand reached to the wine glass and gingerly picked it up.

As another covered dish was put in front of him, Colonel Digby absently took the silver dome from it and laid it aside, his attention on the dish of cooked apples that smelled of cinnamon. Picking up a spoon, he picked at it as a dish was put before Rose, and he looked to her and asked, "A life with me or the noose. Is it such a hard decision?"

She clenched her teeth, looking at the silver dome that sat before her.

The servant assured in a very deep voice, "You'll like this dish, Miss. I prepared it especially for you." He took the knob on the top with two fingers and lifted it just high enough to clear the bowl it covered, then he set it down right beside the bowl.

As Rose saw her dessert, she raised her brow, and her eyes shifted to the tall black man who smiled back at her.

Harold nodded and said, "I loaded it with sweetness and spiced it just right, just for you."

She offered a little smile. "Why thank you. That was very sweet."

"Leave us, now," Digby ordered.

Bowing his head, Harold complied, "Yes sir. You'd better get to eatin' that, Miss, or these guards will pirate it away from you for sure."

She turned her eyes to the guard who stood at the door across the room, fighting to maintain her composure as she recognized him as Mister Mueller.

Mueller noticed her attention and winked.

Fighting back that smile was not easy so she turned her attention back to Digby and allowed it to come. "So, Thomas, same deal as before, aye? In exchange for me life you get to take your pleasure of me whenever you want to." Her eyes remained locked on him as he raised his chin slightly and she watched as he took a sip of his wine. His gaze never left hers. She continued as she picked up her spoon and reached for her dessert, "And I suppose I get servants and everything a woman would want?"

Digby nodded. "Everything you desire, my Sweet."

"Except," she added, "a decent looking man to wake up next to."

He set his jaw and lowered his glass to the table. "You have but two choices, Rose."

"But you don't," she said straightly. "As soon as you tire of me you'll turn me in to Berkley for that reward."

"That would be awkward if you are already reported dead," he pointed out.

"And I'm sure you've already thought of that," she spat. Finally raising her cheek from her hand, she looked down to her bowl and set her spoon down. "I'm tired of being used."

"Then you have my word that you won't be," he assured.

"Except as your personal whore," she snarled. Huffing a hard sigh, she shook her head and looked back to him with a sweet smile. "I don't think so, Thomas. In fact, I'm going to walk out of here and you are going to be a good boy and let me."

With a hearty laugh, Digby picked up his wine glass and shook his head. "You are of wonderful humor tonight, Rose. I shall indulge you and ask why I would let you just walk out of here."

Rose picked the small pistol up from her bowl and pulled the hammer back as she trained it on him, answering, "Because I'll shoot you if you don't."

Digby's eyes widened as they fixed on the weapon. It took him many long seconds to regain his composure, but he finally seemed to with the clearing of his throat, another sip of wine and a raising of his chin. "Rose, darling. What makes you think you will be able to walk out of here even if you shoot me?"

Hearing the hammers pull back on two muskets and at least three pistols, her eyes narrowed and she assured, "Even if they all shoot me you'll be just as dead."

He set his glass down, his gaze fixed on it as he shook his head. "I'd so hoped to avoid any unpleasantness this evening, especially your untimely demise. Guards, see to it that if this woman does shoot me that she is made to suffer as no other has, and ensure that she finds her way to Governor Berkley for the hanging she deserves."

A man stepped from each doorway, and each of them trained his weapon Digby, who set his jaw as he glanced at each of them in turn.

Rose smiled again. "Isn't mutiny a horrible thing?"

His brow held low, Digby assured through clenched teeth, "You will not only all hang, but I shall see to it your families suffer as well. I don't know what she told you—"

"We take our orders from someone bigger than you," Mueller snarled, "much bigger. Now be a good lad and keep that trap of yours shut."

Rose looked to Mueller, her eyes betraying uncertainty as she asked, "So now what do we do?"

He smiled and assured, "We leave." Looking to the kitchen he called, "Harold! We're going."

Harold walked out of the kitchen with a flour sack full of loot from the kitchen over his shoulder, one of the slave girls under his other arm, and a big smile on his face. "I'm taking this with me."

Mueller loosed a sigh and shook his head. "We have to go light, lad."

Raising his brow, Harold argued, "Got many spices in here that will make the Captain's meals much better." His eyes shifted to the table and he lifted his arm from the girl and took a silver gravy ladle from its place, looking it over before he swung the sack from his shoulder and opened it, dropping the ladle inside. "I've been wanting one of these, too."

Before he could close the sack, Rose barked, "Wait!" She set the pistol down and reached for the two unopened bottles of wine, sliding them carefully into the sack as well.

"Are you two finished?" Mueller asked in an exasperated tone.

Rose picked up her pistol and barked back, "We're pirates! It's what we do!"

One of the men motioned to Digby with his chin and asked, "What about him?"

Harold's fist slammed into Digby's forehead hard enough to knock him and his chair to the floor, then he looked to Mueller and assured, "He'll sleep for a while. We'd better be off."

With much of the fort's compliment still returning from the field, the eight of them easily made their way toward through the corridors, and those few who did see them did not question five guards escorting three prisoners toward the front. They even made it outside the perimeter wall without any trouble.

Halfway to the pier, Rose finally looked to Mueller, who walked to her right, and asked, "I trust there is a ship waiting to take us off the island?"

His eyes shifted to her. "We're not out of this yet, Lass."

"We seem pretty clear to me," she pointed out. "Once we reach the pier…"

A thump behind them sounded, and all were alerted to the firing of a cannon from the fort. This was confirmed when a cannonball hit the ground on the side of the road ahead of them and exploded, and everyone ducked down.

"I'd say they're onto us," one of the men shouted.

They all looked back to the fort as three more cannons fired.

Rose shouted, "Get to the pier!"

As they ran the last two hundred yards to the pier, musket fire cracked behind them. Few balls made it that far and those that did hit the ground randomly around them, and one right at Rose's feet.

She looked over her shoulder and yelled, "Everyone spread out! Don't give'em a tight group of us to shoot at!"

With the sun plunging into the sea, they reached the pier and Rose was confident that the cannons would not try to hit them there for risk of damaging the important pier itself. Instead, they switched to solid shot and continued to fire. They all took cover behind crates, barrels and whatever else they could find as cannonballs and musket rounds continued to randomly fall around them from a quarter mile away.

With her back pressed against a barrel of water, Rose looked over her shoulder and flinched as another round hit close by, and she complimented, "They've got excellent range on those things!"

"Too much for my taste," Harold added as he took cover behind a stack of crates, holding the slave girl close to him.

Rose looked around, holding her mouth tight. It was only a matter of time before a garrison of British troops would reach them, and after that… She found Mueller taking cover on the other side of the pier and shouted to him, "We're going to have to get off this pier soon, Mister Mueller! Where's that ship?"

"It'll be here!" he assured in a shout. He had his pistol in his hand and several of the men also had their weapons drawn.

Rose had forgotten about hers, tucked into an undergarment under her skirt and she reached for it, holding it ready for the inevitable.

The cannons stopped, and they all knew what that meant.

Harold asked, "How many will they send?"

Mueller snarled back, "As many as they can spare. I'll not go to the gallows, mates. I'll make me last stand here, ship or no ship!"

The men with them shouted in agreement, and Rose huffed a sigh and looked around the barrel, her eyes widening as she saw forty or fifty men marching down the road from the fort to the pier, four abreast and holding their muskets ready. "Not good," she mumbled, then she yelled, "Boys, we've got company and lots of it!"

Everyone turned and aimed their weapons. Only five of them carried extra ammunition, those in British uniforms. Rose and Harold only had one shot each and no other weapons to call upon when their pistols were empty.

Three more cannonballs hit the ground and one hit the water near the shore just to the right of the pier.

Rose looked to Harold, and when he met her eyes she barked, "Next time, hit him *with* something!"

He smiled and looked around the corner of the crates.

When Rose looked next, the soldiers, not just sixty yards away, had fanned out eight abreast in what appeared to be five columns and appeared to be ready to fan out more and flank them. Looking around her, they would be under the soldier's guns in moments. So close to freedom, and it already looked like their escape was at an end. She did agree with Mueller. She would not be captured again.

Her mind scrambling, she glanced about the pier at anything that she could use to take an advantage. Anything! Nothing was there, no weapons, little cover, nowhere to retreat to.

The fire from the fort stopped and but for the waves and the seagulls everything was eerily quiet for a long moment.

Rose dared to peer around the barrel once more, seeing that the soldiers now formed a semi-circle around them in five groups of eight spaced about five yards apart. The first four of each group was on one knee, already aiming their weapons while those behind them stood ready with theirs.

"All right," one of the British shouted. "You'll be offered leniency, but only once, and only once will I offer you unconditional surrender."

160

Holding her weapon tightly, Rose looked around the barrel, finding the well decorated man in the clean uniform who stood between two of the groups that took aim at them. His was an expression of conceit. He knew he had them cornered. He knew he had already won. His overconfident expression was something Rose had always hated about the British officers, so she shouted back, "You are offering surrender? Very well. Lay down your arms and put your hands up and we'll spare you!"

Many of the British laughed.

Rose looked to Mueller and shrugged.

"I see you still have a sense of humor," the officer observed. "Good form. However, my orders are to bring you in as prisoners or corpses. Please choose wisely and soon. I don't intend for this stand-off to last until dark."

"Then can you come back in the morning?" she asked sweetly.

"Miss O'scarlett," he called back in an exasperated tone, "you don't know this but you are surrounded and in a moment you will all be dead unless you surrender. I have said all I am going to."

Rose raised her chin and countered, "Oh, but you have such a beautiful voice."

"Ship!" one of the men shouted.

They all looked and Rose felt a cold wash through her.

The big sloop was very close to shore, close enough that everyone could see the red uniforms of British officers and soldiers, the white shirts of the crew, and many men on the decks. The swivel guns were manned and aimed at them. The deck guns were manned and aimed. The seven broadsides were ready. At least fifteen men were at the rail with muskets trained on them. And the Union Jack flew proudly from her stern.

Rose felt her heart sink. It was over.

"What say you now?" the British officer shouted.

Mueller wheeled around the crate with his musket and shouted, "Burn in Hell, limey!"

When his weapon fired, everyone followed suit and sent hot lead balls at the British formation. The British returned fire and seven musket balls were met with forty.

Looking back to the sloop as it cruised by, bringing its guns directly in line with the pier, Rose awaited the inevitable. At least it would be quick this way.

The muskets fired first, then the swivel guns, then the deck guns, and finally the broadsides, and all of this deadly fire pounded right into the British positions on the shore.

Looking around the barrel again, Rose saw what was left of the formations in chaos, and retreating! Turning her attention back to the ship, she saw the British flag come down, and the black and white flag flown over the *Black Dragon* ascend to replace it!

"Into the water!" Mueller shouted.

Not waiting for the British to reorganize themselves, everyone abandoned their positions and what they had brought with them and ran down the pier toward the water, jumping into the sea as they reached the end of the pier. A few musket shots followed them, quickly fired and poorly aimed.

The sloop turned hard out to sea, slowing her retreat as four cannons on the stern fired into the British again.

The Fort replied with every cannon she had. Most fell short of the ship, two long, and one hit the pier.

They swam as hard as they could. Reaching the ship looked hopeless under the guns of the fort and the many more soldiers who ran from it toward the water.

The ship finished a sharp turn and brought her starboard guns to bear on the charging British and all of them seemed to fire at once, but not all slammed into the soldiers. A few fired long and actually hit the wall of the fort.

As she swam hard toward the ship and it changed direction again, Rose saw a boat bobbing about in its wake and she smiled and swam harder toward it.

Their retreat seemed to take forever as the ship traded shots with the fort.

Finally at the boat, Rose started to climb onto the stern, only to have her arms grabbed and before she realized she was hoisted aboard by a couple of strong men. Harold had somehow out-swum her and arrived first with the slave girl, and was pulling his mates from the water as fast as they reached him.

When they were all aboard the small boat, Mueller shouted to the ship, "You have us!"

The ship made one more hard turn out to sea, but not hard enough to avoid one cannonball that struck her amidships. Another scored a lucky shot in her rigging and some of it came down, bringing some of the canvas with it. The stern cannons responded, but were already out of range.

A rope that held the boat to the ship was pulled taught and it was jerked along with neck bending force, and before anyone realized, they had been pulled out of range of the fort's guns.

The boat was drawn in and the occupants pulled themselves hand over hand up the rope and to the waiting ship.

Rose made sure she went last as she worried over the rest of the people who had rescued her. As she climbed over the rail of the sloop, a strong hand—a woman's hand—grasped hers and helped her over, and her eyes widened as she found herself face to face with the tall, muscular woman she had encountered with Cannonburg in the tavern a few days before, and this woman looked anything but glad to see her.

She glared at Rose for long seconds, then wheeled around and shouted, "Helm! Give me a course due east at this ship's best speed!"

A man working on the rigging near the top of the mainmast pointed behind them and to the right, shouting, "Sails off the port stern!"

Everyone wheeled around, and Rose slowly shook her head.

Two British ships, one a sloop and one a corvette were in hot pursuit and angling to intercept them, and they were at full sail and slicing fast across the water.

Shielding her eyes against the setting sun, the tall woman squinted as she studied the ships chasing her, then she looked up into the rigging and yelled, "How long to get us to full sail again?"

The man up there simply shook his head.

"Damn," she growled, then looked to Rose and spat, "You'd better be worth all of this, O'scarlett."

As she stormed off, Rose pursued and informed, "I was expecting Captain Jones to come for me, seeing as how he left me there."

"Cannonflash will meet us in the morning," the woman snarled. She stopped at the door to a cabin in the center of the ship and wheeled around, facing Rose with her brow low. "I'll say this once, O'scarlett. I've put me neck out for you only on the orders of Captain Cannonflash. But for that you'd be swinging by your neck or bleeding out from musket wounds by now and I'd not lose a minute sleep over it."

Slowly nodding, Rose offered, "I appreciate your honesty."

Another woman, a shorter, thinner woman who only wore short undergarments and a dirty and sleeveless shirt, ran up to them from the bow and barked, "We'll not make full speed with that rigging damaged so, Captain Angie. We've also had damage to the mainmast below. She'll give out with the next hard push of the wind."

Angie turned her head only slightly, cutting her eyes that way. She was quiet for long seconds as she just stared at nothing, then she wheeled around, facing the two ships that pursued hers. With her gaze fixed on them, she harshly asked, "Can we at least keep some distance between us and them?"

"I doubt it," the thin woman replied grimly.

Rose suggested, "We should lighten the ship, get more speed that way."

With an angry sigh, Angie growled back, "We lightened before we came here to draft in shallower water, and the only thing left to throw over is you." Her attention turned back to the thin woman and she ordered, "Shore up the main mast as well you can and get the rigging in as good a shape as we can. Cut that boat we're dragging loose first and be ready to darken the ship."

"Wait," Rose barked.

Slowly, Angie turned an impatient, hateful look on her.

Rose, however, maintained her bearing and set her hands on her hips. "We keep two lights burning at the back of the ship and have two lamps mounted onto the boat behind us. Well after dark we cut the boat loose and turn a wide circle around them. By morning we'll have opened copious distance and they'll never catch us before we can reach a safe port."

Narrow eyed, Angie set her jaw as she glared at Rose, then she huffed a hard breath and ordered, "Do it." When the thin woman hurried about her task she stepped a little closer and snarled, "You'd better be worth all of this."

 164

Folding her arms, Rose offered a little smile and sweetly said, "I am so glad you and I can be the best of friends."

"You'd be wise not to push your luck with me, O'scarlett."

A cannonball slammed into the sea right beside the ship and a fountain of water shot up over the deck, spraying the side of the ship as it cascaded back down.

Everyone wheeled that way, and someone near the stern of the ship turned and shouted, "Long eighteens, Captain Angie! Probably on that corvette."

Angie's mouth tightened to a thin slit as she watched the ships pursuing her angle in and slowly gain on them. "Damn," she grumbled. "Our guns are still out of range and they can pick us apart from all the way back there."

"You have any chain shot?" Rose asked.

Another man had approached, an older fellow wearing only short trousers, and he replied, "We've about eight rounds, but not enough to do any damage from this range."

"Unless we get it into the middle of their canvas," Rose countered. She raised her chin and added, "It might also keep them off balance if they think we have more than we do." Looking to Captain Angie, she raised her brow ever so slightly.

Angie regarded her coldly, then she looked to the pursuing British again and ordered, "Get a couple of the eighteen pounders to the stern and block 'em up muzzles high. Get your range quick and put all eight rounds into her canvas. Let's see if we can get 'em to back off a little."

The cannons were in position in short order, but the British got a few more rounds off at them in the process. They had the range and it was only a matter of time before they found their mark. The men Angie had working with the cannons now aiming backward were the best she had and one was kneeling at each gun, eying carefully down the barrel and directing the men who worked with the blocks to elevate the guns as much as they could.

Angie and Rose approached them and their captain bade, "Well?"

The older of the men at the cannons looked back and smiled with brown teeth as he asked, "You have a gold piece for the first man to score a hit?"

Raising her brow, Angie nodded and confirmed, "Aye, and a bottle of rum for each shot you put into 'em."

The two men looked to each other and smiled, and the older looked back at her and said, "Awaiting word, Captain."

She looked back at the two ships, and nodded.

The two guns fired almost simultaneously and all eyes were on the corvette. Even at this distance it was easy to see the sails of the larger ship shudder as the chain shot penetrated and tore through the canvas, and one of them slammed into the deck at the rear of the ship, causing untold havoc there.

Cheer erupted and Angie shouted over them, "Give 'em another!"

The ships traded cannon fire and it was obvious that Captain Angie had the better marksmen. As they did more damage to the corvette's sails, it began to slow and the big sloop with it veered away slightly, then back the other way so as not to present an easy target, and this caused it to fall behind.

It was inevitable. Before the sun set completely, one of the corvette's forty-two pounders slammed into the middle of the deck of Angie's ship and penetrated all the way through to the lower decks. The ship shuddered as wood was splintered and disarray erupted on the ship.

Angie found Rose and took her arm, ordering, "Get below and make certain we are not too badly hurt."

Rose nodded and charged that way. When she arrived, she found men with buckets trying to organize a line to start bailing the water out of the ship's belly. The cannonball was lodged in the planks of the ships belly and had thankfully not penetrated all the way through. Repairing the ship as they fled would be impossible, so she helped with the bucket brigade to get as much of the sea as they could out. Glancing around as they sent bucket after bucket to the top deck, she noticed that the keel of the ship was flexing, and a chill washed through her. The ship's keel was broken and it was only a matter of time before she gave up and surrendered to the sea.

Grabbing a young woman who was down there trying to help, she shouted over the noise of all the activity, "Get topside and tell Captain Angie that the ship's back is broken and not to maneuver too hard!" As the young woman headed to the ladder, she took a moment to look around her and mumbled, "This ship is going down."

* * *

A very long night was ahead. Everyone aboard worked feverishly to bail water out of the lower deck, repair the rigging in dangerously low light and hold the ship together as best they could. Rope was used to shore her up below deck, binding the ship together from stem to stern, but they creaked and strained and the wood that made up the ship's spine continued to crack and splinter, growing weaker and weaker as the ship maneuvered to avoid potshots that continued to come even well into the dark of night.

Hours into the chase Rose's plan was executed, the ship was darkened and the boat was cut loose with two lanterns hanging on the rear. The ship had to be turned carefully and could not be maneuvered as hard as needed and the ruse ultimately failed, but it did buy them almost a full mile of water between them and the British.

An early morning glow barely illuminated the East and Rose stood at the bow of the wounded and dying sloop, her arms crossed against the passing wind and her skirt flapping freely with it. Her eyes were blank as she scanned the horizon for friendly sails. All she could see out there were speckles of light reflecting off of the wave tops and small, black shadows that she knew to be islands in the distance. Four more hours of sailing at a good speed and they would arrive, but below they were losing the battle against the invading sea water, and as the ship rode lower and lower in the water the keel was more and more stressed. The ship would not make the islands. The only boat had been used to buy them more time. The British were closing faster and faster as the wounded sloop became heavier and heavier with sea water and slowed a little more each moment. Capture or death was inevitable.

Still, Rose looked sharp to the awakening horizon, clinging to the hope that she would see the double sails of the *Black Dragon* bearing down on the British who pursued her, though moment by moment that hope slipped away.

She glanced at Angie as she stopped beside her, also staring hopefully to the horizon and for a moment the two women simply stared at the horizon. Rose noticed that the tall woman's hair was down for the first time and it was blowing freely to the side on the breeze. Looking fully to her, she also finally noticed how lovely this femme berserker was. Strong features did not hinder her appearance, they enhanced it. Johnny was a lucky man.

Angie finally looked back at Rose, her expression hard and very strained.

"So," Rose started. "Gallows or cannons. What suits you best, Captain Angie?"

"You already know, O'scarlett," Angie replied softly.

"It comes to this," Rose went on. "The two most wanted and notorious women in the Caribbean, Rose O'scarlett and Dreaded Angie shall have their last stand on a crippled sloop against impossible odds. Considering our reputations I'm rather surprised the Reds haven't surrendered to us."

Angie actually smiled, if only slightly. "Aye, me too. In another place at another time I could have liked you, Rose O'scarlett. Since we're going to die together, perhaps we'll die friends."

"And unfortunately sober," Rose added grimly.

The two women enjoyed a good laugh. Cannon fire drew their attention behind and they saw fountains of water blasted from the sea right behind the ship. They could see the Corvette was much closer than they had thought and the war sloop was bearing down on them off the port side from less than a mile away. They looked back to each other, strain and fear of the final battle to come evident in their eyes.

"I'll take the starboard side," Rose offered softly, solemnly.

Angie nodded and they turned and headed to the back of the ship.

Despite being shored up with all the rope they could find, the mainmast cracked from below and leaned heavily into the wind. The ship, now very heavy with sea water, began to sag noticeably right behind the mainmast and the railing began to bow and the deck they walked on began to buckle ever so slowly. All of the cannons that could be mustered were on the deck and were being aimed backward at the shadowy apparitions that were the pursuing ships. Those not working the cannons stood at the rail with muskets or pistols. Every soul on the ship meant to go down fighting. With much of the powder they needed below decks and wet, they would have to rely on the little bit that was salvaged in the night. The cannons would each be able to fire about three times, the muskets, four or five.

As she watched the British sloop close to within half a mile, Rose began to formulate a plan to take it over. The much larger corvette that also pursued them would hinder that.

The corvette fired again, only one gun, this time hitting the wounded sloop at the bow. The cannonball ripped through the planks and timbers all the way to the flooded deck below and out the other side near the water line.

At the same time, Rose and Angie shouted, "Fire!" and the sloop's five remaining guns replied with true aim, two shots hitting the war sloop and three hitting the corvette. Now the British knew this was a fight to the death and they made preparations to end it. Heavy in the bow, Angie's ship slowed more as the sea poured in from the front and the ship began to bow to the sea that meant to claim it.

The sun broke the horizon to the east with blinding brightness and this would hinder the British aim as Angie's ship was sailing right into it. The pursuing ships were in the sights of the pirate cannons and a second salvo did their damage. Now, each cannon had but one shot left, one shot that the men aiming them would make count.

Rose strode behind the men as they moved the guns back into position to fire and she barked, "Aim for the deck and take out as many Reds as you can! It'll be muskets and swords after that, so even up the odds!"

Angie shouted, "Lay all your shots amidships and let's see if we can open 'er hull!"

Each British ship was now only about two hundred yards away. Broadsides and deck guns were turned, aimed at the sinking sloop. Many men were at the rails with muskets, some already taking aim.

Raising her chin, it was Captain O'scarlett who issued the last order: "Fire!"

The pirate sloop fired before the British sloop did and at this range all of the cannonballs found their mark, and suddenly the sloop was torn in half by a horrific explosion that consumed the entire middle of the ship. Bow and stern were blown away from each other. The mainmast careened end over end into the air. Cannons, barrels and men were thrown hundreds of feet.

Angie swung around as she heard the ship explode, then her eyes met Rose's.

Rose just shrugged.

The corvette fired its long guns, but it fired them forward and unexpectedly veered away from the sinking pirate's ship it had pursued all night.

Thunderous thumps were heard from the bow and the entire crew looked that way, shielding their eyes against the sun.

As the corvette turned fully and fired her broadsides into the rising sun, fountains of water blew up from the sea to show that cannonballs had missed, then she was hit by solid shot that ripped into her deck. A moment later the crack of thunder ripped through the air and the side of the corvette exploded in a huge ball of fire and fleeing embers, cannons and shattered timber and planks. Still sea worthy, the battered ship finished its turn and fled, deck guns and muskets firing desperately.

The sun was suddenly darkened by black sails and an ominous twin hull. The *Black Dragon* was moving in for the kill.

Everyone aboard Angie's ship exploded into cheers as the most dreaded ship afloat sailed past at her best speed, pursuing a ship that had been the predator all night.

Much faster and with the wind cutting along her sails to drive her along, the mighty ship closed to nearly point blank range before her guns fired again, and when she veered away to turn and assist the stricken sloop, nothing remained of the corvette but floating, burning wreckage.

* * *

The scene aboard the *Black Dragon* was a jubilant one as the last of Angie's crew was helped aboard. Still in that yellow dress, Rose looked around for Angie, finding her standing at the rail of the ship and looking out into the sea. Slowly approaching, she stood beside her, gingerly grasping the rail as she also fixed her gaze on the dying sloop.

Slowly, Angie's ship rolled to its left side, and as the sea covered her forward deck, a loud crack sounded from her, she twisted, and her mainmast succumbed and fell. From there, the little ship's end was a graceful descent beneath the waves, and in a moment she slipped away. Bubbles marked where she had gone down and a little loose wood drifted back to the surface.

Angie set her jaw, her mouth held tight as she watched the final moment of her ship. Drawing a deep breath, she forced it from her hard, and finally lowered her eyes.

"I'm sorry," Rose offered softly.

Not looking at her, Angie growled, "You owe me a ship."

"Aye," Rose agreed, "that I do, that and more."

Angie pushed off of the rail and turned away, walking toward the other side of the ship.

Rose felt for her, and also felt that the wise thing would be to stay out of her way. As she watched her disappear below, she was not aware of Cannonburg's approach until he was standing right beside her and her eyes snapped to him.

He was also watching after the tall young woman, and he had a mug of ale in his hand. Nodding as he leaned back against the ship's rail, he assured, "She'll be fine, Lass. Not the first ship she's seen sink and probably won't be the last."

"Sure glad you arrived when you did," Rose said straightly. "We were in a hard way."

"Figured something was wrong when you didn't catch up to us last night," he informed.

She nodded, then anxiously asked, "Where is the Captain?"

Johnny motioned to the captain's cabin with his head. "Retired as soon as we took down the corvette. Been in a hard way since last night." When Rose headed that way, he seized her arm and stopped her, shaking his head when he had her attention. "Best to leave him put, Lass. When he's like this he's more likely to put you over the rail than speak kind words to ye."

Staring back up at him, she slowly shook her head and questioned, "What do you mean? He sent people to rescue me, so surely he'd want—"

"Wait for him to be ready to see ye," Cannonburg warned. "Take me word on this, Lass. He goes inside of himself like that and finds him a bottle then he'll not hear what ye say. He can't hear anything beyond the past that put him here."

"Tell me," she insisted.

He huffed a breath and turned away from her, leaning his forearms on the rail as he stared out into the sea. "It's not me place, Rose."

She gently grasped his shoulder. "Johnny, please tell me."

Cannonburg lowered his eyes to his mug, took a gulp, then looked back out to the passing sea. "Twas many years ago. Jones was making quite a living as first mate on a cargo ship shuttling supplies to the American colonies and here to the Caribbean. Had him a nice life and was educated as some kind of engineer. Had a wife and family. Liked the new world enough to move them here from Scotland." He smiled. "Married himself some Prussian beauty and she was his life, her and the wee ones they'd made. He always talked of leaving the sea and starting him a plantation. Wanted to make his living from the land, he did, so he saved every coin he could." He was silent for a long moment, his eyes lowering to the water. When he spoke again, it was with regretful words. "She wanted to visit home, show off the baby they'd made only six months before, so he bought her passage aboard the best liner that crossed the ocean. Ship didn't make it fifty miles."

Rose drew a gasp, her eyes widening as she grasped her chest.

"Didn't go down to storm or sea monster," Johnny went on, "it went down to Navy guns. Heavy frigate ran her down and pounded her until she sank. They left no one alive. Word got back to Jones and he turned himself inside. I've seen grief and madness, but I've never seen it come so quiet to a man. A terrible vengeance was born that day, a vengeance that spawned this very ship."

Mueller, who still wore the shirt and trousers of the British uniform but had shed the coat, had approached unnoticed, also gripping a mug of ale in his hand. With a gentle grasp, he took Rose's shoulder, drawing her attention to him. "That's a man you'd best give a distance when that vengeance speaks to him. Losing a wife and son does things to a man, it makes a man someone else and he loses who he was after a time."

"I've seen that he's still a good man," Rose informed softly.

Cannonburg turned and leaned on the rail, looking back out into the sea as he countered, "A good man lives in there, aye, but the monster dwelling inside is what rules that man. Give that monster time to sleep and wait for him to call on ye."

Lowering her eyes, she nodded, then turned away from them and absently said, "I need a drink."

She found rum in the galley, and a few glasses later could not clear her thoughts, nor could she quiet the voice that begged her to go to the big pirate captain despite the warnings. Though the galley was mostly empty, she found she could not think. Once enough rum was in her, good judgment abandoned her yet again.

Before she realized what she was doing, she had wandered from the galley with the half empty bottle of rum. In a few moments she was closing the door to the captain's cabin as quietly as she could. Her eyes were fixed on the big man who sat in front of the painting across the room, facing the painting that hung over the bed. He was staring up at it, not moving, not making a sound. She stood at the door and just watched him for a time, hesitant to approach but the urge to do so was too strong to be denied.

Her dress ruffled very little as she padded lightly to him. The planks of the floor creaked gently under her bare feet, very softly as if they did not want to disturb the Captain either. At any moment she expected him to order her away, but as she stopped right beside him, her eyes now fixed on the painting, he remained silent.

For a long moment no words were exchanged, no sound but the creaks and groans made by the ship as it plowed through the sea.

Finally, timidly looking to him, she found his eyes fixed on the painting. He held an empty rum bottle in his hands, propped up on his thigh and only his slow, deep breathing gave away that he was still alive. His face was blank, no expression, like he was a living statue.

Turning toward him, she slowly settled her behind on the bed, looking back to the painting as she did. Absently, she raised the bottle to her lips and took a long drink from it, then she lowered it to the bed between her legs.

His voice finally ripped through the silence with, "Ya drink too much."

After long seconds, she countered, "I have my reasons." She took another sip, then offered him the bottle.

Without looking that way, he took it from her and took many loud gulps from it.

Once again they stared at the painting in silence. Rose reached to him and he handed her the bottle and for a few moments they traded the rum back and forth.

His eyes finally slid to her, his head turning ever so slightly. She was staring at the painting, and a tear rolled down her cheek.

Rose glanced at him, then quickly wiped the tear away and turned her eyes down. Swallowing hard, she offered, "Thank you for coming for me."

"I didn't," he corrected. "Sent a party for ya. Got to keep sure that I get me powder."

With a slight nod, she just stared at the floor, then softly said, "You still didn't have to. Captain Angie lost her ship in the process."

He looked back to the painting. "Everyone made it back all right, and I'll get her another ship, so no worries."

She smiled slightly. "You sink everything you run into."

"Not everything," he sighed. "Sometimes they give up without even hearing me cannons."

"That's a shame," she sighed. "They're such lovely cannons."

His eyes cut to her again.

"Will you ever tell me about her?" Rose asked as she stared at the painting.

"Nothin' to tell," he replied softly as he looked back to the painting.

Rose nodded and took another pull from the bottle. Mustering her courage, she drew a deep breath and managed, "I'll not pick at you over it, Captain. I will only hope that you can see beyond that painting someday."

Jones looked to her with those hard eyes.

She returned his gaze with eyes that were soft and vulnerable. "I will hope that you can see what you have in front of you." She stood from the bed, then sank to her knees beside his chair, looking up at him with her big eyes as she propped the bottle on his thigh. "I'll never replace her, Cannonflash, and you'll never replace Jeffrey, but right here and right now we have the moment. We are here for each other when they cannot be here with us."

He stared down at her for a very long moment, then he took the bottle from her and raised it to his mouth as he turned his gaze back to the painting, and he took a long drink from the bottle.

Tears welled up in Rose's eyes as she looked back to the painting herself and laid her head down on his lap, sliding her hand across his legs as the other grasped the back of his chair. Ever so gently, Jones hand found her and gently stroked her long hair and she slowly closed her eyes.

Chapter 9

A MORNING OF DARKNESS

They shared his bed, but he did not take her that night. As they slept, she was curled up beside him and knew even in her dreams that his heavy arm was around her all night.

Cannonflash rose early and without waking her, and when her eyes finally opened she found herself alone in his bed, covered to her shoulders, and she smiled as she saw the empty rum bottle lying on his pillow.

She did not change out of the dress and padded barefoot out onto the deck, stopping as she looked around her at the patchy fog that surrounded them. Glancing about, she saw that the crew looked nervous and the feeling about the ship was unnaturally tense.

Finding a crewman who was at task rolling a length of thick rope, she greeted, "Good morning."

He glanced at her and nodded.

"Where might I find Captain Cannonflash?" she asked.

The man motioned behind her with his chin, finally answering, "Captain's at the helm."

 177

She turned and looked over her shoulder, sure enough finding him behind the big wheel of his ship with both hands gripping it. He had that look about him that he got when he was concentrating, when he was deep in thought. Still, a smile touched her lips and she headed that way, gracefully climbing the ladder and not worried that the passing wind was blowing her skirt about and dangerously high a couple of times.

As she reached the steering deck, she folded her hands behind her and swayed her hips and shoulders as she walked slowly to the Captain, her eyes on the deck before her as she approached. She felt less a ship's captain now, less a woman nearly thirty. There was a playful, flirty teenager within her and she allowed herself to succumb to the feelings that brewed inside of her each time she saw the big pirate captain.

Jones seemed to ignore her and instead kept his eyes forward as he gently worked the wheel of his ship in subtle corrections.

Rose strode with slow steps behind him, running one hand along his back as she passed, and finally she stood by his side with her hands behind her again and just enjoyed the passing breeze in her hair and the caress of her skirt against her thighs. Her eyes cut to him. He was not responding to her presence at all. Something was on his mind and she did not want to stir his ire, but she also wanted him to take notice of her and this conflict tugged at her.

Daring to move just a little closer, she glanced around to make certain no one was watching, and she playfully bumped him with her shoulder.

A moment later he bumped her back with his elbow.

With a little smile on her lips, she looked up at him again, fully this time, but got only a glance in return. Directing her attention forward again, she cleared her throat and asked in a more professional manner, "So what heading do we have this morning, Captain Jones?"

"Easterly," was his reply.

She nodded, then looked around and observed, "Lots of fog today."

"Aye," he answered. Jones raised his hand, glancing down at an old compass.

Rose considered, her eyes glancing about before her, then she looked up at the big pirate captain and hesitantly observed, "That takes us away from Tortuga."

"Aye," Jones replied again.

"May I ask where?" she asked sweetly.

"Nowhere you've been," he answered, "and nowhere you're going. I've something to attend to and then we'll be on our way to Tortuga."

"That worries me a little," she admitted.

Jones loosed a breath, showing his impatience with a clenched jaw.

She continued anyway, "We just need to get there before Smith does."

"I'm aware," he growled.

"May I ask what this place is called?" she dared.

He made a sudden adjustment at the wheel, and at last replied, "Isla de la Mortis."

Her eyes widening, she slowly raised her chin and breathed, "Island of the Dead." She grew more nervous as he sailed on and said nothing more. Swallowing hard, she assured, "Captain Jones, that place is a myth. It doesn't—"

"Been there a few times, I have," he interrupted, "and it's no place you need to go. You'll stay shipside with the rest while I attend me business."

She looked away and said under her breath, "This is insane."

"Go on to the galley," he ordered. "Harold has a stout breakfast prepared for ye."

"Menudo?" she asked grimly, still looking away.

"I think so," he sighed. "Just go and find yourself out."

* * *

Rose entered the galley and took her seat, a blank but fearful stare about her face. Before she realized, there were two men sitting beside her to the left and she looked that way.

Mueller sat on the other side of Harold and they both looked back at her with strained eyes.

"Isla de la Mortis," she said without realizing. "He says he's been there before."

Harold looked away from her and took a long drink from the bottle he held.

Nodding, Mueller leaned his elbows on the table, folding his hands before him as he softly said, "Aye, that he has. Looking for someone, he is, and every time he hopes to find her there."

"Emily," she breathed.

With another nod, Mueller confirmed, "Aye. Emily. That island collects the dead of the sea and they await their turn to move on. Davy Jones'll come for 'em, or the light, or any of many legends about the crossing over. Read the Bible a time or two, meself, and reckon I'd heard of such a place from there." His eyes snapped to her. "Ever heard of Purgatory, Miss O'scarlett?"

A chill ran through her and her eyes widened as she nodded.

"It collects the wrongly dead," Mueller went on, his eyes finding his hands again. "Those who die before their time wait there. Sometimes they rot, sometimes they cannot even do that. They just wait. Can drive a soul mad, it can, and when the soul goes mad it looks for vengeance against the living. They have no laws and any sane man fears the walking dead."

"You've been there?" she asked hesitantly.

He nodded, and so did Harold.

And it was Harold who answered this time. "Went a couple of years back. Thought old Cannonflash could use someone watching his back. Found out I fear the walking dead as much as the next man and they knew it." He shook his head. "Only thing kept them off me was fear they had."

"Fear the dead have?"

His eyes cut to her. "Men fear the walking dead, Missy, but the walking dead fear Cannonflash. Had a run in with 'im, they did, many years ago. Found out he can break the bones of the dead like he breaks the bones of the living. Found out he's a man of terrible vengeance and they're afraid of that vengeance now. That vengeance robs him of the fear he should have for 'em, so they stay clear of him like most living men do."

Rose looked away from them, her thought stirring fear and uncertainty within her. Finally, she asked, "You... You've seen these walking dead?"

"Aye," both Harold and Mueller answered.

Again her eyes darted about, then she stood from her chair and turned around.

Raising his brow, Harold turned toward her as he called after her, "I've some breakfast waiting for you, Missy."

"Not hungry," she replied, "but thank you."

* * *

With a thick fog about that was unnatural and somehow unholy, nobody could tell if the sun was even up, or how high. A glow surrounded this place, an evil glow. Waves could be heard lapping the shore in the distance, but no shore could be seen. No birds could be heard and only the activity of the men and the occasional creak or moan of the ship cut the silence.

The *Black Dragon* was anchored in a lagoon of still water. The place smelled musky, not like the open sea or even the islands they had visited. It was a damp, still odor that was of rot and decay, and somewhere was the occasional whiff of death. A more forbidding place Rose had never seen and as she strode slowly toward the center of the great ship where the dinghy was about to be launched. She had more a feeling of foreboding than she had ever experienced.

She had changed into her tight fitting black trousers, a loosely fitting gray shirt that was left unlaced almost all of the way down her chest and her most comfortable boots. A clean, white skull cap was tied around her head, keeping her long hair under control and behind her for the most part where it was secured into a pony tail. A wide leather belt held her cutlass, two pistols, dagger and two pouches of shot and powder wads. The pistols were, of course, loaded and ready to fire.

As she neared the dinghy, which had been prepared to be launched and was only awaiting Cannonflash to step aboard, she saw the Captain chatting with Cannonburg, and he looked serious. Johnny stiffly nodded, and did not respond otherwise. The feel aboard the ship was somehow even more tense.

One of the crew saw her and nudged the Captain, and when he looked, so did everyone else.

The quiet attention was unnerving, but still she strode right up to Cannonflash, looking up at him with her thumbs hooked in her belt. Reaching him, she asked, "Are you ready to go, Captain?"

"Aye," he assured, "and I'll be goin' alone." He looked to Cannonburg and ordered, "Lower the boat and be ready to shove off as soon as I return."

"Aye, Captain," Johnny assured, turning to his station.

As Jones climbed aboard the boat, Rose strode toward him with angry clops of her boots on the deck as she insisted, "You'll need me along. I'm not—"

"You'll stay as ordered!" he shouted, his predator's eyes locked on hers.

Put in her place, Rose stepped back and watched as the boat and Cannonflash were lowered to the sea without her. She angrily folded her arms, her eyes narrow and a little snarl on her mouth as it reached the sea between the hulls and the ship's Captain began to untie the ropes that kept it tethered to the pulleys.

Jones himself was consumed with what he was doing and his attention was there. Once the boat was released, he raised the sail and sat down on the plank to the rear. Just enough breeze caught the canvas to propel it slowly forward and he steered it expertly between the black hulls of his mammoth ship. Right as he cleared the bows he heard in Captain O'scarlett's voice, "Woo hoo!" and turned his eyes up as she swung down on a rope from the port hull and landed perfectly on the bow of the dinghy.

Throwing the rope aside to make certain it cleared the rigging, she made her way to the back of the boat, a very satisfied little smile on her face as she sat down on a plank directly in front of Cannonflash, facing him as she propped her palms behind her and folded her legs rather seductively.

Staring back at her, he scowled, growling just a little.

"Damn woman pirates," she spat. "They just won't listen to a word you say. Next thing you know they're disobeying orders, seducing you in the night and swinging from every part of the ship."

Jones set his jaw.

Raising her brow, Rose half turned her head and informed, "You've got one aboard your ship who deserves a really good spanking, she does."

He heaved an angry breath and looked past her, making a slight correction to the rudder. His other hand held a rope that controlled the rigging and he let out a little slack as he turned the rudder the other way.

"Want me to help with something?" she asked hopefully.

"I want you quiet," he snarled.

"Yes sir," she barked.

His eyes found her again and narrowed ominously.

She smiled back, ever so slightly. "Okay, Captain Jones, now that you've managed to get me away from the men, I should tell you something."

He just stared back impatiently.

"Fine," she sighed, "I admit it. I like you. I like everything about you. You have a way of growing on a girl. I suppose you dragged me all the way out here to make me confess that."

He looked beyond her again, pulling in on the rigging.

Her hands grasped the plank she sat on right outside of her hips and she looked around into the fog, almost expecting to see something come at them any second.

Moments passed and neither spoke.

"How far are we going?" she asked suddenly.

"Shore," he growled, still not looking at her.

Rose nodded, still glancing about. "So, in this fog, how do we know we've arrived?"

The bow of the boat hit sand and it stopped quite suddenly, and Rose barked a scream as she was thrown over the plank she sat on and slammed back-first into the bottom of the boat. The breath exploded from her and she lay there collecting her wits for long seconds. Blinking to clear her vision, she raised her head and looked at Cannonflash, who stood over her with that same stone-like expression.

"We've arrived," he growled.

She nodded and watched as he stepped over her. Scrambling to her feet, she awkwardly followed and vaulted over the side, her feet landing in shallow water.

This was a sizeable boat and would normally take a team of at least three large men to pull up onto the beach, but Jones took the rope in one hand and jerked it half way from the water with one mighty yank. When he turned around, Rose took his side and looked trustingly up at him.

"This isn't for your eyes," he snarled.

"I understand," she assured, "but I would still be at your side, Captain."

He huffed an impatient breath and strode toward what appeared to be an overgrown jungle.

Visibility was very poor and Rose glanced about nervously. Something that felt like a small tree branch hit her head and she was quick to ward it off with her hand. Stringy moss hung from the trees all around and the smell was horrible, like rotting wood and meat. Death lingered in the air and there was little sound to be heard, no birds nor insects, just the thick air that was heavy with wetness. Everything around was damp and sticky and she touched as little as she could.

The jungle trail opened into a clearing and she entered behind Jones, her breath catching as she found herself looking at what appeared to be an abandoned town of some kind. Even through the thick fog she could make out what looked like an old tavern, a blacksmith shop, a tailor... Her heart thundered as she also saw movement. Following the big man with her as closely as she could, she barely managed to fight off the urge to grasp his hand.

There, through the fog, she could see people walking in front of them. Perhaps this place was not abandoned after all. Swallowing hard, she stayed close to Cannonflash as her eyes darted about and her heart pounded harder with each step. Her mind bordered on blind terror and she made herself draw comfort from the man who she wanted to cling to like a frightened little girl. Of course, dignity would not allow that, but the thought remained.

Jones stopped and Rose, her attention to one side, ran into him, then took a step back and offered him a nervous little smile to respond to the scowl he turned on her.

A breath shrieked into her as she saw three people approaching through the fog. They were no more than ominous black shadows and their steps were slow and deliberate, lumbering along like they were drunk.

They were finally close enough to see through the fog in better detail, and Rose clamped a hand over her mouth as her wide eyes locked on them.

The men who approached were skeletal figures. Most of the flesh had rotted off of them many years ago and what held the bones together was a mystery. Ancient clothing was tattered and gray, hanging off of the living skeletons like the moss that hung off the trees. Leather parts were better preserved. Belts were more or less intact, shoulder straps, and one wore a leather harness that still had two rusty pistols and a dagger hanging from it. Their heads were the most alarming parts of them. There was almost no flesh to them, no eyes, no lips. They were the gray and white of old bones. One of them still wore a mariner's triangular hat. The attention of all three was focused on Jones, but two of them shifted that attention to Rose.

Rose knew weapons were probably of little use against the dead but she grasped the handle of one of the pistol on her hip anyway. She did her best to hide the terror that coursed through her with each heartbeat, but was barely holding her own.

The skeleton with the hat kept its attention on Jones, craning its neck back to look up at him as it pointed a bony finger at him. When it spoke, its voice was strained and distant, and gurgled a little. "Why back here, Jones?"

"Ye know why I'm here," the big pirate captain snapped back. "Move aside."

"He told you not to come back here," the skeleton warned.

Jones countered, "You'll move or I'll go through ye."

The three skeletons focused their attention on him for a tense moment, then they moved aside, the one with the hat warning, "You were told about coming here, Jones."

Cannonflash strode past them, growling back, "You were told about getting in me way."

The skeleton with the hat shook its head.

Rose followed but she kept her eyes on the skeletons. When they all three turned their attention on her, she smiled nervously and waggled her fingers at them in a friendly gesture as she passed by, and the one tipped its hat to her.

Jones strode fearlessly down the main street of the forgotten village and many of the dead paused to watch. Tension was high and Rose's fear was not abated as she kept up with him with quick strides. Her eyes darted around without rest, fearing the dead would attack them at any moment, attack them or worse. Her imagination buzzed about dauntlessly and fed the terror that this place had seeded into her. Still, she would not leave Jones' side even as he stormed to the steps of a dilapidated mansion at the edge of town and up the stone steps that the jungle had spent many years trying to reclaim.

At the top near the front door the fog was not so thick, not there at all. Five skeletons in varying degrees of decay were gathered around an old round table, apparently looking down at some old parchments, one could not tell from this distance.

The ancient wooden stairs creaked and groaned under the weight of the big pirate captain. Jones' eyes were locked on the skeletons in an ominous, impatient glare as he ascended the steps with a dreadful purpose.

The skeletons noticed him from the first step and all five of them turned from the table and watched him approach them. One of them reached for the sword on its belt, but the most ornately dressed of them reached to it and took its shoulder, shaking its head in a silent order to stand down.

Jones never went for his weapon even as he reached the top to confront the five.

Rose wisely stayed behind him, content to peer around his arm and listen from where she was.

The ornate dressed one, wearing an older British uniform with many metals on it and the dilapidated hat of an officer, raised himself up, looking up at the big pirate captain through empty eye sockets as it folded his skeletal arms and demanded in a forced voice, "Why are you back here, Jones?"

Cannonflash seemed to ignore the other four skeletons present and loomed over the officer as he growled back, "Ye know why I'm here, and I'll not take the time for your games."

"Go back," the skeleton ordered. "She's not here, never has been. Crossed over years ago and did not come through here."

"She was taken before it was her time," Jones snapped. "Such spirits taken early by the sea come here!"

"I've no reason to keep her from you," the skeleton countered. "Best way to get rid of you is to show her to you, but she's not here. Go now, Jones. You've no place here. Not yet."

Cannonflash looked away, grumbling, "She hasn't crossed over yet. She couldn't have."

"You've many enemies here," the skeleton informed, "and that number grows day by day. This is no place for you, so be on your way."

Suddenly grabbing the skeleton by the neck, Jones pulled him close and warned, "If I find out she's here and you've kept her from me—"

"What will you do?" the skeleton snapped. "There is no life to take from me. It was taken long before even your grandfather was born." He took Jones' arm and pushed it away from his neck, and Jones seemed to let him. "Thanks to you there are more souls than ever coming through here. I've a hard enough time keeping everything in line and I work until the last of my bones hurts." He turned back toward the table, planting his skeletal hands on the parchments there as he leaned over it. "Go now. You're frightening to the dead."

With another growl, Cannonflash watched the four advisors join the skeleton officer at the table, then he wheeled around.

Rose dodged out of the way as he stormed past her, then she looked back at the skeletons before following at a brisk pace.

"Jones!" the officer summoned.

Cannonflash stopped and turned toward the officer, and Rose nervously did as well.

One would swear that the skeletal face of the officer wore a smile. "You've made many enemies here as I've said, and you've added many more in recent months. Not all fear you when they've nothing but revenge to keep them here."

As he turned back to the table, the other four laughed in raspy, gurgling laughs as they returned to their duty.

His eyes narrowing, Cannonflash turned again, stopping after only a couple of steps.

Rose stopped beside him, raising her chin as her wide eyes saw many of the dead standing before them.

There were six of them, all in different stages of decay. Three wore the aged and tattered uniforms of the navy; others were in the simple and decayed garb of pirates or other mariners. All of them were armed with cutlass, dagger or saber. These walking dead did not seem to fear him as others had, nor did he fear them. They did not advance, but they held their ground right in his path and Rose's.

Clenching his hands into tight fists, Jones ordered, "Stand aside, ye rotted dogs."

One, a British mariner, stepped forward, holding his saber low before him as he countered, "No, Jones. Perhaps it's time you joined us here, seeing as how you put most of us here."

"That's your problem," Cannonflash growled. "You'll move out of me path or I'll do to you what I did last time, savvy?"

Two of the skeletons' attention shifted to Rose, and one pointed to her. "Perhaps that one will stay. She's pretty, and she fears us."

Rose gulped a breath and took a step back. Her eyes could not get any wider and hurt a little, though she was not in a position to do anything about it.

Drawing his cutlass, Jones shouted, "Maybe you'll have another lesson from the man who put you here!"

The skeletons held an advantage this time, and they knew it. Three of them now had their attention focused on Rose while the other three squared off against Cannonflash.

Now is when Rose felt more the helpless damsel than she ever had, but in the presence of the big pirate, she refused to show weakness. Now was the time to courageously make a stand beside the pirate who held her heart. Now was the time to swallow back her fear as she had done many times before. Now was the time to fight to the last. Now was the time to *not* soil herself!

The skeletons advanced, and so did Jones. Two more emerged from the fog to Jones' side and got but a glance from him. He was not afraid of them and this clearly gave them pause. It also fed a little courage into the scared-witless woman at his side.

She forced her eyes to narrow and she crossed her forearms over her belly as she grasped the pistols that were shoved into her belt.

The skeletons raised their weapons and charged. Jones howled an ominous battle cry and swung his cutlass hard, his blade meeting theirs and sweeping them aside in one motion. He half turned and kicked one, knocking it to the ground.

Out of the corner of her eye, Rose saw movement in the fog behind the big pirate and her hands moved in one motion, drawing the pistols as fluidly as if she'd done so a thousand times. Her left hand directed straight ahead while right hand went out to her side with a straight and level aim, and this is where her attention went. The pistols fired together, the right one sending a ball behind Jones and shattering the skull of the skeleton that had emerged behind him with its cutlass held high. It fell quickly. The other ball slammed into the shoulder of the far left skeleton, severing its sword arm.

As the arm hit the ground, all three that were squaring off with her looked down at it, then to the now one armed skeleton as it looked back to the other two, then to Rose.

She tossed the pistols away and drew her cutlass and dagger, her confidence growing a little with each heartbeat.

While the first reached down for its arm, the other two raised their weapons and charged.

Though busy with his own four, Jones arm swung over and he buried the blade of his dagger into the head of the closest one, then he grabbed it by the neck and hurled it into two that he was fighting.

As the first of Rose's opponents worked to get his arm back into place, the other attacked her with the movements of an expert swordsman and she found herself off balance and retreating as she parried over and over and raised her dagger in quick motions to block thrusts and cuts that her own sword could not reach in time. This walking dead man was one who clearly outmatched her and she found herself fighting just to survive second to second. She spun away from a thrust and parried quickly as the skeleton cut toward her with amazing speed. She was tiring quickly, but the dead did not tire at all.

Continuing her retreat, she fought with everything she had, her own blade a blur as it swept to defeat his time after time. An unexpectedly hard slash was caught on her dagger and the hilt was torn from her hand. She gasped a breath and turned again, still retreating as she called, "Jones!" Something stopped her, the solid feel of a tree, and she could retreat no further.

She caught a slash on her blade, then another. Trying to spin around the tree, she hesitated as the skeleton's sword cut downward in her path and she retreated back.

The first skeleton, with his arm reattached, approached on the skeleton swordsman's left, holding his cutlass ready, his whole focus and attention on her.

Unexpectedly, the skeleton she was fighting poised its weapon and backed away a step, allowing the other to come abreast of him. As she stared back at it and tried to catch her breath, it nodded to her and rasped, "Well done, Lass. Well done. You deserve a quick death."

Taking the time for a couple of quick breaths, she poised her weapon before her and insisted, "If I'm to die today then I'll die fighting, thank you."

"As you wish," it accepted.

Both skeletons raised their weapons and Rose prepared to spin away from the tree and retreat anew, and make her way back to Cannonflash who still fought for his own life.

The swordsman thrust at her and she spun to avoid it, raising her blade barely in time to catch the slash that came at her. The second charged and thrust as she parried to avoid the other skeleton's expert swing and she could not get to the thrusting blade in time, but a saber from behind her did.

Her shoulder was grasped and she was pulled backward, behind another skeleton whose blade knocked the swordsman's away, and this skeleton delivered a hard left cross to the swordsman's jaw that sent him stumbling backward. Without missing a stride, he cut his saber through the air with a fluid motion and severed the head of the second that pressed its attack against Rose, then it half turned and kicked the beheaded skeleton hard in the chest.

The skeleton swordsman reset its disjointed jaw and turned its attention back on the newcomer, poising its weapon as it took its stance.

Rose finally noticed that the skeleton that defended her was wearing a British officer's uniform that looked very old, very worn, one that looked as if it had been buried and washed with sea water. Though faded, he still wore it proudly. What did not go unnoticed were the three holes in the back of the coat. As he motioned her back with his free hand, she found herself stepping backward more out of reflex than fear.

The swordsman lowered its head and squared off against its new opponent, warning, "This doesn't involve you."

Answering in a voice that with the same rasp the rest of them and a noticeable Irish accent, the defender countered, "I'm afraid it does, and you'll be told once to stand down."

Something about that voice tugged at her memory and she felt a chill wash through her.

Having none of the threats, the swordsman attacked anyway and his blade was met by Rose's defender. The two dueled savagely and Rose stood dumbly by as she wondered what to do. Movement on the ground to her right drew her attention and she found the other skeleton, still clutching its cutlass, on its hands and knees groping about for its severed skull. Shuffling sideways that direction, she kicked the skull with the side of her boot and sent it rolling away right before its bony hand could discover it.

One of Jones' opponents hit the ground and shattered when it did. Looking that way, Rose saw that he was now only facing two, and these two were backing away from him.

The skeleton that had defended her caught her attention again. It seemed outmatched as well and was backing away, and yet there was a determination to it that told Rose that it would never yield, that it would fight to the finish, whatever that was for the walking dead.

With a thrust that was caught by the defender's blade, the swordsman swirled its blade around and expertly disarmed its opponent, then it directed the tip of its sword at the other skeleton's chest and advanced a step.

Rose's defender barked, "You can't kill me and you know it."

"I told you to stay out of my business, O'scarlett," the other skeleton snapped back.

Rose's breath caught and she raised a hand to her mouth, her wide eyes finding the skeleton who had rushed to her defense. Nothing could have prepared her for that. Nothing! Still holding her cutlass, she looked to the ground where her defender's saber lay and advanced a step, sliding her foot under it, then she froze and shrieked a breath as the blade of a sword blurred toward her and stopped against the skin of her throat.

"Well, now," another skeleton with a French accent observed. "What is this treachery that comes to our midst, eh?"

She cut her eyes that way and saw the skeleton out of the corner of her eye. It was well dressed in the blue uniform of a French soldier, still wearing all of its medals, its ceremonial hat, its ruffled shirt, and it was oblivious to the presence of the big pirate that approached it from behind.

Raising her brow, Rose informed, "I hope for your sake that you can't still feel pain."

The swordsman turned as Cannonflash's blade split the French skeleton from skull to pelvis. Bones and pieces of bones rained down as the skeleton collapsed. As the swordsman turned its weapon on Jones, Rose kicked the saber to the skeleton who had defended her and he caught it by the hilt with perfect form and timing.

When the swordsman engaged Captain Jones it found itself facing an opponent it was unaccustomed to and not prepared for. As it slashed, Jones caught the blade with his dagger and struck back with his cutlass, forcing the skeleton immediately on the defensive. The heavy blade Cannonflash wielded and the massive strength of his arm overwhelmed the skeleton swordsman and in a moment the big pirate's cutlass crashed through its collar bone, ribs, spine. Without ceremony, the swordsman collapsed in pieces.

Jones turned on the last armed skeleton standing and poised his weapon for battle.

Rose's defender slowly raised his hilt to his face, directing the blade up in an honorable salute. When Cannonflash lowered his weapon and raised his chin, the skeleton lowered his blade and motioned him on with his head, insisting, "Get her to safety."

"Jeffery," Rose breathed.

The skeleton looked to her and said with soft words, "I'd hoped you would never see me like this, my Love."

She took the last two steps to him, her mouth ajar and her eyes wide as she slowly shook her head.

He raised his skeletal hand to her cheek, brushing her soft skin with the backs of his skeletal fingers as he said, "You have to leave. Go now before others come."

She grasped his hand, tears rolling from her eyes as she asked, "Why are you here?"

"Berkley," he replied. "Get those documents to the Admiralty in London, finish my work and bring justice to those he killed, and I can move on."

Rose nodded, still clinging to his hand as she strained to assure, "I will."

Sheathing his weapon, he looked to Cannonflash and informed, "His crimes have touched you as well, Captain Jones. I beg you, help to bring him down. Please help her."

Jones nodded, then demanded, "Emily."

"She's moved on," Jeffery replied. "You have to as well. Now go. Get her away from here before they can reassemble and come at you again. Please, just go." He offered Rose's hand to the big pirate and repeated, "Get her to safety. I'll hold them off."

When Cannonflash took Rose's hand, the skeleton drew his weapon again and turned to face the skeletons who had been beaten down, the skeletons who slowly reassembled their parts. One, the skeleton Rose had shot first, was on his knees picking up the shards of its skull and collecting them on its hand. Another drug its torso toward his legs. Still another groped around for its arm and part of its missing skull.

"Please go," Jeffery implored.

"What about you?" Rose whimpered.

Holding his weapon ready, the skeleton informed, "Don't worry over me, Rose, and don't end up here. Finish my work and raise our son to be the fine young man he can be. Live your life as best you can. You are a good woman, now go make some man as happy as you made me." He looked to Cannonflash and nodded once to him, insisting, "Be well, Captain Jones, and good fortune to you. And please watch over her."

Nodding back, Jones agreed, "Aye, Lieutenant O'scarlett. Be well, Sir." With that he turned and pulled Rose along, past the skeletons who labored to pull themselves back together and past those who knew better than to challenge Cannonflash Jones.

* * *

Sundown would find the huge black ship cutting through the water toward Tortuga. The setting sun was on the port side as the ship sailed north and the crew seemed at ease for the first time that day. Jones' return from that island was usually met with days of tension, but this day they could sense that he was not so short tempered and impatient as usual. He was still preoccupied, but his disposition with the crew was far more normal.

On the other hand, Rose spoke not a word as she had come aboard and she did not attend the evening meal. She seemed to avoid everyone on the ship and had only been seen in the galley to fetch a couple of bottles of rum, bottles that stayed with her the entire day.

Finding her at the bow of the ship sitting between two cannons with her feet hanging over the deck, Jones was slow to approach her. Something had happened in her mind on that island, and his as well. Her feelings for that dead husband of hers seemed fresh and an old wound had been freshly opened and bled with all her emotions. Behind her lay her boots, and between her boots an empty rum bottle. Where one of the hundred pounder cannons was to be positioned, she sat in its place with her feet dangling over the deck. Her arm was wrapped around the rail to the side, a rail that was there to keep the crew members from falling overboard in the heat of battle where thick smoke could obscure one's vision of exactly where the deck ended. These rails had once surrounded the different hulls of the ship, but now they were repositioned for the safety of the crew and provided a good point for a drunk woman to keep herself braced against the pitching of the big ship.

Jones stood behind her and leaned on the cannon that was behind her, looking toward the horizon in silence for some time. When she raised the bottle to her mouth and took a couple of gulps, he observed, "Ye drink too much."

She slammed the bottle down beside her and did not look back at him as she shouted with slurred words, "I talked to dead people, Jones! Dead people! And dead people tried to kill me today! There were dead people all over the place and they were just walking around like anyone else would!"

"Told you to stay on the ship," he reminded.

Rose laughed and slapped her thigh over and over. "You're a funny man, Cabinflush, funny man. Did you really expect me to stay on the ship with you marching yourself into God knows what?" She finally turned and looked up at him, rage in her eyes as she hissed, "You just let me go there. You knew what was there and you just let me waltz in with you. Almost got killed! You even care about that?"

He growled a sigh and looked back to the horizon.

Scrambling to her feet, she had the bottle in her hand as she stepped up to him and grabbed his vest, shouting, "I was over him, do you hear me? I had finally moved on! I had finally let him go and there he was! How am I supposed to live with this, huh? How can I live with this? How?"

Jones pulled away from her and turned to walk away.

"And just when I think you and I meant something to each other," she rambled on, "you go there to find your dead wife!"

He stopped, and his hands clenched into tight fists.

Rose staggered up behind him, grasping the back of his jerkin with her free hand as she cried, "And you didn't find her. You went there looking and you didn't find her. And I found someone I had to let go." She leaned into him, crying hard as emotions poured from her. When he turned around, she wrapped her arms around him and held him as tightly as she could. "I'm sorry, Jones. I'm sorry. I wish we had found her. I'm sorry." She turned from him, staggered, and fell against the cannon, then all the way to the deck. Lying on the planks, she looked up at him and sobbed, "It isn't fair."

Jones turned and walked away from her, and as darkness settled, she cried herself to sleep between the heavy cannons of the *Black Dragon*.

Chapter 10

RECKONING AND BETRAYAL

Rose awoke where she had fallen asleep the night before. The chilly morning wind was kept at bay by a gray wool blanket that she found herself tucked into. Her arm had been her pillow and the mostly empty bottle of rum still sat where she had left it and was just within reach. The sun was not quite up and early morning light illuminated the clouds to the east in an orange glow. The sea ahead was still black with glints of white as the retreating moon lit the wave tops.

She pushed herself up and quickly raised a hand to her throbbing head, tightly closing her eyes against the pain of yet another hangover. The ship felt like it was spinning around her and her stomach was queasy.

Struggling to stand, she held on to the cannon to keep herself upright, unsure if the pitching of the ship was the sea or her own unsteady legs. When she looked down and found her boots, she reached to them and picked them up, then the blanket which she threw over her shoulders and wrapped around her, and she left the rum where it was.

Rose entered the galley feeling dizzy, nauseous, and drained of most of her very life. Nobody was there yet at this unholy hour and she sat where she always did, dropping her boots beside her chair and pulling the blanket close to her. Folding her arms on the table, she lowered her head to them and closed her eyes, and for some time drifted in and out of sleep.

A strong hand gently stroked across her hair and she drew a quick breath as she was roused and lifted her head, her sleepy, bloodshot eyes glancing about and finally finding Harold standing beside her.

He smiled and stroked her hair again. "Thought you might come here first, Lass. Looks like you had you a rough night with that rum again."

She nodded and laid her head back down. Shame lanced through her as she stared at the Captain's chair and tears glossed her eyes.

"Something more than all that rum is on your mind," Harold guessed.

Rose slowly nodded. Drawing a breath, she closed her eyes and breathed, "I said such cruel things to him. It wasn't fair of me to talk to him so."

"Oh, don't worry over Captain Cannonflash," Harold scoffed. He patted her shoulder and made for the kitchen. "He's a man of thick skin."

The slave girl who Harold had freed emerged carrying a heavy pot that Rose knew contained some of the cook's famous menudo.

Watching the young woman as she set the pot down and lifted the lid to stir it, she took note of how lovely she was. She was no more than twenty, probably younger, and now there was a light in her eyes that was not there when she had been liberated from the fort.

When she looked to Rose, she smiled and asked in a voice so sweet as to suit her angel's face, "Dat rum got the best of ye, aye?"

Rose nodded.

"Dis make you feel all better," she assured. Looking over her shoulder as Harold emerged with bowls and spoons, she smiled the smile that Rose did when she saw Cannonflash, and that stung at the moment. "Harold," the young woman greeted, "de bread's not done for a while more."

"No worries," Harold assured as he sat in the Captain's chair. "We'll get by. Let's have some of this before more of the crew awakens." He distributed bowls and spoons and looked to the lovely woman he had freed, such a fondness in his eyes that Rose had not seen there before.

They enjoyed a good breakfast, and halfway through the young woman retired to the kitchen and returned a moment later with a plate of steaming bread.

Rose tried to forget about her troubles but they stubbornly clung to her. She enjoyed her time with Harold and the woman he had freed and even managed to laugh with them a time or two. The freed slave reminded her of a flower deprived of sunlight, one that bloomed brilliantly with its first taste of the light, and bloom this woman did.

In time, not quite an hour and as the crew began to collect in the galley for their morning meal, Rose excused herself, picked up her boots and held the blanket tightly to her as she returned to the deck. The sun was up and her nerves were taut as she looked about, anxious to see the Captain and dreading it just as much.

Padding out onto the deck, she glanced around as the crew was rushing about, and finally she realized that they were manning their battle stations. Cannons were moved into position, others were retracted to be loaded and many men with muskets were taking up their positions at the rail. Glancing around, she looked for the big captain. He was always on the deck in the middle of the ship, directing activity and barking orders to the men as needed, usually through Johnny Cannonburg. Today he was not to be seen there and she looked about almost frantically, finally seeing him on the helm deck at the wheel, something she had never seen him do before a battle.

She ran to the ladder, dropped the blanket and her boots and climbed up quickly, holding on as she reached the top when the big ship made a hard turn to port. Looking that way, she saw the tattered sails of a big sloop, one nearly the length of many frigates she had encountered. In the distance so she could not tell if it was friend or foe, but Cannonflash was directing his ship's wrath toward it. Pirates attacking other pirates was a rare thing and this ship did not appear to be one that was carefully kept up by any navy she knew of. Looking back to Jones, she saw him release the wheel long enough to look through a brass telescope at the ship, then he made a minor course correction and the big ship turned slightly in response. Standing near the ladder, she watched as the sloop, which appeared to be only two thirds the size of one of the *Black Dragon*'s hulls, as it actually veered toward them. It was a swift ship and was slicing through the water with a vengeance.

Something about it caught her eye and she squinted to see it better. Finally darting over to Jones, she took the telescope from him and trained it on the approaching ship. She could see men on deck manning cannons, but they were looking behind them, not at the *Black Dragon*, though they must have known of the big ship's presence.

And finally she recognized the ship she was looking at, and she drew a gasp. The flag it flew was a black flag sporting a skull wearing a three point hat with swords crossed beneath it. There was only one ship that flew that flag!

Looking to the captain, she frantically asked, "What are you going to do?"

Jones never took his eyes from the ship as he growled, "She wants to fight, I'll oblige."

"She doesn't!" Rose assured. "I know the man who captain's that ship." She did not even get a glance from the big pirate captain and desperately cried, "Jones, he isn't coming for you, I promise!"

Huffing a laugh, Cannonflash scoffed, "You promise. Holds no weight with me, wench."

She clenched her teeth and looked through the telescope again. The ship was less than two miles away and was at full sail.

Cannonburg strode up to them, his eyes on the Captain as he reported, "She's closing on us fast, Captain, but she's more interested in something behind her."

A crewman who was in the crow's nest high in the *Black Dragon*'s rigging shouted, "More sails, Captain!"

Jones casually looked up toward the rigging, then forward again at the approaching ship. Long seconds passed before he shouted up to the crow's nest, "How many?"

Rose looked up, seeing the man way up there looking through a telescope toward the sea ahead of them.

After a good look, he shouted back down, "Two, Captain. Looks like Spanish colors. Warships, heavy frigates from the look of 'em."

Cannonflash released a heavy breath and adjusted the wheel a little to the right.

"Damn," Rose swore under her breath. Looking toward her friend's ship through the telescope again, she finally saw the two pursuers behind him. A column of water blasted from the sea right behind the ship, then another to one side. She gasped as she saw the ship get hit and shook her head. Looking desperately up at Jones, she pled, "We have to help them!"

Shaking his head, Cannonflash grumbled, "I've no quarrel with the Spanish and no loyalty to that other ship."

Her breath came hard as she grasped his arm, begging, "Please, Captain Jones! Please! That man is a friend of mine! He's seen me through more than I care to remember!"

Jones simply glanced at her again.

A tear escaped her eye and she looked back to Nailhall's ship, shaking her head as it tacked hard to avoid another barrage of cannon fire. "Captain Jones, please! Please help him!"

"To what end?" Cannonflash snarled.

"We are all brethren," she snapped. "If you are to be alone in all of this then get me close enough to get aboard Captain Nailhall's ship so that I may fight with a man with some honor."

He looked down at her again, this time making no secret of his anger and irritation with her.

Clenching her teeth together, she snapped, "Those frigates are no match for this ship. Please, Cannonflash, help me this one time and I'll never ask you another thing."

Jones looked forward again as the ship closed to within a mile, and he snarled, "What's in it for me?"

She reached up and took his face in both hands, forcing his attention back to her as she assured, "Anything I can give you! *Everything* I can give you!"

He just stared at her for a long moment, then he pulled his face from her grip and scowled. "You'll stand down, woman, or I'll have ye in the brig."

"Then put me there!" she barked back, "but please help him. Please!"

Cannonflash stared ahead at the approaching ships without expression but for his brow low over his eyes. There was a tension in his eyes and a decision being weighed behind them.

Rose desperately looked to Cannonburg, who returned her look and gave her but a little nod.

Striding two steps in front of the wheel, Johnny looked to his captain and hooked a thumb in his belt as he asked, "Shall we have the Spanish stand to, Sir?"

Jones did not look at him and for many endless seconds just watched the ships draw closer. Finally, and without looking to his first mate, he ordered, "Go forward and await me orders. We have solid shot in the deck guns, aye?"

"Aye, Captain," Cannonburg answered.

"Make 'em ready," Jones ordered, "and keep the rest at the ready in case they want to fight." As Johnny strode to the ladder, Cannonflash half turned his head and shouted, "Raise the colors!"

The flag the *Black Dragon* flew was bigger than most and that skull with the cannon and cutlass crossed under it was a huge and imposing sight as it took to the wind behind the ship. Forward, the hundred pounders were pulled into position and the entire crew stood ready, many of them with their eyes on the steering house while many looked to Cannonburg.

Still not sure what Jones planned to do, Rose watched him with nervous eyes as the last few hundred yards closed between Bugs' ship and the *Black Dragon*. One pass, one salvo from the huge ship's guns and the *Silver Falcon* would meet the fate of so many of the British she had seen destroyed by this leviathan. Every particle of her being urged her to make one last appeal, but the woman in her knew that this man would no longer listen. His mind was set and anything else she said would reinforce the stubbornness that steeled him.

They were less than fifty yards away from her friend's ship and Bugs' men had seen them and nervously approached that side of their ship.

Rose strode forward and tightly grasped the rail at the front of the wheel deck, her eyes fixed on the smaller ship as she fled, as she turned to evade the two hulled monster that headed her way.

The Spanish guns fired again and three balls missed, one narrowly. One hit the rigging and tore through Bugs' sails, and barely missed the *Black Dragon*.

"Hold onto something!" Cannonflash shouted unexpectedly.

Everyone did as if they expected what was to come.

Rose looked over her shoulder as the big pirate captain wrenched the wheel over hard to the left, spinning it with all his strength and skill.

And the *Black Dragon* responded eagerly with a hard tack to port and everything and everyone not secured was thrown to the right. Any other ship would have listed hard, but this huge catamaran turned very flat and passed only a few yards off of the smaller pirate's port stern.

The Spanish pursuing them turned away and were clearly unwilling to fire again with *that* ship in their line of fire.

"Mister Cannonburg!" Jones shouted. "Have those starboard deck guns send the Spanish our intentions."

With a big smile, Johnny shouted the Captain's will to the men on the starboard side, and the guns relayed that order to the Spanish with a dozen twenty pound balls of steel fired with purpose into the water around them.

The black leviathan had sent them a clear warning and the Spanish ships turned hard in opposite directions to retreat.

Jones shouted up to the rigging, "Set your canvas to bring us directly into the wind." He continued that left turn and his ship had turned completely and found herself pursuing the ship they had saved. Without looking at her, he ordered, "Miss O'scarlett, go forward and signal your friend to raise his sails and stand to, and send him me invitation to come aboard."

Rose could only stare at him for a time, and when he finally turned his eyes to her, she grasped his big arm in thanks before turning to the ladder.

* * *

With the two ships side by side and tethered together, it was easy to see how much bigger the *Black Dragon* really was.

Anticipation swelled in Rose as she waited for her old friend to climb the rope ladder provided by the men of the *Black Dragon* and come aboard. She was standing right beside Cannonflash, but could not look his way. Something was amiss with him and had been ever since their visit to Isla de la Mortis, but she did not know what nor did she care at the moment.

Bugs brought two of his trusted crew with him, and they all boarded the *Black Dragon* armed. One could guess as to why, perhaps a show of strength, perhaps even a show of respect, but in this moment it did not matter. As soon as he was aboard he was ambushed by an eager and dear friend and Rose hugged him as tightly as she could.

Hugging her back, he whispered, "Do I have you to thank for standing here today?"

She whispered back, "I did nothing you've not done for me a hundred times." She pulled away and turned toward Cannonflash, introducing, "Captain Jones, this is my dear friend Captain Nailhall."

Bugs stepped forward with an outstretched hand and it was warily taken by the big pirate captain.

His eyes shifting from Rose to Bugs and back, Jones turned toward his cabin and beckoned them on, ordering, "This way."

Within the captain's cabin, Cannonflash offered them chairs at the wooden table and took one himself. It was clear that he was sizing up the situation between Bugs and Rose, and she was anxious to smooth that situation over.

Captain Nailhall had brought with him a bottle, carried aboard by one of his crewmen, and he pulled the cork with his teeth before setting it in the middle of the table. "With my compliments, Captain Jones. Least I can do for the man who ran off those Spaniards."

Jones took the bottle and took a few deep swallows from it, then he wiped his mouth and handed it off to Rose, but his eyes remained on Bugs.

A very tense and silent moment followed.

Bugs finally, in his usual diplomatic form, took a drink from the bottle and set it on the table before he leaned back in his chair, folding his hands in his lap as he locked his gaze on the big pirate captain who sat across from him. "I suppose I owe you a favor now, aye?"

"If you choose, Captain Nailhall," was Jones' reply. "I've no quarrel with the Spanish or much use for 'em."

With a nod, Bugs nodded and informed, "I try not to be in anyone's debt, and now I find meself there. Feels a bit awkward."

Cannonflash simply, subtly nodded, his eyes fixed on his guest's.

Another awkward, silent moment followed.

This was unnerving for Rose and possibilities of all the terrible things that could happen flashed relentlessly through her mind. With a high arched brow, her gaze shifted nervously from one man to the other and back, though theirs remained unwavering on each other.

Drawing a deep breath, she finally offered, "Captain Nailhall and I have been close mates for many years now. Been through many a close scrape."

"I imagine so," Cannonflash growled.

Bugs picked the rum bottle up and heaved a heavy breath, and finally he said, "Let me make the day easier on both of us, Captain Jones. Rose and I have been associated for many years. I consider her one of me closest mates and she has my absolute trust and I hers." When Rose held her hand to him, he absently handed her the bottle. "There's never been even a smidge of romantic banter between us and likely never will be." He looked to her as she gulped down a few swallows of the rum, and he arched his brow slightly before looking back to Cannonflash. When his host said nothing for a moment, he folded his hands in his lap and offered, "Thank you for inviting me aboard. You seem to want to talk about something, so perhaps we should get that out of the fog."

Turning his eyes to Rose, who took another gulp of rum under his attention, Cannonflash finally asked, "So what had the Spanish chasing ye?"

Bugs shrugged and reached across the table, taking the bottle from Rose as he replied, "I assume the same reason the Brits or the French chase any of us. Quite a bounty offered for any pirates that get turned in and the Reds are payin' better than anyone." He took a swallow of rum and continued, "Many privateers about, and many navy warships who would collect that bounty for themselves." He looked to Jones with hardened eyes. "Even has some pirates turnin' on the rest of us for some quick gold. That's the worst kind of scoundrel, I think."

When Bugs offered him the bottle, Jones took it and had a few swallows himself. For a few seconds after he stared down at the bottle, then he nodded and agreed, "Aye, worst kind. Of course, loyalty is bought and sold with regular ease these days and goes to the heaviest purse."

"Wasn't always so," Bugs said softly.

Jones nodded, then turned his eyes to his guest and informed, "Seems like the days of the lone pirate are comin' to an end, Mister Nailhall. Smart ones are fleeting up these days."

Bugs' eyes narrowed slightly and he asked, "You offerin' Captain Jones?"

Cannonflash shrugged. "I suppose I can put it on the table. Means loyalty is not a commodity to be bought and sold. Means takin' orders from the man in charge. Means paying out a percentage of your takings."

"For the security of many ships," Bugs added. "How would a handful of ships fair against a Navy squadron?"

"Better than just one," Jones replied.

With a little laugh under his breath, Nailhall observed, "Any one ship but this one, I'm thinking. Can't see a fleet standing its own against this behemoth."

"Aye," Cannonflash agreed. "How's your ship fairing?"

Bugs shrugged and answered, "Some holes to patch, rigging in need of attention. Got a few injured but nothing too serious."

Cannonflash nodded and offered, "Ye can remain tethered for a spell and get your ship in order. Some of me men can come aboard and help with your repairs if ye like."

"I would appreciate that," Bugs offered.

Jones held the bottle to him. "Me thanks for the rum, Captain Nailhall. It's of fine quality."

"It's me thanks to you, Captain Jones."

The two men stood and Jones offered, "Enjoy some of me hospitality while your ship is repaired. I've the best cook in the Caribbean."

Nodding to him, Bugs said, "Again you have me thanks, Captain Jones."

They shook hands and Cannonflash informed, "Rose and I will be along in short order. Going to settle a matter and then we'll talk of things, aye?"

Bugs glanced at her and nodded again. "Sounds good, Captain Jones. I'll see you there."

As he left the room, Cannonflash's eyes narrowed slightly and he just watched after the door for a few seconds, then he looked to Rose and ordered, "You'll board his ship and go back to Tortuga. I'll meet you at your stores there in a couple of days."

This made her even more nervous and she looked away from him, advising, "Smith has probably reached the supplies there already."

"And maybe not," Jones countered. "Does Captain Nailhall know of your supplies?"

"I've done business with him for many years, so I'm sure he does. Not the particulars or anything, but he's aware of what I do."

"Fill him in," Jones ordered. "I'll meet you both at that cave in a couple of days."

"So you've said," she said straightly, looking up at him. "I'm not comfortable with this, Cannonflash, especially leaving the ship like this."

"Do you trust Mister Nailhall?"

She nodded.

"Then there is nothing to dislike," he informed harshly. Stepping around the table, he took her chin in his big hand and raised her face to his, meeting her eyes. "You've trusted me this far, Lass. Time to take it all the way now. Ye trust me at all?" When she nodded again he stroked her cheek with his thumb and commended, "That's me girl." With just the hint of a little smile, he raised his chin slightly and said, "This will make sense in a couple of days, and I'll be lookin' forward to it as much as you will."

That finally coaxed a little smile from her.

* * *

Rose had spent time on Bugs' ship before, but this time she found herself distracted as never before. The pirate in her warned of some danger, but the woman in her was anxious and restless. She could not wait to see the big pirate captain again and was sure that this surprise that awaited her was something that would change her life. She could feel it!

They arrived at Tortuga in a day and a half and ignoring the British presence on the island she went straight to her favorite tailor shops. Carrying her big handbag, she finally met Bugs at the tavern at the edge of town where he had been waiting with two of his men, one of whom, an older and rather thin fellow who was far too well dressed for the pirate he was, played cards at a table with six others. Bugs and his other crewman were seated at a small table at the back of the tavern, near the back door where he always sat. The lamp in the middle of the table was turned down low and each man nursed a mug of ale, and their eyes locked on her as she entered.

She was back in that white button up shirt, almost a swordsman's shirt with a big collar, though it was not buttoned, it was tied at the bottom around her belly and hung open about a hand width from the collar to the knot that held it together. She also wore a thin made hot pink skirt that was hemmed just below her knees and belted with a white sash that kept her cutlass, one pistol and her dagger snugly to her. New buckskin boots fit her perfectly and tightly around her ankles, and were only as tall as her ankles, where they showed off the shape of her calves nicely. The hoop earrings she generally wore were not in her ears and at the moment she wore no jewelry there, but she did have a bear claw amulet around her neck, something traded for at one of the tailor shops.

There was quite a spring to her step as she bounded into the tavern and did not even stop to glance around, instead going straight to the bartender and leaning on the bar as she greeted him with a big smile. "Hi there. I need a bottle of the best rum you have."

The barkeep was a rough looking fellow who had not shaved for more than a week, and he eyed her with a mix of confusion and suspicion. With a deep grunt, he turned around and reached to the top shelf behind his bar, taking down a dark bottle that was covered with dust and had a black and gold label. When he placed it on the bar, she flipped him a gold piece which he caught awkwardly.

Snatching the bottle from the bar, she shoved it into her big handbag and turned to approach the table where Bugs awaited her. She was smiling and it was clear to everyone why. "Gentlemen," she greeted as she reached them. "I believe we have somewhere to be."

Bugs and his crewman glanced at each other and Captain Nailhall informed, "We're already supposed to be there, I think, Missy."

She spun around on her heel and summoned, "Well come on, mates. We'd better be on the way."

* * *

Once again an obscure trail through the wilderness led to a hidden cave in the jungle. Surrounded by trees, vines and green things that hid loud birds, buzzing insects and other creatures who called to one another over the noise of others, the cave opened into a clearing and was obscured by vines and a tall tree that grew right in front of it. This was an ideal place to hide anything as the cave was almost impossible to see by those just passing by. One would have to be actively looking for it, and even then it would be difficult at best to find. The clearing itself was semi-circular around the overgrown cliff that the cave opened into was and about thirty feet in any direction. Many large, flat stones littered the clearing and kept the jungle growth at bay for the most part, but machetes had also done their work to keep it clear.

Led by Rose, they marched one by one from the narrow path into the clearing.

Bugs stopped a few paces into the clearing and set his hands on his hips as he scanned the area, commenting as he did, "We'd probably have made better time if you'd traveled a little lighter, Miss O'scarlett."

"He won't be here for at least another hour," she grumbled, setting the heavy handbag down to rest her shoulder. "I'm sure we'll have plenty of time to get things in order here. Besides, I'm sure that Smith has already been here and taken everything he could carry off." She looked to the cave and her eyes narrowed. "Or maybe not." Striding to the cave, she pulled some of the vines away from it and looked inside. There was an old oil lamp hanging from a rusty iron hook on the stone wall just inside that she reached for, then she took the flints from a stone shelf right below it and knelt down to light the wick. Once it was burning, she stood and shined the light inside, looking around at the crates and kegs that were still in there and covered with oil cloth.

Bugs appeared beside her and looked in as well, raising his brow as he observed, "You could outfit a fleet with all of this."

"I suppose we got here before Smith did," she guessed, "or he's forgotten about this one." Shaking her head, she assured herself, "No, he wouldn't do that. This is one of the larger stores."

"Perhaps he thought you would not be able to make it here," Bugs offered. "Could be he thinks you're still on Grenada in the hands of the garrison commander there."

She nodded. "Perhaps so, Bugs." With a little shrug, she blew out the lamp and hung it back up. Sweeping the vines away as she exited the cave, she strode with quick steps to her handbag and snatched it from the ground, turning back to her friend as she said, "I'm going to check something out down the hill. Um, you don't want to follow and I could be gone for a while, so if you need me back quickly just fire a shot into the air and I'll come back up. But tell Cannonflash where I am when he gets here. Oh, and don't go down there because I might accidently shoot you." With a sweet little smile, she spun back around and crossed the clearing with long strides, disappearing into another obscure path that led down the hill.

This was a formidable walk and bordered on treacherous, but she was ready for it and knew just where to step. Somewhere ahead of her she could hear a waterfall and quickened her pace. A smile overtook her mouth as thoughts that had haunted her for two days burned anew within her.

The path emptied out on the grassy floodplain of a narrow river, and on the right was a tall cliff, part of the same mountain the cave was in, and from this a waterfall cascaded from twenty or thirty feet high and into a round pool that radiated about twenty feet from the fall. Ferns and flowering trees and bushes grew everywhere and on the flat of the land that bordered the pool to the jungle was lush grass that looked ankle deep. This was an enchanting place that she had hoped to share with someone dear to her for many years, and it looked as if she would finally have the chance.

Bordering the grass with the water of the pond were two sizeable boulders, the largest of them being almost in the shape of an egg with a flat top and was about twelve feet long by five wide. It was half buried in the soil and nothing grew on it. It was some kind of granite, very smooth to the touch and this is where Rose was going.

Hopping up on the boulder, she looked out over the turbulent water as rings of waves constantly radiated out from the waterfall and across the surface. At some point the water escaped down the tiny river and on its way to the sea, but this was of no consequence. She dropped her heavy bag and reached to the knot that held her shirt together, her eyes straying to the waterfall as she untied it. Her movements were slow and deliberate, her mind wandering about in lucid thoughts kept private just to her. Lowering her arms, she allowed the shirt to slide from her and fall to the stone at her feet, then she reached to her belt and absently unbuckled it. With two pistols hanging from it, she was careful to kneel down and lower it to the stone with gentle movements. Rocking back on her heel, she sat down and crossed her legs, her eyes still on the water as she fantasized about something. With almost haphazard movements, she took the heel of one boot in her hand and tugged until it pulled off of her, then she repeated this with the other. Both boots were put neatly at her side before she reached to her hips. The tights she wore came off easily and with the same slow movements she had used before.

Cannonflash could arrive at any time and she secretly hoped that he was watching her from the trail.

She stood and looked over the clear water of the little pond. It was rather cold water and she did not really fear snakes or crocodiles in it, but always looked anyway. With a quick scan of the far bank, she removed the barrette from her hair and let it fall to her shirt, then she leaned her head back to shake out her long hair. A quick glance over her shoulder confirmed that she was not being watched, though there was someone who she wanted to watch her.

Crouching down, she reached into the bag and removed a clear round bottle of some pink, perfumed bath soap, then she stood and looked over the water once more, and without any warning she ran the two steps to the edge of the boulder and jumped in.

Surfacing with a gasp against the chilly water, she threw her head to one side, then the other, flinging her hair about and water fled in hundreds of droplets as she did. The water came up to her chest here and the first thing she did was pour some of the thick pink soap into her hand. Turning to set the bottle down on a rocky outcropping behind her, she lathered her hair and washed it thoroughly for the first time in a while.

Rose took her time here, moving to shallower water to bathe the rest of her, then it was a short swim to the waterfall. Standing under it where it did not come down so hard, she ran her hands over her head and through her hair as the water showered her in a soothing massage.

She could not know how long she stayed in the water, but almost reluctantly she swam to the boulder and climbed out. Surely Cannonflash had arrived by now. She lay down on her back on the flat of the boulder and flung her hair outward over the rock to dry with the rest of her. With a deep breath, she allowed herself to drift into sweet fantasies again. Perhaps he would find her lying there naked and dozing in the sunlight, and that thought brought a little smile to her lips.

Sometime later she heard the crack of a pistol up the hill where the cave was and she raised herself up on her elbows, looking that way. The alarm in her eyes was not something that was often there and her lips parted as if in response to it. She was quick to try and reason out why it would have sounded, quick to try and reassure herself that it was nothing to worry over. Perhaps they were just telling her that Cannonflash had arrived. Perhaps he did not want to come for her and that was an order to her to go to him. Perhaps...

Another crack from a pistol and she sprang to her feet. Another was more of a sharp pop and she recognized the different sound as a musket. No one had brought muskets!

Quickly reaching for her shirt, she pulled it on with almost frantic motions, shrieking a gasp as three more gunshots sounded, two muskets among them! Without being tied, the shirt dropped almost to her knees and she grabbed her belt, wrapping it around her waist to keep it closed. Dropping to her backside, she pulled her boots on quickly, then sprang back up and drew one of her pistols.

Rose was a little out of breath when she stopped just short of the clearing and crouched down behind a tree where she could survey the area without being seen.

There was no movement and she could see one of Bugs' men lying face down near the cave, shot in the back.

Her eyes swept the clearing once more and she slowly stood, reaching across her waist and drawing her other pistol as she crept into the clearing and toward the cave. Stalking that way, her eyes darted about as she tried to pierce the jungle with her sharp gaze. Breath was not coming easily.

Something screeched behind her and she wheeled around and trained both pistols that way, her wide eyes shifting quickly to find a target. The screech again sent chills through her, and finally she looked up to see a macaw perched on a branch up there. She loosed some of the tension with a hard breath out of her mouth.

Turning back to the man on the ground, she knelt down beside him and set one of the pistols down before reaching for his neck. He had a pulse, weak as it was, and his back moved slowly up and down as he still took shallow breaths. She took his shirt and pulled it up to see to the wound to his back, then she froze and raised her eyes as she heard the distinctive clicks of a musket hammer being pulled into firing position.

Before she could move, a man with a proper British accent and very clear way of speaking advised, "You should think hard about putting that other pistol down." When she half turned her head, he warned, "My orders are to bring you in alive, Miss O'scarlett. That means if we have to shoot you then you'll take our musket rounds in your legs, and that would be frightfully painful."

Rose swallowed hard as she heard the sounds of three more muskets behind her and to both sides being cocked. She heard the hammer of a pistol as well and slowly lowered her other hand, still holding her pistol, to the ground.

"That's a good girl," he commended. "It would be such a pity to have to shoot through such lovely legs as yours. Now, please raise your hands over your pretty little head and stand for me."

With hesitant movements, she complied.

"There's a good girl," he drawled. "See there? That wasn't so hard."

She flinched as two men burst from behind the vines that covered her cave, each one with a pistol trained on her. Hearing footsteps approach from behind her, she raised her chin as someone grabbed her wrists and twisted her arms behind her. Before she realized, something was wound around her wrists, binding them tightly together. This took less than a moment and once done her arms were seized and she was brutally spun around to face the man who had been speaking to her.

He appeared to be in his late twenties and had that same conceited look about him that many officers of the British navy had. She recognized his rank as Commander and he wore his scarlet uniform proudly if not comfortably. He was sweating badly from the heat, but barely seemed to notice. This was a tall man, the tallest of the six present, and she was looking up at him with wide eyes and her mouth agape.

With a little smile, he informed, "We've a short walk to take, Miss O'scarlett. I am hoping you will do me the honor of not trying to run. It would be so much easier if we do not have to carry you after shooting those lovely legs of yours."

She nodded, then glanced down to the man still on the ground and said with a meek voice, "My mate is still alive and needs a doctor."

The officer looked down at him with his brow held high and corrected, "No, I'm sure he's dead. No worries for him."

"But he's still breathing," she argued.

"Hmm," the officer observed. "So he is." Without a second thought, he shot the man again. Looking to Rose, he smiled again and informed, "Seems to have stopped now. Shall we go?"

With her horrified eyes on Bugs' crewman, Rose was pulled brutally along by the arms and to the jungle path toward town.

* * *

Rose was not told where the ship was going, but she knew that it was going to Port Royal. That much was pretty clear. It was a big ship, a warship, but not a frigate. It was also not a ship that saw combat often, if ever. It was pretty inside with fresh paint, plenty of ornate carving on the wood and more cabins in its belly than most warships she had been aboard, especially pirate ships. Despite two decks of cannons and a dozen marines on board, this thing was clearly built for comfort, not combat.

The cabin she was locked in was small, but comfortable. She was allowed out only once and that was under heavy guard and right to a small office at the rear of the ship where she was interrogated for a couple of hours. They asked her about her ship, and she gladly told them all she knew. Asked about others, particularly the notorious Bugs Nailhall, she only shrugged and shook her head, pleading ignorance.

Taken back below to the small cabin with its one small bed and one table that was built into the wall, she remained there undisturbed for the rest of the journey. Before leaving, the guards took her boots and belt, but one was kind enough to give her a length of rope to replace the belt with and she almost reluctantly tied it around her waist to keep her dress of a shirt in check.

Sometime the following day, what felt like late morning, she was awakened by the opening door and looked to see a marine with a pistol in his hand standing in the open doorway and beckoning to her. When she got up from the bed, she did not take her eyes from him as he backed away to allow her into the corridor. Once there, another marine turned her around by the shoulders and pulled her hands behind her. She did not resist as she was put in irons yet again, but she did wince as they were put on very tightly this time.

Escorted to the upper deck by the two men, she squinted against the morning sunlight and was pushed along to the gangplank that would take her to the pier the ship was tied to.

Once on dry land again, she looked about and her eyes froze on the imposing Fort Charles, a place that was waiting for her. Instead, she was taken to a waiting carriage, a fine white vehicle with ornate artwork, curtained windows and was drawn by two white horses. This was the Governor's carriage and she raised her brow as the driver jumped down and opened the door for her. Helped inside, she sat down on the red, deep cushioned seat and leaned back as best she could against her chained hands, keeping her legs tightly together as the shirt she wore—it was still all she wore—rode up a little and uncovered her thighs almost all the way up!

The two marines got in after her and sat across from her, and they kept their eyes on her as the door was closed and the carriage lurched forward.

The ride to the Governor's Mansion would not be a long one, but it felt like an eternity. She glanced around inside the carriage, looking anywhere but at the two marines who watched her like a hawk would watch its prey and with hungry eyes.

When the carriage finally stopped, the marines exited first, one out each of the doors. The door to the left was closed while the other remained open. Rose just sat where she was and kept her eyes on the red carpeted floor. Cooperation was called for, anything she could do to buy as much time as she could to figure out a way to escape, and to that end she would do nothing without specific orders from someone.

The guard cleared his throat to draw her attention, which he did. Stepping aside, he stared at her with stern eyes and gave an unspoken command for her to dismount.

She did so carefully as she was unable to use her hands and stumbled into the marine as she stepped out. Shrieking a gasp as he took her by the throat and drew his dagger, she tensed up, bracing right before he slammed her into the carriage and held the dagger to her chest. Apparently her reputation had these men nervous. When the other marine came around from the back of the carriage, the first put his weapon away and took her arm with a painful grip and she was led forcibly to the whitewashed stone mansion.

Located within a circle of thick stone walls, it was a big structure that was built to impress, built for comfort. Two levels made it up and the upper level sported three stone balconies just outside of double doors that led out to them. The front door was huge and made of oak and stone steps led up to the patio area that had several raised flower boxes lining it, all planted with colorful flowers and small trees. Larger trees surrounded the structure and all of the many windows stood open. Two guards flanked the front door and both had their eyes on Rose as she was escorted up the step toward them.

Inside, the mansion was lavishly decorated. Some of the best furnishings she had ever seen were set up in the open area just inside. The floors were stone with huge carpets covering that stone for the most part. Paintings were hanging where bookcases and other tall furnishings did not cover the walls. It was lit largely by chandeliers but also had lamps about in areas that would otherwise be dark and shadowed. Busts and statues also decorated this large room, some on their own pedestals.

She had seen this room and it did not really impress her this time, either. Escorted through it and up the stairs that spiraled gently upward, she really took little notice of what was around her, only acknowledging some of the weapons that hung on the walls and how many guards were about.

The door was opened to a spacious office and she was taken to the center and made to stand right in front of the huge oak desk that dominated the room. This place was at least twenty feet by twenty feet and was yet another room that was made for comfort. A leather couch was to her right, two chairs of the same design were on her left. Book cases flanked the two big windows behind the desk that stood open to allow the breeze in and smaller ones were right beneath them. Many books were in their places on them, but so were many trinkets and swords and pistols displayed on wooden stands. Paintings hung on the walls above the couch and chairs.

Sitting behind the desk was a man in proper dress with a white shirt and a dark blue jacket that was decorated with gold and white embroidery. He was rather a big man but not muscular so much as just bulky from too many meals. Thinning hair was well groomed and gray at his temples. He did not have features that made him especially attractive. In fact, he was not an attractive man at all. Clean shaven but for long sideburns, he had a rather plump face and full lips. When he finally put down his pen and looked up at her, she wanted to cringe, but she had seen him before and did not change her expression as her eyes met his.

He raised his chin and looked her up and down, then finally looked to the guards and ordered, "That will be all. Close the door on your way out."

They turned without reply and left the room, closing the door as ordered.

Resting his elbows on the desk, the big man folded his hands before him as he studied her a moment longer.

Rose looked away. This day had been long coming and at this moment seemed as if it had always been an inevitability. She had stood here before and did not like it then, either.

"How have you been, Rose?" he finally asked, his accent proper and his words spoken as if he was English nobility.

She shrugged, taking a few seconds before she replied, "It's been a rough couple of weeks."

"I see that," he agreed. "So what of your ship?"

Still not looking at him, she released a little sigh and reported, "It's been... Mister Smith saw fit to take over command. It's his ship now."

"Your crew mutinied," the man said for her. Shaking his head, he sighed, "Well, I do suppose it was to happen sooner or later. What crew of pirates would follow a woman for long, after all?" He stared at her through the silence that followed and finally observed, "It looks like we have a problem, doesn't it?"

Rose nodded.

"At least you do," he added. "I'd say that I'm about to become a hero. I've stopped the notorious Rose O'scarlett and now the Caribbean is a safer place."

She set her jaw and looked toward the painting over the couch.

He leaned back in his chair, never taking his eyes from her. "You did well for a while, I'll give you that. You are far more resourceful than I had anticipated. In fact, I never thought it would take three years to catch you. It was truly a wonderful chase."

"Glad you enjoyed it," she snarled.

He smiled. "Oh, I'm going to enjoy what happens next much more."

Clearly growing uneasy, her features showed strain that she fought hard to conceal, though it was useless. "What do you want me to do," she asked softly.

Raising his brow, he replied, "Why, I want you to hang, Miss O'scarlett, and hang you will."

Her mouth tightened to a thin slit.

"Unless," he added, "you can give me something that will keep you from the gallows, something that will convince me to spare you."

"And live as your whore," she grumbled. "No thank you."

He huffed a laugh. "You still think you'll bring me down someday, don't you, Rose?" Shaking his head, he continued, "You'd rather go to the gallows than stay with me. I can give you a new life and a stable home. No more running." When she still just stared at the painting, he drew a breath and looked down at his desk, raising his brow as he informed, "I really didn't expect the chase to end like this. Kind of puts me in an awkward position. Of course, you could escape and continue your exploits, couldn't you? It wouldn't be the first time."

"No, it wouldn't," she agreed in a low voice.

"Give me something," he offered, "and a careless mistake could lead to yet another miraculous escape by the famed Rose O'scarlett."

"What do you want?" she asked, turning her eyes down.

"You know what I want," he countered. "Your husband was foolish enough to plot against me and I know of the missing manifests and the other documents he stole."

"And you killed him because of them," she snarled.

"His death was an unfortunate accident," he corrected.

"Just get to your point, Governor Berkley," she insisted softly.

He smiled anew. "Perhaps we can continue the chase for a while longer. Give me those documents and you will be out of your cell by midnight."

"I don't have them," she admitted. "And if I did, you would never get your stinking paws on them." When he laughed, she looked to him, her eyes widening as he opened a drawer and produced the brown envelope she had safeguarded for four years.

"How unfortunate," he drawled. "I swore I'd have your obedience or I would break your will before sending you to your death. Looks like it's time to break your will, little girl."

She breathed in labored breaths through her mouth and could not look away from the envelope. Slowly, she shook her head as she realized that the last card she had to play was gone.

Berkley looked to it himself and shook his head. "It's such a shame that an intelligent and cunning woman such as yourself would so easily put her trust in the wrong place." His eyes snapped back to her. "It seems that the man who turned you in had this in his possession."

"What?" she gasped.

With a conceited little smile, he slowly nodded and informed, "I've a new accord with Commodore Jones. I believe you know his son, a man who calls himself Cannonflash."

Something horrible welled up in the pit of her stomach and tears blurred her vision.

"Captain Jones was more than happy to turn you over to me," Berkley continued, his eyes back on the envelope. "Of course, when he told me he had this as well, I just had to talk him out of it. It cost me more gold than I wanted to pay, but it was well worth it." His eyes snapped back to her, his brow low over them. "He's even helping me with my conquests here. You see, he's sailed north to rendezvous with his father the Commodore. They'll raid shipping along the American colonies from now on. So now I've captured two notorious pirate captains to be hung and I've run off the most feared lot on this side of the world. I'll be a hero in London, probably even be knighted by his Majesty. It could not have worked out better." He looked to the oil lamp that burned on his desk and lifted off the chimney. His attention on what he was doing, he held the envelope over the fire until the corner of it burned, then he tossed it to the corner where there was no rug over the stone floor.

Rose watched it burn to ashes and with it her last opportunity for absolution and revenge for her husband's death. Her heart was broken and her will with it. Her brow held high and arched over eyes that spilled tears, she drew a broken breath and asked in a voice that wept, "What about my son?"

"Oh, little Jeffy?" Berkley smiled and leaned back in his chair, lacing his fingers before him. "Children can be so cruel, especially to those with criminals as parents. I had to look out for the boy's well being, so I put him on a ship and sent him to the American colonies." He lowered his eyes to his hands and shook his head. "Silly me. I put him on a ship that had a history, one that might be sought out by those who hunger for revenge." His brow low over his eyes, he looked back to Rose and informed with harsh, serious words, "Sea travel is not as safe as it once was, my dear. I'm afraid the man you gave your heart to not only betrayed you, but he sank the ship that carried your little son to safety."

A gasp shrieked into Rose and she took a step back, her wide eyes locked on the Governor.

Raising his brow, he looked back to his desk and heaved a heavy sigh. "Such a pity. He was upon them before they knew what was coming and they never had the chance to defend themselves. This man you think you loved killed your son the same day he handed you and your friend Captain Nailhall over to me, the very day he collected a sizeable fortune in gold."

"You're lying," Rose hissed, tears streaming from her eyes.

He fixed his gaze on her with an artificial pity in his eyes. "Dear Rose, there is no reason to lie to you now. Your trial is over and you have been condemned to hang the day after tomorrow. Admiral Peterson is coming to witness it, the very man you needed to talk to about me. Of course, he'll not arrive in time. When he gets here you'll be hanging by your pretty little neck at the mouth of the harbor as a warning to others. You'll be so close, and yet when his ship is seen, the lever will be pulled, the floor will drop from under your feet and you will be dead just like that. Of course, I could have them shorten the rope so that you strangle. I would enjoy that much more than watching your pretty little neck get broken."

"You are a monster," she whimpered. She wanted to harden herself, to not cry in front of him, but it was to no avail. He had what he wanted. He had won.

"Let me give you some comfort, my dear," he offered. "The Admiralty in London received my letter regarding your Cannonflash Jones a month ago and I received word that my request has been approved. In two days you will have your revenge on Captain Jones."

She looked away, drawing a broken breath as tears formed rivers out of her eyes.

"You see," he continued, "some time ago requested a ship, the *HMS Goliath*, and now that the Spanish are in their place once again it was no longer needed in England. It will arrive at the same time as Admiral Peterson, the same day your neck gets stretched, and it has orders to hunt down and sink the *Black Dragon* and kill everyone on board."

Rose managed to huff a laugh and look back at him. "I hope you're on that ship when it attacks him, that way you and this *Goliath* can die together."

"Oh, we won't, my dear. The *Goliath* is the largest and most heavily armed warship in the world. She is not like the ships your Cannonflash has faced before. She will also have many escorts and many guns. The man who commands her, Captain Doom, is a personal friend of mine, and unbeknownst to the Admiral he has orders from me to hunt down this *Black Dragon* and end her once and for all, and take no prisoners in the process." He smiled. "With the *Goliath* in my fleet I'll have no equal on this side of the world."

She just stared at him for a long moment, praying that this was all lies, and knowing it was not. Closing her eyes, she half turned to the door and asked between sobs, "May I go now?"

Berkley stood and slowly strode around his desk toward her. The look in his eyes was different, and was something she had seen before. Stopping right in front of her, he folded his hands behind him and looked her up and down, then smiled and informed, "You may leave as soon as our business here is done."

"I have no more business with you," she breathed.

"Perhaps not," he agreed, reaching to her face with both hands, "but I have business with you."

With savage movements he grabbed the collar of her shirt and tore it open, pulling it brutally from her shoulders. She backed away and he pursued, taking her by the throat and forcing her down onto the leather couch. When she tried to struggle away and screamed, he slapped her hard enough to crack her neck and consciousness tried to slip away from her. She was barely aware of him untying the rope she used for a belt but knew it.

He opened her shirt fully and stared down at her bound and naked form with sickening eyes.

When she felt his hands on her she was sure she would be ill if there had only been something in her stomach. Tightly closing her eyes, she turned her face away from him and braced herself to endure his lust for the last time.

Berkley grabbed the back of her hair and forced her head around, bringing his mouth close to her ear as he whispered, "I'm far from done with you, sweet Rose." His breathing was heavy and his other hand clawed its way down her body and back up, taking her breasts with a rough touch. When she struggled anew, he grabbed her by the throat and took her mouth with his.

It was all hunger and lust. There was no passion.

Some time later she was pushed into a small cell in the basement of Fort Charles, one separated from the regular jail and only five by seven feet in size. Her shirt dangled from her shoulder. She held her head low and her eyes were on the ground before her. One of the guards unlocked her hands and she was finally unchained, but she was too despondent to even notice and absently rubbed her sore wrists.

As the door behind her was closed and locked, she finally looked to the crude bed that was mounted to the wall and held up by a couple of chains. There was only a blanket on it and she would sleep on the aged planks that made it up. Nothing else was in there. Slowly turning, she sat down on it and closed her shirt with both hands, holding it tightly so as if to protect herself from the pain of what she had just endured. It was not the first time she had been raped, but with the betrayal weighing down her heart, this was the worst.

The door opened again and two scraggly looking guards entered the room. They were unshaven, unattractive, and grinned at her with chapped lips and teeth that were mostly rotten. These men were unkempt and stank of liquor and wore their uniforms with no pride or dignity.

The closest of them set his hands on his hips and looked her over, then informed with a thick and low brow accent of someone of very little education, "The Governor sent us to keep you company, puppet."

As the other closed the door, she shrank away, her brow tense over wide eyes that shifted in terrified glances from one man to the next.

Chapter 11

PIRATES TO THE GALLOWS

Rose slept as much as she could. No more guards bothered to visit her over the next couple of days and there was nothing to do but drown in the sorrow of her betrayal, her capture, the death of her son. The only thing left to look forward to was her imminent death and the end to the pain that racked her shattered heart every second. When she could not sleep she worked on mending her torn shirt, using knots where the buttons were missing to keep it closed. With her rope belt gone she had carefully torn out the entire lower hem of the shirt and used that. Once that was done she spent her time in the very dim light that was offered through the window in the timber door just sitting on her bed reminiscing about the last of the happy memories she'd had. She shook and hurt and sweat poured from her that whole first day as her body demanded a drink of rum, but she endured it absently as the pain in her heart overwhelmed everything else she could feel. Her last meal consisted of a tiny bowl of beans, a chunk of stale bread and a cup of water. After, she lay back down and closed her eyes. After two days, she still cried herself to sleep.

Startled from a deep sleep and sweet dreams by the unlocking of her door, she sucked in a gasp and raised her head. She was lying curled up on her side with the blanket wrapped around her. Even in the Caribbean the rooms underground were cool and constant, a little too much so for comfortable sleep.

The door was pulled open and the hinges creaked and groaned. Two guards in new looking uniforms entered and one reached for her as she sat up, seizing her arm and pulling her from the bunk. He was not gentle at all with her and pulled her by the arm outside into the corridor where he turned her and slammed her chest first into the wall. Once again her arms were twisted behind her and her wrists bound there with just enough rope to keep them there. It was done quickly and given enough time she could free herself, but time was one of many things she no longer had. Today was the day.

When they emerged into the sunlight, she squinted against it as it burned her eyes, turning her face away but she was not allowed to break stride.

Taken to a large common area near the back of the fort, she was greeted by the jeers and shouts of the thousand or so spectators who were crowded into it and who watched from the perimeter wall, the second level balconies of the main fort itself, the lower walkway along the wall… They were everywhere, and none were friendly.

Turning her eyes ahead, she could see the gallows that waited for her. They would hang people one at a time while the crowd watched, and lined up at the stairs that would take them to the top level and to the rope and trap door were four others, four people she knew. She was escorted to the back of the line, right behind a thin man with white hair, and her heart managed to break a little more.

Bugs looked over his shoulder at her and raised his brow. "I see you made it. We were so worried that you would miss your own hanging."

She turned her eyes down. "Wouldn't miss it for anything, Captain Nailhall." She loosed a hard breath and shook her head, offering, "I'm sorry for this, Bugs."

He smiled and assured, "This is how pirates end, Rose, at the gallows or blown to bits in a good sea fight."

"I'd rather have the sea battle," she said softly.

"Aye," he agreed, "but this will be quick, and we'll go out to the cheers of our adoring public."

She raised her eyes to him. "I'm why you got caught. I wish you were still out there."

Bugs turned fully to her. "That's not for you to worry over, Miss O'scarlett. Things are as they are."

"But I trusted him, Bugs. You warned me and I… I gave him my heart. I gave him my trust and here we stand, just like you said. Giving my heart to the wrong man was just one more in a long line of mistakes that we must both pay for now."

He managed a little smile and countered, "We both lived fast lives, my dear, lived hard lives. Don't meet your end with such regrets. I'll never regret our friendship or anything we went through together. Never."

He had managed to pull a little smile from her. "You know, Mister Nailhall, perhaps the only regret I'll harbor is not letting you bed me."

His smile broadened and he shook his head. "No, Miss O'scarlett, I'll not regret that a bit. I'm sure it would have complicated our friendship in ways we'd never recover from." He turned around to face the gallows and added, "Besides, I'd only ruin you for all other men."

Facing death by hanging, Rose giggled.

An entourage of soldiers and well dressed officials, of clergy and one big fellow wearing black trousers, heavy boots, a long robe over his thick frame and a black hood over his head strode toward the gallows, all directing their attention forward. Behind him were two nuns who held their heads down and appeared to be praying, and two more men who carried a litter with what looked like burial shrouds piled on it.

Rose drew a nervous breath as she saw them and murmured, "Here we go."

"Don't give it a second thought," Bugs advised. "Find your happiest memory and stay there until it's over."

She guessed, "You'll be at the helm of the *Falcon* on a calm sea, I suppose."

He shook his head and corrected, "No, I'll be drunk in some brothel."

She laughed this time, provoking looks from those around her, especially the three men in front of Bugs.

Looking over his shoulder, Bugs ordered, "You'll find your own, O'scarlett. Had a difficult enough time keeping you out of me rum when we were still alive, so stay out of me brothel."

"No promises," she laughed. "Bugs, you're the dearest friend I ever had. I love you with all my heart."

He nodded and confirmed, "And I you, Lass."

Governor Berkley strode up to the line with a broad smile and set his hands on his hips. He was wearing his best suit with a dark blue overcoat and frilly shirt beneath it. This day he wore no hat and his thinning hair was somewhat uncooperative in the slight breeze that managed to snake over the wall and get to them.

"Well, now," he started with jolly words. "Looks like we're in for a glorious day of watching pirates get their necks snapped. Glorious day." He looked to the gallows as the priest and nuns slowly ascended the stairs behind the hangman. Turning his attention back to the condemned, he raised his brow and asked, "Everyone ready for their big moment?"

No one spoke or even looked his way.

"Splendid!" he declared. Looking back up at the gallows, he called, "You there, hangman-chap." When he had the hangman's attention, he ordered, "Be sure that Miss O'scarlett here is the last to hang. I want her to see her mates get theirs first." He looked to one of the guards beside him. "See to it she watches. If she turns away even once feel free to stab that bayonet into her."

The guard nodded.

"Very good," Berkley said loudly. "I'll be watching from the shade of the balcony up there. It's getting beastly hot today, but I suppose that won't bother you much longer, will it? Well, cheerio."

Rose finally turned her eyes to him as he spun around and left with half the entourage he had come with, and she snarled, "You'll get yours someday, you conceited bastard."

The hangman came down the steps and walked the line of people slowly, looking to each of the condemned in turn before he stopped at Rose, and she gulped a breath as he took her arm and pulled her along with him.

As they ascended the steps, she reminded, "I'm supposed to go last." To that he jerked on her arm and said nothing to her.

At the top, she was pulled to the trap door and positioned carefully in the center, and the hangman was sure that her feet were inside the faded black square that was painted there. Without ceremony, the rope was slipped over her head and he slowly pulled her hair out of it, then he pulled on the knot and tightened it around her neck.

Drawing a deep breath, Rose tried to calm herself and her eyes darted about, finally finding Bugs Nailhall. He was staring tenderly up at her, and offered a reassuring little nod. This calmed her a little and she nodded back to him, one last goodbye to her dearest friend.

One of the nuns approached her. Holding her head down and a small wooden cup in one hand and a little round wafer in her other hand. Rose could not look at her and turned her eyes away.

"You will go before God for judgment in a moment," the nun said in a soft, low voice. "Will you accept Christ and be forgiven for your sins?"

A tear spilled from Rose's eye and she nodded.

"Pray with me, my child," the nun said softly, almost in a whisper.

Storming to the gallows, Governor Berkley shouted, "Stop! I said she is to go last!" He got to the top of the stairs terribly out of breath and strode right up to the hangman, standing less than a foot away as he shouted, "You incompetent imbecile! I told you she goes last! Were you not listening?" The hangman towered over him but he was not intimidated.

The nun finished, "Take her into your house, oh Lord, and watch over her in your glory forever." She slipped the wafer into Rose's mouth, waited for her to finish it before raising the cup, then she looked to the governor as he continued to shout at the hangman.

"Can you not follow simple instruction?" Berkley yelled. "I was sure that all around me were not so mentally feeble, but I can see you are!"

Rose glanced that way, then noticed the nun was holding the little cup to her lips.

"Drink it all," the nun ordered.

Rose complied, and as she swallowed she turned astounded eyes to the nun.

Raising her eyes to meet Rose's, Angie offered her a smile and a wink and whispered, "Thought you might prefer rum over sacramental wine."

"And take off that ridiculous hood!" the Governor shouted. "I want to see your face so I'll know who I'm sending to the remotest post I can think of!"

Slowly, the hangman raised his hand to the top of his head, and just as slowly removed the hood.

Governor Berkley's eyes consumed much of his face as he stumbled back a few steps and declared, "Jones!"

Drawing a gasp, Rose looked up at him, her mouth hanging agape as she saw Cannonflash staring down at the Governor with hard, deadly eyes.

The big pirate captain tore the robe he wore open and pulled it off with horrible intent. Beneath he still wore that jerkin and his huge cutlass and pistols hung from his belt. With quick, menacing movement, he grabbed the hilt of his cutlass and drew it with a terrible metal on metal ring, then he grabbed the lever that would swing the trap door beneath Rose's feet open and kill her!

Rose cringed, then she watched as he swung the cutlass high and buried it in the beam above her. She ducked a little as the rope fell onto her, then she barked a scream as Jones pulled the lever and she fell through the gallows. Managing to hit feet first and crumple hard to her backside before rolling to her back, she looked up through the trap door opening and shouted, "You could warn a girl!"

Sitting up was a problem and she was aware of a horrible commotion all around her. As someone grabbed her shoulder, she shrieked and looked back, seeing Bugs kneeling behind her and looking down at her hands.

"Gave your heart to the wrong man?" he scoffed. "I'd say you hit the mark, Little Missy."

He untied her quickly and they stood.

The two men with the litter tore the burial shrouds from it and grabbed the swords that were there hidden beneath them and they threw two swords toward Bugs and Rose before taking more for themselves.

"Just like old times," Bugs yelled almost happily as they swung around to engage five soldiers who charged them with bayonets. Backing away toward the men with the litter, they held their weapons ready, not thinking about being outnumbered or even the chance of dying in battle. They were consumed by the exhilaration of the moment.

As the five soldiers passed under the trap door, a nun fell from above and crushed two of them to the ground, then she swung her arm hard and slammed her fist into the face of a third, sending him to the ground as well.

Bugs and Rose charged and steel rang as they engaged the last two.

More soldiers charged from the fort and cannon fire from the wall slammed into their formations, stopping their charge cold.

As she dispatched her opponent, Rose looked up to the wall to see battles erupting up there as well.

"To the right!" Bugs shouted as he took down his opponent.

She turned and saw three more soldiers charging them. They were intercepted from the air as well by the clergyman who swung by a rope off of the side of the gallows and slammed into the men feet first and felled all of them. Rose and Bugs charged and the fight with the three British soldiers was brutally short.

Rose looked to the clergyman as he approached her and raised her brow as she greeted, "Mister Mueller!"

He smiled back at her.

She smiled back. "You look good."

"Thank you, my child," he replied. "Blessed art thou."

Two more soldiers ran toward them, but this time they stopped on the other side of the gallows and took aim with their muskets. Mueller, Rose and Bugs turned toward them and froze, not knowing in those tense seconds just what to do as they stared down the muzzles of those big bore muskets. Right before the soldiers fired the screaming Governor slammed into them from atop the gallows. Muskets fired into the ground as the three men collected into a pile where they fell.

Dropping from the trap door, Cannonflash slammed into the ground boots first and poised his weapon for combat as he made his stand between the soldiers and Rose. As they pushed the Governor off of them and got to their feet, three more joined them, these with sabers drawn. Rose took his left side, Bugs his right, and Mueller was behind them struggling to free himself from the priest's robes. Outnumbered five to three, the pirates held their ground as the British soldiers charged.

Steel rang as it met mid-air and still Rose shouted to Cannonflash, "You have a lot of gall, Jones!"

Fighting two of the soldiers with expert movements and brutally powerful blows from his heavy cutlass, he growled back, "What's that supposed to mean?"

"You turn me in," she yelled as she parried and thrust in response, "you collect all of that money for the bounty on me, you hand over the documents that I need to get to the Admiralty, and then you come back for me."

"Couldn't let you hang," he countered. "Ye still owe me those five kegs of powder."

"Ha!" she scoffed, countering her opponent's blade high. "You think I'm paying you now?"

"If ye know what's good for ye, wench!"

"Stop calling me that!"

"I'll call ye what I please."

"I almost got hung! You handed me right over to Berkley for that reward and I think you meant to all the time!"

"You would complain about a sunny day, wouldn't ye?"

"Only if you were in it!"

Jones dispatched one soldier with his blade, kicked the other to the ground and swung his cutlass to engage a third. "You act like all of this was a surprise."

"Did I expect you to turn me into the British? No I didn't!"

"Can't read, eh?"

She glanced at him, then spun around and swung hard and the soldier she fought slammed his blade into hers just in the nick of time. "What's that supposed to mean?"

"Everything was in the note." Cannonflash grabbed the soldier's arm, blocked his blade with his own and pulled him brutally forward, slamming his knee into the man's gut.

"What note?" she cried as she barely dodged away from the saber she faced.

"The note in the cave!" he shouted back. "Ye didn't read the note?"

"I didn't see a note!"

"I nailed it on the first crate at eye level as you go in. How did ye miss it?"

"Your eye level or mine?"

He growled and dispatched his last opponent, then he turned on the one fighting Rose and took him down with a single blow.

When Mueller finished off his, Jones took Rose's arm near her shoulder and directed her toward the stairs that led up to the wall.

Leading the way, she looked to the top of the stairs, seeing many red uniforms waiting for them and she hesitated. Pushed along by the big pirate captain, she protested, "Cannonflash, there are, um…"

"They're ours," he informed harshly. "Get yourself up there, O'scarlett!"

"How did you—"

"Just get up there!" he shouted.

More soldiers poured from the main buildings of the fort and streamed toward the stairs of the perimeter wall.

Reaching the top, Rose could hear the sounds of the sea and smell the salt air and she paused to look out over the blue water even as battle was erupting around her. Coming to her senses as she was pushed aside, she glanced about and noticed that the cannons had all been turned around and were manned by rough looking men in British uniforms as well as those adorned more like pirates, and they were all turned inward toward the fort! Bugs had already been taken up there as well as his men and they were aiming muskets into the British positions.

Even as the British soldiers fired up at them, the cannons were all fired into the common area with devastating results, but despite the early successes, it was clear that their luck was about to take a bitter turn. They were atop the wall with the British storming it from both sides, British in the courtyard below, and the sea on the other side.

Jones yelled to his men, "Send 'em down!"

His men atop the wall responded quickly, the largest of them ganging up on cannon barrels and hoisting them over the wall to the courtyard below or into the sea. As the soldiers ran up the steps, cannons were sent down there as well and other men fired into the scattering ranks.

On both sides of the wall Rose could see powder kegs stacked up like barricades and she raised her chin. This looked like a last stand, but the big pirate captain had one more order to give.

As the British soldiers relentlessly closed in, Jones yelled, "Fire 'em and go!"

With that, torches were thrown into the powder kegs and men began to jump over the wall into the sea.

Rose leaned over the wall and looked into the water far below, and gulped a breath. Men were hitting the water feet first beyond the rocks and already swimming out to a couple of ships that were clearly British warships! Looking back at Jones, the terror in her eyes was quite clear as she cried, "You can't be serious!" He grabbed her arm and the next thing she knew she was plunging toward the deep water below and screaming the whole way down with her shirt blowing up all the way to her shoulders and over her head.

Hitting the water, she torpedoed in about ten feet under the surface and began to struggle back up. With her lungs screaming for air, she fought harder back to the surface and was near panic when someone grabbed onto her arm and pulled her up the rest of the way. She broke the surface and filled her lungs with a deep gulp of the wind and barely had time to get her bearings when she was pulled along by that same strong hand.

Two explosions thundered from the wall and she turned to see smoke rising from the fort where they had just been. There were also two sizeable holes in the wall and stones and debris still raining down onto the water.

"Quit your doddling," Jones ordered.

"I don't swim well!" she barked.

He hesitated and turned an almost confused look to her. "You've captained a ship for three years and you can't swim?"

"I can swim," she corrected, "just not well."

Shaking his head, he growled and pulled her along with him, grumbling, "Women like you are why men drink."

Musket balls began to randomly hit the water around them. Only a few of the soldiers had managed to get into position to fire on them but the British were known to be notoriously accurate, even at this range. The ships answered with cannons and hammered the wall with twenty pound balls.

It seemed like a long swim and Rose was exhausted by the time she was hauled aboard. Glancing around, she noticed that this ship had recently been in battle and was quickly patched back together. This made her think of her son, killed in a fight with the ship commanded by the pirate who had come to her rescue. Gratitude yielded quickly to her rage. As sails were dropped and the ships took the wind and began to turn away from the fort, she looked to the rail to see Jones climbing on board, and when he looked to her and their eyes met, she quickly turned away, storming to the bow of the ship.

Reaching the bow, she grasped the rail and leaned on it hard, feeling the wind blow into her face as the ship cut across the water. Tears blurred her vision anew. This rescue was meaningless now. Her son, whom she had protected from afar for more than three years, was dead.

"I'm sorry, Jeffy," she whispered. "Mommy did her best." A moment later someone grasped her shoulder and she recognized the powerful grip as belonging to Cannonflash. Quick to shrug it off, she twisted away and swung her arm to ward him off, crying, "Don't touch me!"

Jones nodded and turned to lean his hip on the rail, folding his arms as he stared back at her with narrow eyes. "Well now. There be gratitude for ye."

She turned away. "Just leave me alone."

He nodded, then asked, "Would you like to return to the fort?"

Rose looked down to the water, to the dolphins that rode the wake in front of the ship. Jeffy loved watching the dolphins and could watch them for hours. Suddenly she hurt a little more. "I guess you expect me to thank you. You saved my life and I suppose I should be grateful." She wiped tears away and then turned on him as she shouted, "And what of my son?"

"What of him?" Jones growled back.

"He was on that ship you attacked a couple of days ago!" Rose yelled. "You blew that ship out of the water and killed all aboard! You killed my son, you bastard!"

Cannonflash raised his brow and looked to the horizon ahead of the ship, to the ship they followed. "Killed him, did I?" He looked back to her and motioned behind her with his head, asking, "Then who is that?"

Rose spun around, her wide eyes finding the nine year old boy who was smiling up at her, and she covered her mouth with both hands.

The children at the orphanage where he had been kept all wore the same uniforms: Black trousers and a white shirt that almost never fit right. He was wearing those black trousers and the poorly made boots he was issued, but no shirt, instead wearing a black jerkin similar to the one Jones wore. It appeared to have been made quickly out of some old trousers or perhaps a heavy shirt and the boy wore it proudly. He also wore a very proud look in his eyes as he stood there with his fists resting on his hips as Rose had seen Cannonflash do on many occasions. Around his head and covering his dark brown hair was a dirty bandana, again worn like Jones wore his.

Rose spun back to Cannonflash, still holding her hands over her mouth. She could not speak and new tears filled her eyes.

Jones looked down to his hand and informed, "I guess you'll be owin' me an apology now, aye?"

She looked back to the boy and slowly sank to her knees, extending her arms to him. When he ran to her, she wrapped her arms around him as tightly as she could. He hugged her back, burying his face in her neck. Rose wept uncontrollably and this only made the boy hold her tighter.

Finally, Jeffy pulled back from her and asked, "Mommy, why are you crying?"

She offered him a little smile and replied, "Sometimes mommies cry when they are happy."

The boy looked up to Cannonflash, who only shrugged.

The two embraced again and a moment later the big pirate captain ordered, "Mister O'scarlett, take your mother to the galley and get her something to eat."

236

Pulling away from his mother again, the boy shouted back, "Aye, Captain!" He took his mother's hand and tugged on her until she stood, ordering, "You heard the Captain. We got to go eat now."

As she was pulled along, she looked back at Cannonflash and offered him a big smile even as tears still streamed from her eyes.

* * *

Jeffy simply would not let her help so she sat at the small table in the galley with her elbow on the table and her cheek resting in her palm as she watched him labor away like a boy possessed with whatever breads and fruits and cheeses he could find. In short order he had assembled a small collection of foods on the table and two mugs full of water. He finally joined her there and over a meal of whatever he could find they talked at length about his ordeal at the orphanage, how it was not quite as bad as she had imagined. He was most interested in telling her about the sea battle that had won him his freedom, how the mammoth black ship had snuck up on the ship he was on in the night and only made its presence known with its cannons as the sun was coming up. After a few warning shots they had surrendered and Cannonflash and his men had boarded without further conflict and taken the ship. The other orphans and the entire crew had been put ashore a few miles from a settlement somewhere in the American colonies and the ship itself was taken by the pirate crew and they all sailed away. Always he spoke very highly of the big pirate captain and had hardly left his side since they had met.

Still chewing on some gravy soaked bread, he continued, "We were sailing really fast with the black ship and it had to keep slowing down so that we could keep up. The pirates who rescued us put on British uniforms and the other day we met up with another ship, this one I think that already had men in British uniforms on it and then we went to the fort and a bunch of men went ashore and the rest of us waited out here until it was time. I even got to shoot a cannon!"

"They really had this planned out," she observed with a little smile, "didn't they? Wait. They let you fire a cannon?"

"Uh, huh. And I hit the fort with it too!"

Her hand slid over her eyes and she mumbled, "Oh, dear God."

One of Jones' men, still wearing the shirt and trousers of a British soldier, burst into the galley and looked to Rose. He appeared to be in a bit of a hurry as he announced, "Captain'd like to see ye, Miss."

She stood and turned to him. "What's the problem?"

He swung around and made for the door he had entered from. "We've sails behind us closing fast. Best ye get to your station."

Rose rushed out behind him and once on the deck she stopped and turned to the boy who followed her. "Jeffy, where are you going?"

"With you to see Captain Cannonflash," he answered straightly.

She drew a breath and calmly said, "I need you to stay below now and attend to the galley, okay?"

The boy folded his arms and raised his chin. "Captain Cannonflash told me to stay with you and he's the Captain."

"And I'm your mother," she reminded.

Jeffy's eyes narrowed and he countered, "He's still the Captain, Mommy."

Rose looked aside, then turned and continued on her way with her son following.

They arrived at the stern to find Jones looking through his telescope toward the horizon, toward the three white sailed ships that followed.

Grasping the rail, Rose looked sharp at the ships that followed. They were a quarter mile apart one from the next and less than two miles behind them. "British?" she asked.

Still watching them through the telescope, Jones replied, "Aye. Two war sloops and a light frigate from the look of 'em."

"More than a match for our two ships," she observed.

"Maybe so," Cannonflash countered. "Mister O'scarlett. Go forward and find Mister Mueller."

"Aye, Captain!" the boy barked before turning to run to the bow.

Rose looked back at the boy as he hurried to his task, then she turned to Jones and folded her arms. "You let him fire a cannon?"

"Aye," Cannonflash answered. "Let you fire one too. What's the difference?"

"He's nine years old!" she cried.

"He's a stout lad," Jones grumbled. "Just cut the apron strings and let him grow up."

"And I guess you don't see a problem with putting him in the middle of battle like this."

Cannonflash lowered his telescope and looked to her. "They catch up to us and we lose this fight then it won't matter if he stays below."

She felt a chill at his words and looked to the ships behind them. "So what are we going to do? I guess you don't plan to attack them head-on."

"No," he replied, still staring at them. "We'll do that when we've evened things up."

"And when will that be?"

"The *Black Dragon*'s waiting for us southeast of Cuba. We reach her and they'll break off."

"If we reach her." Rose looked up at him and softly said, "By the way, Captain, thank you."

He slowly turned his eyes to her.

"You didn't have to do all of this," she continued.

With a slight nod, he raised the telescope to his eye and turned his attention back to the ships that followed. "Ye still owe me that powder."

She smiled just a little and looked that way herself, replying, "Yes sir."

Mueller, back in the clothing he was most comfortable in, arrived with Jeffy and reported, "I'm here, Captain Cannonflash. Ye have a plan?"

"Aye," Jones confirmed. "I'll need at least ten of this ship's biggest cannons back here, loaded and ready as quick as ye can get 'em here. See about disguising 'em and get word to Captain Angie to do the same."

Mueller smiled and nodded as he replied, "Aye, Captain. Sounds like they've a nasty surprise comin' aye?" He looked to Jeffy and said, "Come on, Lad. We've a fight to plan for!"

As the two hurried off, Rose did not even have time to protest as Cannonflash took her arm and ordered, "Let the boy have his fun, Missy. He's earned it."

"He's nine years old, Captain Jones!"

"Holds his own just fine, Lass."

She huffed a sigh and looked back to the ships behind them. "How long do you figure until they overtake us?"

"Some time in the night," was his direct answer. "We need to be ready for 'em."

Rose nodded, then glanced at him and asked, "If I told you I had a plan, would you listen?"

"I would."

Raising her brow, she looked to him barked, "Really?"

"Angela tells me you had some tricks for 'em before that took 'em off guard. I'll hear what ye have to say, Lass." He looked to her as she just stared at him. "Why do you look so surprised?"

She shrugged and looked to the horizon, a little smile on her lips as she replied, "Just surprised that you would trust me so, especially since my own crew didn't."

"This Smith bloke sounds like an idiot."

"Well, I also wasn't sleeping with him, and I'm sure he wanted me to."

"Can't say I blame him for that."

She cut him a flirty glance. "Can't blame him, huh? Did I impress you so?"

He shrugged. "I suppose so. I think I impressed you more."

"And why do you think that, Sir?"

"You were much louder than I was."

She burst into girlish giggles and bumped her shoulder into him.

* * *

The glow of early morning had barely begun to illuminate the East and brought a frightening sight.

The faster of the two fleeing ships was a half mile ahead of the other, and the British war sloops were moving into position to flank the straggler. Their cannons were at the ready, their decks lined with marines who held their weapons at the ready, prepared to clear the deck of opposition and board the ship without damaging it too badly. It was a smaller warship, not quite a match for either of the sloops, but considering the losses the British had suffered the last year it would be a wonderful prize. The light frigate had fallen back and veered east another quarter mile but was still close enough to charge into the action should it be called upon. Sometime in the night, the frigate had been joined by two more ships, heavy galleons by design that flew French flags. All five pursuing ships flew flags beneath those of their nations, white flags with black X's in the centers.

Looking through the telescope from the lead ship, Mueller shook his head and admitted, "I can't see 'em well in this poor light, Captain, but I can tell ye they're not flags I recognize, not from any nation in this part of the world."

Jones growled as the morning light grew brighter. "Those are definitely French ships. Can't see 'em in league with the Reds, but there they are."

"Unless something's changed in the last couple of years," Mueller pointed out. "Strange times we're in, Captain."

"Aye."

Rose looked to Mueller and asked, "What if it isn't an alliance with the crown. What if Berkley's forged an alliance of his own with them?"

Everyone looked right at her, and everyone was clearly pondering her questions.

Jones looked back to the ship behind them, one that was tethered to the one they were on by a quarter mile of rope and chain, whatever they could find the night before. Running along it was a thinner cord, held in place by twine. His steely eyes were locked on the ships and his brow tensed as he informed, "They've grappled her."

Rose watched as he took the thinner line firmly in his grip, then she looked back to the ships behind them as the British pulled their captive in close to them.

A moment passed. When the hulls nearly touched the soldiers sent volleys of musket rounds into the captured ship from both sides. Another moment passed, and finally they boarded from both sides.

His eyes narrowing, Cannonflash gripped the twine tightly, wrapping it around his hand, then he took two steps back to remove the slack. Looking to Rose, he murmured, "Let's hope this works," then he gave the twine a mighty yank.

241

The flash and thump that came from the captured ship reached them in short order and a second later the ship exploded in a horror of thunder and fire. The flames and smoke consumed the two war sloops and cannonballs ripped into them from both sides of the stricken ship. Silence followed, broken up only by debris hitting the water, the crackling of burning wood and the groans of the dying ships behind them. As the fireball boiled upward and slowly burned out, it illuminated the sight below it. The captured ship was gone. The sloop to the right had received the worst of it as its side was completely gone, its hull was burning and its masts were flattened. The sloop to the left had fared little better. Its masts and sails were also gone and what remained of the side that had been tethered to the captured ship was engulfed in flames. A few men scrambled onto the deck and after surveying the situation they jumped overboard.

Rose and Cannonflash watched the carnage behind them in silence for a moment, then Rose finally folded her arms and turned a very self satisfied look up to him.

He only glanced at her as he ordered, "Cut the line and let's have some distance."

A couple of crewman ran to them with axes and began chopping the tow line away, and when it was severed the ship lurched forward as it was no longer burdened with the task of towing the explosive laden ship behind it.

Mueller took Jones' side and remarked, "Two down, Captain. Still the matter of that frigate and those French ships."

"Bought us some time," Cannonflash observed.

"We're still running heavier now," Mueller reminded.

Bugs joined them with Angie walking at his side and he observed, "Seems to have worked. I'd say that'll give 'em something to think about."

"Not enough," Jones grumbled. "They're comin' for us come hell or hurricane, and they can't afford not to catch us."

The morning glow had grown a little brighter and the lookout who was perched close to the top of the mainmast shouted down, "Captain Cannonflash!" When Jones looked up at him he reported "We've sails ahead of us and you'd better look to the East!"

Everyone followed him to the starboard side and he grabbed onto the rail, his eyes narrowing as he could already see the sails of four ships.

"They've got the wind," he grumbled.

Rose took his side and whispered, "I wish you hadn't come for me now."

He glanced down at her and informed with authority, "We're not dead yet, Missy." Spinning around, he barked, "Quit your standing about and get to stations! If this is to be our last fight then we'll give 'em a fight that will haunt this sea forever!"

The crew cheered and shouts rang out from all over the ship.

As the sun began to turn the eastern sky orange and slowly bring light to the sea and the few clouds above, the ship was readied for battle and the pirates aboard were prepared for one glorious last stand. Rum and ale flowed freely and cannons and muskets were loaded and made ready. Rose herself was not ready to die anymore and even as she made preparations and watched her son as he did the same, her mind scrambled for a way out. No land was within swimming distance and floating about in a boat in the middle of a battle with people who she knew would kill her on sight was not an option either.

When everything was made ready and they watched their enemies close in for the kill, the ship grew silent. Jeffy stood beside Cannonflash and both of them had their arms folded as they watched the four heavy frigates, three of them French, close in on them from the East.

Rose padded up behind her son and grasped his shoulders, pulling him back into her as she stroked the boy's hair.

He half turned his head and looked up at her with a big smile, assuring, "Don't worry, Mother. We're going to win, you know."

She smiled back at him and patted his shoulder. "Aye, son. We'll prevail, won't we?"

He nodded and looked back to the attacking ships.

Looking to Cannonflash, Rose sought some kind of reassurance from him, and when he looked back at her she did not see it. She did see his iron resolve, though, and this began to infect her. She offered him a nod, and he responded in kind.

The attacking ships would be in firing range in moments. They were huge and even from half a mile away Rose could see the activity in the decks forward as cannons were moved into position. They had seemed to have been joined by two others, smaller ships that had been behind them the whole time and were veering a little out of formation to attack from a different angle.

Jones looked forward, seeing the shadows of three ships ahead, and leading the way was a British heavy frigate, a ship of the line that was obviously a ship of some great importance, and his eyes narrowed.

The ships attacking them from the East began to turn into firing position.

"Captain Cannonflash!" the man atop the mainmast shouted. When everyone looked up at him he pointed ahead and yelled, "Captain, the *Black Dragon*!"

Before he and Rose could even look that way fountains of water were blasted from the sea right beside the closest of the French warships. A second later a solid hundred pounder slammed into her side and ripped into her hull with devastating results. Smaller shot also hit the water and the side of the ship, fired from different cannons. When all eyes turned forward they were amazed at the sight of the *Black Dragon* and the British war frigate both firing on the French ships with their forward batteries—and they had the range!

The *Black Dragon* veered east to plunge right into the middle of the six ship formation while the British frigate continued toward the fleeing pirate's ship. It eased to port and at full sail passed within fifty yards. The men on the frigate's deck were holding their weapons up and cheering the pirates as they sped by each other while the men forward were reloading the cannons and making ready for another salvo. Like the *Black Dragon*, this ship had two decks of broadsides as well as heavy deck guns, swivel guns and marines armed with muskets at the rail.

Cannonflash and Rose watched in stunned silence as the British frigate charged into battle against the three ships behind them. Slowly looking to each other, they still could not speak for long seconds. Looking to the other side, they saw the *Silver Falcon*, Bugs' ship, also charging into battle against the ships behind them.

Finally snapping out of his stunned haze, Jones wheeled around and stormed toward the stern, shouting, "Angie! Swing this thing around and get us into that fight!"

The crew exploded into cheers and Angie, who now wore a huge smile, worked the wheel over as hard and fast as she could.

Apparently, the French were not that familiar with the black two hulled ship they were up against. Reasoning that they outnumbered her six to one, they turned hard and split their formation to bombard the huge pirate ship from both sides. The frigate that was already wounded was the first to feel the black ship's wrath as four of the hundred pounders, each now armed with high explosive cannonballs, drove their shot home low on the French ship's hull, blasting it open near the water line and opening the second cannon deck. Fire poured out of the open hull as kegs of powder ignited and secondary explosions started quickly. Two of the hundred pounders found their mark on the second ship in line on that side and the other four opened the hull of the frigate on the left.

Angie turned the ship as hard as it would go and everyone held on to something as it listed over and groaned in a hard semi-circle to join the *Silver Falcon* in the battle behind them.

The *Silver Falcon* tacked in a hard right turn and brought her cannons to bear on the closest ship, one of the French frigates, which turned to respond. They traded fire and the Falcon finished her turn and set a course north, and as the frigate turned to pursue she found herself under fire from the ship Cannonflash commanded and Jones' men proved their marksmanship with the cannons, sending many of their shots right into the frigate's cannon ports. Jones' ship also turned as if to flee. As it again turned to pursue it found that the *Silver Falcon* had turned a complete circle and had brought the cannons on her other side to bear on them.

While this one frigate maneuvered wildly against the two smaller ships, the British heavy frigate that had arrived with the *Black Dragon* engaged the other two. While the French ship held its ground, the British ship with it turned to retire, heading at full sail back south toward Port Royal.

The battle lasted a quarter hour and two damaged French frigates turned tail and limped back out to the open sea, still harassed by the guns of the *Black Dragon*. The British heavy frigate had found itself in a close-in slug match with the French galleons but the odds shifted in the English ship's favor when a salvo from the *Black Dragon* blasted the side of the first French ship open, obliterating her cannon decks on that side. With two of its masts down, the second crippled and burning French ship, now facing four enemy ships, surrendered. Rather than take it captive, the British and pirate vessels leisurely turned south and sailed away.

An hour later both the British heavy frigate and the *Black Dragon* signaled that they were dropping anchor, and the two smaller ships followed suit.

Jones took a boat with a few of his men and Rose to his ship, stopping at the *Silver Falcon* to allow Bugs and his crewmen to return to their own ship.

Climbing aboard his ship, Cannonflash strode with purpose toward the wheelhouse where he hoped to find Johnny Cannonburg, but he stopped and raised his chin as he saw his first mate approaching him with a well decorated British officer in a red dress uniform adorned with gold embroidery and decorated lapels. Brass buttons were perfectly polished and a ceremonial hat that was lined with some kind of white feathers was held in his hand. A saber hung on his belt, a fine looking blade in a well decorated scabbard that looked almost too ceremonial to be a real weapon. This was a pleasant enough looking man. Apparently in his fifties, his light brown hair was streaked with silver at his temples and he regarded the big pirate captain with blue green eyes beneath well groomed eyebrows.

He stopped about a yard away, right beside Cannonburg, and he raised his chin slightly, saying in a proper English tone, "Captain Jones, I presume?"

Cannonflash nodded, his eyes narrowing.

"Bit of an odd thing," the British officer observed, "English navy fighting alongside notorious pirates and all that. If I may introduce myself, I am Admiral Stewart Peterson of His Majesty's Royal Navy. Might we go somewhere to have a word?"

Still eying him with suspicion, Jones growled, "This way," as he walked past the Admiral toward his cabin.

Once inside, he looked to Cannonburg and ordered, "Have Harold send over some of that rum,"

"No need," Peterson corrected. "I brought over a couple of bottles of brandy. Took the liberty of having them delivered here to your cabin." He extended his hand to the table and sure enough there were two crystal bottles with crystal stoppers and four glasses waiting for them.

Jones stared at them for a few long seconds, then he looked to Rose and asked, "Where's the boy?"

She replied, "He stayed behind to help Angie with repairs." She smiled. "He thinks she's really pretty and it looks like he wants to give Johnny a good run for her."

With a nod, Jones strode to the table and pulled a chair out, which groaned under his weight as he sat down. Extending his hand to the others, he invited everyone to join him without a word, and they did.

The Admiral reached for the first bottle of brandy, pulling the stopper and filling the first glass. As he did, he informed, "It seems we have a problem, Captain Jones, and you and I are neck deep in it."

Taking the glass from Peterson, Cannonflash took a drink and growled back, "How so?"

He filled the next glass and offered it to Rose, then reached for a third. "The documents Commodore Jones left in my care weave quite the troublesome tale."

Rose's eyes snapped to Jones. "Wait a moment. You gave those to Berkley. He burned them right in front of me."

Jones huffed a laugh and took another sip from his glass. "He should have read what was inside first."

A little smile touched her lips.

Filling the last glass, the Admiral finally put the bottle down and looked to Cannonflash. "What you sent my way confirmed our fears and suspicions about the Governor. Seems he's building his own world down there and he's using England's resources and money to do so." His eyes shifted to Rose. "So he does not know I have the documents?"

She shook her head and replied, "He thinks he's burned them."

Admiral Peterson half smiled. "I see. Sounds just splendid." Turning his eyes back to Jones, he went on, "We still have the issue of what he's doing and how you are a part of it." Looking back to Rose, he finished, "Both of you, Captain O'scarlett."

Rose's neck stiffened and her breath caught. Taking a gulp from her glass, she asked, "So what is to become of us?"

Reaching into his coat, Peterson produced a folded document that was closed with a red drop of wax that had the royal seal pressed into it.

Jones stared at it for a second before asking, "What's this?"

"A full pardon," was the Admiral's reply.

Cannonflash and Rose exchanged looks, then they looked back to the Admiral, not knowing what to think about this offer.

"Yes," Peterson confirmed, "it is a legitimate offer. You get a pardon in exchange for your services as a privateer to bring down Governor Berkley."

Looking away, Jones growled, "I'm no privateer and I've no use for you reds."

"Understandably," the Admiral sighed, looking to his glass. "Of course, according to the documents we received you have much more of a grievance against the Governor than anyone."

Rose raised her chin slightly, looking to Cannonflash as his eyes slid to the Admiral.

Peterson took a sip of his brandy and looked to her. "You as well, Miss O'scarlett. It is quite clear that your husband, the late Lieutenant O'scarlett had uncovered Berkley's activities early on. I'm sorry to say he paid the price for his loyalty to the crown."

She nodded, then asked, "Am I to be pardoned as well?"

Admiral Peterson released a deep breath, just staring at her for a moment before he answered. "I'm afraid your situation is a little more complicated, Miss O'scarlett."

Rose looked to Cannonflash, then across the room as she drank down the last of her brandy.

Jones regarded the British Admiral coldly as he growled, "You'll have her help you bring this Berkley down and then send her to the gallows when it's done."

"I said her situation is complicated," Peterson corrected, "not hopeless. My hands are not exactly tied in this matter and I've been authorized by the crown to take certain liberties." He met Rose's eyes and assured, "I shall do my utmost to keep you from the gallows, Miss O'scarlett, and you have my word on that. However, there are still unresolved matters concerning you that must be attended to at some point."

"Unresolved matters," she grumbled. "Berkley created the pirate I am today, Admiral Peterson."

"And after that," the Admiral informed straightly, "your actions were your own. I'm not saying that he did not have you cornered as far as the path you were put on, but what you did when you were on that path was a matter unto itself. But, we have time to settle that once the current crisis has been resolved."

With his fingertips, Jones slowly slid the document across the table back to Peterson. "We'll resolve it now, if you please, or you'll attend to this crisis on your own."

The Admiral met Jones' glare with one of his own, then he looked to the pardon and informed, "That is a new start for you, Captain Jones. It would be foolish to throw it away."

"I was foolish to trust you reds before," Cannonflash growled.

Still staring at the document, Peterson huffed a sigh and finally conceded, "I shall personally see to the matter with Miss O'scarlett. Her husband was a lieutenant in the Royal Navy, after all. It would be poor form not to take care of his family." He slid the document back over to Jones and asked, "So, Captain Jones. Do we have an accord?"

"Aside from that pardon," Cannonflash demanded, "why would I put me neck out for you reds? Why would I risk me ship and men for you?"

"For the same reason you do what you do," the Admiral replied straightly. "You want revenge. I'm offering you that opportunity *and* a full pardon from the crown. According to the documents provided by Miss O'scarlett, the ship your wife and son were on, the *Swordfish*, was listed by then Captain Berkley as one that was involved in piracy activities."

Jones slowly raised his chin.

Peterson continued, "Of course, the listing took place after she was sunk, just like so many others. His report was suspect even then but he managed to see to it that no investigation was pursued. Your wife and son were killed by that man, Captain

Jones, and now you have the opportunity to see him humiliated and taken to the gallows for his many crimes."

Looking to Rose, Jones considered hard what an alliance with the British would mean, and what he could accomplish with it.

"It is entirely up to you, of course," the Admiral went on. "Just bear in mind that you have a deal with the man who killed your family and he means a rather ghastly double cross. You see, there is a new squadron of ships on its way from England. They should already have arrived, actually. Have you heard of the *HMS Goliath?*"

Rose answered, "Berkley mentioned the *Goliath.*"

"Most powerful ship afloat," Peterson informed. "Took two years to construct her. She's not like the frigates you are used to dealing with, Captain Jones. She was purpose built to engage your *Black Dragon*, and then to assert England's power all over the world. Only one tiny problem."

"And that is?" Jones asked in a low voice.

Raising his brow, the Admiral replied, "Well, it seems that Governor Berkley's influence reaches all the way to London. He requested the specially built ship to be constructed specifically to deal with you, then he was able to maneuver certain officers to the front of the line to command her. We think that everyone on that ship is more loyal to Berkley than the crown. We also fear that he intends to break away from British rule with the aid of his new found friends the French."

Rose's eyes narrowed. "So, if you suspect this—"

"He's a man of great influence," Admiral Peterson interrupted. "Dealing with him has been both a chore and quite the delicate matter." His eyes found Jones again. "He must not have the *Goliath* in his hands. That ship has no equal and if he controls it then the Caribbean and whatever else he has his hands into will be lost, and there will be little we can do about it."

Jones looked down to the pardon in front of him again and stared at it for long seconds. Finally, he gulped down the last of his brandy and set the glass back on the table before asking, "And you want me to put me ship between Berkley and this *Goliath.*"

"She'll have to be captured or sunk," the Admiral informed straightly.

"And you think the *Black Dragon* is the ship to do this."

"From what I've seen, Captain Jones, this ship is the only ship that can stand against her and have any hope of success."

Cannonflash nodded slowly, his eyes still on the document before him. "He'll not give up without a fight to end all." His gaze shifted to the Admiral. "We stop this *Goliath*, there's still the matter of him at that fort. He's not one to just come out and surrender, I think."

Raising his brow, Peterson stared across the room and agreed, "No, I can't expect that he will."

"But we can sure flush him out," Rose said with a little smile. When all eyes ended up fixed on her, she added, "It just takes the right touch."

* * *

Evening found the four ships at anchor just off of Tortuga, two of them for much needed repairs and all of them for resupply— and to drop off a few passengers who would not be well suited to the heat of the battle to come. The sun was setting as Rose led the way down one of the main streets of the village, one that was lit with torches on a few of the stone buildings. Dressed in red trousers and wading boots, she had her hair restrained with a red bandana and had strain in her eyes as she walked, her hand tightly gripping her son's as he walked beside her. He seemed upset as well, but said nothing. Jones strode behind her, talking over what was to come with Johnny and Admiral Peterson, who on the advice of the pirates around him had abandoned his uniform and wore black trousers, a white swordsman's shirt left open at the chest and an older pair of boots. Bugs walked with them, but said nothing as he listened.

They reached a house that was just outside of the main square. It was a quaint place with whitewashed stucco walls and two windows that each had a wooden box planted with flowers below. An oil lamp burned outside the well made wooden door, awaiting the coming night.

The boy sniffed and turned his eyes down.

Turning toward him, Rose knelt down and took his shoulders, fighting back tears as she softly said, "Jeffy, Mommy needs you to be brave now."

"I want to come with you," he whined.

"I know you do and I wish you could, but this time you have to stay here."

He would not look at her as he cruelly reminded, "That's what you said last time and I didn't see you again for years."

The words stabbed at her and she clenched her teeth, finally admitting, "I know, Sweetheart, I know. I wanted to come and get you all that time, I just couldn't."

"Then why do you have to go now?" he questioned.

She drew a breath, then grasped his jaw and turned his eyes to her. "I have to make sure that the bad people who separated us can never do it again. I need to be sure that they'll never try to hurt either of us ever again."

Jeffy took deep, difficult breaths, tears finally rolling from his eyes as he sobbed, "But why can't I come with you? Why can't you just stay here?"

Her brow arched, a tear finally escaped from her eye as she gently stroked her hand over his hair and admitted, "I wish I could, Sweetheart. I wish I could."

"Then don't go," he whined. "Just stay here with me this time."

Heavy boot steps hitting the ground announced the approach of Captain Jones and they both looked that way, up at the big pirate.

Setting his hands on his hips as he loomed over the boy, his features were as they always were. He just stared back at Jeffy for long seconds, then he ordered, "Walk with me, boy."

As Jones turned, Jeffy pulled away from his mother and took the big pirate captain's side and they strode down the street a few paces. All could hear Cannonflash talking to him, but he was speaking in a low voice and no one could make out what was said.

Rose stood as she watched her son and this huge pirate speak. Jeffy nodded often as he stared up at Jones and would occasionally reply with something. She worried over what was said, what this pirate was telling her son, but she knew she dare not interrupt.

A couple of moments later Jones extended his hand and Jeffy took it, and they nodded to each other, then Jeffy turned and strode back to his mother, his features more stone like and his head held high with a certain pride. Looking up at her, he set his hands on his hips and straightly said, "I'll be waiting here for you when you return, Mommy. You watch yourself out there, aye?"

She was a little astounded and glanced at Jones before she responded. "Um... I will. You watch yourself here, okay?"

"I will," he assured.

Glancing at Cannonflash as he approached again, she asked her son, "What did you two talk about?"

Jeffy looked over his shoulder at the huge pirate, then back to his mother and answered, "It was man stuff, Mother. Nothing you should worry about." He took her arm and pulled her down to him for a good hug.

Rose struggled to maintain her composure as she hugged him back as tightly as she could.

Cannonflash strode by them and knocked on the door, and when it opened a rather plump woman wearing a blue dress and a white apron opened it, her eyes widening as they locked on Jones. Her white hair was restrained in a bun and had a blue ribbon tied around it.

Pulling reluctantly away from her son, Rose turned to the woman as she grasped Jeffy's shoulder and greeted, "Thank you for doing this, Irene. I'm in your debt."

Tearing her eyes away from Jones, the woman smiled and shook her head. "You've been a dear friend of us for a long time, Rosanne. We're glad to help ye in any way we can."

She smiled back, then looked to her son and introduced, "Jeffy, this is Irene Greun and she is a dear friend of mine. She has children who are waiting to play with you."

Jeffy nodded and turned steely eyes up to his mother, informing, "We'll be sure to have fun." Looking to Irene, he greeted, "Good to meet you, Ma'am."

Irene nodded to him and offered him her hand. "Come along, Jeffy. We've a hot meal and many toys awaiting you."

He turned to his mother once more, gave her one more hug, then turned and strode confidently into the house.

Rose met Irene's eyes and nodded to her.

With a nod back, Irene assured, "We'll take good care of the boy, Rose."

"Thank you," Rose managed.

 253

* * *

Entering Mister Greun's tavern, Rose was very quiet and lagging behind the men. Her eyes were on the ground and her thoughts were distant even as they found a large table at the rear of the tavern that would accommodate them all. As the men talked absently about the events of the days to come she remained quiet and not really paying attention.

Bugs, sitting beside her and opposite Cannonflash, nudged her and drew her attention to him.

She was tight lipped as she regarded him distantly and only with a short look.

"He's in good hands, Lass," Bugs assured.

Rose nodded and confirmed with a soft voice, "I know. It's just hard to leave him again."

"I can only imagine," he said sympathetically.

Admiral Peterson vented a deep breath and shook his head. "Even with that monster of yours I can't see us getting through the screen of ships he commands. With the *Goliath* among them I can't see even a squadron of heavy frigates succeeding."

Jones growled, "You just worry over the rest of his fleet and let me take this *Goliath*."

"A sound plan, Captain Jones," the Admiral commended, "and it was in my thoughts already, but I'm afraid the best the rest of us can do is keep most of the rest of his fleet off of you while you engage *Goliath*, and that would be a twitchy plan at best. I have three more ships coming, but Berkley is known to control ten times that number."

"Thirty against seven," Bugs said as if to himself. "Even with the *Black Dragon* among our numbers we'd stand little chance, especially with two of our ships in need of repair."

Rose looked toward the bar, clenching her teeth. "The *Scarlet Dragon* would be a good addition to our fleet, if I still had her."

Peterson's eyes snapped to her. "*Scarlet Dragon*. A French-built frigate?"

She looked to him and nodded.

He raised his brow. "That ship was in a firefight with two of my ships east of Cuba in the Windward Passage a few days ago. She was captured and sailed to Port Royal."

"Her crew?" Rose asked hopefully.

Peterson shrugged. "Interned there, I suppose."

Giving Cannonflash a glance she asked, "Can I have her back?"

"I don't see how we would arrange that," the Admiral said hesitantly. "Truly, I don't see one more ship that size doing us much good."

"What about a dozen?" Bugs asked.

Jones looked to him. "Have some favors to call in, Mister Nailhall?"

Raising his brow, Bugs informed, "This Governor Berkley has been a thorn in the side of many a good captain out there. I'm sure we could rally more to our cause with a little inspiration."

"And still go in outnumbered," Peterson grumbled.

Jones took a couple of gulps of his ale, then looked to the Admiral and informed, "The Commodore will be heading this way with his ship and two more just like her. He can rally more to us."

Angie entered the tavern and stormed to the table, slamming her hands down on the table beside Rose as she shouted, "You are the worst luck in a firefight I have ever seen!"

"Mind your manners, little girl," Jones growled. When she looked to him he asked, "What is it that's got your ire up this time?"

Standing fully, she set her hands on her hips and cried, "Cannonball came through right in the middle of the hull and severed the mainmast below decks! Again! Two of 'em hit the inside of the hull and fractured main planks and they gave way an hour ago. The damn thing is out there sinking!"

Cannonflash vented a sigh and looked to Rose, raising his brow as their eyes met.

Admiral Peterson finished his drink and pushed away from the table, informing as he stood, "I am expected at Port Royal. I'll do what I can once I get there, but remember that he cannot take possession of the *Goliath*. That must be avoided at all cost."

"Agreed," Jones said straightly.

As the Admiral took his leave of them, Angie watched after him, then looked back to Jones and stamped her foot as she cried, "That ship was supposed to be mine and now it's sinking!"

Looking to her, Cannonflash growled, "Just mind your place, Angie. I'll get ye another. Until then you'll serve aboard the *Dragon*."

She looked away and folded her arms, grumbling, "Serve on the *Dragon*. I should have me own ship and now I'm not even to be first mate."

Rose gulped down her drink and stood, grabbing onto Angie's arm as she ordered, "Let's go. Gentlemen, we'll rendezvous with you tomorrow."

They watched as Rose towed the big blond girl out of the tavern and Bugs looked to Cannonflash, shaking his head as he observed, "You get women together like that and no good can come of it."

Jones huffed a laugh and took a gulp from his mug.

Chapter 12

SCARLET'S FLIGHT

Governor Berkley threw the door to his office open and stormed in, wheeling around as he shouted, "You'll have them back here by tomorrow or I'll have your heads decorating the front gate to this fort!" He slammed the door and wheeled around, stomping toward his desk. He had papers in his hand that he slammed down onto the desk. Turning to the small table on one end of the desk, he picked up a glass and poured it full of brandy from one of the crystal bottles he had there.

Rose ordered from behind him, "Pour me one, too."

Berkley froze before his glass could reach his lips. Ever so slowly, he looked over his shoulder, toward the couch against the wall to his right and behind him, and he half turned.

Rose was lying on the couch with her boots crossed at the ankles as she stared back at him. Her left arm was lying over the armrest while her right slowly rose out of her lap, gripping a pistol. Wearing that white shirt she was before, this time freshly cleaned and belted at the waist, and now in those scarlet tights with wading boots that reached to her knees, she was an alluring sight, especially with her shirt open between her breasts. She was

 257

also something of a deadly sight as her thumb slowly pulled back the hammer of her pistol.

He stood frozen where he was as he looked her over and finally moved his gaze to her eyes and he raised his brow. "Brandy?"

She shrugged. "Whatever you're drinking." Rose watched him warily as he turned back to the table and set his glass down to pick up another. As he poured her a drink, she smiled slightly and asked, "How have you been, James?"

"Under a little pressure about your escape," he answered frankly.

"Oh," she drawled. "That's unfortunate." When he turned back to her with a glass in each hand, she trained her pistol on him and held her other hand to him, offering, "Thank you," as she took her glass.

Berkley backed away, keeping his eyes on her as he took a sip from his glass. "You know, Rose, if you shoot me then the guards will be alerted and you'll—"

"You'll be just as dead," she interrupted. "Believe me, it's the least you deserve."

"I see," he said softly. After another sip of his brandy, he asked, "What is it you plan to do now, Miss O'scarlett? We both know you aren't getting out of here alive."

"That remains to be seen," she countered. "First things first, Governor. I heard my ship was captured a couple of days ago. I want her back."

Berkley raised his brow.

Half smiling, Rose continued, "You don't want the chase to end any more than I do, James. We can call it another miraculous escape by the notorious Rose O'scarlett."

"And make me look like a fool," Berkley pointed out.

Rose smiled broader. "That would just be sugar in the tea, James."

Staring down at his glass, the Governor reminded, "Jones aided you in your escape, Rose."

"Yes," she confirmed. "I owed him a substantial debt, one that he knew he would never collect if I was hung."

"And you paid this debt to him despite his killing your son."

She took a sip of her brandy before answering, "His cannons killed my son, but I blame you for that. You've taken everything from me, James. My husband and son are dead because of you, the life I loved as a wife and mother is dead because of you, and no matter where I go or how carefully I try to hide myself I'll always be a wanted woman and always be looking over my shoulder for the next soldier or bounty hunter who recognizes me."

He finally turned his eyes to her.

She continued, "I have nothing left but the sea. If I'm to live a fleeing woman then I want the pirate's life you forced me into."

Berkley just stared at her for a long moment, then he nodded slightly and looked back to his glass. "This will be a complicated undertaking, Miss O'scarlett."

"Captain O'scarlett," she snarled. "I saw my ship moored at the end of the pier and I'm guessing my men are under the fort here somewhere."

"They are," the Governor confirmed with a nod.

Rose finished her brandy and set the glass down on the floor, then she stood with fluid, sultry movements and approached him with slow steps, keeping the pistol trained on his belly and her eyes locked on his. Once within arm's reach, she stopped and just stared up at him for long, tense seconds. Adding to the tension, she smiled at him and assured, "Don't worry about a thing, sweetie. Rose will handle the details tonight. Oh, and one other thing." Her left hand was a blur as she slapped him hard in the face and snapped his head around, and she snarled as she hissed, "Don't ever touch me again unless I say you can."

Slowly, carefully, he raised a hand to his stinging cheek as he looked back to her.

She grabbed his throat right under the jaw and warned, "And the next time you'd better pleasure me or I might just cut it off, savvy?"

He tensed up more but managed to ask, "And when will this next time be?"

Rose smiled a flirty smile and ran her fingers over his lips. "It will be when I say it is, James, and not before. Now I'm going to leave and you are going to sit down at your desk and do whatever it is you—"

The door burst open and Rose swung around as two British marines stormed in with their weapons trained on her. The distraction was all Governor Berkley needed and he snatched the pistol from Rose's grip before she realized and before she even had time to react the two men each had an arm and she was held firmly in their grips. Turned back to the Governor, she stared up helplessly, her eyes wide and her pouty mouth slightly ajar.

Berkley smiled as he held the gun on her and he shook his head. "That was a brief chase, Rose. Looks like you'll be standing back on the gallows in the morning." He raised a finger. "But this time I'll be ready for Jones and his men when they come, if they come. And, of course, I'll let you watch your old crew hang before you, one by one. Sounds like a ripping good time, eh?" He looked to the marines who held Rose and ordered, "Keep her under heavy guard and shoot her if she so much as coughs, but only wound her." His venomous eyes found her again and he raised a hand to cup her cheek. "I want to watch her get her pretty little neck snapped in the morning. And this time Admiral Peterson will be in attendance. He arrived an hour ago. Such a pity that the two of you will not have time for that chat before your date with the hangman's noose." He looked back to the marines and motioned with his head for her to be taken away.

As they brutally turned her toward the door to escort her out, she looked over her shoulder back to the Governor and spat, "You'll get yours one of these days, Berkley! Mark my words you'll get yours!"

He laughed under his breath and shook his head as the door closed behind her. Looking down at her pistol, he shook his head again, then strode over to his desk and shoved the pistol into a drawer as he sat down.

* * *

Morning found the Governor in excellent spirits as he strode from his suite and into his office to take care of the day's issues before he would attend the hanging of Rose O'scarlett. Once again he was wearing his best suit and polished boots and a ceremonial saber hung at his side. He would see her face to face as last time, watch from the balcony and his men would be ready for any ambush. Ships blockaded the harbor in the unlikely event they would try to rescue her again. Cannons stood loaded and ready, this time facing out to sea as they were supposed to. Every guard and soldier at the fort was on duty by his order and many of them even patrolled the village in squads of four. The fort was abuzz with activity.

The window to his office overlooked the harbor and the two piers that jetted out, and after quickly finishing up on some paperwork and signing off on requisitions, he wore a big smile as he stood and spun around to look over the water. Two ships were moored at the pier taking on supplies.

Slowly, his smile straightened until his mouth was tight slit beneath his nose.

The *Scarlet Dragon* was gone!

Bursting through the door to the jail cells below the fort with six armed guards following, he looked around him at empty cell after empty cell. Made of flat iron that was riveted together, each cell was about ten feet by ten feet and had bunks on opposite walls. Each one on the left had one window that was high on the wall as most of the rooms were under ground. The aisle between the rows of cells, four on each side, was a stone and dirt floor and the bottoms of the cells themselves were covered in straw. There was one table and one chair in the middle of the aisle halfway in with a lamp burning in the middle of it, and the guard at the table stood as the Governor strode angrily up to him.

This man was not especially tall, rather old with thinning gray and white hair and had not shaved for a few days. His uniform was not in good order and he did his best to straighten it before he asked, "What can I do for ye, Governor?"

Berkley looked around him once more. The third cell to the right still had one man in it.

Lying on one of the bunks, Mister Smith looked back at him with blank eyes.

The Governor shouted, "Where are all of the prisoners?"

The jailer tensed and replied, "They were transferred out last night, Governor!" He turned and took a document from the table, offering it to Berkley with a shaking hand.

Snatching it from him, Berkley opened it and read with narrow eyes. He clenched his teeth as he saw the Governor's seal—his seal—on the document, and a very close forgery of his own signature on the bottom. Slowly, he crumpled up the document and bared his teeth as he turned back to the door and stomped toward it. He was grumbling, but nobody could quite make out what was said.

Chapter 13

A PRICE OF LOYALTY

With the *Scarlet Dragon* cutting through the water at her top speed and the wind from her stern, things seemed to be looking up. Rose was at the wheel, holding it with one hand as she raised a rum bottle to her mouth with the other. This was good rum! It was very stout, very flavorful, and when half of the bottle was in her she felt the effects of a whole night of drinking. Relaxed and feeling good, she just enjoyed the wind in her hair and the gentle rolling of her ship beneath her on a restless sea.

Angie struggled up the ladder with a rum bottle of her own and when she was on the steering deck she walked with some difficulty to the ship's captain and took her side. Her bottle was also half empty and she raised it to her mouth to pull another swig from it.

They watched the horizon and the wind in the sails in silence for a time, and finally looked to each other.

Holding her bottle to Angie's, Rose commended with slurred words, "This is some really fine rum ya snitched."

Touching her bottle to the Captain's, Angie agreed, "Aye, it is, the best that Berkley could offer. Got us four cases, I did!"

Her mouth tightening to a thin slit, a teary eyed Rose said with solemn words, "You are the best first mate I ever had."

They touched bottles again and drank.

One of the marines who had escorted Rose from Berkley's office ascended the ladder and approached the women, his eyes on the ship's captain as he greeted, "Captain O'scarlett."

With an unsteady gaze, she looked to him and announced, "Aye, you'd be addressing Captain O'scarlett. State yer business!"

He reached her and folded his hands behind him, looking down to the bottle before he said, "To be honest, Captain, I'm a little surprised to see you drinking. We're in waters that are heavily patrolled by the Navy and we should all be ready for action at a moment's notice."

She nodded and looked forward again. "Let me get this straight, General. I'm at the helm of a stolen ship with a crew that's already mutinied once and in hostile waters and you think I should face all of that sober." She looked to him and shook her head. "What's wrong with you?"

He turned his eyes up. "Just concern over what is to come, Captain."

Angie spat, "You just let the Captain worry over that and go guard something!" Looking to Rose, she nodded, and Rose nodded back."

He glanced behind her and nodded himself. "I should do just that, then. By the way, we've a ship behind us."

The two women spun around.

Sure enough, a two mast sloop with its sails full of the wind was in pursuit and cutting across the water with alarming speed.

Rose and Angie looked to each other, their eyes wide with fear and indecision.

The marine removed a small telescope from his belt and held it to his eye. After studying the ship for a moment he raised his brow and said, "Looks like the *HMS Kestrel.* She's a fast ship with a shallow draft. Should be eight marines on board along with her compliment of twenty officers and men."

Angie asked, "So she's not an open sea ship?"

The marine shook his head, still studying the pursuing ship. "Coastal patrol. Not well suited to ocean crossings."

Rose shook her head. "But suited well enough to chase us across the sea. Can we outrun her?"

Looking to her, the marine shook his head and replied, "No. Your *Scarlet Dragon* is a fast ship, but not as fast as that one. She'll be on us within the hour."

"Damn," Rose grumbled. "How well armed is she?"

"She'll easily match your firepower," the marine replied. "She's also far more maneuverable."

Her eyes narrowing, Rose snarled, "That means lighter built." Looking to Angie, she ordered, "Let's take a page from Captain Jones' book on sea battle and move all the cannons we can to the bow. And hide them. Make the Reds think that we're moving in for a close-in broadside."

Angie smiled and nodded. "Now I see what it is that Captain Cannonflash likes about you, O'scarlett."

As Angie hurried off, Rose looked to the Marine and asked, "How many muskets aboard?"

He shrugged and answered, "I haven't taken an inventory, but I suppose I can do so." Looking back to the ship behind them, he raised his telescope again and examined the ship once more. "Many men on deck forward. Your flag seems to be drawing them right to us."

Rose looked up where the skull and crossbones flew proudly on the back of her ship and she barked, "Who the hell ordered that thing up there?"

"You did," the marine replied dryly, still examining the ship behind them.

"Shut up!" Rose shouted. She took another drink of rum and stared back at the ship herself.

The marine suddenly raised his head and lowered his telescope. Raising it back to his eye, he said with enthusiasm, "We need to stop!"

Rose looked to him.

He looked back. "They are signaling us to stop. We should cease all hostile activities and let them come along side."

"Like hell I will!" Rose barked.

"Captain," the marine explained, "they are not asking for us to surrender."

She raised her chin, staring at him suspiciously, then she looked back to the pursuing ship.

"The *Kestrel* may not be loyal to Berkley," he said. "I think they are looking to join us."

Rose stared back at him for a moment. Despite being intoxicated, she felt in her gut that this man was telling her the truth. Looking forward, she shouted, "Angie! Bring this ship to a stop and stand to!"

"What?" Angie shouted back.

"Stop the ship!" Rose yelled.

"Why?"

"Because I'm the Captain and I said to!"

* * *

They were overtaken in less than a half an hour and the war sloop slowed and drifted up beside them, lowering its own sails as lines were thrown across to tether the ships together. A plank was extended and a well decorated officer, a smaller man with short black hair, strode across it. He wore a saber on his belt but no pistol and his men watched nervously as he crossed from one ship to the other. He looked young for his position, a handsome, pleasant looking fellow who bore confidence in his eyes as well as strain. His red officer's hat was decorated with the white feathers of his position and he held it onto his head with some difficulty as he crossed, and finally aboard his shiny black boots solidly on the deck of the *Scarlet Dragon*.

Rose was standing by and closed the space between them with three steps, her left hand resting on her cutlass, her right resting on the pistol shoved into her belt. Raising her chin as she made eye contact with the young officer, she ordered, "State your business."

He politely removed his hat and greeted, "I am Captain Wilson of the *HMS Kestrel* and I bring word from the fort. You are Captain O'scarlett?" When she nodded he continued, "Admiral Peterson sent us to find you. He's been arrested and is to be hung in the morning."

Her eyes widened and she took a step back.

The marine approached from behind her and demanded, "Arrested on what charge?"

"Treason," Captain Wilson replied. "Governor Berkley accused him of helping you escape."

"Which he did," the marine grumbled, looking away. "That will leave Commander Wallace in command of his ship. He's not that experienced in these matters and will simply follow orders, and his ship is now in the hands of the Governor."

Rose turned and strode away a few steps, grumbling, "Everything is playing right into Berkley's hands. Everything!" She huffed a breath. "He has to know we'll come for the Admiral."

"And he'll be expecting you," Captain Wilson informed.

Rose considered, her eyes darting about as her lips tightened in anger. Her hair flailed out as she wheeled around and she demanded, "Does the Governor know where your loyalties lie?"

"He thinks they're with him," Wilson replied. "*Kestrel* was sent because she's the fastest ship he has there. Captain O'scarlett, we cannot allow him to hang the Admiral."

"I know," Rose agreed.

"Sweet Mother of God!" someone on the other side of the ship yelled.

Everyone looked that way and strode quickly to the far rail.

Her eyes widening, Rose raised her head as she saw the many sails just barely on their side of the horizon. She snatched the telescope from the marine's belt and held it to her eye, fixing her gaze on the biggest of the ships which sailed in the middle. "Oh my God," she breathed. "That thing's huge!"

Captain Wilson squinted to see the distant ships better, and his brow lowered. "The flotilla that is escorting *Goliath* to Port Royal."

"Damn," Rose snarled. Looking to the stern, she shouted, "Get that flag down and raise the Union Jack before we're seen!"

Two of the crewmen sprang into action at the ship's stern.

Angie approached from behind Rose and grasped her shoulder. "Well, we don't dare attack, not against that many ships and that monster among them. Captain Cannonflash would but we won't fair well with these ships."

Captain Wilson informed, "*Goliath*'s broadsides are forty-two pounders and she has long thirty-twos up front, the largest guns ever put to sea."

Rose and Angie slowly looked to each other and raised their brows.

"She also has sides that are double thick and solid oak," he continued. "The chances of getting shot through them are pretty slim. She can win against any ship, even if she's outnumbered five to one."

"We'll see," Rose snarled. "Angie, take the Scarlet Dragon back to Tortuga and tell Captain Jones that we've sighted the *Goliath*. Also tell him that Admiral Peterson is to be hung in the morning and I am going to get him out."

Angie grabbed her shoulder and turned her. "I should be with you, O'scarlett."

Grasping the girl's arms, Rose shook her head and countered, "I need someone I trust in command of my ship, and if I don't make it back the *Scarlet Dragon* will need someone of aggression and wits in control of her for the coming battle."

With the slight raise of her chin, Dreaded Angie's eyes showed the same steel resolve that was often seen in Cannonflash's eyes, and she hesitantly nodded. "Just don't get yourself killed, Captain O'scarlett." She smiled. "We've still a couple of cases of rum to drink."

* * *

The *HMS Kestrel* eased up to the pier just outside of Fort Charles and was moored with the efficiency that made the British Navy legendary. As the men labored away an entourage followed Governor Berkley down the pier and right up to Captain Wilson as he disembarked.

Wilson snapped to attention and greeted, "Good afternoon, Governor."

Berkley folded his arms and snapped, "Well?"

Shaking his head, the Captain reluctantly reported, "She wasn't to be found, Governor. No sign and no sails on any horizon."

Raising his chin, Berkley's eyes narrowed as he regarded the smaller man with suspicion and disbelief.

Wilson continued, "We stopped and boarded one ship but it was a merchant vessel leaving Haiti. Nothing out of the ordinary."

"And no sign of O'scarlett?" Berkley questioned.

"I'm afraid not, Sir. The ship we stopped had no women aboard and her cargo and manifests were in good order. With your permission I'd like to take on provisions and go back out after her, perhaps check the port at Tortuga. I hear many pirates consider it a safe haven."

Berkley just stared at him for long, uncomfortable seconds.

Raising his brow, Captain Wilson asked, "Should I go or should I remain here in the event she attacks the fort again?"

The governor drew a breath and stared at the smaller man for long seconds more, then he ordered, "Take on six more cannons and round up some volunteers, then go after them. If you find the *Scarlet Dragon* then she is to be captured or sunk. In fact, don't come back here without news that Rose O'scarlett is your prisoner or her body bound to the bow of your ship."

Nodding, Wilson said, "Understood, Sir. I shall see to it at once."

Berkley turned to one of his aids and growled, "See to Captain Wilson's cannons and whatever else he needs." Looking back to Wilson he ordered, "I will have her back here or you can take her place in a cell."

Captain Wilson watched him spin around and storm back toward the fort, and he smiled ever so slightly and nodded.

* * *

Being an admiral in the Royal Navy, Peterson was not sent to the jail under the fort despite the charges against him. Instead he found himself confined to the suite he was to sleep in anyway, under heavy guard. Two men were outside with orders to shoot him should he emerge. It was rather a nice room he was in with a large bed, a desk, a sitting area and even a fireplace. Paintings hung on the walls, a vanity and water basin were near the bed and a vase of flowers decorated the small table where he would eat his meals. The one window was rather large and arched at the top with a heavy timber shelf about two feet wide at the bottom. It was three feet wide and at least that high and ringed in carefully cut limestone. A silver pot of tea sat in the middle of the table with fine china cups, a small bowl of honey and a few pastries. Though a prisoner, his comforts were seen to.

At the table was where he sat, writing out his last orders in the hopes that they would somehow arrive at the Admiralty in London. His coat was laid out on the bed behind him and his shirt was open at the chest for comfort against the still air inside the room. Once in a while he would blot perspiration from his forehead with his sleeve, then resume putting pen to paper as he recorded his thoughts. With the *Goliath* anchored a half mile off the pier outside his window and the forty ships with her he knew there was no chance that the pirates he had enlisted to aid in the overthrow of Governor Berkley could attack and get to him in time. With no hope left, he simply wrote down his orders and clung stubbornly to the dignity that seemed a trait of all of the officers of the English Navy.

A click at the door drew his attention and he looked to it as it opened, raising his head as a small wooden cart that was covered with a long white cloth that swept the floor was pushed in by a young woman with long black hair and bronze skin.

She was wearing a simple white dress of a very light material and a faded blue apron. Her long hair shrouded her face and it seemed her attention was fixed on the silver dome that covered the platter in the middle of the cart. She wore no shoes and her skirt brushed back and forth just above her ankles as she walked in. A little hunched over, one had only to guess that she was not treated well by those above her. Behind her was a soldier in a red uniform, and his eyes were on the young woman as she strode to the Admiral.

Peterson, out of reflex more than anything, stood when he saw the young woman enter but quickly turned his eyes to the soldier.

"Last meal, Sir," the soldier informed. "Governor Berkley also wanted to make your last night memorable so he's arranged some company for you." He grabbed the girl's arm and pulled her toward him, smiling as he observed, "This is a pretty little thing, don't you think?"

The Admiral raised his chin, but kept his voice under control as he offered, "Thank you. That will be all."

Laughing under his breath, the soldier turned and strode out, closing the door behind him.

Peterson looked the girl over and she cringed under his attention. "Not to worry, Miss," he assured. "I'll not be a party to adding another victim to Berkley's list."

She nodded, still not showing him her face.

"I suppose you'll be safe here for a while," he observed. Venting a deep sigh, he finally sat back down and asked, "Would you do something for me?"

She shrugged.

He picked up his pen and looked back to the parchment. "I would ask that you get this to the Admiralty in London somehow, or to an officer or soldier who is still loyal to the crown." He looked back to her. "This is very important, Miss, and no one can know you have it."

She nodded again.

His mouth tightened and he asked, "Can you speak?"

"Oh, she can talk," Rose answered from the window.

Peterson sprang to his feet and wheeled around.

Rose was lounging in the window with her back against the cut stone of the window opening, one leg dangling inside, her other foot planted on the window shelf and her hands clasped over her knee. She smiled as she met the Admiral's eyes and continued, "The hard part is getting her to shut up once she starts."

The girl finally looked up and brushed her hair back from her very pretty face, her big brown eyes wide as she barked in a slight Spanish accent, "Rose! I don't talk that much!"

"And it starts," Rose mumbled as she hopped down. "Okay, Admiral, it's time to get changed. It's about time to go."

He raised his brow. "Go where, Miss O'scarlett? There are guards outside the door, and soldiers all over the fort who are waiting for someone to try and break me out of here."

She folded her arms and smiled slightly. "Yeah, it's a shame you won't be leaving." Striding past him to the cart, she removed the silver dome to reveal the folded uniforms beneath it. Looking back to him, she informed, "You'd better get changed. We haven't much time."

"Those pants look too small for him," Maria observed.

Rose looked down at his waist and squinted slightly, approaching slowly as she observed, "Yeah, they might be." Unexpectedly, her hand shot toward him and she grabbed his crotch.

He jumped and took a step back, his eyes locked wide on Rose as he barked, "Miss O'scarlett!"

"Quiet!" she hissed.

"Madam," he growled in a low voice, "I am a married man!"

Rose looked to Maria and smiled. "And his wife is a *very* satisfied woman."

Maria giggled and approached him as well, sliding her hands onto his shoulders as she purred, "We don't have to have him out of here until morning. Maybe we can share him."

He pushed away from them and backed away. "Ladies, this is horribly inappropriate."

Setting her hands on her hips, Rose locked eyes with Maria and raised her brow. "Well! That's the second time this year I've been rejected by a man." She turned and took the first bundle of clothing from the cart. "Very well, General. You just turned down the best thing that could have happened to you. Let's get changed and be quick about it. Much to do."

In short order he was in the uniform of a British soldier, not one of much rank, either. Rose was something of a distraction as she also changed—right in front of him. Rose and Maria had changed into black tights and loosely fitting black swordsman's shirts. Maria remained barefoot as she was clearly comfortable that way. Beneath the clothing was a small metal flask that Rose picked up as soon as they were changed.

Looking to the girl, Rose ordered, "Maria, go knock on the door and get the guards in here." She turned her eyes to Peterson and tossed him a triangle hat, ordering, "You'll need to keep that low over your eyes."

He nodded.

Maria knocked on the door as hard as she could, then backed away.

The door was unlocked and the guards entered again, the first one declaring, "What the hell?" When the other rushed in, the first slammed his elbow into his gut and Maria was quick to close the door.

Before the second guard realized what had happened he was backed up against the wall and Rose had her pistol trained on his face.

She smiled sweetly and held up the flask, ordering, "You be a good boy and drink this all gone, okay?"

His eyes darted from one in the room to the next.

"Go ahead," she ordered. "I really don't want to have to shoot you."

He finally complied, swallowing all of the liquid within.

Rose motioned to the bed and ordered, "Go lie down. In a few seconds you're going to need to, anyway."

The other guard and the Admiral exited the room cautiously and stood by the door to await the next guard change, which was expected at midnight. Taking the rope that still dangled from a hook that was set deep into a space between the stones just under the window, the two women slowly made their way down the wall and to the ground some thirty feet below. From there they darted into and out of the shadows toward the water.

Aboard the Admiral's flagship, which was anchored a long swim away from the shore, the two women stayed to the shadows, avoiding the sentries whose loyalty was a mystery. Rose had abandoned her boots, leaving them under the dock before they began their swim out and she was able to walk much more quietly on the ship without them. The second in command would have his own cabin and all they had to do was find it. The ship was very big, very solid, but still the deck creaked in places as they padded lightly toward the lower deck.

There was not much light, only a few lamps, but ahead of them there was a door that led into a room where there seemed to be quite a bit of activity. Light sprayed from all around the door and muffled sounds could be heard from within.

Her eyes darting around, Rose motioned behind her for Maria to back away and they crept back toward the ladder. Halfway there, they turned around and froze as they came face to face with a half dozen marines who had sabers and pistols trained on them.

Maria backed away, right into Rose, and as the soldiers advanced she raised her hands before her and pled, "No habla English!"

A half hour later they found themselves inside the spacious room that was on the other side of that door. It seemed to be nearly the breadth of the ship with a seven foot ceiling and was easily twenty feet deep. Another door at the other end of the room led somewhere but was closed. A large table was in the center of the room and was covered with maps and drawings and was surrounded by eight of the ten simple wooden chairs that normally ringed it. Rose and Maria sat in these last two with their backs against one wall and their hands bound behind them. Four armed marines were in the room with them along with two of the ship's ranking officers.

Rose watched the better decorated of the two, a tall man with low sideburns, broad shoulders and black hair and wearing black trousers and a white shirt, as he paced in front of them. His eyes were on them almost constantly as he appeared to be thinking about what to do with them.

When his gaze fixed on Rose, she raised her brow and asked, "Is this a bad time to ask what you are going to do with us?"

He stopped pacing, his eyes narrowing as he replied, "I think it is a good time."

Another officer approached them and his eyes shifted from one to the other a few times before he growled, "They cannot be allowed to leave the ship. If they've figured out what we're doing then everything could be in jeopardy."

"Agreed," the ranking officer said frankly. "I suppose we can keep them here or in the brig until everything is finished and then deal with them later."

Maria arched her brow and whimpered, "No habla."

Rose looked to her and barked, "Maria, just stop! You barely speak any Spanish, anyway!"

The ranking officer strode to Rose and folded his arms. "So, clearly you are in charge. What we have here is a problem and we will be taking care of that in short order. You will start with your name."

She raised her brow. "My name?"

"Am I looking at anyone else?" he countered.

She glanced at Maria and stammered, "I'm, uh… I'm Angie… Jones. Yes, that's my name. Angie Jones."

He raised a brow ever so slightly. "So you are the dreaded Angela Jones, wanted by the crown for piracy and a host of other crimes."

Rose stared dumbly up at him for long seconds with her mouth hanging open, then she hesitantly shook her head and corrected, "No, I'm not that Angie Jones. I'm, uh…" She looked to Maria again, who just shrugged.

"Another Angela Jones?" he asked.

"Yes," she replied. "It's a really common name." She smiled. "I get mistaken for her all the time."

He nodded. "Of course you do. And I suppose you are not a notorious pirate, either."

Rose shook her head and declared, "Nope! I hate being at sea."

"So naturally you snuck aboard one of his Majesty's ships."

She swallowed hard and hesitantly nodded. "Yeah, kind of got lost. We were looking for another ship with a man on board we are supposed to, um…" She smiled a flirty smile and leaned her head, batting her eyelashes as she said, "Well, a girl's got to make a living, govna."

He nodded again. "I see. Who is it you are looking for to make this living?"

"His name," she stammered. "Have you ever heard of Captain Wilson?"

With yet another nod he confirmed, "I know Captain Wilson quite well."

"Oh." She glanced at Maria again. "Well, it isn't him."

"We are getting nowhere," the officer grumbled as he turned away from them. "Lieutenant, when we have the Admiral back on board and we are out to sea, make sure that these two—"

"Wait!" Rose barked.

He looked over his shoulder at her.

"You're going after Admiral Peterson?" she asked in an almost frantic tone.

He slowly turned back to her and folded his arms again.

Staring up at him, she guessed, "You must be Commander Wallace." When he nodded, he continued, "Captain Wilson had some kind words about you."

"The same Captain Wilson you meant to pleasure for money tonight?" he spat back.

Rose drew a breath and shook her head. "Commander, I couldn't tell you who I was because I did not know where your loyalties lie. I didn't know if you were—"

"On Berkley's side," he finished for her.

She nodded. "I had to be sure."

"Then tell me who you are."

Glancing at Maria again, she swallowed hard, knowing that she was about to take an awful risk, then she softly replied, "My name is Rose O'scarlett."

Wallace turned his eyes aside, his features tense. "O'scarlett. I know that name from somewhere."

"I'm a good friend of Admiral Peterson," she continued. When he turned around and took a few steps away, she informed, "I know. I'm the notorious pirate Rose O'scarlett with the huge price on her head, the price put there by Governor Berkley. That's how you know me. Right now we have a common enemy and we..." She stopped as he raised his hand.

"O'scarlett," he breathed. Spinning around, he asked, "Was your husband in the navy?"

She raised her chin, tears glossing her eyes as she slowly nodded. "The Governor had him killed."

His eyes narrowing, he prodded, "What was his name and rank?"

She answered, "Lieutenant Jeffery O'scarlett."

His eyes widening slightly, Wallace took a step back, then he spun around and ordered, "Cut her loose."

One of the men strode forward and turned her chair and she looked over her shoulder as he began to untie her.

Not facing her, Commander Wallace offered, "Will you accept my apologies, Mrs. O'scarlett?"

Rose looked to him and assured, "None needed, Sir. You had to be cautious and I understand. How did you know Jeffery?" She pulled her arms in front of her and gently massaged her wrists.

Wallace vented a deep breath, just staring across the room as he replied, "Jeffery and I served together on the *HMS Valliant* when we first took to sea. It was his first assignment, and mine. He was a fine man, Mrs. O'scarlett and I am deeply sorry for your loss."

She stood and padded to him, and when he turned she slid her arms around him and laid her head on his shoulder, offering, "Thank you."

He hesitantly hugged her back, and finally tightly embraced her as he whispered, "He was a good man and a fine officer."

She nodded and a few tears leaked from her eyes.

Wallace motioned with his head to Maria and the same guard began to untie her. When Rose pulled away from him, he smiled and observed, "You've worked up quite the notorious reputation, Mrs. O'scarlett."

She smiled back and shrugged. "Long story, Commander, and please call me Rose."

"As you wish," he said softly. Turning around, he looked to his men and ordered, "Okay, gentlemen. We've cleared up this issue, now it is time to go and get our admiral back."

Rose looked to Maria and raised her brow.

A knock on the door preceded its opening and a crewman in a white shirt and triangle hat entered, alarm in his voice as he reported, "We've a dinghy approaching, Commander. Looks like two men aboard."

His eyes narrowing, Wallace folded his hands behind him and ordered, "Prepare to receive them, sabers and bayonets only."

"No," Rose barked, and when everyone looked to her she strode toward the door and dryly informed, "It's probably the Admiral. We got him out of there a couple of hours ago."

Everyone looked to each other.

Maria followed her and added, "Well you didn't think we would leave such an important thing for the Navy to do, did you?"

Up on deck Rose was the first to greet Admiral Peterson as he climbed on board, and he greeted her with a big smile as he informed, "Been a while since I was so neck deep in such affairs."

Rose added, "I'll bet it's also been a while since two beautiful women broke you out of a heavily guarded fort."

"That it has," he laughed. Looking behind her, he raised his chin and asked, "Commander Wallace, is everything in order here?"

"Yes Admiral," the Commander reported.

"Excuse me," Rose began, "I'm sure Commander Wallace is an excellent officer, but don't you usually have a captain in command of your ship, Admiral?"

"I did," Peterson sighed, "but we put him ashore after he was injured in battle with a French Man-O-War. Mister Wallace, have the officers assemble in the war room. We've plans to make."

As he strode to the ladder to take him below, Rose took the Commander's shoulder and asked, "He was wounded in battle?"

Wallace raised his brow and looked to her. "Slipped on a mop and broke his arm."

She laughed, "Oh, dear God. Well, here's hoping you get promoted soon to replace him."

* * *

With Maria drawing the attention of most of the men, Rose followed Wallace into the war room where she and Maria had been detained and stood by the door with her arms folded as she listened to the officers debate their situation. The Admiral sat at the head of the table and listened as well, his brow high as he listened to his officers try to work out their situation.

Wallace insisted, "Most of the blockade is at anchor and looking out to sea for threats there."

"And those who are patrolling beyond them?" a lieutenant countered.

"We'll have to find some way past them," Still another insisted. "A ship this size will be seen either way, even in the dark."

Rose rubbed her eyes and grumbled, "We don't have time for this." Looking back to them, she loudly asked, "May I offer something?" When they all looked to her, she suggested, "Why don't we just join the patrols outside the blockade?"

Again, the men at the table glanced about at each other.

She looked around at them and continued, "It wouldn't be that unusual for one more ship to be added, would it? And when they're comfortable with us being there we can just slip away."

No one spoke for a moment.

Finally, Admiral Peterson cleared his throat and said, "Commander Wallace, get us under way to the blockade, if you please, and make certain that everything that is happening on the deck is of a routine nature. Dismissed, everyone."

The men stood and Rose stepped aside to allow them to leave, and many of them gave her venomous looks as they left. Commander Wallace smiled and patted her shoulder as he brought up the rear.

"Miss O'scarlett," he summoned, and when she looked to him he raised his brow again and said, "Your little plan is reckless and very brazen. Now I can see where your notorious reputation really comes from."

She smiled back at him.

* * *

Slipping away from the blockade took more than an hour, but slip away they did and before long the big ship was cutting across the water at her best speed for its rendezvous with a feared and notorious pirate vessel.

Commander Wallace opened the door to his cabin slowly, cringing a little as the hinges creaked. A little bit of light swept into the small cabin from the lamp outside and illuminated the small desk, the vanity with the water basin and pitcher, the two foot wide wardrobe and of course his bed, which was occupied. He smiled slightly and folded his arms.

Rose was curled up on the edge of the bed with Maria right behind her. They slept soundly with Maria's arm draped limply over Rose's waist. These were two women who were simply exhausted and he really wanted to allow them to sleep longer, but duty called.

Wallace crept in and gently took Rose's shoulder

She awoke with a start and looked up at him with wide and fearful eyes, her breath coming with some difficulty as she got her wits about her.

Maria also stirred and sat up, rubbing the sleep from her eyes as she did.

The Commander whispered, "Admiral would like to see you."

Rose nodded and swung her feet to the deck.

Still in the war room, Admiral Peterson looked up as Rose opened the door. He was alone in there and had been studying charts, drawings and diagrams of ships and many other papers all night, and most of them were still scattered about. His eyes were strained and hollow as they fixed on her and he asked with a weary voice, "Would you close the door please?"

She complied, then padded into the room and took the chair beside his.

"How many ships would you say we have on our side?" he asked straightly.

Rose shrugged. "I don't know for certain. My ship, Captain Nailhall's ship, the *Black Dragon*, of course... Whatever ships the Commodore could muster. I think Jones said something about two just like the Commodore's along with it, and they are formidable heavy frigates."

The Admiral nodded, just staring at her for a time before he spoke again. "I'm not sure it will be enough, Miss O'scarlett. It may take everything we have just to contend with the *Goliath*, and then there are the forty ships with her."

She raised her chin and assured, "You shouldn't worry over the *Goliath*, Admiral. Just leave her to Captain Jones and the *Black Dragon*."

"I wish I could," he said softly. "I've seen what that *Black Dragon* can do to other ships, but this isn't some other ship. She is purpose built to deal with Captain Jones' behemoth."

"She won't survive the battle as she went in," Rose said straightly. "Even if she sinks the *Black Dragon* she'll be so shot up that the rest of us should be able to take her down."

"And her forty escorts?" Peterson asked. "I don't see us going in with more than a dozen ships."

"Including yours," she reminded. "I'm certain that many of your captains will think twice before firing on an admiral's flagship."

With a slight nod, he said in a low voice, "Let's hope so."

The door burst open and a young sailor with wide, fear filled eyes barked, "We've sails off the stern, Admiral!"

Peterson and Rose sprang to their feet.

The sailor continued, "Commander Wallace has us at stations."

They rushed up onto the deck, finding Wallace standing behind the steering assembly with a telescope raised to his eye and his gaze fixed on the many sails behind them. The sun was barely up and shrouded by clouds and a fog bank to the east and to the ship's starboard side. Right in the middle of the two score of sails was a set of masts that was almost twice as tall as any of the others. *Goliath* was coming out to fight!

"And no sign of our fleet," Wallace said grimly.

Rose clenched her teeth and said under her breath, "I need a drink."

Admiral Peterson glanced at her and assured, "I've more of that brandy, and if we survive the day you are welcome to join me."

She smiled slightly and offered, "Thank you, Admiral."

Lowering his telescope, Wallace turned to them and said, "Now just to survive the day. I'm sure that is the *Goliath* among them and they've a squadron of corvettes leading the way."

Another of the crewmen approached, an older, rough looking fellow who had clearly spent most of his life at sea. Shaking his head, he informed, "I'll bet they've lightened those ships of everything they didn't need. They'll run us down in a few hours for sure."

"We only have to make Tortuga," Rose assured.

The crewman added, "And then they'll take down everyone there. That Berkley's built him a fleet that half the Royal Navy couldn't contend with."

"A considerable lot of them are French," Wallace informed as he raised the telescope to his eye again. "Perhaps when the shooting starts they'll surrender."

Rose patted his shoulder and laughed, "Let's hope they live up to that dubious reputation, Commander."

"In the meantime," Admiral Peterson cut in, "Let's see about..." He raised his head, then turned and headed toward the bow of the ship, barking, "Someone bring me a telescope!"

Everyone followed, and once at the bow Commander Wallace handed his telescope to the Admiral, who raised it immediately to his eye.

As he stared ahead through the telescope, he mumbled as if to himself, "Fog bank. Could be the lucky break we've been looking for."

"Will we reach it in time?" Rose asked softly.

Lowering the telescope, the Admiral shrugged and replied, "That remains to be seen, Miss O'scarlett."

They watched the approach to the fog bank in silence for a time. The whole ship was quiet but for the wind in the rigging and the occasional creak of the hull.

A crack of thunder from behind drew everyone's attention.

Though a very big ship, the *Goliath* had pulled ahead of her escorts and fired a warning shot from one of her forward cannons. The sea a hundred yards behind the Admiral's ship exploded as the massive cannonball slammed into the water.

"We are damn near in their range," Wallace grumbled.

"How far to the fog bank?" Admiral Peterson asked grimly.

Shaking his head, Wallace replied, "Over a mile, Admiral. I don't think we'll make it before they have the range on us."

The old mariner added, "And just one shot from a gun that size will cripple this ship and kill half of us."

Wallace looked to Admiral Peterson, who nodded to him. Raising his chin, the Commander shouted, "Get to stations and prepare for battle!"

Rose grasped his shoulder and pointed out, "We don't stand a chance against that thing!"

He regarded her solemnly and countered, "It's better than being shot to pieces while we run."

Spinning back to the fog bank as men ran about the ship to prepare it for its last battle, Rose willed the *Black Dragon* to emerge from the fog as it had before, to come to her rescue and tilt the scale once again. She stared hard into the mist ahead of them and whispered, "Cannonflash, please come for me just one more time."

Thunder sounded again and this time water exploded from the sea beside the ship. *Goliath* had the range!

Tightly grasping the rail, she looked hard into the fog and begged in a whisper, "Please don't let it end like this." As the frigate began to turn to port for its final fight, a shadow broke through the fog and Rose's eyes widened. Shaking her head, she murmured, "No," as the *Scarlet Dragon* charged from the fog a half mile off their starboard bow. Another ship emerged, one she knew had to be the *Silver Falcon*, then another, a black ship that she recognized as the *Black Revenge*. Another, one she recognized as yet another pirate, a galleon that was a privateer that had once hunted her west of Cuba. Still another, one the same design and size and color as the *Black Revenge*.

As she watched, slowly turning her head to keep her attention on the emerging ships, her heart raced, pounding as it never had. Hope sprang back to life and she turned and shouted, "Commander Wallace!"

He looked. Everyone did.

When Rose turned her eyes back to the fog and the ships that emerged from it, she grinned broadly as another black shadow parted the fog, a shadow in the form of a giant black catamaran with ten huge cannons directed forward, and once again it was coming right for them.

Seeing the *Black Dragon*, Wallace spun around and shouted, "Hard about! Give that ship a wide berth!"

With the Admiral's frigate speeding out of the way, the two biggest warships in the world rapidly closed for battle. The *Black Dragon* had the *Goliath*'s full attention. The smaller ships, even the four heavy frigates in Commodore Jones' group, veered away in two directions to stay out of the way of the two massive ships as they closed head-on.

Looking to the *Goliath*, Rose finally saw that it was truly huge. Four masts held rigging that suspended sails that were angled to maximize the use of the wind. She listed over slightly as the wind approached largely from the side. Twice as wide as the heavy frigate she was on, it seemed to ride low in the water and yet moved with tremendous speed for a ship so big. Six massive guns, long barreled bronze cannons that were at least sixty-four pounders—not the long thirty-two pounders they had been told about—faced forward and were elevated for maximum range. The front of the hull seemed to be formed around them and thick timbers guarded them from frontal assault. Six more guns, forty-two pounders, protruded from open hatches in the hull a deck below the main deck. With twelve guns just facing forward, she wondered if the *Black Dragon* was indeed a match for this thing.

As they veered from its path, her eyes widened as she saw two decks of broadsides. Arranged in a line on the second deck down were what appeared to be twelve twenty-four pounders, and on the deck below them were what had to be forty-two pounders, eight in number. She seemed to be more than a match for the *Black Dragon* in a broadside slug match and confidently sailed right toward her enemy.

While Rose wanted to send the Admiral's frigate into the *Goliath* to help her pirate captain, she knew that such an attack would be suicide. Looking back to the *Black Dragon*, she bit her lip as doubt of the outcome squirmed within her.

Closing to within a quarter mile, the *Goliath* struck first with all twelve of her forward guns firing a murderous barrage right into the upper decks of the *Black Dragon*. Debris was kicked up and the rigging on the right hull shuddered as it was hit. Two of the massive cannonballs splintered the hull on the left right below her big cannons. Even before the smoke cleared the *Black Dragon* replied with a horrible vengeance and ten solid hundred pound cannonballs ripped across the deck of her massive enemy. Debris flew up and one of the solid balls slammed into the heavy timbers high on her bow, which nearly succumbed before repelling the huge shot ball.

At less than two hundred yards the *Goliath* tacked hard to bring her twenty broadsides to bear on the huge pirate vessel. It stood to reason that the *Black Dragon* would respond in kind, but instead she turned slightly to port and directed her bow right at the *Goliath*'s side. With her hundred pounders still reloading, this looked like suicide.

"What are you doing?" Rose whispered.

No one had noticed the concealed hatches on the front of the *Black Dragon*'s hull. When the first swung open, the maw of a long barreled cannon, another hundred pounder, pushed forward and stopped with its muzzle a good six feet from the opening. Another hatch on the other side of the hull opened, then two on the other hull. Four long barreled, bronze cannons were suddenly in firing position, and as the *Goliath* fired the first of her broadsides, these four guns replied almost simultaneously. This time, four high explosive cannonballs slammed into the *Goliath*'s side and ripped into timbers and planks. Not all of the broadsides had the opportunity to fire before the ship's hull was opened and many of them were knocked out before they got off their first shot. Though she had thick sides, the explosive cannonballs had done their destructive work.

With fire and smoke pouring from the wounded ship's side, the *Black Dragon* finally turned hard to starboard, bringing her twenty-four guns to bear on the *Goliath*. They fired in a sequence from bow to stern, aiming carefully for the damaged and smoking sections of the *Goliath*'s hull. Many opened the hull further while many more fired right into the holes and detonated in the big ship's belly.

As they passed, each turned aft facing guns on the other and fired with true aim. It was clear that the *Black Dragon* was taking damage this time, but it was also clear that she was dispensing far more.

The two massive ships turned complete circles to have at each other again. Tighter in a turn, the *Black Dragon* brought her port cannons to bear first and fired at less than a hundred yards away, and explosive cannonballs did their work again, this time on *Goliath*'s starboard side. The angle of the attack saw glancing shots as many of the hatches for the ship's cannons were blown off and it appeared that a few of her guns were put out of action. As *Goliath* completed her turn, she replied with her own broadside. Normally a ship would veer off to avoid a counter stride, but the *Black Dragon* continued her hard turn into her enemy. Solid iron cannonballs ripped into her hull where they struck high and two slammed directly into her open cannon hatches. An explosion on the first gun deck belched fire out of three open cannon hatches.

Though wounded, the *Black Dragon* continued to turn hard into the British Man-O-War and as the *Goliath* tried to evade to port, the big forward guns of the pirate ship lined up and fired again, and this time they all fired high explosive shells almost point blank into the *Goliath*'s side and over her upper deck, opening both in violent explosions. Secondary explosions below decks tore at the ship further.

The forward guns of the *Black Dragon* retreated and men rushed to the front rails of the ship, aiming their muskets as best they could. Chaos gripped the wounded *Goliath* as musket balls raked over her deck and many men fell. British marines rushed to that side to respond, then ran back as the bow of the *Black*

Dragon slammed into the *Goliath*'s side near the stern. Deck guns from both ships fired at point blank range and men on both sides fell dead and wounded. Swivel guns fired, muskets, and as the *Goliath* turned, the big ship that had rammed her turned the opposite way, and this time it was her starboard broadsides that fired, and each shot had been well aimed.

Once again, high explosive cannonballs detonated deep in the *Goliath*'s hull and explosions ripped through her upper deck and threw debris, men and cannons into the air.

Even as far away as they were those aboard the Admiral's ship could hear the roar of the men of the *Black Dragon* as they charged over the rail and onto the burning *Goliath*. Other men stayed behind to snipe at the *Goliath*'s men with muskets. From there, it would be hand to hand.

And there was no time to watch the outcome.

Outnumbered four to one, the ragtag fleet of pirates and privateers charged Governor Berkley's flotilla head-on. The British had not thought about putting big guns facing their bows but the pirates under the command of Commodore Jones had— and Jones' ships were each packing four hundred pounders forward!

From the bow of the Admiral's flagship, Rose watched anxiously as the gap between Berkley's fleet and the ship she was on rapidly disappeared. They would face many smaller ships, but many more ships and Berkley had at least as many heavy warships as the privateers who faced him. Her eyes swept from one side of the line facing them to the other. It seemed hopeless, and yet she had been in such hopeless situations before and somehow prevailed.

Her hair flailed out as she spun around and rushed to the wheelhouse where Admiral Peterson was quickly working on some kind of strategy with Commander Wallace and a few other officers. Halfway up the ladder she stubbed a toe and stopped, shouting, "Ow! Damn!" Not pausing long, she continued to the top and hurried to the men, calling, "Admiral!"

He turned to her and raised his brow. "In need of a task, Miss O'scarlett?"

"Do you have any captured pirate flags aboard?" she questioned.

Commander Wallace answered, "We have a couple, I believe. They are trophies from a couple of years ago."

"I strongly recommend that you raise at least one of them beneath the English flag."

Raising his brow, Admiral pointed out, "That is a trite illegal, Miss O'scarlett, especially for Englishmen to serve under a pirate flag."

Wallace raised his chin, his eyes locked on Rose as he countered, "Under the circumstances, Admiral, I would recommend that we bend the law and raise the Jolly Roger. We wouldn't want our pirate and privateer allies mistaking us for Governor Berkley's ships."

With a slow nod, Admiral Peterson conceded, "I do see your point." Looking to one of the officers he had in attendance, he ordered, "See to it our pirate flags are hung both fore and aft." As the man hurried off, he looked back to Rose and raised his brow.

"What else can I do?" she asked.

Venting a breath, Peterson looked about the ship, seeing everyone and everything at the ready. "Well, the men are well trained and everything is attended to. I suppose you should step in where you see an opportunity to help. I would hate to see your talents wasted."

"I could use a couple of pistols," Rose informed, "perhaps a musket and shot for them. Maria and I can get shots off at the men on the decks as we pass."

The Admiral looked to Commander Wallace and raised his brow.

Wallace nodded to him, then turned to one of the sailors who stood by and ordered, "Take Mrs. O'scarlett to the armory and get her whatever she needs."

Right before the shooting started, Rose and Maria were sitting cross-legged on the deck in the middle of the ship loading muskets. Both knew their way around firearms and had commandeered two full crates of new muskets that were bound for Port Royal, but had never been unloaded from the ship. They had seven of them loaded and ready to go and Rose had two pistols shoved into her sash.

A couple of marines happened by and paused to watch them.

Rose looked up at them, then motioned with her head to the loaded muskets beside her, offering, "If you'd like extra then now is the time to take them."

The Marines glanced at each other, then each slung the weapon he had and took one from the deck beside Rose, one of them offering, "Thank you, Miss."

She smiled at him and resumed her labors.

Before the first shots were fired, Rose and Maria had all of the guns loaded and had extra shot and powder slung over their shoulders. Admiral Peterson was a conventional war fighter and even as the ships commanded by Commodore Jones fired from the bow and maneuvered to avoid being hit, this ship was content to turn her guns against the first largest ship she encountered, going broadside to broadside. Cannonballs were exchanged and Rose and Maria joined a dozen marines at the rail to return musket fire with the men aboard the enemy frigate.

Ships all around exchanged gunfire and many of the British and French ships under Berkley's banner were shot up and on fire in the first few moments, but there were many more to replace them. The privateers and pirates were also sustaining damage and four of them retired in the first quarter hour, pursued out of the fight by their enemies.

Rose fired a round into the ship that slugged it out with the Admiral's ship, then looked beyond it to see the *Silver Falcon* limping out of the fight with one of her masts down and smoke pouring from one side. Her lips tightened as she saw two ships in pursuit. The fight was not going well. A thunderous explosion drew her attention to the other side of the ship and she turned that way, her eyes widening beneath an arched brow as she saw one of the privateer corvettes belching flames from amidships and rolling over to sink.

A salvo from the enemy ship hit the deck close by and Rose and Maria were thrown to the deck. Pushing herself up, Rose looked back to find Maria lying where she had fallen and bleeding about the head and shoulder. Scrambling to her, she tore her shirt open at the shoulder and clenched her teeth, then she grabbed onto the shiver of wood that was stabbed deep into her friend's shoulder and pulled it out. Tearing Maria's sleeve away, she fashioned a bandage with it and bound the small woman's wounds as best she could.

The other side of the ship was hit and the flagship replied, pounding the French galleon at her side, but taking more fire from the bow from another French ship.

They were sorely outnumbered and Rose looked about again to see even one of Commodore Jones' ships retiring from the fight.

The big British frigate they had been fighting turned sharply to bring her broadsides to bear one more time. Both it and the Admiral's ship were badly damaged and many men on both sides lay dead or wounded.

Rose heard Commander Wallace shout orders to turn her side to the enemy ship and reply. He knew this was a hopeless cause, and yet he seemed intent to go down fighting in true English fashion.

As the enemy frigate took aim, her bow blew apart at the water line with a terrible boom and the top deck was lifted from the hull like the mouth of a great beast opening to belch smoke and fire. It peeled up about a third of the way down the ship, the forward mast fell and the upper deck settled back down onto the hull, collapsing to the water line with a great splash as the ship began to quickly settle down by the bow.

"Fire!" Commander Wallace shouted.

The Admiral's flagship did just that and pounded the crippled frigate with a full broadside from her lower guns, her deck guns, swivel guns, and the surviving marines fired muskets into her for good measure.

Rose knew that only one thing could do that to a ship so large and looked aft, smiling as she saw the *Black Dragon* charging into the fight and taking aim at the French ships.

As the Admiral's ship veered out of the way, the *Black Dragon* fired her big forward guns again, splitting her fire between the two galleons with horrific results.

Looking behind the giant catamaran, she saw the damaged *Silver Falcon* turning to get back into the fight, and the two ships that had been pursuing her sinking, one on its side and the other going down by the stern, and both were burning.

Admiral Peterson strode to the middle of the ship and stopped right behind Rose, looking around him as he shouted, "The day shall be ours! Fight on, men, and let's give that traitor Berkley a reason to fear the sea!"

A great "Pazzah!" was raised by the crew and the big frigate took the *Black Dragon*'s side to charge into the thick of the remaining flotilla.

The surviving pirates and privateers formed up with them and three of the ships that had retired were turning to rejoin the fight.

As Commander Wallace had predicted, the French ships saw the *Black Dragon* rejoin the fight after dispatching the *Goliath* and all of them turned to retreat.

"Admiral!" a cannon man shouted, and when everyone looked he pointed to the stern of the *Black Dragon*.

And there, hanging beneath the pirate banner Jones sailed under were the colors of the English Navy—the Union Jack.

Looking about, Rose saw other ships flying the British flags beneath their respective pirate flags. As she looked forward and saw the *Scarlet Dragon* speeding back into the battle and trailing smoke from a few more holes in her sides, she saw the same flags flying from her highest mast, and she smiled.

As Admiral Peterson's flotilla closed in on the remaining British fleet, their enemy turned their flanks and lowered their flags—and the pirate and privateer fleet erupted into cheers. The French squadron sailed away as fast as the wind would take them. Many of their ships were wounded, burning and bleeding smoke, and a few were missing masts and sails.

Within a half hour all of the ships loyal to Governor Berkley were under the control of Admiral Peterson and the English crown once again. The men aboard were not held at fault, but the captains of these ships were taken aboard the flagship to answer a few questions.

With the battle over, Rose helped Maria to the medical section of the flagship where she could be properly treated, then she accompanied the Admiral to the *Black Dragon* as the ships came alongside each other. The *Black Revenge* also came along the *Black Dragon* and everyone aboard the huge ship made ready to receive the Admiral and Commodore.

Still wearing the black trousers and loose shirt from the night before, a barefoot Rose O'scarlett strode proudly between a British Admiral and Commander who wore their best uniforms. They met Cannonflash and Commodore Jones in the center of the ship among the cheers of the ship's crew and the crews of the ships tethered to her.

Jones' attention was on the British officers and his expression was as hard as it always was. The Commodore stood beside him with a look of pride. Both men had their huge arms folded and Rose could clearly see the resemblance between them.

As she and the Admiral and Commander reached the big pirates, Rose turned her eyes up to Jones, keeping her arms at her sides. A little smile found her mouth as he looked down at her. She knew her three year ordeal was almost over. Almost.

The men extended their hands to one another, passing on congratulations on a battle well fought. Rose simply folded hers behind her and never took her gaze from Cannonflash.

Admiral Peterson raised his chin as he looked to Jones and said, "It would seem that I find myself in your debt, Captain Jones. It would also seem that the crown is in the same awkward position."

Shaking his head, Cannonflash corrected, "No, you've handed over that pardon for me men and me. We be even, Admiral."

Peterson nodded and agreed, "It would seem so, Sir. Of course, that pardon shall extend to all who helped win the day today, as will an offer of employment."

Jones' eyes narrowed and he glanced at the Commodore.

"Thanks to Governor Berkley and his reckless exploits," the Admiral explained, "the fleet in this part of the world is horribly depleted. Now we'll have the French and Spanish to contend with. We'll definitely need someone to fill in for the missing ships."

Commodore Jones set his jaw and asked, "You would have us privateer for you British?"

"I would," Admiral Peterson replied. There was a steel resolve behind his words. "You pirates know these waters better than anyone and it would seem you are already the most feared lot on this side of the world."

Cannonflash asked, "How will your King feel about this?"

Raising his brow, the Admiral informed, "He's given me license to do so. After scrapes with both the French and the Spanish it could take years to rebuild the Royal Fleet to its former glory. That means many years of lucrative employment for someone who can pull together a collection of warships that can defend our interests here." His gaze fixed on the Commodore and he raised his brow again. "Very lucrative." Looking down to the wedding ring on his hand, he added, "And if your ships happen to raid or capture a Spanish or French ship once in a while under a pirate's banner... Well, I think I could just look the other way."

Meeting his son's eyes, Commodore Jones raised his brow and asked, "What ya think, boy? You ain't at war with 'em anymore, may as well get paid for doin' what ya do."

Cannonflash stared back at him for a moment, then he turned his eyes to Rose and nodded, assuring, "We'll follow ye as always, Commodore. Just give the word."

Patting Captain Jones' big shoulder, the Commodore looked to Admiral Peterson and extended his hand, saying proudly, "We have an accord, Admiral!"

The crew exploded into cheers once again as the men shook hands.

A horrible succession of cracks was heard; the sounds of splitting timbers and snapping planks, the creaking of wood under massive stress that would be the final sounds of a ship in its death throes and everyone looked aft.

The *Goliath* twisted amidships and the stern rolled to port, sending her aft masts toward the water. The stricken ship's midsection lowered in the water and the upper deck there was slowly swamped by the sea. The ship's bow turned upward and ever so slowly she began to disappear beneath the waves. Many boats rowed frantically away from the dying ship as other men who had jumped overboard clung to floating debris and also paddled away as fast as they could.

Admiral Peterson sighed and informed, "Captain Jones, I was about to thank you for capturing the *Goliath,* but I see you were content to sink her."

"Was as gentle as I could be," he growled.

Everyone flinched as the midsection of the ship exploded, then another horrific blast tore the bow apart and sent parts of the ship skyward.

Angie ran to them from the boat that had been raised to the center of the ship, shouting, "Commodore!"

As the men turned to her, she threw herself into the Commodore and wrapped her arms around him, and as he hugged her back she cried, "Did you see?" She pulled away and smiled broadly up at him. "We unleashed hell on them and came about sinking two of 'em! Captured a British corvette, we did! May I have her?"

He smiled and shook his head. "No, Angie, that one'll have to be returned to Admiral Peterson."

She stepped back and shouted, "What? That isn't fair!"

Cannonflash stepped toward her and yelled, "You'll mind your manners, little girl!"

Angie looked to him and set her hands on her hips, stomping her foot on the deck as she cried, "Papa, that isn't fair! I lost me ship and you said you'd get me another!"

Rose's eyes widened and she murmured, "Papa?"

Captain Jones stepped up to her and jabbed a finger into her chest, growling, "What's fair is what I say is fair, savvy?"

She glared back at him for long seconds, then she turned her eyes down and nodded, softly conceding, "Yes, Papa." Looking to Rose with daggers in her eyes, she snarled, "You still owe me a ship, O'scarlett!"

Rose folded her arms and countered, "No, Angie, I don't." When the girl's eyes narrowed, Rose continued, "The *Scarlet Dragon* is yours. We're square now."

Angie's eyes widened and she stepped back with her mouth wide open.

Looking to Cannonflash, she saw him raise his brow, then she smiled slightly and looked back to Angie. "That ship needs a woman in charge and that crew needs someone who will keep them in line, and I think you're the woman they need. She's yours, Dreaded Angie."

Angie looked to Cannonflash and the Commodore, and they just stared back, and finally her father nodded to her. Unsure of what to do or say, she stormed to Rose and took her arm, dragging her toward the rail of the ship as she said, "Come on." Reaching the side of the ship, Angie finally released Rose and folded her arms again staring out at the *Scarlet Dragon* that sat at anchor a hundred yards away.

Rose grasped the rail and also stared at her old ship, one that still looked like it was in dire need of repair.

Both women were silent for a time, standing side by side in an awkward moment.

"I know why you're doing this," Angie finally accused. Turning her eyes to Rose, she snapped, "You want to stay here with me father, don't you? You get rid of me and your ship at the same time and he's stuck with you. That's what you're planning, isn't it?"

Lowering her eyes to the water, Rose shook her head and softly replied, "No. I'm just tired of running, tired of looking over my shoulder all the time. I'm tired of a crew that could mutiny on me. But I won't lie to you, Angie. If Captain Jones wants me then I'm his. If he doesn't..."

"If he doesn't," Angie cut in, "then he's a fool." When Rose's eyes snapped to her, she smiled unexpectedly and bumped her with her shoulder. "You're quite the catch, O'scarlett. He could do much worse."

Rose smiled back, a strained smile. "Thank you, Angie."

"You still have to get me blessing," the girl warned.

Nodding, Rose softly agreed, "Aye." Looking back to the *Scarlet Dragon*, she sighed and grumbled, "Now there's only one more issue to finish this thing."

"Berkley?" Angie guessed.

Rose nodded. "I think the Admiral means to storm the fort to get at him. Many people will be killed when that happens and I think he'd rather die than give up all that power he has."

Angie slipped an arm around Rose's shoulders and agreed, "Aye, it will be messy. Of course, I think you should just go in there and give yourself up." She looked to Rose, meeting her eyes. "Beats storming the place."

Hesitantly, Rose shrugged.

"Excuse me," Admiral Peterson bade from behind them, and when they turned to see Commander Wallace and four marines with them, he folded his hands behind him and raised his chin slightly, his gaze locked on Rose as he said, "Miss O'scarlett, we should talk about your part in all of this as it weighs against the warrants for your arrest."

She turned her eyes down and nodded, then looked out to sea, her spine going rigid as she saw the French ships turning back to fight, and they had been joined by others. "Um, Admiral, perhaps we should discuss it later."

Chapter 14

VILE CONSEQUENCES

Evening brought long shadows and eight ships limping back into Port Royal. Governor Berkley anxiously waited at the dock for the first of his warships to tie onto the pier. The closest of these was a small corvette, one that had been battered by cannon fire and would likely be at the dock and under repair for some time. One mast had been hastily patched and halfway up was at a slight angle where the splices of timber had been tied on with generous lengths of heavy rope.

A ramp was extended and men began to file off the ship, the first of them carrying litters that bore the wounded. He watched them pass by him on the way to the fort, watched other men who disembarked, and finally set his hands on his hips as he saw the ship's captain and a few other officers step onto the pier.

The Captain strode up to the Governor, looking rather frazzled as he greeted, "Good evening, Governor." He was young for his position and had the look of a man who had gone into battle for just the first time.

"Well?" the Governor snapped.

Raising his brow, the young captain reported, "It was a fierce battle, Governor. We lost many men and many ships."

 297

"Did you stop that traitor Peterson and his band of pirates?" Berkley snapped.

"Aye, Sir," the Captain assured. "They put up quite a battle until they lost that big black ship."

Berkley almost smiled. "So Captain Jones' ship has been dispatched?"

"Yes sir. Cost us the *Goliath* and two other ships, but the monster was sent back to Hell where it belongs."

"Very good," the Governor commended.

Something proud took the young captain's eyes and he added, "We also took a few prisoners, and I have one who I think is of some interest to you." He turned back toward his ship and shouted, "Get her off my ship!"

Still wearing the black trousers and shirt, Rose was escorted off of the ship by two marines. Each of them held one of her arms and her hands were shackled behind her. Her hair looked to have been recently dried and not brushed or combed. She kept her eyes down as she was taken directly to the Governor and she did not resist the men who had her.

Looking down at her like she was some prized trophy, Berkley smiled and folded his arms, nodding as he said, "Well, now. It would seem you've brought me something of great interest indeed, Captain... What is your name?"

"Stryker, Sir," the young captain replied. "She was aboard the Admiral's ship and was one of the few survivors left when it went down. We wanted to capture the ship, but I suppose a lucky shot got to her powder magazine and she blew apart."

"Unfortunate," the Governor said, his eyes still on his prisoner.

Rose sheepishly turned her eyes up to Berkley's, looking like a woman with little left. Finally, she whimpered, "I thought I was doing the right thing."

"Of course you did," he drawled. Looking to the men holding her, he ordered, "Take her to the fort and lock her in a cell."

"Wait!" she cried. "I have information!"

"Quiet!" Stryker growled through bared teeth.

As she was taken toward the fort, she struggled against her captors and called back, "Peterson isn't dead and he's coming for you!"

"Silence her!" Stryker ordered.

"Stop," the Governor barked, turning toward Rose and the soldiers as they stopped and turned her. He slowly strode toward her, his eyes narrowed and locked on her as he demanded, "Admiral Peterson is still alive?"

She nodded. "Yes! The pirates didn't flee as he told you and they were not all dispatched. After—" She stopped as the Governor raised his hand to her.

Turning to the young captain, Berkley folded his hands behind him and raised his chin, and his expression was not one of a happy man as he glared at Stryker.

Captain Stryker swallowed hard and looked back to Rose. "She'll say anything to keep from getting her pirate neck stretched, Sir. We won handily out there! The *Black Dragon* has been sunk and—"

Rose interrupted, "And what will you tell the Governor when he storms the island and takes the fort, huh? He's going to be here any time if he isn't already here and I'm sure you'll be one of the first he shoots!"

Berkley's eyes never left the Captain and his expression was one that looked like it had been carved in stone. "Captain Stryker. Perhaps you will explain to me exactly what happened out there, and if you are not telling me the truth then you can hang with this pretty little pirate." He raised a finger. "In fact, I want to see you in the fort in an hour and I will question you and the other ship's captains individually. That might give you time to get your stories straight. Go there now."

Stryker shot Rose an uneasy look, then he stormed past them toward the fort.

Turning back to his prisoner, the Governor raised his brow and sighed, "And now you."

"Please, James," she begged. "I... I have more to tell you. I know their plan. Don't send me to the gallows and I'll tell you everything."

He smiled. "Pleading for your life. That's what I like to hear, my girl."

She looked away, then back to him and softly said, "I have nothing else left but you. I have nothing left."

* * *

Within the fort, the Governor had a simple study where he conducted some of his official business. This one was made for comfort but was lacking many of the things his study in the mansion had. Plush chairs were there, a comfortable chair behind the desk and a few lamps to light the room where the sun did not reach.

Rose was escorted without incident to the middle of the room and she kept her eyes down. The expensive looking rug beneath her feet was a nice feeling, but she did not allow herself to dwell.

Governor Berkley entered behind them and ordered, "Wait outside." He just eyed the bound woman before him as they left and waited for them to close the door before he spoke. "Very well, Rose, what information do you have? What happened during the battle?"

She did not answer for long seconds and he slowly approached her. Her body quaked as she wept and bowed her head.

With narrow eyes, he took her shoulders and repeated, "What happened during the battle?"

Finally, slowly raising her head, she softly replied, "He told me the truth."

"The truth?"

"About Jeffery, about what really happened five years ago."

Berkley glanced aside, his brow low over his eyes. Taking her arm, he turned her to him and ordered, "Go on."

She raised her eyes to his. "When the second attack came he told me he wanted me aboard his ship, then things went badly. We were hit too many times and our mainmast was down." She sniffed and looked down. "He said he'd never surrender, that I deserved to die with him for what Jeffery had done. And…" She shook her head. "I had no idea, James. I'm sorry. I didn't know."

He took her chin and gently lifted her face. "You didn't know what, Rose?"

She stared back into his eyes for long seconds before she answered. "The manifests and other papers he had stolen, what he meant to use to extort you with."

Raising his brow, Berkley stammered, "Ex… Extort me with?"

Rose nodded. "Peterson told me everything, how Jeffery was stealing from the crown, how he meant to turn evidence against you to cover his crimes." She slowly shook her head as tears welled up in her eyes. "James, I'm... I'm so sorry. I loved him so much I... I suppose I was blind to what he was doing. I really didn't know. I didn't know you took little Jeffy to protect him and..." She looked away. "I should have listened to you."

He stroked his hand over her hair. "It's all right, Rose. What of Admiral Peterson?"

Staring across the room, she shrugged and replied, "I jumped overboard before the last engagement with... before the ship exploded. I watched the rest of the battle from the sea."

"And Captain Jones?"

She lowered her eyes. "I don't know. His ship went down and I don't know if he got off of it or not. Would you take these off of me, please?"

His eyes narrowed again and he slowly grasped her hair. "And why would I do that, Rose?"

"You made me an offer once," was her answer. "You offered me a nice life with you. I owe you at least that, and I have nowhere else to go." Finally looking up at him, she breathed, "Take me to your mansion. Take me there right now! I... I need you. I need to know that you still want me. Please, James. I'll do anything, anything you want me to, just let me know that you still want me."

His eyes remained fixed on hers and he did not move or even blink, but a slight smile curled his mouth and he said in a low voice, "The mansion."

She nodded, everything about her face looking like a begging child.

Berkley drew a breath and turned his eyes to the ceiling. "The mansion," he said loudly, then he looked down at her and jerked her head back by the hair.

She barked a scream, horror now joining her begging expression.

Baring his teeth, he hissed, "That's where they're waiting for me, isn't it?"

"What?" she gasped.

"Go ahead and play coy, Rose. We both know you're lying." He jerked back on her hair again. "Oh, but I enjoyed the game, little girl. The mansion. You're going to spend the night in a cell and in the morning I'll be eating breakfast as I watch the trap door drop from beneath your feet!" Turning, the threw her brutally toward the door, looking on her like an enraged animal as she slammed into it and stumbled to the floor. He stormed to her and grabbed her hair again, hoisting her from the floor. "This time, little girl, that rope is going to be nice and short. Your pretty neck will stretch slowly and I shall enjoy the performance as you spend the last moments of your life strangling. Guards!"

The guards burst into the room, their weapons ready.

Berkley looked to one of them and ordered, "Alert the garrison. I want every available man armed and marching on the mansion immediately! Do it now!" As one man turned and hurried about his task, the Governor looked to the other and growled, "Escort us below."

The dungeon of Fort Charles was just as Rose remembered it when last she had departed. Mister Smith was even still in his cell and raised his head as she was pushed by the hair down the corridor between the cells.

Governor Berkley pointed across the aisle from Smith's cell and growled, "Over there. I want her across from this other pirate."

"James, please," she begged. "I'm not—"

"Quiet!" he roared. Turning her, he slammed her back-first into the cage she was to be imprisoned in and grabbed her throat. With an evil smile, he shook his head and hissed, "Not this time, Rose. Not this time. You'll not escape and your Cannonflash Jones will not come for you. You're going to the gallows, you will hang and I will display your body at the dock as my trophy." He stroked her hair, then seized it near her ear and yanked her head over. "I did enjoy the chase, though. Perhaps I'll visit you tonight when your pirate friends have been attended to. One last romp before I put you to death. Yes, that's a delightful idea." He looked to the guard and ordered, "Open it."

The guard pulled the door open and Berkley led Rose by the hair to it, standing in the open doorway with her for a moment as he scanned the cell. "Your last sleep will be in here, Rose, and I'll be the last man you ever lay with." He released her hair and turned her toward him, taking her waist and pulling her to him. "Oh, but I'm going to enjoy you."

She smiled and countered, "Oh, I don't think you will." Her hand swung from behind her and she slammed the empty shackle into the side of his head, and as he staggered backward she grabbed his coat and hurled him into the cell, watching him collapse to the dirt and straw floor.

The guard seized her arm and pulled her away, slamming the cage door before Berkley could get back to his feet.

Rose looked to the guard and extended her hand to him, and he took her hand in his. With a big smile, she informed, "I'll be sure to tell Commander Wallace that you get extra rations of ale from now on."

He raised his brow as he shook her hand. "Or you could buy a round or two for one of his Majesty's soldiers."

Bowing her head to him, she assured, "It would be my pleasure, kind sir."

They both looked to Berkley as he approached the cell door, and they both smiled at the horrified look in his eyes.

"Oh, James," she drawled. "I enjoyed the chase, too, and it ended just as I'd always hoped it would."

Berkley looked to the guard and snarled, "Your neck will stretch as well if you don't open that door right now!"

Looking to Rose, the guard told her, "I'll give you a moment with him."

As he turned and left, Governor Berkley shouted after him, "This is treason and I can assure you that you will die for it!" When the door closed, he looked back to Rose and grasped the iron cage he was in, demanding, "Open the door. Open it now!"

She just stared back at him for a moment, then she turned to the small table where the duty guard usually sat, the table where the keys lay. Pulling the chair out, she turned it and sat down, folding her arms and crossing her legs as she continued to stare at him.

"Rose," he implored, "it does not have to end like this. You can still have your revenge against Peterson and I can facilitate it."

Looking down at her fingernails, she still would not speak to him.

"Rose!" Berkley shouted. "Listen to me! That life you want is still within your grasp."

Finally she said, "Oh, I know it is." She turned venomous eyes to him. "Jones didn't kill my son and he didn't sink that ship.

He reunited me with my son and right now little Jeffy is waiting for me in Tortuga. That's the life I want, James, the life with my son that you took away from me." Her eyes cut toward the door as it opened.

Admiral Peterson strode in with four soldiers behind him, each of whom had his musket at the ready.

The Admiral had his gaze locked on Governor Berkley as he slowly approached with his hands folded behind him.

The two men stared at each other for a moment and said nothing.

Raising his chin, Admiral Peterson informed, "As you can see, Mister Berkley, you are under arrest. Rest assured you will receive a fair trial, a last meal and a nice public hanging. Until then, here you will stay." When he cleared his throat and extended his hand, one of the soldiers handed him a thick envelope full of documents. It was heavy white paper and tied off with twine. The Admiral displayed it in front of Berkley for long seconds before he spoke again. "By the way, Mister Berkley, these are the documents you thought you burned in front of Miss O'scarlett. You really should have read what Captain Jones gave you a little more carefully. Your actions brought about his and based upon that he has received a full pardon from the crown, as have all who helped topple you."

Berkley clenched his teeth, pushing away from the bars with a low brow and a scowl.

"You'll be formerly charged in a day or two," the Admiral continued, "just as soon as all of the charges are collected and documented. Good day, Mister Berkley." As he turned toward the door, he called, "Come along, Miss O'scarlett."

"Wait," she barked. Snatching the keys from the table, she sprang up and spun around, striding with quick steps to the cell across from the one holding the fallen Governor. Smith rolled from his bunk as she unlocked the door and pulled it open. She strode in, grabbed his shirt and backed him up against the wall across the cell, glaring up at him as she snarled, "You even *think* mutiny again and believe me you will be shot! You got that, Mister?"

He swallowed hard and nodded to her.

Her eyes narrowed as she scowled and ordered, "Get your butt back to the ship." She released him and strode to the Admiral, looking up at him with a smile as she took his side.

* * *

Evening found her in her favorite yellow dress with her hair restrained behind her by a pretty white bow. A banquet was under way aboard the *Black Dragon* as it sat at anchor a hundred yards off of the pier at Port Royal. Men drank and enjoyed themselves on all decks of the ship and smoke poured from the chimney that vented the galley as Harold had many people cooking to keep up with the demands of those on board. Among those on board were Bugs Nailhall, Commodore Jones, Dreaded Angie, a bandaged Maria, Commander Wallace and Admiral Peterson. Cannonflash Jones, holding a pitcher of ale by the handle, stood near the ship's bow talking with Johnny Cannonburg as the ship was abuzz with activity. For the first time it was British sailors and soldiers enjoying themselves with Caribbean pirates.

Wearing his best dress uniform, Admiral Peterson found Jones and strode up to him, greeting, "Captain Jones. Thank you for inviting me aboard. This is a ripping good party."

Jones nodded to him, then looked to Cannonburg.

Johnny gave his Captain a nod and said, "Excuse me," as he turned to rejoin the party.

"Wanted to see how you're fairing," Peterson said. "Seems that you're in for some changes, sailing under the English flag and all that."

Jones nodded and agreed, "Aye," then took a drink from the pitcher.

The Admiral looked across the ship where Rose stood with a bottle of rum in her hand, talking and laughing with others. "Seems you've another important decision to make, Captain."

"And what is that?" Cannonflash growled.

Still looking to Rose, Peterson smiled slightly and replied, "If I held the heart of such a woman I would be sure not to allow her to get away." He took a drink and looked back to Jones. "And believe me, Captain, if I wasn't already married, I'd have her on my arm for sure."

Cannonflash just stared at the Admiral as he nodded and turned to rejoin the others, then he looked to Rose, and caught her looking at him.

She offered him a little smile, then turned her attention back to the men she was talking to.

He just stared back at her for a moment, and took another gulp from his pitcher.

Chapter 15

MEMORIES TO THE SEA

Morning light sprayed into the captain's cabin and Rose found herself awakening alone. Curled up beneath the linins, she was slow to open her eyes, feeling the first pounding aches of yet another hangover. Rubbing her eyes, she pushed herself up and groaned as she grasped her temples with one hand to cover her eyes against the morning light. Finally blinking, her eyes widened as she looked around her, finding the entire cabin awash with a strange fog that blanketed the floor.

She finally threw the covers from her and swung her feet to the floor, looking around for her dress. It was on the floor beside the bed somewhere, but the entire deck was covered with that eerie fog which seemed to glow an unnatural blue. She groped around through it and found what she sought.

Quick to dress, she rushed to the door, tripping over her boots after only a few steps and disappearing into the blanket of fog with a succession of thumps as her body crashed to the deck. "Dammit!" she spat as she pushed herself up.

Finally reaching the door, she pushed it open and rushed a few steps out, freezing as she found the entire ship surrounded by that fog. The deck was quiet and nobody seemed to be moving

 307

very fast. Carefully padding to the ladder, she climbed up to the wheelhouse through a waterfall of that fog that also covered the steering deck. Once at the top she found Johnny Cannonburg at the helm, and she did not like the nervous look on his face, and that look told her where they were going.

"Johnny?" she called almost in a whimper.

He just glanced at her.

"We're on our way to Isla de la Mortis, aren't we?" she asked fearfully.

He nodded and replied, "Aye. Captain's at the bow."

And to the bow is where she went, groping along in the fog.

Unable to see well, she thought she was almost there when she ran into someone's back and offered, "Excuse me."

The man was in a clean and perfect British sailor's uniform, the uniform of an officer. As he turned, she recognized his insignia and his rank as lieutenant—and she recognized his face.

Blue eyes stared back at her and his clean shaven and very handsome face wore a smile as he greeted in a slight Irish accent, "Hello, Rose."

She took a couple of steps back, her wide eyes on his as she gasped, "Jeffery!"

"This is how I wanted you to remember me," he said as he stepped to her. Taking her hands, he went on, "It's time, my Love."

"Time?" she whimpered.

"Time for me to go," he replied. "You've taken care of everything that kept me here including the one thing that you couldn't know would keep me from crossing over."

"What…" she stammered, "what was that?"

He smiled a little broader and raised her hand to his lips, kissing it ever so gently. "You've let me go and opened your heart to another."

Tears filled her eyes and she whispered, "You aren't angry?"

"Far from it," he answered. "Rose, you are a wonderful woman. You deserve to love again. Just love him with all your heart. Show him what we had and be happy again. I think he's a good man to take our son under his wing as he did, and to take you into his own heart."

Her eyes now spilling tears, she nodded and agreed, "I think so, too."

"I love you, Rose," he said softly, stroking his hand over her hair. "Thank you for letting me go." He looked behind her and raised his chin. "And thank you for helping her, Captain Jones."

Rose swung around, seeing Cannonflash a couple of feet behind her with his solemn eyes locked on Jeffery. This was awkward and for a moment she found herself standing between two men she deeply loved.

Jones nodded to him. "Aye, Lieutenant."

Jeffery reached to Cannonflash and took his hand, then he placed Rose's hand in the pirate's. "Take care of her. Take care of each other." With one more smile to them, he turned and walked toward the heavy mist at the ship's bow, only to stop again and look back at Jones. "I bring a message, Captain, one from someone you've been looking for."

Cannonflash raised his chin.

"She says she's always loved you and the time for vengeance is over. She had to cross over, Captain Jones, to take your son to where he needed to be. Now it's your turn. Let her go. Give her memory to the sea and your heart to Rose. You both deserve to be happy."

Tight lipped, Cannonflash nodded to him.

"Be well," Jeffery said as if from a distance. The mist began to consume him and he became the mist, adding, "And be warned. The dead are restless." Bright light consumed him and Rose and Cannonflash shielded their eyes. In an instant the mist was gone and they found themselves sailing into the sun, due east.

Turning to Jones, Rose could only stare up at his eyes, eyes that looked out to the sea and were glossy with tears for the first time since she had met him. She raised a hand to his cheek, expecting him to shy away, but he allowed her to turn his face toward her, and finally their eyes met. She found she could not speak, had nothing to say to him, so her eyes would have to speak for her.

Jones finally turned away and ordered, "Head up to the wheelhouse."

She nodded and obeyed his order without word or a second look.

Joining Mister Cannonburg there, she simply stood beside him and stared at the sea as he corrected the wheel slightly to turn the ship gently to port.

Moments later, Cannonflash ascended the ladder with the painting of Emily. Rose and Johnny watched him stride to the back of the ship and look down at the painting once more, then he lifted it over the rail and let it fall. As he stared down into the churning sea behind the ship, Rose slowly strode to him and slipped her arm around his back, laying her head against his big, solid arm as she also looked down there, and when he lifted his arm from her, tears slipped from her eyes as he wrapped it around her shoulders and pulled her to him.

"I love you, Cannonflash," she whispered.

He pulled her tighter to him and whispered back, "I you, Lass."

For a long moment they stared at the passing sea, then their thoughts were torn from each other by the distant sound of cannons and they both swung around.

Mister Mueller raced up the ladder, shouting, "French Man-O-War, Captain! Got a schooner in her sights that flies the Union Jack!"

That familiar snarl took the Captain's mouth and he ordered, "Mister Cannonburg, get us to quarters. Time to earn our pay."

"Aye, Captain Cannonflash!" Johnny shouted back as he abandoned the wheel and raced back down the ladder behind Mueller.

Jones strode with heavy steps to the ship's wheel and took it in his hands, scanning the horizon for the ships he sought. With narrow eyes he turned the wheel hard to the right and the ship responded eagerly with a hard starboard turn.

"Captain!" someone forward shouted. "You should see this!"

"O'scarlett," he growled. "Take the helm."

She eagerly darted to the wheel and took it with both hands as he stepped away. This was the biggest ship she had ever helmed and her eyes were wide and darting about the horizon as she held a steady course. She did not see Jones return to her and she gasped as he jerked her head back by the hair and savagely took her mouth with his. She could barely breathe as he kissed her with a commanding, animalistic hunger, something she found herself craving more and more, and ice ran up her spine as his hand slid up her belly to her chest and around her back. She released the wheel to grasp his shoulders as he arched her backward.

He finally pulled away and snapped, "Both hands on the wheel, woman!" When she complied and looked back up at him, he ordered, "Bring those port guns to bear on my order, and until then give us a true course into that Man-O-War."

"Aye, Captain," she replied.

His eyes narrowed and he snarled, "And don't forget you still owe me that powder."

She giggled and confirmed, "Yes Captain, I won't forget." As he turned and strode toward the ladder, she abruptly asked, "Will the Captain wish to have me again tonight?"

He stopped and looked over his shoulder, smiling a rare smile back at her before he headed down the ladder.

Watching him storm down to the lower deck, she smiled as he strode to the bow of the ship, then she looked down to the wheel and tightened her grip on it, smiling even broader. Grasping the helm like this, she could finally feel the *Black Dragon*'s power, its soul, and she nodded slowly, saying to herself, "Aye, a girl could get used to this."

63538424R00190

Made in the USA
Lexington, KY
10 May 2017